Y0-BSX-859

REVENGE & REDEMPTION

A NOVEL OF LOVE AND CONFLICT IN THE CIVIL WAR

BRAD E. HAINSWORTH

DESERET
BOOK

SALT LAKE CITY, UTAH

This is a work of fiction. Characters and events in this book are products of the author's imagination or are represented fictitiously.

© 2007 Brad E. Hainsworth

All rights reserved. No part of this book may be reproduced in any form or by any means without permission in writing from the publisher, Deseret Book Company, P. O. Box 30178, Salt Lake City, Utah 84130. This work is not an official publication of The Church of Jesus Christ of Latter-day Saints. The views expressed herein are the responsibility of the author and do not necessarily represent the position of the Church or of Deseret Book Company.

DESERET BOOK is a registered trademark of Deseret Book Company.

Visit us at DeseretBook.com

Library of Congress Cataloging-in-Publication Data

Hainsworth, Brad E.
  Revenge and redemption : a novel of love and conflict in the Civil War /
Brad E. Hainsworth.
    p. cm.
  ISBN 978-1-59038-744-3 (pbk.)
  1. United States—History—Civil War, 1861–1865—Fiction. 2. United States—
History—Civil War, 1861–1865—Secret service—Fiction. 3. Religious fiction. I. Title.
  PS3558.A3323R48 2007
  813'.54—dc22   2007000160

Printed in the United States of America
Publishers Printing, Salt Lake City, UT

10   9   8   7   6   5   4   3   2   1

REVENGE & REDEMPTION

For
Jacquelin (Jackie) Webster Hainsworth
Daughter of God
Faithful Latter-day Saint
Constant Wife and Mother
Eternal Companion
Best Friend

PREFACE

★　★　★

For Americans, there is no greater story to be told than their own. The American story is, by and large, a story of triumph achieved at great cost. It is the story of an embryonic nation of emigrants who sought freedom and strove for opportunity, a future widely dreamed of throughout the ages, but rarely found. Over the years, what was achieved on this continent became and has remained the envy of the world.

Throughout the tumultuous history of this great nation, people from around the globe have sought its shores and its opportunities, not to remain what they once were—encumbered with old loyalties—but to become renewed, to slough off the old, to reach unhindered for the future—to become *Americans*.

Revenge and Redemption is a work of historical fiction. The plot revolves around characters who are engaged in perhaps the greatest struggle that, until only recently, ever divided this nation. The issue then, as now, was whether this was to be a nation composed of free Americans living in a United States of America, or whether it was to be a country divided by bickering regionalism, spurious political divisions, and/or ethnic loyalties, its people forever unable to abandon the old, diverse cultures and economic interests that mitigated against the very freedom and opportunities they sought.

The result was a bloody civil war. But with the conclusion of that horrendous four-year struggle for identity, former enemies eventually overcame their lingering animosities and strove to move forward, forging a new nation, under law, that would become the economic and political envy of the world. While many issues remained—conflict over the meaning of human rights, individual freedom, and equality of opportunity—the character and identity of the American people was forged.

Today, daily observance of the news can easily drive one into the depths of pessimism, if not despair. But pessimism and despair, now as then, are the enemies of that endurance essential for a free people to remain free and to prevail against those forces that threaten to bring about their sure destruction.

The alarming question now before us is whether the United States can successfully meet the challenges currently raging against it. As in the past, the outcome will be determined by the character of its people, their commitment to law, their sense of unity—not diversity—and their allegiance to the idea that has been and must continue to be America, to the exclusion of all else.

Perhaps few things can help more in our current struggles than an awareness of American history. The value of historical fiction is that it enables the reader to experience the great issues of the past, as if actually present, almost as a participant-observer.

Within these pages, readers can interact with a few of the giants of our past, as well as those unheralded Americans who worked loyally to make things happen. Here, at least to some degree, the reader can glimpse the pressures that confronted these earlier Americans and forged them into what they became.

It is my hope that this work of historical fiction will, in some small way, put readers in touch with an important chapter in this nation's past and help point them toward an enduring commitment to its future.

Brad E. Hainsworth
Kanab, Utah Territory, 2007

ACKNOWLEDGMENTS

★ ★ ★

Though it is the author's name alone that appears on the cover of a book, there is an army of talented professionals working in support of his efforts, who too often receive little or no public recognition. Foremost among these are those executives burdened with the unenviable responsibility of deciding whether or not any hopeful author's work is worthy of publication—a difficult and often thankless task that strikes at the very heart and soul of any would-be author.

If and when a manuscript is accepted for publication, there are those sturdy souls whose talents go into the preparation of the manuscript for printing. With the completion of those efforts, the team of hardworking individuals in marketing and sales sees that the book is presented to the reading public in an artful and appealing way.

To every member of this worthy organization of talented professionals at Deseret Book, I owe my thanks. There are, however, two exceptional people who merit special mention. These are men with whom I have worked closely now on two books, and who throughout the process have become personal friends. On Cory Maxwell's shoulders rested the burden of initial acceptance or rejection. That he has looked upon my efforts favorably is not only a wonder to me but a blessing in many ways. Then there is Richard Peterson, an editor of exceptional talent and commitment, without whose help my efforts would lack the polish so essential to any Deseret Book publication. In addition, it was his initial evaluation of my work that moved the whole process forward. Special thanks to him.

Richard Erickson and Laurie Cook must also be given special mention. They put the finishing touches to the whole project, Richard as designer and Laurie as typesetter, making the final product appear appealing to anyone looking for a good book. Their work is then put into the hands of marketing specialists Gail Halladay and Liz Carlston, who work their magic in bringing the finished book to the attention of the discerning consumer.

To these wonderful people and all others involved, my heartfelt thanks.

★   ★   ★

Verily, thus saith the Lord concerning the wars that will shortly come to pass, beginning at the rebellion of South Carolina, which will eventually terminate in the death and misery of many souls; And the time will come that war will be poured out upon all nations, beginning at this place.

—Doctrine & Covenants 87:1–2

PROLOGUE

★ ★ ★

John Hay, President Lincoln's young secretary, tapped
lightly on the gleaming white door and stepped from his office
into the president's cramped study. To avoid the intrusion of job-
seekers and sycophants who seemed to roam the mansion without
hindrance, Lincoln had insisted that the outer door to the wide
central hallway be kept locked. Even a full year after his taking
office, and in the middle of what was proving to be a hellish war,
the favor-seekers would give him no rest.

The small office, tucked away in the southeast corner of the
Executive Mansion's second floor, was cluttered and somber, much
like its over-burdened occupant. The president, in an effort to rid
himself of the painful headache that had suddenly come upon
him, had drawn the heavy velour drapes across the room's three
narrow windows, further increasing the gloominess that constantly seemed to envelop him. Such headaches were not uncommon and, if anything, were becoming more frequent with the

constant confusion that had surrounded him since assuming the presidency.

"Come in, John," the president said, in response to the light knock, his usually high-pitched voice etched with fatigue. "Come in and sit down."

At age twenty-four, John Milton Hay had quickly become the president's closest confidant and unofficial advisor. Hay's Springfield law office had shared a common hallway with Lincoln's and, not long after taking office, the new president had appointed the young lawyer his private secretary.

"Feeling poorly, Mister President?"

"Oh . . . no more than usual," Lincoln said, rubbing his temples, a sigh escaping his lips as he spoke. "Just another of my cussed headaches."

"Sorry to bother you, sir," Hay said, declining the invitation to sit and crossing the small room to the desk, "but I have some requisitions here. They were just delivered, and the messenger is waiting."

"Let him wait; the rest'll do 'im good. A soldier, is he?"

"Yes, sir. A young private."

Lincoln chuckled. "He ain't in any hurry then. Sit down, son."

"Something troubling you, sir?" Hay queried, taking a seat while looking more closely at the gaunt figure slumped behind the desk.

"Mmm," the president murmured, closing his eyes momentarily against the pain. "I don't know, truth be told. I've been sitting here wondering about a troublesome vision I had not long after the election. I keep tryin' to forget it, but the memory of it plagues me still. It came on me three times."

"A dream, sir?"

"No, not exactly a dream—a vision is what it was, I think.

Yes—a vision, it was," the president said, his eyes searching the dimly lit room. "I'm positive I was awake each time it happened, so it couldn't have been a dream. One way or the other, it's had me and Mother plain worried—Missus Lincoln, especially. I was just sitting here thinkin' on it when you came in."

"Has it occurred lately, sir? The vision, I mean?"

"No, John, not recently. No. I think the fact that I had it three times has troubled me as much as the vision itself."

The gangly president leaned forward and rested his elbows on the desk. "I had come home late one night and lay down on the lounge in my bedchamber. Opposite to where I lay was a bureau with a hinged looking glass on top of it—you know the kind. From where I lay, I could see myself reflected nearly full length. But my face, I noticed, had two separate and distinct images, the tip of the nose of one bein' about three inches from the tip of the other. I got up to look closer in the glass, but the illusion vanished. Yet, when I lay back down again, I saw it a second time—plainer, if possible, than before. It was then I noticed that one of the faces was paler than the other. I got up to look closer again, but the thing melted away, as it had before.

"Well, I went off, and got busy and forgot all about it—nearly, but not quite. Every once in a while, the thing would come to mind and give me a little pang, as though something uncomfortable had happened. A few days later I went back to that couch and lay down again to see if the image would appear again—sort of an experiment, y' see. Well, sir, sure enough, the thing came back again, but for the last time. I never succeeded in bringing the ghost back after that.

"When I told Missus Lincoln about it, I tried to show her—tried very industriously—but the image wouldn't return. I'm afraid the whole matter has worried her more than it should.

More than it has me, I think. She's convinced the vision was a sign."

"A *sign,* Mister President?"

"Uh-huh. A sign. She thinks it's sayin' that I'll be elected to a second term of office, but the paleness of the one face is an omen that I will not live to finish that last term."

Hay thought for a moment, not knowing quite how to respond. "Well . . . what do you make of it, sir?"

"I don't know," Lincoln shrugged. "I just don't know. I guess only time will tell. I feel better talkin' about it, though," Lincoln said, straightening himself in his chair. "But keep it to yourself, John. Such things are best not bandied about, especially where the president is concerned—especially one as popular as I've been," Lincoln chuckled. "It might give some folks more hope than they ought to have."

Hay leaned across the desk and handed Lincoln a piece of scratch paper. "I'll not say a word, Mister President."

"What's this?"

"Your note regarding Clay Ashworth, sir. It was telegraphed to Fort Union early yesterday. Their response arrived this morning. Ashworth and his Mormon cavalry left for Salt Lake City a day or so after the fight at Glorieta Pass."

"Did you send a telegram to Brigham Young?"

"I took the liberty of doing so, sir—signed your name."

"Good. If anyone can find Clay Ashworth, Brigham Young can. Ain't much west of the Great Divide gets past his nose. What I could accomplish if I had his system of intelligence gathering. Gotta wonder how he does it. I'll tell yuh one thing, John, I'm glad the man's on our side in this fracas. Yessir, I'm glad of that."

★ ★ ★

"Stay seated, Ben," Brigham Young said as he entered his sun-lit study and took his seat at the large, ornate table that served as his desk. Outside, it was a cloudless, early-spring, mountain morning, invigorating and uplifting. "What have you got there?" Young said, glancing out of the window to his right, appearing almost resentful of being confined inside on such a day. "Does it feel as good outside as it looks, Ben?"

"Yes, sir. It surely does." Leaning forward, Benjamin Pratt Kimball, one of the Mormon leader's most trusted assistants, slid a yellow sheet of paper across the massive table's polished surface. "This arrived within the hour, President Young."

"Mmm. The Executive Mansion,"[1] Young said, scanning the telegram. "Any idea where Clay Ashworth is, Ben? Has he arrived yet? Aren't they due in Salt Lake any day now?"

"Clay and his troop of cavalry left Fort Union two days after the battle at Glorieta Pass, sir, and that's been more than three weeks, now. The only thing I can say for sure is that he'll be more than a little anxious to get back to his ranch and his new bride, when he does arrive. They had very little time together before he left for New Mexico."

"Oh, yes. A beautiful young woman—Mexican, I think."

"Yes, sir—a true Hispanic beauty. High bred and well educated, too. Her father was the governor of Sonora before his death, as I'm sure you recall."

"Yes, that was a nasty piece of business, the vicious murder of her parents. What a shock for that young woman. If there is anything worse in this world than manipulation among nations, I can't imagine what it would be. Signs of the times, I'm afraid."

"Well, she certainly suffered for it. It's lucky she had Clay to fall back on."

Brigham Young's chair squeaked as he leaned back. Heaving a

sigh, he studied the room's ceiling for a long moment. Finally he said, "Well, Ben, we've got to find him, and quickly. Beautiful young bride aside, apparently his life is not yet his own. It would appear that Mister Lincoln has a more urgent need of him than she does."

"Yes, sir. I've already sent a messenger to *Rancho los Librados*. If he hasn't arrived there, I'll send riders east."

"Excellent, Ben. Oh . . . and what of Porter Rockwell? I take it, since I haven't seen him, the marshal has not returned?"

"Well, sir, Rockwell being Rockwell, his whereabouts can take some guessing. As you know, Port finally chased Wolf Striker to ground. That was before the Glorieta battle. He had taken him to Fort Union for hanging."

"Yes . . . Fort Union," Young said, lightly tapping his desk. "Porter didn't get himself involved in the Glorieta fight, did he? His involvement could raise all sorts of unnecessary difficulties."

"Port knows better, sir. I expect he'll show up here before too long. He might even be returning with Clay Ashworth's cavalry troop."

"And Striker? What of him?"

"Well, sir, when Port gets back, we'll know for certain. There's been no word of any hanging. It wouldn't surprise me if the man had escaped in the confusion of the fight, or even before it. If that's the case, Port's gonna be fit to be tied."

"Mmm . . . well," Young said, pushing back his chair and striding to the far end of the room, where he stood gazing out the window toward the mountains to the east. "What has worried me since Porter left is the thought that those two might just be too much alike. I can't help but wonder what happened when they finally met."

"Rockwell is Rockwell all right, President Young," Kimball

said, turning in his chair to watch the Mormon prophet. "The mold got broken when they made him. One thing's for certain, Port's no murdering renegade. And Striker has shown himself to be without conscience."

"I don't mean to imply that he is, Ben," Young said, turning from the window. "I trust Port implicitly, but catching Striker is one thing, hanging him may be something else again."

"Port will prove more than his match, sir. That's my guess, anyway—knowing him as well as I do."

"Striker is a Southerner, Ben," Young said, glancing over his shoulder. "Did you know that?"

"No, sir," Kimball said, a look of surprise crossing his face. "He was supposed to be commanding a Confederate force at Platte River Station, but the truth is, the man struck me as nothing more than a murdering mercenary—the whole bunch of them. With the exception of those two Rebel officers, I guess."

"A man with a past, no doubt of that," Young said, heaving a sigh. "But I think, down deep, he's something more. Striker is a born-and-bred Southerner—South Carolina, Charleston, the very heart of southern sedition, or so I've been told. If anything can, this so-called civil war might just bring him back to his roots— along with many of his fellow countrymen."

"Well . . . from what I saw, the man must be pretty far gone. Judging from the murdering mess he left behind, I mean."

"This conflict is going to tear at the very fabric of the United States, Ben. Before it's over, it will do terrible things to people— fracture treasured institutions, tear families apart, cause men and women to question their loyalties, their very identities—bring instinctive loyalties to the surface that weren't even recognized before this all started."

"Do you really believe it will last that long, President Young?"

"Ben, before we see an end to the violence—and it won't be over for a good long time—men and women are going to be forced to search their souls as never before. This Civil War, as they're calling it, could well prove to be the beginning of the end. Just the beginning, mind you, but the beginning nonetheless. Revelation tells us as much."

"I guess it takes men like Striker to cause this kind of evil."

"Yes, but stop and think, Ben. Even if the worst is true of Wolfgang Striker—and we have no reason to believe it's not— could such a man get anywhere near a fight between Confederate and Union forces and not find a way to get into it? I don't think so. And would it be only for the perverse thrill of shedding blood? I can't think that, either. No, Ben, I think you may very well be right about his possible escape. But what little I know of our Mister Striker tells me there's more to the man than meets the eye."

Ben Kimball watched the Mormon leader pace his study. Ben never ceased marveling at the man's ability to see beyond the facade, behind a person's skin, into the real meaning of events and history. "I'm afraid you see more to him than I do, sir. All I know is what he did at Platte River Station. From all we're told he led that murderous raid, despite the presence of those two Confederate officers."

Brigham Young stopped at the window for another longing glance outside and then, with a sigh, returned to his desk. "Perhaps you're right, Ben. Maybe he is no more than a murdering scalawag selling his skills to the highest bidder. But somehow I don't think so. I think he's much more. Much more."

"Yes, sir," Kimball said, leaning forward in his chair. "Something like that might explain why Port's not back yet. If it's as you say, and if there was any way for Striker to get into that fight, judging from Platte River Station, he would likely have stopped at nothing."

"Well . . . it's one possible explanation for Porter's tardiness."

"The more I think about it, President Young," Kimball said, scratching his chin, "the more I wonder just what has happened. Porter Rockwell left here to see justice done—one way or the other. He left Utah a man on a mission.

"Striker, or that gang of thugs with him—those so-called Confederate patriots—murdered Will and Luke Cartwright without provocation and then illegally occupied Platte River Station. They shot them down in cold blood, and Port would never forget that. He loved those two like they were his own sons. Those boys were just doing their duty as the town's sheriff and deputy. No, sir," Kimball said, shaking his head emphatically, "Porter Rockwell's out to see justice is done, and one way or the other, he'll do it, President Young. He'll do it!"

"Yes, he'll do his best, but where our Mister Striker is concerned, he's been underestimated before. How else could a man like that have survived? It's always a hard lesson to learn, Ben."

"What is, sir?"

"Too often we base our assessments of others on assumptions, and those assumptions all too frequently prove faulty. It's a dangerous thing to do, making hasty judgments. A man—any man—should never be underestimated. I think that might be doubly true of Wolf Striker."

PART ONE

★ ★ ★

CHAPTER 1

★   ★   ★

Lowering the .52-caliber Sharps rifle from his shoulder, the sound of its brutal discharge ringing in his ears, Porter Rockwell carefully slid on his belly a few inches back from the edge of the cliff that overhung Johnson's Ranch, the Confederate staging area at the west end of Apache Canyon. From the rocky ledge where he lay, Orrin Porter Rockwell had witnessed the unexpected Union attack on the now-smoldering Confederate supply wagons below, waiting for the opportunity to finally bring Wolf Striker to justice.

The ranch lay some four miles down the canyon from Glorieta Pass and a couple of miles more from Pigeon's Ranch, just on the other side. The entire canyon had been the scene of bloody fighting over the past three days. But earlier in the day, a Union force had unexpectedly stormed like a plague of biblical locusts down the cliffs on the far side of the wide canyon. *Deadly* locusts!—catching the handful of Confederate reserves and wounded completely by surprise. The mountains surrounding the canyon and pass were so rugged the Confederates had thought their supplies safe from any flanking attack, and a Union assault on their rear had been given little or no consideration.

For an exhausted Rockwell, aching to bring the chase to an end, the surprise Union attack had been one of the slickest maneuvers he had ever witnessed, not only resulting in the complete destruction of the invading Confederate army's supplies, but putting Wolf Striker right where he wanted him—squarely in the sights of his trusted Sharps.

After watching Striker ride into the Confederate camp and begin giving orders, pushing his weight around, Rockwell had been prepared to walk into that nest of Texas Rebels and capture or kill Striker on the spot—whichever proved easier. But those screaming blue bellies had blown his not-so-carefully-thought-out plan completely away, along with all of the Rebel forces' badly needed supplies, and denied him the chance to settle things up close and personal. And now, Wolf Striker lay among the rubble and wreckage of the Confederate camp, unmoving and most likely dead.

Bringing Wolfgang Striker to justice—the man he had hunted for so long, the man guilty of the slaughter at Platte River Station—and seeing him lying dead in the dirt below, Rockwell at last hoped to feel a longed-for sense of vindication.

In reaction to the scene below, his pale blue eyes—eyes almost lost between the heavy brows and the thick, bushy beard—had grown colder, fading to the even more pale hue of hard-frozen ice. "Hanged, if that didn't feel good," Rockwell muttered to himself, as he started to turn away.

But something held him, turning him back toward the canyon and the devastation that lay below. Somehow the sight of Striker lying helpless, crumpled and broken, in the chill of the dying light of day, did not truly feel all that good. He was kidding himself, and he knew it. That deadly shot did not bring with it the sense of final victory he had so long anticipated.

The chase had been long and exhausting, first losing his quarry, then capturing and jailing him, only to have Striker escape from the military prison at Fort Union and join with the Texas Rebels in the fight at Glorieta Pass. Bringing the hunted to ground, making the criminal—any criminal—pay for his terrible crimes was a wonderful thing, and it should have brought a certain satisfying sense of justice—of justice-at-long-last-achieved—with its unequivocal finality and closure.

But what now nettled Porter Rockwell as he lay beneath a twisted juniper was the realization that there was no real sense of satisfaction from what he had just done. *Curse that man if what I just did don't really seem any good at all,* he thought, the annoying twinge of regret following too closely on his deadly shot.

It was the growing feeling of remorse that moved him once more to the ragged edge of the rocky shelf. Deep inside himself, Porter Rockwell knew that in spite of everything, over the months he had come to respect Wolf Striker as a worthy foe. Chasing him through weeks of hardship had given a sense of purpose to Rockwell's days, of motivation that was seldom felt.

Confound it, he thought, *any other way, maybe we could have been friends. Get right down to it, he had it in 'im, alright—a man to ride the river with. Tarnation, anyway. So what if I hadn't of shot 'im? Doin' it didn't change a bloody thing.*

★ ★ ★

The thought slowly surfaced within Wolf Striker's cold, nearly dead brain that nothing was blacker than black velvet. Was it? What could be? That beauty down in Sonora, she always wore black velvet. Why she did that—wore black velvet—would not come to him, or who she was somehow would not come to him, either. Maybe she didn't even exist, never existed except in the dark. But the dark for some reason was not as black as before. Maybe that was the answer.

That tiny pinhole of light was the obvious explanation, confusing as it seemed. It must have appeared over the ages. Maybe it had come to save him. Illumination does that, they say—it could be God, or God's doing. That's the first thing they teach you in Catholic school, but that was equally confusing. What did he know about Catholic school? It wouldn't come to him with any degree of certainty, but he did not think he was a Catholic—not now, not for years, anyway. Whatever—that tiny, bright twinkle gave him something upon which to focus, something in which to find meaning, if only for the moment.

Wolfgang Striker slowly reached for his aching forehead. His hand was heavy and unwilling, and for some reason his head seemed far away, the distance so great that finding it was going to be a problem . . . but it hurt so. The strange touch felt oppressive, almost crushing, and sticky.

It was then the soldier within him awakened, and he realized that he, Wolfgang Striker, soldier of fortune and Confederate officer, had been shot, and that pinpoint of chimerical light was only a star—existential in its meaning, at best. *Existential? Where the devil did that come from?* "Twinkle, twinkle, little star," he muttered, rolling onto his side, struggling to sit up.

Blasts of pain repeatedly jolted through him, bringing with them the full realization of the bloody battle of Glorieta Pass.

Then a flood of memory: the meaningless destruction of Platte River Station; the shooting of the sheriff and his deputy; dodging Porter Rockwell, that Mormon marshal from Salt Lake, clear into New Mexico Territory; the butchering of the Indian children by other renegade Indians and some of his own men. It had been too much.

Lying in that ditch, helplessly watching the slaughter of those little innocents had drained him of any will to fight. It had been then that the meaningless horror of his life had finally caught up with him, and he knew full-well there was just no point to his existence, to what he had become.

The realization that he'd be better off dead had seeped into his mind like some enervating stain. *Better to be dead—dead with those little Indian kids.* For him, how could there possibly be any redemption? The answer was all too simple and obvious.

Porter Rockwell had finally caught him—if you could call it that—found him more dead than alive, shot through and half frozen in the snow, and had taken him for hanging to Fort Union. And none of it meant anything. It was as if a light had gone out. There was just no point to going on. Hanging seemed as good an end as any, when you got right down to it. It seemed a painful truth, but any end would be better than the emptiness he had been enduring.

But it had been news of the pending fight between Union and Confederate forces somewhere along the Santa Fe Trail—a place called Glorieta Pass, at the southern end of the Sangre de Cristo Mountains—that had begun to put the old military starch back into him, restoring to his jaded mind a reason for living; and he had escaped from jail. Life had suddenly again become worth living, as if he had sucked in a huge breath of clean, brisk, invigorating air.

It had been a barn-burner of a fight, Glorieta: a soldier's dream, a chance to bring all of his education and training and experience to good purpose. Rank, the command of fighting men, the sounds of war, and the rush of life in his ears had brought him back from the brink. And now, here he was again, here in the dirt, exhausted in mind and spirit, bleeding, hurting, his battered body almost unwilling to move. They had failed, he had failed; the battle was lost, and the Union troops might yet come charging out of the canyon to crush them completely. And yet—

"Shoot, man, we thought you was dead."

"I'm not dead?" Wolf said, groggily trying to focus. "You're telling me this isn't hell?"

"No, I ain't sayin' that," someone near him said. "I'm just sayin' you ain't dead. Not like we thought you was, anyway."

"How many ways are there for a man to be dead?" Wolf mumbled, half to himself, his throbbing head threatening to explode with every unmerciful beat of his heart. Not only was the surging pain nearly unbearable, his head was alarmingly unsteady on his shoulders. Just holding it up required a degree of effort almost beyond his ability. "Where am I?—we? Where are we?" he groaned, looking around.

"We-all are here, at Johnson's Ranch, and it prob'ly ain't gonna be long before them Yankees come stormin' outta that canyon yonder. Best you get up and get outta here with the rest of us before they do."

The growing rumble of a retreating army, the unmistakable sounds of panic, almost unnoticeable at first, had suddenly made the need to do something immediate, and as Wolf Striker struggled unsteadily to his feet, the canyon behind him suddenly began disgorging Confederate men and horses from its mouth into the charred remains of Johnson's Ranch. They came in a rush, man and animal alike, their eyes wild, their bodies tumbling through what was left of their once-orderly staging area in a dirty cloud of unmitigated chaos.

Staggering behind a half-burned horse barn, Wolf watched the pandemonium with disbelief. What was once a determined Confederate army, organized for victory, was now gone, lost in the unholy terror of defeat. Any effort to control the fear-stricken horde would only get a man trampled to death; that much was obvious.

Leaning back against the charred side of the barn, Wolf closed his aching eyes and slid to the ground. Drawing his knees up to his chest, he laid his pounding head on his folded arms, his mind empty, save for the recurring thought that the Confederate cause—his rebirth—should not end this way.

The ground beneath him trembled from the riot of disintegration that swirled around him. Horses stomped and complained, and the air was filled with the cries of men caught in the horror of the moment, oblivious to any sense of resolve, each seeking some idea of where to go, what to do next.

"Get up, Major!"

Wolf looked up at the man sitting atop what seemed an enormous horse. It was Bill Scurry, the Confederate lieutenant colonel who had been in command, and from Wolf's dusty vantage point the man did not look as if all had been lost. In fact, he almost appeared to be an island of rock jutting up out of the sea of confusion that swirled around them—some sort of Confederate statue cut from stone. "Time to get these men organized and move out for Santa Fe, Major. If we don't, one way or the other, we'll perish here."

From where Wolf sat, the man began to look and sound like a pompous jackass, braying out orders as if nothing disastrous had happened. The loss of their supplies had caused the loss of the entire Glorieta campaign. The Confederates could have carried the day, if it had not been for Scurry's failure to leave a sufficient guard with the wagons. Because of his stupidity—bad judgment would be more generous, if Wolf had been feeling the least bit generous—the entire expedition was in disarray and could easily be slaughtered if the Union troops chose to attack. "For want of a nail . . . ?" Wolf grumbled to himself.

"Are you hurt, Major?" Scurry said, dismounting.

"Yeah," Wolf said, struggling to stand, swallowing the urge to give Scurry the full benefit of his low estimation of the man's leadership. But the urge to explode in Scurry's face quickly diminished as the pain once again threatened to overwhelm him. "I'm afraid I got shot. Oddly enough, from the other side of the canyon, I think."

Scurry glanced over his shoulder at the steep hillside behind them as he bent to help Wolf to his feet. "But they didn't come down that way."

"I'm aware of that, Colonel," Wolf retorted, slumping against the barn. His reply to a superior officer, no matter how derelict the man may have been, was a little too abrupt, and he knew it.

Wolfgang Striker had been a professional soldier all his adult life. He was now; and wounded or not, he always would be. For that fact alone, he knew the responsibility of rank; he knew the terrible burden of command in the heat of battle; he knew what it was to fail; he knew the anger of spiteful subordinate judgment before all the facts were known; and he knew how to address a superior officer on the field of combat. All of this he knew, even as he passed out from the overwhelming pain.

★   ★   ★

Three weeks of hard riding brought Clay Ashworth and his troop of Mormon cavalry from New Mexico to the gaping mouth of what had become known as Emigration Canyon. Throwing his right arm into the air, he brought the small cavalry troop to a halt on a promontory overlooking the thriving and rapidly growing settlement of Great Salt Lake City. Clay gestured toward the now-fertile but snow-covered valley that sprawled before them. "Not many sights more welcome or beautiful than that city down there, Jeb."

"Not for me there isn't, Clay." This from his second-in-command mounted next to him.

"Wasn't it about here that Brigham Young told his people, 'This is the place,' or something like that? What, fifteen years ago? And look at it now."

"Yeah, about here," Jeb Smith said, filling his lungs with the crisp high-country air. "That long ago."

"I guess you were too young to remember, huh?"

"I'm only nineteen, Major. We came here several years later—from England. There was already a sizeable settlement here then . . . back when we came into the valley."

From somewhere in the restless group, someone said, "Men are getting anxious, Major."

Clay turned in his saddle to look at his command. "Gather around, men," he shouted.

Horses stomped and blew, and equipment clanked as the troop pressed around Ashworth and Jeb Smith. Such times were always hard for Clay—saying good-bye after a campaign. These were the men he had fought with, risked his neck with, the men with whom he shared his most basic values. Clearing his throat, he said, "I'm not sure what the future holds, men. Because I don't, I'm not going to ride into Salt Lake and take any chances on being seen," he said, with a chuckle. "If Brigham Young knows I'm back . . . well. . . . Instead, I'm leaving from here to head south and home. I suggest each of you do the same.

"Jeb, here, will bring you word if we are to reassemble as a troop. I doubt that will happen, but with what's going on back in the States, one never knows; and I need to spend some time with my bride. That so-called Civil War seems like a long way off, but as we all know, it can reach out and burn us all. It has once, and it can do it again.

"Before we split up, I want each of you to know how highly I prize your loyalty and friendship. Better men can't be found on the face of the earth. At Glorieta you fought with distinction; you are a credit to your families, your church, and the Territory of Utah. I hope we don't have to do it again, but if it becomes necessary, I want always to fight next to men such as yourselves."

Offering a casual salute, Clay reined his horse around to his left and touched his spurs to its flanks. The gray responded with a bound and scrambled over and down the steep slope. Muddy snow and rocks scattered violently as the big animal plunged headlong toward the bottom, horse and rider disappearing into a stand of snow-blanketed oak brush. *Rancho los Librados* lay nearly a full-day's ride to the south, and Clay Ashworth would spare neither himself nor the powerful horse beneath him in getting there—home, into the arms of his Consuelo, his Connie.

★   ★   ★

It had snowed lightly during the night, and the ranch house lay snuggled beneath the sheltering stand of Ponderosa pines that surrounded it, just as he remembered—just as he would always remember it. Beneath each window of the ground floor, oblong splashes of light gave the wet, heavy snow a soft, golden hue. Only the plop of snow falling from the over-burdened trees could be heard. All was still, a place of safety and rest.

Wet and cold as he was, Clay sat quietly in his saddle, savoring the moment. First, he would put the big gray in the barn, rub him down, and give him a generous helping of sweet oats—the large horse's favorite treat. Then, he would sneak into the house. He wanted it to be perfect. Emily would be there to squeal and run into his arms, all the while scolding him for tracking snow and mud into her house. Prior to Connie, she was the one woman who had filled his life, made him a home, been a mother to him, and he loved her with all of his heart.

But it was Connie—Maria Emilea Consuelo Salinas Ashworth—his Connie, who now filled the center of his being. He wanted this to be just right. They had only been married a few weeks when he was called away to the war in the New Mexico Territory. At the time, it felt as if he had been torn away from her—torn in half, in fact. And now he was home, and he had to be careful. He had to make his entrance back into her life just right.

The first step onto the rear veranda was his undoing. He had asked both Robby and Chet at one time or another to fix that warped board. He had intended to do it himself, but his return from Mexico had been too full of more pleasant things to occupy his—and his bride's—time. Now it was too late."

"Who's there? Talk fast, because I got a shotgun right here, *me entiendes?*" It was Emily in her scariest voice. Every time Clay heard the old woman's maximum effort at sounding tough and scary, he could not keep from laughing out loud.

"Emily . . . put that thing down before you hurt yourself," he chuckled.

"Clay Ashworth? Clay? What you doing there?" she shouted, throwing the screened door open and disappearing into his arms. "One of these days you gonna get yourself shot, *tú sabes?*"

"Oh, little one," he said, lifting her off the floor in a mighty bear hug, "you'll never know how much I've missed you." Setting her down, Clay held her back to where he could plant a kiss on her forehead.

Then he asked, "Where is she?"

Emily wagged a finger at him. "Now, you be quiet, Clay Ashworth. Things no the same around here any more, and it's late at night, *tú sabes?*"

The grin drained from his face. "What's wrong?" His breath caught, almost robbing him of speech. "Where is she? Where's Consuelo? Is she sick? Is she hurt?" The words came in a rush, leaving no time for an answer. "If anything's happened to her, I'll—"

"*Sí,* something's happened, Clay Ashworth, an' it all your fault. You're the one, *tú sabes?* She's upstairs in your big bed, but she no alone."

"She's what?" The words caught in his throat.

"No, sir, Clay Ashworth, she no alone."

"Whaddayuh mean, *she isn't alone?*"

"She going to have a baby."

"A bab—"

"*Sí,* a baby. What you think all that laughing and giggling was going to bring? Huh? You no think I knew—but I knew. I coulda tol' you, but not me. Oh, no, I mind my own business, *tú sabes?*"

Clay's face was the color of putty. "A baby? Oh, Emily," Clay said, setting the little woman aside, heading for the stairs in the big front room. "I've got to see her. "I've got—"

"Now, you wait down here. She—"

"Clay?"

★   ★   ★

Brigham Young turned from the window, filled with the wonder of a spring night in the tops of the mountains. The hour was late, but the Mormon leader's evening was yet to end.

"Well, who can blame the man? I don't think he had more than a couple of weeks or so with her. It took a man of some strength and conviction to leave his wife and ride off into the middle of a war, to say nothing of what it took on her part. There she was, a new bride in a strange land, and all alone, but for her husband. She's a beautiful, intelligent woman, and I know how hard it was for both of them. They were both here in this office just before he left, you know."

"Yes, sir, I know. But do you want me to send for him, sir? President Lincoln's message sounded—"

"No, Ben," Young said, slumping into the big chair behind his desk, his voice heavy with resignation. "Wars have a way of just going on with or without us, and I'm afraid this one's going to be long and bloody. It's true, Mister Lincoln's telegram had an air of urgency to it—but not all that urgent. Not if you read it just right, anyway. I'm sure at this point, from where the president sits, everything appears urgent, but I think we'll give Clay some time—a couple of weeks, maybe."

The Mormon leader continued. "Young Missus Ashworth is going to have a baby, you know, and she's not been having such an easy time of it. I've had Doc Richards down to see her at least twice a week since I learned of her condition, and he's concerned. No, Ben, right now Clay's young wife needs her husband far more than Mister Lincoln does, I think. I can't stretch the point too far, but we'll let them alone—for a little while, anyway."

Ben Kimball arose to leave the office, then turned. "President Young, should we reply to Mister Lincoln's telegram?"

"Umm . . . yes, I suppose we'd better." Young studied some object or defect on his office ceiling for a long moment, sighed, and said, "Tell President Lincoln . . . use these words, Ben: 'Mister President, I will send a rider to seek out Ashworth when we are more certain of his circumstance.' Yes," Young said, with a chuckle, "that'll do nicely, Ben—vague enough to cover a multitude of meanings."

★   ★   ★

"Clay?"

Out of the darkness at the top of the stairs came the sound of the only voice that could make Clay Ashworth forget that anything else mattered. "Clay? My darling, is that you?" Only she could so completely disarm him.

He could not remember scrambling up the stairs, but suddenly she was in his arms, her body pressing against his, his face buried in her soft hair, her tears dampening his shirt.

"Oh, Clay, I've missed you so."

Enveloped in his arms she seemed so small, so fragile. When he held her close, it felt as if he could wrap himself completely around her, as if she would disappear altogether in his being. Only her intellect, her capacity to challenge him, seemed large; but those qualities only added to her desirability, her completeness as a woman and as a companion.

From the moment he had been torn from her side to join the war in New Mexico, he had dreamed of nothing but this moment:

the sound of her voice, the softness of her body held closely against his, the fragrance of her hair and skin. She was his, she always would be—nothing could ever harm her or tear her again from his embrace.

Lifting her in his arms, Clay laid his wife gently on their big bed and lay down next to her. "What's this I hear you've been up to while I've been away?" he asked, brushing a wisp of hair from her damp forehead and kissing her warm cheek.

"Well . . . you did your part before you left," Consuelo whispered, a couple of sniffles punctuating her words, "and while you've been away, I've been doing mine. We are going to have a little one."

Some combination of her physical beauty, her slight Spanish accent, and the soft richness of her voice completely captivated him. Her perfection was complete, right before him. She was the most unfathomable mystery of his life. If she had a fault, he had not found it, nor did he think he ever would.

"Say it again."

"What?"

"What you just told me."

"You and I are going to have a little one, my husband."

"And she been told many times to stay in bed, too. And you going to see she does, Clay Ashworth," Emilly scolded, her bluntness shattering the magic of his perfect moment.

"Huh?" Clay said, lifting his head from the pillow, as if reluctantly emerging from a beautiful dream.

Emily stood silhouetted in their bedroom doorway. "You hear me? You two got to behave like you is going to be parents, *tú sabes*? She no be doing so good, Clay."

Swinging his legs over the side of the bed, Clay motioned the little woman into the room. "Light a lamp, Emily, and let's sit here and talk about all that I've been missing."

"It's been kinda hard for her, Clay," Emily said, lighting a lamp and moving across the room to light another, "an' it no going to get much better prob'ly."

Too suddenly, the joy of the moment had changed, and Clay felt something catch in the pit of his stomach. "What's wrong, Consuelo? What's Emily talking about, sweetheart?"

Consuelo reached up and pulled him down to her, lightly kissing his lips. "Nothing is all that terribly wrong, my dearest. It's just what women now and then experience when they're in this condition."

"Experience what?" he said pulling away.

"Oh, now see, Emily, we've gotten Clay all upset, and he just got home, too."

"She been having pains, Clay. Pretty bad ones, too."

"Well, is everything all right?" Clay said, his voice strained with concern.

"It's just that I've been having what Doc Richards calls contractions. It's like the baby is anxious to come much too soon. But I've been staying right down in bed, like the doctor said, and the pains have stopped . . . almost."

"What do you mean, *almost?*"

"She means *almost*," Emily said, her voice half-full of reproach. "So you no getting her upset, Clay Ashworth. You gotta leave her be. I no understand how come men ain't so smart when it comes to this kind of stuff."

Lying there in the dim light, her beautiful face nestled in a halo of dark hair against the white pillow, Connie looked to him like a fragile doll, one that could easily be broken. And he quickly began to feel like a clumsy ox, worrying people that he was going to break things, and it seemed as if he had only been home ten minutes.

It was just plain bewildering. His had been a world of men and horses, of cattle and mountains and open spaces, of guns and conflict, and now here he was standing in his own bedroom, confronting the most frightening situation he had ever faced.

Political intrigue, fighting off attacking Indians, cavalry charges, these were what he knew, each almost second nature to him. It was a world where control was always within his grasp, where he could shape things to fit his demands; but this . . . Here, in his own home, he was facing a circumstance that was almost beyond his understanding, let alone his control.

To further his confusion and consternation, he felt as if his feelings were spinning out of control. How could a man be so happy, so completely bewildered, and so scared all at the same time? If he were to lose Connie, his life would be over, and it would be his fault. It wasn't that he had taken things so lightly. She was more precious to him than life itself. It was just that . . . they had experienced such joy in one another. Wasn't that the way of things between a man and his wife? She came so late into his world, and all through his lonely years he had anticipated the joy of sharing everything, life itself, with this one special woman. It was just that Consuelo had fulfilled all of his dreams. It was just that his life was only complete when she was in his arms. It was just that . . . who could have expected this? She was his wife, and without her, he would have nothing to live for—nothing at all.

Consuelo's face darkened, and lifting her knees slightly and turning her face away from Clay, she moaned softly into the pillow.

"What? What is it?" Clay asked, his voice breaking with anxiety. "What's the matter? Consuelo? Emily?"

Relaxing after a moment, Consuelo smiled up at her anxious husband. "It's alright. It just happens now and then. Everything's going to be fine."

"Emily?" Clay said, his concern growing. "What's the matter? Emily, what should we do?"

"Do? What you mean, *do,* Clay Ashworth?"

"Oh, for goodness sakes, Clay. I'm alright. It was just a passing pain. And don't be so nervous. Doc Richards will be here in the morning. He always shows up on Thursday mornings."

"Emily," Clay stammered, his face pale with anxiety, "is tomorrow Thursday?"

"Either Clay must be very tired, Emily," Connie snickered, "or this pregnancy must be very hard on him. You might need to help the poor man find his nightshirt," she teased, "and get him tucked safely into bed."

CHAPTER 2

★ ★ ★

I<small>T WAS THE THIRD DAY</small> of the battle, cloudy and hot—and dust, thick and choking, hung in the air, clogging the nostrils and stinging the eyes of man and beast alike. The lone Union officer lowered his binoculars, wondering if so little ground had ever before been so hotly contested. It was late in the day, his body ached with fatigue, his spirits sagged, and it had gotten too dark to see anything clearly in the bloody confusion below. No matter; the second battle of Bull Run was all but over. Napoleon said it, and the past three days had proved the point: war truly is "the business of barbarians."

Sent by Mister Lincoln as his personal observer, the young cavalry officer, Major Jonathan Wickham Duncan—Johnny to his friends—had spent three long days in the saddle, watching from various vantage points the battle's development and progress, the ebb and flow of determined warfare, in all its violent brutality. Four years as a West Point cadet had taught him about war and soldiering, but nothing had prepared him for the shocking reality of what he had witnessed here amidst the beauty of the northern Virginia countryside. To have been in the struggle, fighting for one's life, if not for the Union, would have been one thing. But to have witnessed the carnage and not been a part of it was an experience for which he had been totally unprepared.

At the request of the president, Jonathan Duncan had been ordered to serve as an unattached observer, free to move about the fields of engagement without hindrance. Several field commanders had questioned his presence, but the special presidential commission tucked safely inside his blouse ended any further inquiry or objections.

Sitting back in the saddle, Duncan put the field glasses in their case, removed his hat, and wiped the perspiration from his grimy forehead. Just four years out of West Point, and he was already a fieldgrade officer, a major of cavalry. Say what you will about the horrors of war, for a young professional soldier aspiring to greatness, there was a positive side to it: rank advancement came faster when lead balls filled the air, and he had been in all the right places to reap the benefits. His father, an Illinois lawyer and friend of Mister Lincoln, had seen to that. That Cadet Duncan, upon graduation, had opted for and been assigned cavalry duty, had done him no harm, either. The majority of his classmates had wound up as infantry officers, and the few he had encountered over the past three days—all still company-grade officers—had shot him glances that ranged from envy to disapproval, just as one might have expected.

But even more disturbing was the number of men with whom he had walked the halls of the nation's military academy who were now wearing butternut gray and shooting back at their fellow alumni. This was a crazy war, to say the least. One thing seemed certain, though: it was going to be a long one. Those who thought the fight would be over in a matter of months, if not weeks, were just plain nuts. What he had witnessed here at Manassas Junction, sixteen months into the war, certainly would put an end to that kind of speculation.

During the previous three days, Pope's Federals had fought bravely, as had McDowell's more than a year earlier, when the Confederates had sent the Union force back across Bull Run in confusion, if not outright panic. This time, though whipped again, Pope's beleaguered Army of Virginia had ended the day holding Henry House Hill and the line of retreat to Centreville.

It had been one gut-buster of a battle. Shortly before 4:00 P.M., Longstreet had launched a massive attack against the leading Federal units. Anderson's division and part of Hood's had pushed forward north of the Warrenton Turnpike and crossed in front of Jackson's embattled right. The rest of Hood's forces smashed into Warren's New York brigade, the only Federals remaining south of the pike. Then, shortly after 5:00 P.M., the bulk of Longstreet's command had been hurled against a hastily formed Federal line on Chinn Ridge. It was a dangerous flanking maneuver, but in less than an hour the Confederates had swept the ridge clean.

With the ridge lost, Pope's entire left had begun to collapse, his troops retreating toward the Warrenton Turnpike. By 6:00 P.M., Jackson had attacked both the center and right of Pope's army, and the day was all but lost for the Union.

Though some units struggled to hold on, the Union line had largely crumbled, falling back toward Bull Run. Only brigades from divisions commanded by Reynolds, Sykes, Reno, and Schurz had kept the Union army from complete disaster by stubbornly holding the Manassas-Sudley Road and the slopes of Henry

House Hill, keeping the Confederate right from reaching the turnpike and blocking the Federal line of withdrawal.

Yet, after a bitter day of bloody fighting, when all was said and done, Pope's army had been beaten, but not routed. As darkness fell, little was left for the Union force but withdrawal and humiliation. Bull Run had again witnessed a Union defeat. But the fight had been bloody, Confederate forces advancing only at great cost. Union divisions, brigades, and even single regiments had made heroic stands in an attempt to cover the withdrawal and stall the Confederate advance. In the end, however, Pope's forces had been no match for either Jackson or Longstreet, and certainly not the two together.

From where the young Union observer sat, things looked bleak, to say the least. It was a discouraging thought, but the longer the war dragged on, the more apparent it became that the southern rebellion was not going to be easily crushed. With this defeat, the way to the defenses surrounding the northern capital now appeared to lay open, and after the events of the past three days, it was becoming obvious that this new Confederate general, Robert E. Lee, was showing himself to be a military leader the Union had better take seriously. It was true that Lee had taken the reins of the Army of Northern Virginia only a short time before, but if the last three days were indicative of anything, it was that the South had the military leadership to fight—and fight well.

Just how much of a threat Lee would become remained to be seen, but he had already succeeded in taking the pressure off Richmond; and now on the offensive, he had put the squeeze on Washington. Under lackluster leadership, the Union Army seemed to be getting a constant mauling by the Confederates, and with Lee's army now standing near Washington, even Union victories in the West were beginning to lose their hopeful significance.

After three long days of watching the fight develop, it had begun to appear to the young Union observer that the Confederates seemed to have in some abundance that most precious of all commodities: battlefield intelligence. Between Stuart and Hampton, it appeared as if the two cavalry units had provided all the information Lee needed to take the fight to Pope's boys. No matter where they fought, it looked as if Confederate commanders somehow understood the field of battle as no Union commander had yet come to do. It almost was as if there were Confederate eyes and ears everywhere, as if somehow the Rebel commanders stood above the entire countryside and could see everything. From where Lincoln's young observer sat, that was perhaps the most disturbing part of the entire second battle of Manassas.

Of course, it wasn't so. Lee and the other Confederate commanders had the same problems as those faced by Union generals: a debilitating lack of information, their excellent cavalry aside. There had been misunderstandings in moving troops to their best advantage, and at times Lee had seemed to hesitate when he should have pushed ahead. Still, they had risen above such difficulties, at times even appearing to stumble into victory when those with more troops and better equipment somehow managed to fail.

Yet, in the end, with little or no organized effort to collect information on the enemy, fighting a war successfully was more a chance of luck based on insufficient information. However, Lee and his commanders were beginning to appear doubly blessed where Union commanders too often fell short. The really disturbing question was, why? Was it lack of information, or lack of leadership? Or both?

Straightening in the saddle, the Union officer reined his horse about to begin the difficult journey back to Washington. Exhausted as he was, he knew it would be an agonizing ride, made even harder by the necessity of making his way along winding country roads clogged with bedraggled and wounded troops, struggling to leave behind them the fields of their humiliation.

From where he had last observed the battle, the weary soldier was faced with the necessity of making his way past Centreville, then through the northern Virginia countryside to Fairfax Courthouse, then to Falls Church, and finally to Washington City.

Picking his way through some dense stands of timber, down a slope strewn with the wounded and dying, and across one field after another, each heavily scarred from the battle, he finally reached the Warrenton Turnpike and the stone bridge spanning Bull Run. The road was jammed with retreating troops, many of whom could hardly walk because of their wounds, and the stone bridge looked to be completely choked with horses, wagons, and men, all struggling to reach the perceived safety of the other side. It was a pathetic sight he would long remember.

The ride quickly proved to be a nightmare, but the young major deeply felt the need to reach the Executive Mansion before the president received the full story of the defeat. Earlier in the day he had learned that three times during the fight, Mister Lincoln had wired his generals hoping for some word. But as far as he knew, even at this late hour, the president's messages had not been answered.

The man in the Executive Mansion needed to know what had happened and some competent eyewitness analysis as to why. And as far as Johnny Duncan could tell, there was no one else to provide that information—no one, at any rate, without an ax to grind, something to hide, or a picture to paint that would not be entirely truthful.

What might have brightened Lincoln's day at this bleak juncture of the war, had anyone been able to assess it, was the fact that General Robert E. Lee's victory at the Second Battle of Bull Run would prove to be the quickest and the easiest decisive victory he would ever achieve. But who could have guessed it? There was no way to know. Communication was a major problem. Little information of any kind was getting into or out of the federal capital, and even if there had been, no reasonable basis for such a heartening analysis existed.

His lanky frame slumped in his chair, his face gaunt, his hand frequently straying to his forehead, the sixteenth president of the United States listened intently to the young officer standing at attention before him. Another of Lincoln's headaches was coming on, and what he was hearing was doing nothing to lift his spirits. Twice the president had invited Duncan to take a chair and relax a bit, but the young major remained stiff as a pole, the words spilling forth with uncontrolled energy as he described the battles he had witnessed. There was just no stopping him.

At this juncture in the rebellion, Lincoln knew he simply could not allow himself to reflect on where it was all heading. To allow this nation, not yet a century old, to completely disintegrate into the throes of suicidal sectionalism was simply not acceptable. The nation almost would die aborning. With a weak central government at the constitutional mercy of thirty-four separate, squabbling states, how could the country ever fend off or compete with grasping European powers, let alone become a world leader in its own right?

No one who has held this office, Lincoln gloomily thought to himself, *has ever had such a load dumped on him. Where do I look for any help, any example?* The corners of Lincoln's mouth lifted ever so slightly. *Oh,* he thought, *there was Buchanan—poor Buchanan. But Buchanan really couldn't be looked to. The man was no example of executive leadership. No, no help there. I have to face this . . . alone.*

"The truth is, Mister President," the young major finally concluded, intruding into Lincoln's gloom, "they were just better than our boys. Their leadership . . . somehow smarter."

Lincoln's hand momentarily dropped to the arm of his chair. Something in the way the young solider had said it somehow caught his attention. "What do you mean, *better,* son?" Lincoln's hand again strayed to his forehead. "*Smarter,* you say. Smarter in what way? We've got leadership problems, it's true, but where could you find a better-trained officer corps—at least among those trained at West Point?"

Not sure the president had been listening, the question caught the young officer by surprise. "Ah . . . well, sir, I guess . . . on the other side. I mean, I saw some of my old classmates and a few West Point faculty members across those killing grounds, sir. Why, General Lee was Commandant of West Point the year I entered the academy, sir."

"Yes, of course," Lincoln said somberly. The headache was getting worse, and he was feeling the need to darken the room and maybe rest for a while. "Yes . . . I'm aware of that. Too many of our best officers have chosen to stand with the rebellion. But they come from the same military background, for the most part."

"What I mean, sir, is they somehow seemed to understand the field of battle better than our commanders. I don't have much experience, Mister President. Well, truth be told, I don't have any experience to speak of. But it seems to me, sir, that more must be done to out-think the enemy, and I don't see how that can be done when our men are facing theirs across some field and the battle has already started. I mean . . . it seems to me, we need more information . . . more intelligence, or something, so we can beat them to the punch. Maybe just better maps would do the trick. I mean . . . sometimes there aren't even any maps at all. I guess I'm not making myself very clear, sir."

Oh, to be young again, Lincoln thought, as he watched the young officer across his desk. *To be his age again, and to be in his shoes. I think I could win this war by myself if I could just. . . .*

"Mister President, are you feeling okay, sir? You don't look so good, if you'll excuse me saying so, sir."

The President leaned forward, his elbows on the desk. "Young Major Duncan, I think you've hit on something important, something that's been bothering me, as well. And don't worry too much about your inexperience, son. Sometimes coming fresh to the field of battle enables a man to see what others have failed to see—or been too blind to see. I've been thinking for some time now that more often than not, it's the old dogs who don't get up and move when they should who cause the most problems.

"Now, Major," Lincoln said, indicating the door, "if you'll excuse me, I'm not feeling too chipper. Don't leave town just yet, son. You'll stay attached to the Executive Mansion for the time being."

★　★　★

The message from President Lincoln of the rapidly disinte-grating United States had been on Brigham Young's desk for sev-eral days. The telegraph line from the East had reached Salt Lake City some ten months earlier, but there were times when such modern, efficient communication was something less than a blessing. This was such a time.

The Mormon leader slid the telegram across his desk toward Doctor Richards. "Take a look at this, Doctor, and tell me what you think. Can Clay Ashworth be taken from his wife's bedside yet?"

The doctor read the short telegram, then read it again. "Well, I just can't say, Brother Brigham. She's in an extremely delicate condition, as you know, and no wife should be denied the pres-ence of her husband just at the time her baby's due. I know that's not the usual practice, but I firmly believe a woman in labor needs her husband close at hand."

Young leaned back, the weight of his thick body causing his chair to complain loudly. The room fell silent as he studied some spot on the ceiling, the other men in the room sensing this was not the time for talk. Finally, leaning forward, he asked, "Just what is the nature of her problem? When last here, she appeared healthy enough. Though, at that time, I must say, I had no idea she was with child. I'm not sure anyone did."

"It's not all that unusual, President Young. She's been threaten-ing to deliver the child early—for at least two months, now. That surely would have been disastrous, but now she's about to term, and I think the baby could safely come at any time. I'd feel much better, though, if she were here in town where I could watch her closely."

"Is Clay aware of all of this?" the prophet asked, his concern obvious.

"He is. In fact, I don't know when I've seen an expectant father more attentive and concerned than Clay Ashworth. Come to think of it, I don't think I ever have." Richards grinned. "In some ways it's almost comical."

"Mmm . . . one seldom thinks of a father as *expectant*," the Mormon prophet said, a grin also crossing his face.

"Well, if the description fits anyone, it more than fits Clay Ashworth," Richards chuckled.

For a long moment Brigham Young seemed lost in thought, his mood growing more serious. "Doctor, I want you to go down to their ranch and bring her back here. We can put them both up right here until the baby comes.

"Jeb, I'd like you to go with Doctor Richards. You were with Clay at Glorieta Pass, and the two of you are fairly close friends. Clay will appreciate your concern. I'd like you both to leave at once. In the meantime, I'll see that a room is prepared for them here in the compound."

Seeing no need for further talk, Jeb Smith rose from his chair and turned toward the door. "Are you coming, Doc?"

Richards leaned forward in his chair. "You see, Brother Brigham, it's not just her coming to term that worries me."

"No? Well, what then, Brother Richards?"

"The greatest danger to Mrs. Ashworth will be after the birth of her child. As you well know, the death rate among new mothers is extremely high, in some places reaching alarming proportions. The problem is one of infection and inflammation. It's called puerperal fever, or childbed fever."

A frowning Brigham Young sat with his elbow resting on the arm of his chair, a forefinger tapping his chin, staring intently at the doctor. When at last he spoke, he said, "The number of children in this household . . . well, that has not seemed to be an insurmountable problem, has it, Doctor? I mean, stop and think, Brother Richards. You can't blink at that kind of success."

Returning to his chair, Jeb Smith asked, "Have you got some new kind of medicine, Doc?"

"No. Believe it or not, it's much more simple than that, brethren. I'm fortunate to have gotten my hands on an article only recently published by a professor of obstetrics at Budapest University. Ignaz Philipp Semmelweiss is his name. He has found that puerperal fever, in all likelihood, is spread by physicians who simply do not wash their hands before examining their patients, something I've long suspected. Proof lies in the fact that with those who do—wash their hands, that is—the death rate among their patients drops dramatically. Yet the solution seems so astoundingly simple, it's hard to believe that many doctors refuse to do it."

"Humph," Young grunted. "Does that kind of arrogance really surprise you, Doctor?"

"Frankly, no. However, I've been doing it all along. That and boiling bed sheets to get the blood out. Up to now, I've always thought it almost a fetish, but I can't stand dirty hands. My wife thinks I'm just an old fussbudget, but filth anywhere, on anything, has always bothered me. Not out of any training I've had, mind you. It's just that the cleaner my hands and tools are, the better I feel. I know now that is undoubtedly the reason why incidents of puerperal fever—and perhaps a host of other diseases—have not been a problem in what I do."

A look somewhere between surprise and disgust crossed the Mormon prophet's face. "Well, it's been long noted, Brother Richards, that cleanliness is next to godliness. And it seems a truth so obvious that it's a wonder to me that more so-called 'men of science' have failed to even stumble upon it. Unfortunately, truths have a way of becoming trite. Maybe that's the problem."

"Trite, perhaps, but all too true, it would seem. Well, the short of it is, Brother Brigham, if we can keep her here and keep her clean—and keep me clean—the danger will be minimized, and Clay Ashworth will have a happy, healthy baby. And a happy, healthy wife."

"Yes," Young said, glancing at the telegram on his desk, "healthy, but I'm not so sure about happy. I'll have to share this message with Clay. The decision will be his . . . theirs."

It was the most difficult night of Clay's life—the night their baby girl died only moments after birth—and his wife lay near death in the next room. How could Clay tell Connie how beautiful the baby had been before that tiny body had been taken from his arms? How could he ever explain the hollowness he felt inside, as if, when that little body was taken from him, his very soul had been wrenched from him and taken with her? How could Consuelo, his Connie, ever know how deeply he loved her, how desperately he needed her, to feel her safely in his arms, forever in his life?

All throughout that evil night, listening to the muffled sounds of his beloved's terrible struggle, Clay's mind kept going back to that wonderful evening in San Francisco, when he had first seen her. It had been at the gala dinner party hosted by Senator and Mrs. William Gwin for their closest friends and secessionist allies that Clay had first met her.[2]

She and her parents had just entered the Gwin's vestibule, and from where Clay stood, on the far side of a very crowded living room, the flash of her red dress had caught his eye as she removed her cloak. He knew then he was looking at the most exquisite woman in the world, and he knew as she glanced up and their eyes briefly met—as he knew now—life without her would be unthinkable; without her any future would be destitute, forever incomplete.

Maria Emilea Consuelo Salinas was the most perfectly stunning woman he had ever met—ever laid eyes on. If anything, her beauty was exceeded only by her intelligence. Almost from the moment they sat down at dinner and she overheard her father speaking with him, she had begun challenging him, needling him on every subject, jabbing at him, especially where the Territory of Utah and Brigham Young were concerned. There was just no letting up. But with each provocative word from her perfect mouth, he had fallen more deeply in love. Before they had left the table that magic evening, she had taken him completely captive, and she would hold him so for as long as he lived.

It was Brigham Young who quietly persuaded Clay to at last relinquish the tiny body to the waiting arms of a distraught Chet Langtree who, along with Robby Robshaw, Clay's two closest friends, would see to any necessary final preparations. They would take the small bundle south to *Rancho los Librados* for burial near the large ranch house that was to have been the child's home.

Brigham Young sat next to Clay, listening to the big man's broken sobs, his hand lying softly on Clay's trembling shoulder, hoping his quiet presence would offer some comfort. How long the two sat there, neither could have said, but when Clay at last became aware of the Mormon leader's presence the shadows of the day had grown long.

"Why, President Young? Why? She was so perfect, her little hands, her beautiful face, her tiny feet? But . . . there was no life, only for a moment or two." Clay's voice failed him, and the sobs broke through his struggle for composure. Catching his breath, his voice high with emotion, he said, "I held her little face next to mine, but there was just nothing. She was gone. She never came, really."

"So much must be taken on faith, Clay. Only the Eternal Father can answer such questions, and you'll need to approach Him for that. In our faith, we know there is a purpose to all things, even such tragedies as this. There is a meaning to it all. That little spirit gained her body, and for now, that was sufficient. But the time will come, Clay, when that perfect little person will rise again, just as the Son of God did, and where she'll be, we will all want to be. With sufficient faith, you and Connie can have her as yours, at last."

Neither spoke for some time, the mood too somber for words. At last, Clay asked, "But how, President Young? How? How do I explain that to my wonderful wife? How do I explain it to her?"

"Perhaps now is not the time, Clay. We'll save that for another time, a time when your grief has abated somewhat. Now is the time for mourning and for comforting your sweet wife. She still must be told. You need to be with her when she awakens."

Clay heard the screened door of the big ranch house bang shut but thought nothing of it until Consuelo sat down next to him. He had spent much of the morning sitting on the split log bench that weeks before had been placed at the side of their baby's small grave. In the nearly two months since that terrible night, hardly a word had passed between them. Clay had not known what to say to comfort her, and Connie had withdrawn to a place where he wasn't invited.

From the moment Clay had told Connie of the death of their baby, and she had turned her head into her pillow, their lives had begun to slip apart. At a time when each desperately needed the love and understanding of the other, a dark gulf of depression had opened between them that neither knew how to cross. On the surface, Connie had seemed at first to rally from the shock, but inside she was emotionally devastated and unable to communicate her deepest needs—even to the man she loved.

Neither knew how to deal with the loss alone, but neither of them knew how to comfort the other, not beyond words that in the end somehow sounded hollow and meaningless. And as the days crawled by, the silences had grown longer and the gulf wider. Finally, to give his wife the solitude she seemed to seek, Clay moved out of their bedroom, and the silence had become total.

For the longest moment neither spoke. Each sat alone, isolated, staring at the only thing they now held in common, the small mound of earth at their feet. Only the sough of the wind through the large Ponderosa pine trees surrounding the small grave could be heard, its lonesome sound adding to the sense of emptiness each felt. Neither reached out for the other, no hand finding the touch that was so desperately needed.

It was she who finally broke the silence. "Clay . . . I'm going back to Mexico."

Her words caused Clay to stir, to force away the numbness that had so deadened his mind and body since that terrible night. "Mexico?" he said, like a child hearing the word for the first time. "But why? It's so far away. You belong here. This is our home. Here is where our child is buried."

"I don't know," she said, her gaze falling to the small grave. "Maybe that's why. To get away from here. From her."

"*From her?*" Clay said, unsure of what he was hearing. "But you're her mother."

Connie's breath caught and tears welled up. "Maybe that's what I mean, Clay. I'm not a mother. I'm nobody's mother, and I can't deal with it. I don't know how to deal with it, Clay. There are too many memories here," she said, stifling a sob, "and I don't know what to do."

For the first time since their baby's death, Clay Ashworth's mind began to clear, to push away the heavy burden of grief that had taken him down, and he reached for her hand.

"No. Don't," she said, snatching her hand from his, rising from the bench. "I'm going, that's all. Please don't try to stop me."

Grief was suddenly supplanted by a sense of terror that Clay had never felt before, and the words spilled out, words that had been dammed behind a wall of stunning shock and despair. It was happening again; something he loved was slipping from his grasp. "You can't run away, Connie. You belong here. You are my wife, and *Rancho los Librados* is your home—our home."

Connie stood looking down at her husband, as if she were looking at a stranger. "I need to go. Don't you understand? There's an emptiness here that I can't deal with . . . that's all."

Clay got to his feet, and she reluctantly allowed him to pull her into his arms. "But, Connie," he said, holding her as if for the first time, "that's all life is—memories—the now and the then, and not everything can be expected to be good. And what of our future? What do you expect to find back in Mexico?"

She stood stiff and unyielding in his arms, and he knew something had closed between them. "Have you forgotten the evil done to you and your family by Zamora, the murder of your parents? Have you forgotten the happiness we found together?"

"No," she said, pulling herself free and turning toward the house. "I haven't forgotten."

She was gone. Only some hint of her having been there remained in the air, but the sound of the screened door banging shut behind her shattered even that, leaving him with a crushing sense of finality.

Clay knew there was nothing he could do but let her go.

CHAPTER 3

★ ★ ★

Major? Major Striker?"

Wolf Striker's eyes fluttered, and wishing nothing more than to be left alone, he managed to respond to the newest irritant in his life with something between a grunt and groan.

A gentle hand rested on his shoulder. "Come, Major, you need to wake up now. You Confederates need to move on before our Union troops begin arriving."

The delicate touch was accompanied by a soft, cultured voice—a woman's voice. But it wasn't so much the distinctly feminine voice as it was the threatened arrival of Union troops that momentarily overwhelmed all other sensations, and with renewed effort, Wolf Striker strove to focus on his unfamiliar surroundings. "*Our Union troops,*" he croaked. Wolf grappled with the thought for a moment, then struggling for some understanding blurted, "You mean, Yankees?"

"That's right, Major—*Yankees*—and they'll be here before too long. You need to hurry."

As his mind slowly began to clear, Wolf Striker realized he was looking into a pair of bright, sympathetic, blue eyes. "Who're you?" he rasped, the discordant sound almost unintelligible. "Where the blazes am I, anyway?"

"Never mind who she is." Lieutenant Colonel William Scurry abruptly retorted. "You just get up and get dressed, Major. We are in Santa Fe, and we need to be out of here within the hour."

"Oh . . . yeah . . . Santa Fe," Wolf stammered, struggling with the tangled bedding, his head throbbing from the effort. "I didn't know you were here, Colonel. Where'd you come from, anyway?"

"Best you leave now, Mrs. Canby," Scurry said, with a nod toward the door. "And once again, ma'am, please accept our heartfelt thanks."

"If you're sure, Colonel. I do hope everything's all right. He certainly doesn't look very well, does he? I'm sure the infection has not—"

"Everything's fine, ma'am, and thank you so much for all you've done. I'll help Major Striker, here, get into what's left of his uniform."

"Who'd you say that was?" Wolf mumbled, still trying to get a focus on his surroundings.

"That fine lady," Scurry said, nodding toward the woman as she stepped from the room, "is Missus Louisa Canby, the wife of Colonel Edward Canby, the Union departmental commander in these parts. She—"

"Canby? The Union commander?" Wolf repeated, renewed pain crowding his consciousness, his mind again receding into gray fuzziness.

"That's right. She's literally the Angel of Santa Fe, where we're concerned. She and other wives of Union soldiers have played angels of mercy to our needs."

"Huh," Wolf grunted, indifferently.

"I tell you, these women are amazing, Wolf. It was of little concern to them that we are Confederate soldiers. These wonderful women saw our need, and their humanity saved a good many lives these past few days. Yours among them, I might add. However, Major, I don't think her husband and his men will display such a Christian attitude toward our presence here, so just you concentrate on getting dressed, you hear?"

"The Union commander?" Wolf echoed, his mind suddenly flooding with memories of the lost battle at Johnson's Ranch. "We're not prisoners?"

"No," Scurry said, finding Wolf's boots and setting them next to the bed. "You were grievously wounded at Johnson's Ranch, and when we started evacuating, you passed out. You've been unconscious for several days, and it's a good thing, too. It took both Doctor Jordan and Doctor Matchett a good deal of time figuring out how to patch you up, and your wound is still badly infected. For some reason, it refuses to heal—perhaps that's the worst part."

"Jordan?"

"Uh-huh. Along with everything else, he's a doctor. Knows his stuff, too—had to dig a chunk of lead out of you big enough to kill a grizzly. It's here on your bed stand," Scurry said, plucking the blood-stained object off the table. Examining it for a moment, he handed it to Wolf. "Looks to be a .52 caliber slug—slightly used."

Trying to focus on the misshaped object, Wolf rolled it around in the palm of his hand. "Yeah . . . that's what it is, all right."

"Not exactly army issue," Scurry casually observed. "How do you suppose you got in its way?"

Avoiding Scurry's question, Wolf placed the ball on the bed stand and turned to struggle with his boots. "Maybe I ought to keep that thing for a souvenir," he mumbled, half to himself. "Never know when something like that might come in handy, paperweight or something."

Scurry studied his subordinate for a moment. "Didn't you tell me that shot came from the other side of the canyon, opposite the cliff down which the Yankees attacked?"

With a deep sigh, Wolf sat back on the bed, weak from the effort of attempting to dress himself, and looked at his superior officer for a long moment, watching the bearded visage slowly slip from focus. "Colonel Scurry, sir," he at last said, a sigh of fatigue escaping his pale lips, "how many men in this war have a past, do you suppose? One they would like kept in the past . . . infected, you say?"

"Mmm . . . ," Scurry responded, watching Wolf more closely. "You all right, Major? You're looking rather poorly. Major?"

★   ★   ★

It was a sharp poke in the arm that once again began to stir Wolf's awareness. It wasn't painful, but it wasn't pleasant—annoying is what it was. Nor was the rude jab accompanied by any soft, feminine voice. For some reason the jabs and the prodding just kept coming, as if an attempt were being made to punch a hole into him through which to pour the same irritatingly repeated question or demand. "Major. Major? Come on, Major, the vacation's over. Time to think of your future."

How long he had lain there, how long he had been unaware

of his surroundings, was unclear to Wolf, but with each goading jab, a certain urgency began penetrating his stuporous brain. The last thing he could remember with any degree of clarity was the struggle with his boots, as Colonel Scurry warned him of an approaching Union invasion—at least he thought that was what he had heard. And to add to the confusion, this new annoyance was not accompanied by Confederate Lieutenant Colonel William Scurry's irksome drawl.

"Come on, Major. We have your future, and the future of your remaining men to discuss."

"*My* men?" Wolf said, his mind refusing some implied sense of ownership or responsibility, his voice little more than a rasping croak.

"Major, you and some of your men are still in Santa Fe. The rest of you rebels have evacuated New Mexico and are headed, I suppose, back to Texas. Now, the issue is, Mister Striker, what am I to do with you?"

Wolf slowly turned onto his side and struggled to sit up. His body, slow to cooperate, was suddenly shot through with renewed pain. "Oh . . . Jehoshaphat," he mumbled, half to himself. "I can't . . . Here, let me sit up," he said, attempting to clear his throat, his voice unwilling to return. "I need to get things straight here."

"Yes, you do," the Union officer said, taking Wolf by the arm. "Here, let me help you. We need to make some decisions, you and I."

"Texas, you say? I don't—"

"Major Striker, you need to snap out of it. As of now, you are the ranking Confederate officer here in Santa Fe, and we need to discuss the status and disposition of you and your men."

Attempting to focus on the blue-clad officer before him, Wolf shook his head, and asked, "Who the devil are you?"

"I'm Colonel Benjamin Roberts. I'm commander of the Northern District of the Department of New Mexico. I have just arrived in Santa Fe—only yesterday, to be precise—and have established the Federal military presence here."

Wolf tried to concentrate on the man's face as it slowly swam in and out of focus, and his thought processes slowly pushed aside the pain and sluggishly began functioning. "You must forgive me, Colonel," Wolf drawled, his mind fighting the effort. "You see . . . I'm afraid I'm not myself. How long did you say I've been this way?"

"Well, so far as I know, it's been several days—perhaps longer. I really can't say, but you do need to get control of yourself, and we need to—"

"How many men? How many wounded . . . anyway? I . . . I have no clear recollection of the past day or so."

"Several days ago, Captain James Ford and his Colorado Volunteers rode into town with eighty-four Texans—at least I think they're all Texans—captured at Apache Canyon and Glorieta Pass. They are still with us, and you're the senior officer remaining here in Santa Fe."

"But what of—"

"Those who earlier arrived here with you, after the battle, have all headed back to Texas. The latest word is there has been a fight down along the Rio Grande somewhere. However, I have no idea how things have gone for them since leaving here.

"The point being, Major Striker, there are problems we must deal with—here and now. For starters, we are faced with an alarming lack of medical supplies and a rapidly diminishing store of food. As you can understand, I have my own men to think of. We are at war—their needs must now come first."

Wolf's hand felt heavy as he rubbed his forehead, where the

pain seemed about to break through his skull. His vision was again dimming, and he began feeling himself slipping back down out of the light. "Colonel . . . with all due respect . . . I don't think I—"

"Yes, I can see that," Roberts said, a sense of futility overcoming his desire to get on with things. Attempting to negotiate through the Confederate officer's weakened condition was getting them nowhere. "Look here, Major, you appear to be bleeding—your wound must have opened. I'll send someone in to see to your needs. But, Major, I can give you only until morning—after lunch, say."

Wolf let himself fall back onto the bed. "Yes. Thank you . . . morning."

"Just let me say one thing more, Major Striker," the Union officer said, leaning over Wolf's prostrate form in an attempt to make himself understood. "None of your men has been molested in any way while under my command, nor shall you be. Do you understand what I'm saying, Major? No one has been molested. However, your status, and that of your remaining men, must be clarified as soon as possible. Do I make myself clear, Major? Major Striker?"

Molested? Who'd he say was molested? Wolf's shock-numbed mind seized on the word, as if it would give him some half-hoped-for buoyancy, as if it might yield some important memory, some clarity of understanding he could grab onto.

But slipping beneath the surface, away from the face of authority blurring into darkness above him, once again sinking away from the light, Wolf Striker knew nothing could save him from his torments, the least of which was physical pain. Deep in his fevered brain the recurrent, agonizing thought would give him no rest: *molested . . . Chapultepec . . . death.* Was he truly beyond redemption? *Long is the way And hard, that out of hell leads up to light.*

In the end . . . did it matter?

★   ★   ★

Through the open jail cell door, Marshal Orrin Porter Rockwell recognized Ben Kimball's footsteps the minute he heard them on the boardwalk approaching his office. For some reason, the man always walked with a heavy-heeled manner. Which was okay, because Kimball was not a man to throw his weight around or try to bulldoze or bluff anyone, it was just his way. In fact, there were few men Rockwell liked more.

Benjamin Pratt Kimball was a solid citizen, one Rockwell knew he could trust with his life—and he had done so on more than one occasion. The trouble was, he was certain Kimball would be coming from Brigham Young's office, and that could only mean the prophet wanted an accounting—not a welcome thought to a man just awakening from a miserable night's sleep on a hard, cold, jail cell bunk. And not after a long, grueling trip through the mountains from Santa Fe. A trip that in more ways than one he could not count as successful.

As Kimball entered the outer office, Rockwell rolled onto his side, facing the rough stone wall, not wanting to deal with whatever the man was bringing with him.

After a long moment, Kimball tapped on the iron doorframe. "Come on, Port," he said, settling onto a stubby wooden chair just outside the cell, "you're being rude again—still, actually."

"Huh," Rockwell grumped.

"President Young would like a few minutes with you."

"I was comin' up later this mornin'."

"It can't get much *later this mornin'*," Kimball bantered. "It's almost noon."

Rockwell lay silent, as if contemplating his options, then heaving a sigh, rolled over and sat up. "Not that much t' tell."

"What little there is, he'll want to hear it."

"Well . . . I ain't so sure."

Thirty minutes later Ben Kimball and Orrin Porter Rockwell sat in Brigham Young's office while the Mormon leader stared out through a window pondering what he had just heard.

Looking contemplative, Young turned, and said, "So . . . you're not certain if Wolf Striker is dead or alive? Is that correct?"

"No, sir, there's just no way to be sure," Rockwell said, shifting in his chair. "He escaped before he could be brought to justice at Fort Union."

"Mmm. By *justice,* you mean hanged?"

"Yessir. Like I said, the place was in such a mess of confusion—troops arriving and all. I trailed him as far as a ranch located at the east end of the canyon, where the trail climbs into the mountains, up to Glorieta Pass."

"But you never followed him farther?"

"No, sir. Not up the canyon, anyway. But when Clay Ashworth and his boys caught up with me, the two of us sort of decided it would be best if he looked for him during the fight. I mean, a real brouhaha was lookin' about to let loose between those Federal troopers from Fort Union and them Texas Confederates on the other side of the pass. In the middle of that was no place for me t' get caught."

"So, you let it go at that, Port?" the prophet asked, the look on his face leaving little doubt he already knew the answer. "Frankly, it doesn't seem like you to let go quite so easily, especially after what Striker had done at Platte River Station."

"Truth is, Brother Brigham, I couldn't just let go."

"No," Young chuckled. "I thought not."

"Wasn't easy, but I got finally around on the north side of the canyon, above where the Confederates had their supply wagons, over on the Santa Fe side, and in the confusion of the Union attack, I got a bead on 'im. He dropped right in his tracks, but there's just no way of knowing if I killed him—brought him to justice, that is, for killing those Cartwright boys and all the others."

"Well, it's hard to argue that he didn't deserve being called to account, somehow. What he and those hoodlums with him did at Platte River Station can't be called an act of war—not by any stretch of the imagination. It was a bloody assault that resulted in the death and suffering of innocent people—not to mention the Cartwright brothers, who were just doing their duty." Young watched Rockwell for a moment, attempting to read the man's reactions. Then, finally, "Right, Port?"

"Yessir," Rockwell said, half lost in thought.

"But what, Port?"

Rockwell sighed heavily and said, "When I first caught up to him in the New Mexico mountains, the man was more dead than alive, shot through, bleeding, and nearly frozen stiff. Fact is, I thought he was dead. I mean, even after patching him up, thawing him out, and getting some food into him, there was just no fight left. It was as if shooting him would have been doing him a favor. He said as much, in fact."

"Mmm," Young said, sensing Rockwell's softened, almost remorseful, attitude. "Well . . . since you could have, why didn't you?"

"I dunno. There's just something about that man. I don't know what it is, but I almost liked the cuss. Still do."

"Well," Ben Kimball said, leaning forward in his chair, "maybe he's still alive. His kind somehow always seem to survive."

"What do you want me to do, President Young?"

"What is there that can be done, Port?" Young said, with a shrug of resignation. "Very little, I think. You should have brought him back here. Under the circumstances, shooting him would have been wrong, Port. It was nothing I condoned.

"My hope, for some reason, is that the man survived. What little I know of our Mister Striker, I've learned from others, but somehow I have this odd feeling about him. I think I agree with you, Port. There's just something about him: a kind of depth, some quality—something worth saving."

"I ain't so sure I can live without knowing," Rockwell said, his eyes searching Brigham Young's face, "if you know what I mean. One way or the other, I'm gonna need to find out."

Brigham Young stood up from his desk and, taking a deep breath, turned toward the window. "I need to get Clay Ashworth up here. Mister Lincoln has asked for his services once again. His circumstances are now such that I think he will respond to the call. When I get him here in the next few days, we'll see what he thinks."

★   ★   ★

The bedroom had grown dark, but somehow it didn't matter. Clay could not move; he had no desire to move, no reason. In truth, he had no idea how long he had sat there staring at the bed—his and Connie's bed. He hadn't slept in it since the day she and Emily had left for Mexico. How long that had been, he couldn't say. Days, nights, whatever—things just seemed to run together. With Connie's leaving, all had been lost, and time had become meaningless, his grasp on reality shattered, his reason for living gone.

With the death of the baby and Consuelo's—Connie's, forever his Connie—consequent inability to cope with their terrible loss, Clay's once perfect world had crumbled around him.

Emily had done her best to soften the blow for both of them, especially for Connie. In fact, that was why Emily had gone with her to Mexico, to help bring her back—back to life, back to Clay. But neither love nor reason had reached her. No matter what was said or done, there was just no spirit left from which anyone could draw.

It was not that Connie blamed Clay for the baby's death. If she had, it might have given him a means of reaching her, an avenue of communication, however tenuous. Instead, she had simply withdrawn, as if there were no love or life left in her, and the world had grown cold and empty. Since that bleak day, time had meant nothing, nor did he think it ever would again. The baby was dead, and the two women he loved beyond measure were gone. There was just no reason for him to go on.

It was the sound of boots on the stairs that brought him out of the melancholy stupor that had seized him and had held him down for so long. Why the hollow thumping of boots on the stairs would do that, he had no idea. Unless it was the sound of so many boots that had startled him; it wasn't just one person on the stairs. The growing rumble—the din, in fact—had to be made by an entire army, a mob invading his sanctuary of misery.

Clay looked up as indistinct forms flooded into the dark bedroom, crowding into his grim solitude. The oppressive horde quickly grew in size, giving him an uncomfortable sense of vulnerability, closing around him, hovering above him like some hard-breathing beast with many heads, and finally growing silent.

At length, one of the specters spoke. "Boss? Well . . . yuh see . . . we was wonderin' when you was gonna come out of it, like, and . . . we . . . well, we—"

"Clay," Robby butted in, "what Chet is tryin' to say is . . . Clay, you need to snap out of it. We need you. The ranch needs you, and folks are beginning to wonder what's going on. Things are happenin', and you're needed—seems like everywhere. President Young has even sent word that he wants to see you—something about Mister Lincoln needin' you."

Somewhere in the room someone struck a match and lit a lamp, and the dark heads before him gradually assumed familiar features. It struck Clay that this must be what it's like awakening from near death, a coma or something, and finding yourself surrounded by everyone you ever knew or counted as a friend. The sensation was almost overwhelming.

★   ★   ★

Two days later, Clay Ashworth slid the yellow telegram back across Brigham Young's desk. "Would you be kind enough to telegraph President Lincoln and tell him I'll be on my way in a few days?"

"Certainly. The telegram was addressed to me," Young said, watching Clay closely, "so I should respond. I've waited too long as it is."

"Yes, sir, and I apologize for that. I sort of lost contact with reality after Consuelo left."

"Yes. So I've heard. Oddly enough, Clay, this war between the states back east may be just what you need to let things sort themselves out. Time and circumstance can be great healers."

"I hope so, sir. I certainly hope so."

Seeing Clay Ashworth in such an obvious state of distress was more than Brigham Young had anticipated. The big rancher was thinner, more worn, and disheveled-looking both in manner and dress. The man almost looked defeated. But that simply could not be. Clay Ashworth was a man equal to any task, a man who had proved himself many times under the most difficult conditions. To see him so emotionally and physically drained when so many were relying on him was alarming, and it was all too obvious he could not be allowed to leave before something was said or done to help him reclaim some stability, his feeling of self-worth, some sense of purpose.

There was only one place to begin. "I don't know your wife well, Clay, but she struck me as a woman of great refinement and depth."

"Yes . . . yes, she is," Clay said, sitting straighter, the tone of his voice growing stronger at the mention of his wife and leaving no uncertainty as to his feelings. "I've been around a good deal, President Young, but I have never encountered anyone like Consuelo Salinas, nor will I ever again," he said, his voice almost wistful.

Even as he spoke, he could see her, just as if she were standing before him and there was no one else in the room. "She is the most beautiful woman I have ever met, just perfect in every way. But I think what I have always loved most about her is her sharpness of mind. She has kept me on my toes from the first moment I laid eyes on her, and she has made the world live for me ever since."

Clay's voice broke, and for a moment he could say nothing. Finally, struggling with his emotions, his gaze searching the room, he said, "I don't know what I'm going to do without her, President Young."

Only the ticking of the large clock in the corner could be heard as Brigham Young studied the man before him. That Clay

Ashworth was heartbroken was more than obvious, but that he was also a man of great character and resilience could not be doubted. After a few moments of silence, President Young said, "You won't be long without her, Clay. Of that, somehow, I am sure."

Clay looked up, relief flooding his drawn features. "But, I—"

"But for now, you're going to respond to your country's call and give your sweet wife time to heal. And, Clay, I am certain that's all she needs, time to heal, in a place that to her has always meant peace and safety—a place of comfort and stability. Think about that for a moment. After every adventure in her life—her education, her travels—where did she go?"

"Home. Like we all do, I guess."

"Yes. Like we *all* do. She's gone back home, her home, the only home she really has ever known."

"But her home is here. With me."

"Clay, things can happen too fast, too suddenly, for any real emotional adjustment to take place. My guess is she has just become overwhelmed—meeting the man of her dreams, the death of her parents, leaving the only real home she ever knew.

"Think of it, Clay. In just a few short months she met and married you, came to a strange land, and almost immediately suffered an extremely uncomfortable pregnancy, without the nearness and solicitude of her husband. And then giving birth to the child she had carried for so long, and with such difficulty, only to lose it at the moment of birth. When you add it all up, that sweet woman you love so much has suffered a devastating shock."

Clay drew a deep breath and let it out slowly. "I needed to hear this, President Young. I've had a hard time trying to sort things out, to make sense of it all. I guess it all happened too fast—for me, as well."

"Perhaps so," Young said, rising from his desk. The two men walked to the door, and Brigham Young drew Clay to him in a fatherly hug. "The truth is, Major Ashworth, I think right now she's trying to find herself; and with you leaving again, it may be best that she and Emily are in Mexico, the one place where she will be surrounded by what she has always thought of as her home."

Clay studied the Mormon leader's face. Brigham Young was, indeed, a true father figure, not only to his people, but in truth Clay felt that way about him as well. In fact, he felt a part of all the man before him stood for. "Do you really think I will ever get her back? Do you honestly think so?"

"I most assuredly do. Give her time, Clay. In Mexico she's going to discover that things are not the same as when she left; not what she expected; not what she thought she was returning to. The warm familiarity she's looking for will no longer be there—at least, not to the degree she's expecting. Her parents are gone, you're not there. Who's going to fill that void? At that point she's going to start thinking of the man she loves, and then her thinking is going to change. Believe me, her next move up here will be permanent. Of that I am sure. In the meantime—"

"Yes, sir." For the first time in weeks, Clay felt as if an almost unbearable burden was being lifted from his shoulders, and he could once again straighten up and stand without slumping like the old man he felt he had become. Maybe there was meaning to life, a purpose to be found in his wife's behavior—something he had not fully understood before—and a new resolve for himself: he was needed. She would always need him; his country needed him. For the first time in weeks, he felt a sense of hope.

"If you will tell Mr. Lincoln that I'm on my way, I'd appreciate it."

"Good as done, Clay," the Mormon prophet said, as the two men embraced. "But you be careful. You have a lot of loose ends to tie up. Some you may not yet be aware of."

★   ★   ★

Roberts leaned back in his chair and contemplated the ragtag assembly of Confederate soldiers standing before him. "Am I to understand, Major Striker, that you are now officially requesting Union assistance for you and your men?"

It had taken a full two weeks for Wolf to recover sufficiently to take command of the handful of Texans remaining in Santa Fe. Once his wound had sufficiently healed and the fever had abated, Wolf had assessed the situation he and his companions faced, and it did not make a pretty picture.

It was all too apparent there were few alternatives to their present circumstance. Not officially prisoners of war, their indeterminate status gave them little bargaining power. While he had been incapacitated, many of his former companions had been exchanged, paroled, or had left with the first contingents for Texas. Only the wounded had remained.

"Would you say I have any alternative, Colonel?"

Ignoring Wolf's question, Roberts leaned forward. "Major, I will do what I can to meet your immediate needs, but please understand that I must now consider you and your men to be prisoners of war. Your appeal for help and the issuance of supplies makes your status official. Have you any questions, Major?"

"No, Colonel, I don't. Obviously, at this point we have no reasonable alternatives."

Summoning his adjutant, Roberts arose from his desk. "Captain, issue these men whatever supplies they need, and have them taken to their place of confinement. They are now to be considered prisoners of war and are to be kept under guard. However, I want it fully understood by all that their needs are to be met, and they are to be treated with due regard. Am I making myself clear, Captain?"

CHAPTER 4

★ ★ ★

THE MILITARY AMBULANCE crested the hill and, relieved of the uphill strain and feeling the wagon beginning to crowd them from the rear, the horses broke into a gallop. Jamming his foot on the brake handle, the driver hauled back on the reins as the creaking rig jolted down the steep incline toward the dry riverbed at the bottom, its irritable occupants in the rear profaning him loudly. Over his shoulder, he hollered, "If you Rebs don't like the accommodations, you can get out and walk."

Having absorbed all of the punishment he could stand in the back of the stuffy, enclosed wagon, Wolf climbed over the back of the seat and settled next to the driver. "Take it easy, Corporal. It's hot and dusty back in that sweatbox, and three weeks is a long time to get your hind end pounded into blisters."

"I reckon," the man responded, noncommittally.

Wolf looked around at the flat, unappealing countryside. "Where the devil are we, anyway?"

"Ain't much more t' go, Reb," the teamster said, squirting a stream of black tobacco spittle off to the side of the wagon. "In case yuh think you've died and gone t' hell, well, you ain't. We've jest been crossin' Kansas, is all. That there," he said, nodding to the settlement a few miles off in the distance, "is Fort Leavenworth? and that, what yuh see off over there, is the Missouri River, ol' Big Muddy."

"Leavenworth. . . ." Wolf said, his voice trailing off.

"What'd yuh say?"

The large military compound was not a welcome sight to Wolf. Just a glimpse of it in the distance was enough to stir dark memories. "Oh, nothing," Wolf said. "Ugly place, isn't it?"

The corporal looked at Wolf and rolled his quid from one cheek to the other. "Well, as forts go, it ain't s'bad. Compared t' some, it's downright elegant," he said, giving the heavy reins a flip. "I spent some time there once—a couple of months, in fact."

"Me, too. Several years ago."

"What outfit was you with?"

"I wasn't exactly with an outfit."

"Oh," the soldier chuckled, glancing at the Confederate officer sitting next to him. "That kind of time, huh?"

"Yeah . . . *that* kind of time."

"Well, Reb, that's what yuh get fer choosin' the wrong side."

The wagon seat on the ambulance was so narrow Wolf's hip and shoulder rubbed up against the smelly driver next to him as the man struggled to control the four big horses that were getting anxious to reach the fort. "Mmm," he said, thinking how easy it would be to shove this dirty blue belly right off the wagon, or dump him into the back, where some mighty unhappy Confederate soldiers would quickly relieve him of all his worries.

When Wolf didn't respond to what struck him as an inane

comment, the driver observed, "Well . . . I reckon we all make mistakes."

Wolf had seen the man's nervous glances and sensed his growing unease. "Yuh know, Reb, you ain't supposed t' be up here anyways. Maybe you better get back in there where yuh belong. 'Cause, if you're of a mind t' try somethin', you wouldn't get ten feet 'fore them outriders shoot yuh full of holes."

Twisting on the seat, Wolf surveyed the cavalry troop that had accompanied the caravan of five enclosed wagons since leaving Fort Union. The Union troopers had been fairly easy on their Rebel charges, but there had never been any doubt of their willingness to do their duty if anything went amiss.

Giving the Union corporal a knowing grin, Wolf threw a leg over the back of the seat and, slipping back inside the wagon, said, "Do something to a sweet guy like you? What could I possibly do that wouldn't get me killed, as you have so cleverly pointed out?"

The stockade was just as Wolf remembered it: solid, overwhelming, and completely demoralizing. Confinement in such a place has many evils, one no worse than the other, really. But permeating everything was the constant stench: the ever-present odor of unwashed bodies, the rotten food, the slop pots. Inside, there was nowhere a man could breathe clean air. The vermin-infested cells were damp and cold in the winter, unbearably hot in the summer, and always filthy.

The only relief came with being assigned to a work team out in the yard, sometimes even outside the compound. But then there was the palpable hatred of the guards, made all too real by frequent and unnecessary beatings. The slightest offense—a word, a look—was all it took. Aside from the physical brutality, there could be days in the hole, a filthy pit where the sun never shined.

Still, time in the Leavenworth stockade could be good for a man—the right man—if he knew how things worked, how to avoid the hostile glances of the guards, how to keep his head down, how to do what he was told and never complain. In short, how to work the system without being obvious. But of even greater importance was the skill to glean whatever scraps of information might prove useful to a resourceful, determined soldier.

Wolfgang Striker was just such a soldier—all soldier—educated, trained, and experienced in taking the fight to the enemy, surviving when and where few could. Survival in Leavenworth required such skills, and he had endured worse. Getting back into the war was the single driving force that invigorated Wolf Striker's entire being. Day after miserable day, it was the sole motivation that kept him alive. Regardless of what he was forced to bear, Wolf let nothing distract him—not the brutality, not the filth; not the sometimes overwhelming sense of damnation, the gnawing thought that there was no world beyond this terrible place.

But the weeks can pass quickly for a man dedicated enough to keep his vision focused beyond the stockade walls. And as the weeks passed, Leavenworth gave Wolf time to listen and think and make a few useful acquaintances, among whom was a Union sergeant who years before had fought alongside him in Mexico, a man for whom he had once covered during a bad time for both. The man had not forgotten.

The heavy cell door complained loudly as it swung inward. "Mister Striker! Out in the hall, and be quick about it!"

Wolf rolled over on his cot, letting his feet drop to the floor. He was dead tired, and every muscle and sinew in his body screamed out for rest. "Yeah, right. Okay," he said, the small, still voice in his head whispering caution through the fog of his fatigue. "What is it this time of night?"

"You'll find out. Just get out here. And no funny business."

As Wolf stepped through the narrow doorway, a hand shot out of the darkness, grabbed his arm, and shoved him further into the blackness of the stone passageway, away from the stairs that led up and out of the dungeon-like row of cells.

"What the—"

"Don't say nothin', Major," a voice whispered. "Jest follow me, and stay quiet."

"Granby?" Wolf hissed. "I wasn't sure it was you, Sergeant. I guess by now I ought to know that whiskey voice anywhere, though—especially in the dark."

"Yeah, it's me, sir," the formless smudge responded, keeping his voice low. "This way. We need to make as little noise as possible."

As the two carefully felt their way further down into the inky darkness of the passageway, Wolf said, "Sort of brings back old memories. Didn't look to me as if there was anything down here."

Stopping, Wolf's guide struck a match and lit a small torch. The darkness remained oppressive, but the smoky, flickering light revealed what looked to be a solid iron door. "There ain't nothin' down here," Granby quietly responded.

"But—"

"Here, hold this," Granby said, eyeing the massive iron obstacle and handing the fitful torch to Wolf. "The dang thing's all but rusted shut. Aside from me, ain't nobody been down here in months, I'd guess."

The two men leaned into the heavy door as Granby struggled

with the badly corroded latch. The hinges creaked from age and neglect as the door grudgingly gave way.

"Quick . . . down here. We gotta hurry."

The air got worse as the two descended a narrow, stone stairwell that emptied into a low, tunnel-like corridor, deep underground. In the dim, flickering light, the rusted iron doors of several cells could be seen hanging open along one side.

"What's down here?"

"This is where they used to keep the real bad ones."

"Well . . . this can't be the way out of here."

"Oh, yes it is, Major. For you, anyway, it's the only way out. And if I get caught doin' this, they'll be keepin' me down here permanent, fer sure—in one of these fancy cells, more'n likely."

The door of the second cell hung at a precarious angle, supported by a single, badly corroded hinge. Wolf followed Granby's dim torch into the narrow, rock-lined keep. The cramped space was nearly filled by two dilapidated wooden bunks, one along each wall. A rotted scrap of canvas—what looked to once have been the side of a wedge tent or half of a pup tent—hung in tattered shreds from the rear rock wall, between the bunks.

"What is this place?"

"It's your way outta Leavenworth. And, Major, you gotta get out before morning slop, four or five hours from now."

"But—"

"*But* nothin'," Granby grunted, as he tore the grimy scraps of canvas from the wall, revealing a small hole or tunnel. "You want out, Major, this is it. Two or three years ago, a couple of desperadoes dug this here tunnel and escaped.[3] It goes under the outer wall, on the river side. Comes up just outside the wall."

"'Two or three years'?" Wolf hissed. "Is it still open?"

"I checked it best as I could last night. You can make it. But you sure don't want to spend much time in there, believe me."

"You mean to tell me they didn't have this thing filled in?"

"Them two outlaws killed a guard and drug him in there after 'em, and that's where they left him, to sort of clog the hole, like. Well . . . t' make things short, we finally got 'im out, the guard, I mean. But, bein' shorthanded, what with the war an' all, well, there just never seemed the time or need to fill the hole up proper like; so, they jest shut these cells off and forgot 'em, I guess. Hole should of caved in on its own by now, but it's still pretty much there."

Wolf bent down and peered into the dripping blackness of the hole. "Yeah . . . that's what's got me a little worried. How long is it? Where does it come out?"

"Maybe fifteen yards."

"*Fifteen yards?*" Wolf hissed with unbelief.

"Yeah. Well . . . maybe ten, and it comes out jest the other side of the stockade wall. You might have to push your way up, but the hole's still there—only partly caved in, near as I can tell.

"Look, you can make it, Major. Jest do it."

"Sergeant Granby, I didn't come all this way just to die in some hole under this miserable prison."

"Major, you gotta get outta here, or you'll die *in* this miserable prison. You know what I mean?"

"Yeah, yeah. I know what you mean."

"There's some around this place that's gonna settle some old scores with you, Major Striker, if'n you hang around here much longer."

"Fifteen yards, you say?"

"Maybe less," Granby said, in an effort to offer some encouragement. "Once you get out, make your way down t' the river an' get yourself lost. They ain't gonna miss yuh fer maybe five or six hours—if you get out now, that is. If yuh stay here, sure as the devil hates little kids and puppies, you'll die here.

"Now I gotta go," Granby said, offering his hand. "I gotta get back before I get missed. Good luck, Major." Taking the flickering torch, Granby backed away from the tunnel entrance. "And, Mister Striker, this squares us."

"Yeah . . . it does."

"I mean, it's war now, Major, and you and me's on opposite sides."

"We're square, Granby. And thanks."

As Granby quietly slipped through the cell door, Wolf turned and knelt down, the darkness now total. The tunnel, if it could be called that, felt scarcely large enough for a man to enter, let alone crawl through, and it stank of mud, rotted vegetation, and he could not guess what else, nor did he want to.

The impossibility of his situation was suddenly depressingly clear. He had no choice. It was this hole or worse. He could not risk going back to his cell. If he did, unreasoning confinement and death surely awaited him there. If he was ever going to get back into the war, this muddy, foul-smelling tunnel offered some hope, however scanty.

Stretching out on his belly, his face at the slumping shaft's mouth, its fetidness almost overwhelming, the thought came to Wolf that he had been in worse places. "I just can't remember where," he grumped to himself. With both hands he reached tentatively into the confines of the dank hole and struggled to pull himself in. *Only one way t' get this done—one way or the other.*

His shoulders barely fit, and the foul air closed around him like something wet, dank, and slimy, like something almost alive, as if he were suddenly caught in the narrow gullet of some horrid beast. There was no feeling of air on his skin, no draft, no disturbance at all, and the darkness was total and terrifyingly disorienting. To turn his head was impossible, his arms and shoulders preventing any movement. All he was able to do was inch forward toward whatever lay ahead of him.

It was as if the world had abruptly ceased to exist. Though he could feel the tunnel tightly confining him, any hint of orientation was gone. Curiously, he could no longer tell where his body was, his sense of self gone with the light. He thought his feet might still be hanging out into the cell behind him, but it was as if nothing real existed.

A feeling of total helplessness began to smother him, until Wolf's mind suddenly exploded with panic. Whether he screamed or not, he could not tell, but a half-crazed frenzy seized him, and he struggled for freedom, grasping at the mud, the water, the slime, anything that slithered over or around him. But his tortured, struggling body remained mired in the total darkness.

Like a thing alive, the mucky throat squeezed him in its gluttonous embrace until his frenetic struggles ended in near exhaustion, and his captivity seemed complete. He could not move, the hole's devouring, death-like confinement—black, wet, airless—seemed hideously absolute.

Any sense of time had ceased to exist, as had any other welcome sensation. But at length a thought seeped into Wolf's now leaden mind: *All hope abandon, ye who enter here.* It was a dark thought, but it was Dante's thought, not his; yet the thought persisted. But what else he knew of Dante, if anything, in his struggles would not come to him.

Hope was what he had existed on day by day, minute by minute. How could he abandon hope now? Hope was his nourishment, the very air he breathed. Was he now to give up, abandon all hope, helplessly consigned to hell—Dante's or any other?

Perdition. Is this perdition? Am I in perdition? Maybe someone will pray me out of this hell. This must be perdition. But confused from terror and exhaustion, Wolf did not know what to do with this new idea. *Perdition? Where did that come from?* he thought. *I don't know anything about perdition.*

If this was perdition, someone would have to pray for him. Who there was that would pray for him would not come to mind, and the thought brought him again to the edge of terror.

He paused in his struggles, closing his eyes and willing himself to be calm. Who could he ask to pray for an indulgence? *Indulgence? Who was there who would pray for me? Holy Mary, Mother of* . . . He tried to picture the mother of Christ, but no vision appeared. There must be someone who would have some scrap of positive feeling for him.

Saints. His mind grasped at the word. *Saints. Brigham Young has Saints—lots of them, but* . . . Somehow, his jumbled mind could not envision the Mormons praying for him, though why they would reject him, he couldn't remember. It might have something to do with a place called Platte River Station, but just what, in his panicky state he couldn't recall. Still, perhaps they wouldn't reject him; they were an interesting people—he knew none better.

Porter Rockwell. Yes . . . *Porter Rockwell was a Mormon.* A bearded, hairy visage suddenly flooded his mind. Rockwell might pray for him. But, no, that made no sense. Rockwell was the Utah lawman who had been so set on seeing him hang.

Yet somewhere he had heard that there were Saints that prayed for soldiers like himself. But who? *Yes* . . . *think* . . . *there's Hadrian* . . . *there's Joan of Arc* . . . *or Martin of Tours. Yes, they were soldiers, but how to . . . or even Ignatius Loyola. They were Patron Saints, weren't they? Intercessors of some kind. But how do I get them to . . .*

How long Wolf struggled with the idea of perdition and the need for someone to intercede for him, he could not have said. He had seldom felt the need to rely on anyone other than himself, and when he had, it had almost always ended in disaster. In fact, he had never really felt the need to pray. Relying on others, even God, had always struck him as a weakness, one a soldier could not afford.

Still, the nagging thought persisted, that if he were ever to get out of this tomb, prayer might be the answer. Perhaps he should pray for himself. But what were the words? From his childhood, he could vaguely remember snippets of prayers someone had recited at his bedside. *Now I lay me down to sleep. . . .* But the words would not come.

His entire being seemed to shrink from his spiritual frustration. Yet, somehow, the walls seemed less oppressive, and he felt a sense of renewal, almost of succor. Determined not to yield to the darkness, Wolf gasped for air and tried to concentrate, to summon the energy and commitment to do what he knew had to be done if he were to survive: to crawl forward.

"Please, Father!" The words seemed to come from deep within him, bursting forth in a plea only a *Father* would understand, and he began to gather strength. For him there was no alternative. He had to renew his struggle, to fight the evil, to reach up and out of the tunnel.

Rain suddenly splattered off his head, and he raised his face. It was the most wonderful sensation he had ever experienced— the large drops almost sacramental in their insistent, cleansing touch—yes, a kind of baptism, washing away the filth that had surrounded him. And air—fresh, clean air—filled his lungs.

This must be what the resurrection will be like, Wolf thought, struggling to pull himself free of the black grave that had fought to consume him and out onto the wet prairie grass, where he lay on his back, letting what was quickly becoming a thundering downpour saturate his filthy, mud-soaked clothes.

Luxuriating in the relief and the cleansing rain, Wolf gave no immediate thought to discovery. Never had anything felt so cleansing, so liberating. Not only was he free, he was being made clean. It was a sensation of true deliverance, of absolution, of renewal—almost of purification—that seemed to permeate his entire being, as the filth was washed from his body.

The rain poured steadily from the dark sky above him, though a dim grayness in the east, beyond the river, warned of the approaching day. Still, Wolf could not will his aching body to move. He felt heavy from the inside out, as if he had nothing left to give, his limbs refusing his weight. His mind, however, would not rest.

What's happening to me? he wondered, as the soothing rain continued to soak life back into his exhausted body. *What's this fixation on religion? I was scared, but not that scared. Religion is for weaklings. Not since that first year in seminary—what's that about? Most of a lost year I have tried to forget, then nothing.*

"Maybe I need to find a priest," he mumbled half aloud. "No . . . not a priest. No . . . I know . . . I'll find Porter Rockwell. Yeah," Wolf chuckled, "Rockwell will know. I'll talk to that Mormon marshal that caught up with me in New Mexico.[4] That bearded preacher was a regular Samson. I've never seen a man so torn between hanging my body and massaging my soul."

Wolf had no idea how long he had lain there lost in thought, the rain bathing his aching body, when somewhere a door slammed and voices gradually grew louder. Rolling onto his stomach, he froze. Two men rounded the stockade wall, not twenty feet from where he lay, approaching him, the slickers over their heads shrouding their faces.

"I tell you, it's serious," he heard a voice saying. "The Union's got to control the entire Mississippi River if we're ever going to bring the Confederacy to its knees."

"Yes . . . well, who'd argue with that? The real issue is *how,* not *if.*"

"Vicksburg."

The men sloshed past him in the darkness, not ten feet away, heading toward a gate at the far end of the wall.

Vicksburg? What about Vicksburg? Wolf wondered.

Opening the gate, one of the men stepped from sight, as the other said, "Control Vicksburg; you control the river, and you split the Confederacy in half."

Exhausted, Wolf lay still, his ravaged body slumped, but his mind racing. *Vicksburg, a world already gone, already shredded beyond recognition, and now the Yankees are going to finish it off— my world, and Ellen, gone.*

Wolf got to his knees, wondering where it was all going. Why was he even fighting to stay alive, to stay free? What was there left to which he could ever return if he did survive? Can one ever return? Without Ellen, did he even want to return?—and to what?

I wonder, he thought, *how many other beautiful worlds have been torn apart by this war, or any other form of human conflict, misery, and misunderstanding?*

Staggering to his feet, shaking his head to clear his mind of the doubts that had suddenly assailed him, Wolf began to focus on his surroundings. One thought did, however, persist. *Something good will come of all of this. It always has. After all, time has always had a way of healing all things—or so they say. And if that's true, maybe there is a God. Maybe there is some form of human redemption.*

CHAPTER 5

★   ★   ★

A T A PLACE WHERE THE RUTTED road turned up a gentle slope to pass through the orchard, toward the main compound of the sprawling Salinas *rancho*, Consuelo Salinas Ashworth ordered the driver to bring the coach to a halt. The sight of the heavy, ornate iron gate through the trees and the big *casa* it guarded was something she had been hungering for since crossing into Mexico.

Throughout her childhood, this orchard and its dusty, rutted lane had always been a place of mystery, adventure, and sometimes even danger. But now it seemed as if she were seeing it all for the first time, and everything was different, almost colorless. Now a mature, experienced woman and not a young girl, she was no longer able to see these things as they once were, not without thinking of the night Clay Ashworth had passed this way and into her heart. He had changed everything, and she suddenly realized that nothing could ever be the same again. How could she ever have thought otherwise?

For most of the past two days, they had been traveling across lands that were part of the Salinas ranch, and now, climbing down from the coach in the growing dusk, she at long last could see the familiar house with its graceful arches and adobe facade just beyond the gate, the light from its windows promising the warmth of a loving welcome. It was the home of her childhood, once a place of refuge, a place to which she had always returned as she grew to adulthood—returning each year from months away at school, extended trips abroad, and after enjoying the pleasurable absences of the privileged life she had always taken for granted.

"Here we are, Emily," Consuelo said, her voice husky from the dust of the day's travel. "It is so beautiful. Just as I have always remembered it," she sighed, a sense of resignation deepening her mood. "Quickly, come and see before it gets too dark."

The long, difficult journey across the great expanse between the Utah Territory and Mexico, along with the emotional strain of the past months, could be seen in her movements, and there was a sadness in her beautiful features that even the joy of this much anticipated homecoming could not hide. Something, someone, was missing, making everything incomplete, almost empty.

From the day she had ridden away from *Rancho los Librados,* her heart had ached with misgivings. She loved Clay more than she could put into words, and not a day had passed that she did not think of ordering the coach to turn about. Yet, deep inside, she knew this was a journey that had to be made. It was not something she could have put into words, but she felt compelled, nonetheless. And now, seeing the home where she had grown to adulthood, the weight of her misgivings seemed to grow heavier. The relief or peace or escape she had hoped for was not here.

Stretching to relieve the accumulated aches of the long days of travel, she stepped to the front of the coach and leaned against one of the horses. The nearness of the big animal somehow felt familiar and comforting as it gently leaned toward her touch. The horses were Clay's, all six of them, and she loved them. "Oh," she sighed, "I thought this awful trip would never end, but now we are here, and it's so beautiful. Don't you think so, Emily?"

Turning, Consuelo reached back to help Emily as, with some difficulty, the older woman stepped down from the coach and turned to look up the road toward the house.

"Here it is, Emily, the home where I was raised. I know I've bored you half to death with all of my chatter, but at last we're here," Consuelo said, taking Emily's hand.

"Oh, if only my mother and father were here. You would love them, and I know they would love you, but you'll soon meet Uncle Lazaro and then we. . . . Emily? Emily, is something wrong? You look faint. Are you ill? Here . . . let me help you."

Holding her hand to her head, the older woman slumped down onto the iron step of the coach, almost as if she were shrinking in size. "My name is Maria Emilea Consuelo Salinas Montoya," she said softly. The look on her ashen face showed no emotion, as if she had just awakened from a long sleep. "My name is Maria Emilea Consuelo Salinas Montoya," she slowly repeated, almost to herself. "Consuelo . . . that's me . . . who I am."

"What? Are you all right, Emily?"

"I . . . I remember. You no see?" Emily said, looking up at Consuelo, the color slowly returning to her face. "Suddenly I remember. I know who I am!"

Consuelo knelt beside the older woman. "But, Emily, that's my name. What do you mean?"

"Yes . . . you no see? I am a Salinas. I have been to this place before. It is the *rancho* of my brother, Luis, and you, my sweet niece, were named after me."

"But, Emily, I—"

Dust swirled around the two women as a beautiful bay stallion was reined to a sliding stop nearly on top of them, and Lazaro Salinas swung down from a heavily silvered saddle. As a confused Consuelo got to her feet in an effort to embrace him, Lazaro caught sight of Emily.

"*Madre de Dios,*" he said, crossing himself. "What am I seeing? Maria, is it you, *hermana carnal,* or am I seeing a ghost?"

"No, Lazaro," she said, rising as he took her hand. "I'm alive. Here. Now."

Taking her in his embrace, half choking with emotion, he said, "But we thought you were dead. These many years—we thought you were dead. How can this be?"

Stunned, Consuelo watched the emotional reunion unfolding before her, unsure of what she was witnessing.

"Oh . . . Lazaro . . . I don't know how to begin. I was—"

"Not now, my dearest sister," he said, turning to bring his confused niece into their embrace. The two women stood enclosed within his arms as tears dampened his face. "Nowhere are there two treasures I love so much.

"Come," he said, turning the two women back to the coach and motioning to the driver. "The two of you get back into the coach. You are home now, my sister, and there is so much to speak of. But first we must get the two of you up to the house, where you can refresh yourselves, rest, and food can be prepared."

Turning, Consuelo looked up at her uncle. "Uncle Lazaro, I don't—"

"Not now, my sweet," he said, patting her cheek affectionately and turning toward his horse. "How wonderful of you it is to leave your husband and return home to bring your aunt back to her brother. I am most anxious to hear all about it."

Climbing into his saddle and spurring his big horse, he hollered to the driver, "*Vamanos, muchacho.*"

The dinner that night was a confusion of emotions for Consuelo. The conversation had been entirely in Spanish, and though it was her native tongue, for some reason its use only added to her feelings of somehow no longer belonging.

The evening had been intended to be a celebration of Emily's return, her lost memories restored by the sight of the Salinas ranch and seeing, for the fist time in many years, her last surviving brother, Lazaro Salinas.

However, as the sumptuous meal progressed, Consuelo's mind kept drifting away from the conversation. She would laugh when the others laughed, and she listened intently, or at least appeared to listen intently, as her aunt and uncle recalled family experiences and reflected on lost opportunities. But aside from an occasional nod, she participated little. In truth, throughout most of the evening, she was back in Utah—with Clay.

"Consuelo?" Lazaro said, as the laugher at the table died. "Consuelo? Is there something wrong?"

"Wrong?" Consuelo said, trying to appear as if she knew what had just been said. "No, uncle, nothing is wrong. Why do you ask?"

Lazaro looked at Emily and winked. "*Why do you ask,* she asks me. Why, indeed?"

Reaching over, placing her hand on Consuelo's arm, and continuing to speak in Spanish, Emily said, "My dear, you don't appear to have been here with us much this evening, and your face is so long, so unhappy."

Emily's Spanish was flawless, and that only added to

Consuelo's sense of loss. Along with everything else she had turned her back on, she missed Emily's unique way of trying to express herself in English. Her struggle with the English language was one of her most endearing traits.

"What is it?" Lazaro asked, watching his niece closely.

"I know what it is," Emily said, her voice soft with understanding. "It's Clay. He's no here."

Consuelo smiled. "No. It's not that he's not here. It's that I'm not back there, with him, where I should be. I ran away, like a silly schoolgirl, when I should have remained by his side."

"My dear," Emily said, patting her arm, "I know Clay Ashworth like a son, and I know how much he loves you. When the time is right, he will come for you."

"What do you suppose he's doing right now?"

"I have no idea, but it's probably best that you are here with us. You need time to heal—in your body and in your head."

Wiping away a tear, Consuelo said, "Do you really believe he will come for me, when I was the one who ran away?"

"As surely as I know anything. He needs to do some healing, too."

Clay Ashworth sat in front of a window in one of the dark, cheerless room's two easy chairs, where he could gaze out at the storm that had been drenching the stricken nation's capital for most of the past week. His was a corner room on the fourth floor of the elegant Willard Hotel, and he could see in both directions along Pennsylvania Avenue.

Off to the east, the magnificent Capitol Building was just visible through the storm and heavy, gray haze. The most prominent feature of the imposing edifice, what little could be seen of it, was the not-yet-completed massive, twin-shelled, iron dome. The top tier of the three-tiered dome was encircled by a skeletal scaffolding, making the structure resemble a splintered skull, the top of which was open to the hostilities of the weather—not unlike the fractured nation whose representatives it housed. Around to his right, if he strained a bit, Clay could see the Executive Mansion off in the distance—Mister Lincoln's sanctuary of misery.

The Willard was one of the nation's fanciest hotels—"The Residence of Presidents," as it had become known. It had housed also many of the nation's notables. In fact, the story continued to circulate around Washington that Lincoln had used his first paycheck as chief executive to settle his $773.75 hotel bill. He had been a guest at the Willard on several occasions before becoming president. How true the story was, one could only guess. There were too many around the nation's capital willing to spread any story they could where the gaunt man from Illinois was concerned, a fact that thoroughly disgusted Clay.

Arriving late the previous evening, Clay had spent a restless night in the large, comfortable bed. Anticipation of the next day's meeting with the president had kept sleep away. Not knowing exactly what to expect, he had repeatedly thought through every possible scenario, finally dropping into a fitful sleep in the early hours of the morning.

The rain spattered against the hotel window with renewed force, and Clay rose from his chair to look down onto the cheerless street below. It was not a sight to lighten the heart nor lift the mind. Several days of heavy rain had left the city little more than a quagmire, and only a few people could be seen scurrying here and there, hunched against the unforgiving downpour.

Watching the scene below, Clay couldn't help but marvel at

the determined activity up and down the mucky street. Carriages and streetcars, in some places nearly hub deep in the muddy runoff, their teams struggling to keep their footing, made slow progress. Anyone afoot attempting to cross the street not only risked a soaking from the rain, but an unwelcome mud bath as well.

Just below him, two bedraggled street urchins were earning tips sweeping away mud and water as ladies in their long skirts, and gentlemen willing to pay to save their polished boots, signaled their desire to cross the storm-drenched street. The sight was enough to bring a slight smile to Clay's face. Free enterprise was alive and well in the federal city, despite the war and the debilitating political and economic conditions threatening to tear the young nation apart.

Where were they all going in such weather? What secrets did they carry with them? What loyalties were so urgent that they would venture out into such a tempest? "Stay home by your fireside bright," Clay muttered half aloud. But then, this was a city of many intrigues and secrets. What was true of him could be no less true of others.

Stretching, in an effort to relieve some of the aches and pains acquired during the past weeks of travel, Clay turned and crossed the room, stopping to light one of the fancy gas hurricane lamps near the bed. The bright glow immediately brought some much-needed cheer to the otherwise comfortable room.

Turning, he caught sight of himself in the elegant mirror hanging above an ornately carved chest of drawers. Looking back at him was a troubled man, one who somehow seemed to resemble the weather outside: gray, dismal, unhappy. In the weeks since Connie had returned to Mexico, he had lost too much weight, lost focus, and lost touch; and he could not seem to pull himself out of it.

Brigham Young had tried to console him, make him see things for the best. The wisdom of the man constantly amazed him. The Mormon leader had a way of getting right to the heart of any issue, and before their conversation had ended, Clay had come to realize that Consuelo's absence was both only temporary and necessary.

Clay knew his wife had suffered a terrible shock, and he knew that time to heal was what she needed most. But it had taken an afternoon with the Mormon prophet to make him fully appreciate what he finally came to see as obvious. Yet her leaving had created a hole in his world that robbed him of any interest in living, and nothing or no one could fill that terrible void but her.

He saw it as his good fortune that Mister Lincoln had sent for him. He would lose himself in whatever mission or responsibility the president had in mind, but getting Consuelo back was the only thing that would heal him. In the end, nothing else truly mattered. She represented his entire world, his only happiness.

The trip from Salt Lake to the stricken nation's capital had not helped. It had been miserable at best, the roads rutted and bumpy, and even the big Concord coaches, where available, were too crowded and dusty. The rail service, where it existed, was no better. Clay had hoped that the demands of the trip would lift his spirits, but travel gives a man too much time to think.

To occupy his mind, he had read and reread the president's telegrams until the ink had begun to fade. At every stop, he had purchased whatever newspapers were available, some of them weeks old, reading them over and over again. The war news was not good, and by all appearances it was going to be a long one.

From what little he had been able to deduce from the

disjointed and uneven news stories, the Confederacy was proving to be a formidable force. Subduing the southern rebellion was clearly not going to be easy. It was nearly all bad news, but it helped to give him a boost. There was little doubt that here, at least, he was needed. There would be a way for him to serve his country in all of this chaos.

"Too bad my wife doesn't feel the same," he grumped to himself. It wasn't fair to her, and he knew it.

What he needed right now was a future, one that would bring renewed vitality and focus to his troubled mind, and it was Mister Lincoln who would provide that focus for him.

The hack came to a stop under the North Portico, and Clay stepped out to be greeted by a black liveryman and escorted into the Executive Mansion. In the previous hour, the rain had slackened considerably, to the point that Clay had given some thought to walking the relatively short distance to his meeting with the president. But a discouragingly cold and persistent wind had arisen out of the north.

Following a uniformed steward, Clay took the marbled stairway to the second floor and was ushered into a small anteroom outside the president's office.

"Please wait here, suh," the man said, indicating a wingback chair, overstuffed and covered in red velvet. "Someone will be with you shortly."

Clay settled himself onto the comfortable chair, hoping for enough time to relax and compose himself before his session with the president. As always, however, the atmosphere of the Executive Mansion was not unlike the portentous stillness at the center of a raging storm, making any attempt at some kind of mental tranquility nearly impossible.

Behind each door the buzz of wartime government administration could be heard: voices barely audible behind closed doors, people coming and going out in the main hallway—a dozen congressmen had passed him on the stairs—and he could hear what sounded like the president's high-pitched voice on the other side of the door across the room to his right. There was little doubt from his surroundings that he had stepped into the center of things, and it felt good.

Sensing he could be in for a long wait, Clay leaned back and, from a disorderly pile of reading material on the table next to his chair, picked up a recent copy of *Frank Leslie's Illustrated Newspaper*. A weekly paper full of illustrations and commentary, *Leslie's* made for some enlightening reading, though a quick glance through the paper's sixteen pages made it obvious that ten cents could buy a Union loyalist a lot of bad news. The illustrations, and there were a good many, might be quick to cause a chuckle, but their obvious message was no laughing matter. Things were not going all that well for the Union or for Mr. Lincoln.

Folding the paper and tossing it back on the table, Clay's attention was drawn to a worn copy of *Harper's Weekly* partially buried in the untidy pile of papers and magazines—others had obviously been here before him. What had caught his eye was a pen and ink illustration of gunboats on a river, closing on an obviously doomed fort. It could have been almost any fort on any river, but turning the page, Clay found a story describing the Union capture, the previous February, of two Confederate fortresses.

February, Clay thought to himself, his eyes losing focus above the edge of the paper, not so distant memories beginning to stir.

My whole world has changed since then, he thought, as an image of the bloody fighting at Glorieta Pass crossed his mind, only to be followed by the sight of his wife walking away from him the day she had said she was leaving, the screened door slamming behind her.

A noise somewhere out in the hall brought him back to the paper he had momentarily forgotten he was holding, and his attention was drawn to a short but surprisingly positive story about the recent fall of two Confederate fortresses. Forts Henry and Donelson were located in what was being called the western theater of the war. Fort Henry commanded the Tennessee River, and its capture opened the river to Union gunboats and shipping as far as Muscle Shoals in Alabama. Fort Donelson, on the Cumberland, some eleven miles distant from Fort Henry, had fallen a few days later.

Now, thanks to what the story called an "obscure" brigadier general from Illinois by the name of Ulysses Simpson Grant, there were two major water transportation routes open into the Confederacy's heartland, which was bounded on the east by the Appalachians and on the west by the Mississippi River.

From everything Clay had read and heard in recent months, the war in the east was not going all that smoothly for the Union. The fault, in large part, seemed to be that of the Union commander, General George B. McClellan, whom Clay knew to be an able staff officer but who was apparently proving to be too fainthearted in the face of the enemy.

On the other hand, the new Confederate commander, General Robert E. Lee, was showing himself to be an audacious military leader, as anyone who knew him would have expected. Clay both knew and respected Lee, as a man and as a soldier. The day Lee had resigned his commission as a colonel in the United

States Army and returned to his beloved Virginia was a tragic day for the Union. A man of valor and moral rectitude—for whom the most sublime word in the English language was *duty*—Lee was going to make a formidable foe.

Clay couldn't help but smile at what he read regarding Grant. The man might easily be dismissed as obscure, given the fact he had been out of the army for some time. But now, with his leadership, the progress of the war in the west was considerably less dismal than in the east. Perhaps Grant's obscurity would turn out to be the Union's strength, at least before his military astuteness and outright audacity became too widely recognized by his Confederate counterparts.

The thought brought a smile to Clay's lips. "Obscure? Yeah, right." *Maybe to these guys,* he thought, thumbing through the paper, *but not to me. I remember old Sam way back when. And Lee? Anyone the least bit familiar with the American military knows who this guy is.*

"Any good news, Colonel? Uh . . . Colonel?"

Glancing up from the paper, Clay saw the trim figure of John Hay, the president's private secretary, one of the few men in whom Mister Lincoln placed absolute confidence. "Sorry. Were you speaking to me?" Clay said, lowering the paper and glancing around the empty room.

"Yes, sir, I was," Hay said, a smile splitting his closely trimmed goatee. Hay had the kind of face that looked good with a goatee—in Clay's opinion, few men did. "Obviously, you didn't get the word."

"The *word?*" Clay responded, rising from his chair, unsure of Hay's meaning.

"I'll let the president tell you. He's ready to see you now, sir."

The president of the United States sat slumped behind his

cluttered desk, his face even more gaunt than Clay remembered. In a subdued voice he said, "Come in, Colonel Ashworth. Come in and sit down." Glancing at Hay, he said, "John, will you please see if Major Duncan is around? And have Mister Pinkerton join us, if you can find him."

"Mister President, I'm afraid you've caught me—"

"Sir," Hay said, as he turned to leave the room, "Mister Ashworth does not yet know of his appointment."

"Oh, is that so?" Lincoln chortled, leaning forward, a slight smile lighting his craggy face and the hollows of his deep-set eyes. "Well, I hope you'll be as delighted as I am with the news. Nothin' I like better than doing a good man a good turn, and then tellin' him about it."

He paused a moment before continuing. "A couple of months ago, Clay, I appointed you a full colonel of cavalry—unattached, of course—and a regular army appointment, to boot. To tell the truth, I'm not surprised the word never reached you. Things are in a terrible mess."

For a brief moment, Clay was taken back by the generosity of the appointment. It was not all that unusual in wartime, but he had not expected anything of the like. "I'm at a loss for words, Mister President. *Thank you* seems almost too little, but . . . well, thank you. Thank you very much, sir."

"Oh, well, Clay," the president said, his smile too quickly fading, "there are few men in whom I place more trust. It's not as if it were a political appointment, is it? Lord knows I've had to make enough of those, and most of 'em turn out to be failures, anyway. But you . . . you're a graduate of West Point, and a professional in every sense of the word. Though I'm havin' my share of West Point disappointments, too," he added.

"Well . . . again, thank you, sir. I'll do my best not to be one of them."

"Maybe you'd better wait a bit to thank me, Colonel," Lincoln chuckled. "You need to know right off, your appointment's about all the good news you're gonna get because I'm afraid I've got some difficult work for you, my young friend," Lincoln said, his usual solemn look having returned. "Before this thing is over, you're probably gonna need all that rank and more."

"Mister President, right now I'd welcome just about any responsibility. It couldn't have come at a better time in my life. I'll take any assignment you give me, as a matter of course."

"Oh, Allan," Lincoln said, rising behind his desk and waving Pinkerton into the office, a young army officer close on his heels. "Both of you, come in."

Rising with the president, Clay quickly found himself enveloped in the big Scotsman's bear hug. "Clay Ashworth, it's been a long time, and you've been doin' us some fine work, lad. It's good to see yuh." Though Pinkerton had been in the United States for many years, his Scottish heritage still could be heard in every word he uttered.

"I'll be truthful, Allan, I never thought I'd be happy to see your whiskers again, but I surely am."

"And this young man," Lincoln said, pointing over Pinkerton's shoulder, "is Major Jonathan Duncan."

"Yes," Pinkerton said, turning toward the young soldier. "Hardly out of West Point and he's a major already, and he's not been slow to be of real service to us either, I don't mind sayin'."

Greetings and preliminaries over, the three sat facing the President of the United States, slumped in his chair, seemingly lost in thought, the fingers of his right hand drumming an almost funereal cadence on his desk. Finally, as if seeing the men before him for the first time, he leaned forward, and said, "Clay, you're here because of my aggravation with the way things are goin', and I need your help for matters we're soon gonna be facing. Allan, you tell him."

"Well," Pinkerton hesitantly began, "I'm not sure just where to begin. But—"

"Manassas," Lincoln spat, high voice rising. "Begin with Manassas. Best example of a military foozle I know of."

"Yes, sir. Well, last August, at Bull Run, we . . . uh . . . the president, that is, sent young Major Duncan, here, to observe the fighting, and for three days he moved around the field of battle as much as he could, and—"

Clay knew exactly where this was now going. Leaning forward, he said, "Let me guess. Mostly he saw confusion and little observable evidence that things worked out according to any plan of battle—on either side. Right, Major?" he said, glancing at Duncan.

"Colonel, there aren't any maps to speak of. There are few existing roads; but the farther out into the countryside you get, you can hardly call them that. Of course, there are rail lines, and they are helpful—if you happen to be going where they're going. Without a good cavalry, no commander can tell where the enemy is, where he's coming from, or what his strength is."

"Mmm . . . well . . . that's war for you," Clay said, a little too lightheartedly. Then, sensing the depth of the young soldier's concerns, he continued, "But let me make another guess, Major. The Rebs seem to be way ahead of us where cavalry is concerned?"

"Yes, sir. But to be honest, I couldn't be everywhere at once. Making such a judgment is unfair, and I'm hardly qualified. Still, the Rebs seemed to have an edge."

"Jeb Stuart?"

"Yes, sir. But there was General Bayard's cavalry. I must tell you, it was hard for me to tell how either of them were being used. Until our troops withdrew back down the Warrenton Turnpike, the whole thing looked like opposing armies bumping into each other, then shooting, then maneuvering—I don't know."

"Well, Major, don't get discouraged. War has always been a wonder to me."

"Colonel," Duncan said, exasperation in his voice, "out at Manassas last August, it seemed like just one mistake after another."

"I'm sure," Clay offered. "But if you—"

Duncan went on. "When King's division marched its left flank directly across Jackson's line—just for instance, Colonel—it was a disaster in the making, and there was nothing I could do but sit and watch.

"Late in the afternoon," the young major continued, words piling upon words, "Longstreet attacked and occupied Chinn Ridge, and the entire federal line began to collapse, troops retreating back toward the turnpike, and then the whole thing seemed to cave in. Before it was over there was so much confusion, I almost rode headlong into General Jackson on the ridge above the turnpike where he and some of his staff were observing the fight."

"Well, if it's any solace to you, Major Duncan," Clay said, hoping to quell some of the frustration the young soldier was obviously feeling, "I'd be willing to bet this same conversation is taking place right now somewhere on the Confederate side, as well."

"There are too many such stories, Clay," Lincoln said, leaning forward in his chair, "but the point is, I've got to know what's going on, and most of the time I feel like a blind man stumbling around in broad daylight. I had no idea how the fight was going until it was over. My commanders would not respond to my appeals. I know things are happening, but I can't tell what, and when I do get word, it's mostly rumor."

"I don't need to tell you, Mister President, that war feeds on rumor," Clay offered. "It's difficult enough for the commanders in the field to know what's going on, just as Major Duncan experienced at Manassas. I mean, even they may not have known what exactly was happening."

"Well, Clay," Pinkerton said, "what's the solution?"

"Allan, you know as well as I do, the answer lies in planning, getting out in front of events. I know of no other solution."

"You're right, Clay," Lincoln said, a sigh revealing his exhaustion and frustration. "But it has to go further than that. Look, in the months since McClellan failed to take Richmond, there have been three major battles. There was Shiloh in April, Bull Run last August, then Antietam—all of them bloody. It's as if all that spilled blood has gotten us nowhere, and at tremendous cost.

"Congress got on McClellan's back last March," Lincoln continued, his frustration obvious, "and the complaints are still comin'. I've even confronted him in the field. But it's not just me. The Committee on the Conduct of the War, and the Jacobins. . . . Wade threatened me with a revolt in Congress because of McClellan's excuses.

"So, to make a long story short, back in March I had to do something, so I relieved him as commander in chief, but I left him in command of the Army of the Potomac. And still all he has offered is more of the same. The man just has the slows, I guess."

Lincoln leaned back in his chair and studied the ceiling of his office for a moment. "Well," he said to no one in particular, "I've had to look to the future. General McClellan's not getting the job done."

No one in the room was quite sure of what they had just heard, but to each it sounded mighty like an ax falling.

Not quite knowing what to say, but wanting to break the uncomfortable silence that had descended on the room, Clay offered, "Mister President, General McClellan is a very able planner. As a staff officer, there is—"

"Tell 'im about the fight in the West, Allan," Lincoln said, with a dismissive wave of his hand, not wanting to hear more about McClellan.

"Well, as you probably know by now, Clay, the western theater is where our best fighting seems to be taking place, at least as far as we can determine back here in Washington. We've got a general out there who knows how to fight."

"Yes, I've been reading about him."

"U. S. Grant's his name," Lincoln offered. "Kind of ironic, those initials, huh?" he chuckled.

"Clay, the Mississippi is our great hope right now," Pinkerton said, thumping the arm of his chair. "Grant has taken Fort Henry and Fort Donelson, opening the Tennessee and Cumberland rivers. And now he's aiming for Vicksburg. It's the key to the control of the entire Mississippi River."

"Last May, Admiral Farragut opened the lower Mississippi," Lincoln said, tapping his desk with a bony finger, "and General Butler occupied New Orleans. Then in June, Admiral Davis took Memphis, so we now command the upper Mississippi as well. That leaves Vicksburg smack dab in the middle. It's the main link between the Confederate states east and west of the Mississippi. If Grant takes Vicksburg, he will have split the Confederacy, and victory will be within our reach."

"Just weeks ago," Pinkerton added, some enthusiasm finally

in his voice, "Grant won two brilliant battles, one at Iuka and the other at Corinth, forcing the Confederates to retreat south."

Lincoln leaned forward, his finger punching the air for emphasis. "But things are in such a state of flux, Colonel, we really have no idea what's going on. I've worn a trail between here and the War Department trying every day to get the latest word from the telegraph over there. But too often I get it from the newspapers before I get it from my commanders in the field."

Leaning back, Lincoln paused, then with a sigh, continued, "Clay, it's essential that Grant take Vicksburg." Looking at Pinkerton, he said, "Now, tell 'im what you want, Allan."

"Colonel, we need you to try and make your way to Vicksburg and reconnoiter the situation between here and there," Pinkerton said, thumping the desk. "From what we are able to determine back here, the fighting keeps goin' back and forth between Memphis, Corinth, and Vicksburg—back and forth, back and forth."

Clay couldn't believe what he was hearing. "You want me to be a spy, is what you mean?"

"Call it what yuh want, lad," Pinkerton said, with a wave of his hand, his Scottish burr thickening, "but that's what's needed, and you're the man t' do it. And there's precious little time t' do it in."

"But there's more," the president said, leaning forward in his chair, "and this is the most important part. Somewhere between here and there, the Confederates are getting their lead, vast amounts of lead for their bullets. We need to know where all of it is coming from. If you were to discover that much, your mission will have been a success."

The room fell silent as Clay tried to absorb all he had heard in the past two hours.

Watching Clay closely, Pinkerton continued, "Take a southern rail route, lad, and keep your eyes open. We've not really penetrated the southwestern tip of Virginia, southeastern Kentucky, and northeastern Tennessee—all that region. We know the Rebs are gettin' tons of lead from somewhere in that area, so keep your eyes and ears open. They're gettin' their musket balls from somewhere."

Lincoln studied the big Utahan's face carefully, trying to read his reaction to what was being asked of him. "Not exactly what you expected, is it Colonel Ashworth?" he said, breaking the silence, a hint of empathy in his voice.

Clay looked up, his decision made. "No matter, Mister President. I'll do what has to be done."

"Yes, it does matter, Clay," the President said. "Vicksburg is going to be one of the biggest battles, if not the biggest battle, of the war. Right now, there is no objective of greater importance to the cause of the Union. Splitting the Confederacy by taking Vicksburg will almost surely weaken it beyond repair—Vicksburg's the key! We need to disrupt their supply sources if we are to be successful.

"And I want you to know, Clay, you were my personal choice for this difficult assignment. Right now, I don't know who else I would ask."

The president turned to Pinkerton and with a wave of a bony finger ordered, "Give him his credentials, Allan."

Pinkerton took several small envelopes from his valise and handed them to Clay. "Here's your papers, lad. There's a set establishing your Union authority and a second set should you be questioned by the Confederates. Keep them with you at all times, and by all means, keep them separate.

"One more thing," Pinkerton interjected. "We're sending

young Duncan here farther north. He'll come down the Ohio to Cairo, then down to Memphis to find you. That's where the two of you should plan on meetin', at Memphis. Last we heard, that's where Grant has his headquarters. Anything you've got, Clay, give to Major Duncan, here. He'll get it back to us."

"And, Colonel, time is of the essence, as us lawyers like t' say," Lincoln said, leaning forward, his finger jabbing the air. "Waste no time—and whatever you do, don't get caught."

"Believe me, Mister President, I'll avoid that at all costs. From what I've heard, Andersonville is everything it's cracked up to be."

The three men rose with the president, the decisions having been made, and Lincoln turned to Pinkerton. "Allan, please give Colonel Ashworth a complete briefing. Give him all the information he needs and whatever resources we can that'll help him on his way."

Clay watched the gaunt chief executive as he stepped from behind his desk and couldn't help wondering if he would ever see him again. "Mister President, I—"

Clay, would you mind stayin' a minute or two longer?"

As the door shut behind Pinkerton and Duncan, Clay stood watching as the president slumped back into his chair.

"Sit down, Colonel Ashworth. I want to share something with you." Pausing for only a moment, Lincoln turned and retrieved a large Bible from a small table behind his desk. Clearing his throat, he continued, "Last evening, just before retiring, I picked up this very King James Bible and sort of let it drop on the bed, so it would open of its own accord. Well, in a way that I couldn't miss its meaning, it fell open to the Book of Revelation, chapter six. You may recall, Clay," Lincoln said, thumbing through the book's delicate pages, "that's the chapter where John the Beloved watches the Lamb open six seals. Four beasts, each in turn, invite him to come and see as each seal is opened."

Clay shifted uncomfortably in his chair, not really knowing where this was going, or why the president had chosen to share such an experience with him.

"Oddly enough, Clay," the president said, looking up from the scripture, "the first verse I saw—it almost jumped out at me—was verse seven. And then came verse eight."

Having little more than a passing familiarity with the New Testament, least of all with the Book of Revelation, Clay somehow knew that whatever those verses contained, they undoubtedly would have some foreboding application, perhaps prophetically so—both for him and the man who sat slumped over the scriptures before him. It was well known that Lincoln had no commitment to any particular church, but his reliance on the King James Bible was legendary. Rumors of Lincoln's almost otherworldly, prescience also abounded. Over the years, Clay had heard many such rumors but had paid them little attention, dismissing such stories as myths, spread for political purposes, fabrications intended to undermine the president's credibility.

As Lincoln began reading, his voice assumed an almost ghostly solemnity, sounding to Clay as if it were a voice from the grave. A chill settled over the room, an inexplicable haunting sensation Clay knew he would never forget. The words described with disquieting certainty the fate they and their country surely faced.

"'And when he had opened the fourth seal, I heard the voice of the fourth beast say, Come and see.

"'And I looked, and behold a pale horse: and his name that sat on him was Death, and Hell followed with him. And power was given unto them over the fourth part of the earth, to kill with sword, and with hunger, and with death, and with the beasts of the earth.'"

The president looked up, his eyes searching Clay's, as if seeking for some glimmer of understanding. "I wonder who he is, that fourth horseman, Death?" Lincoln solemnly queried almost to himself, his melancholy voice trailing off for a brief moment. Then his eyes again returning to the page, he queried, "And I wonder, could this present conflict, our civil war, be the event spoken of?"

"What did it say?" Clay asked, almost in a whisper, his eyes searching Lincoln's face. "'The fourth part of the earth,' or something to that effect?"

"Yes," the Lincoln slowly responded, almost absently. Staring at Clay, he continued, "What color is your horse, Clay?"

The words might have brought a chuckle, had they not been so direct. Thinking a moment, not quite knowing what to make of the president's strange query, Clay answered, "I have a number of horses, Mister President, but my favorite, the one I ride most often, is a big stallion, a quarter horse—a dappled gray."

"Mmm," the President responded, thoughtfully studying Clay's face. "Lee rides a big gray, too."

"Yes. I think he calls him Traveler."

"Yes . . . Traveler."

With a smile he hoped would lighten the mood, Clay said, "I'm afraid mine's a rather intemperate horse, Mister President. I guess that's why I named him Diablo."

It was not the right thing to say, and the room suddenly felt oppressively warm. Clay asked, "Mister President, are you suggesting—"

"Oh, Colonel Ashworth," Lincoln said, a wan smile somewhat

easing the tension, "I'm not implying anything. Except to say that the sixth seal is supposed to reveal the signs of the end."

Clay looked at the solemn man before him and for a moment wondered what the future would bring—for their beloved nation so torn by rebellion, for the tragic man now seated across the desk from him, and for himself and Consuelo.

"The end times, Clay," the President said.

"End times? You mean the end of the world?"

"Truth is, the sixth chapter is intended to reveal the entire history of the world, but it requires a lot more insight than I've got to untangle it, I think."

Clay sat silently, watching the president and thinking of what had just transpired. For some reason, those words Lincoln had read made sense. So much so that they continued to echo in his head. Finally he said, "There's a book of scripture the Mormons use, Mister President. Brigham Young once read a verse to me regarding this war that Joseph Smith claimed to have received from the Lord—back in 1832, I think. In that verse, it prophesied that this war would begin with the rebellion of South Carolina, and that—"

As Clay spoke, the president's eyes took on such a penetrating stare that Clay began to wish he had kept his mouth shut. "You don't say—1832?" Lincoln said, his voice low, stressed with fatigue.

"Yes, sir. But as I recall," Clay continued, more hesitantly, "there was more."

"More?"

"It went on to say that war would be . . . let's see, how did it go?" he said, rubbing his forehead. "It said that war would be poured out upon all nations, beginning at this place."

"This place?"

"South Carolina, I think."

Lincoln sat back, obviously deeply moved by what he had just heard. "What book was that, you say?"

Clay shook his head. "A book of scripture the Mormons use in addition to the Bible—they have several, you know. It's full of revelations received by Joseph Smith. I forget its title."[5]

"Ain't that somethin'?" The president said, obviously lost in thought, his speech momentarily reverting to that of the backwoods lawyer he once was.

"Oddly enough," Clay said, unsure of his feelings, "General Lee and I are not the only ones to favor gray horses. I know someone else who rides such a horse. A fellow by the name of Wolf Striker—and Death could well be his name."

PART TWO

★ ★ ★

CHAPTER 6

★ ★ ★

Something bumped hard against the heavily laden flatboat, jarring Wolf into a groggy awareness; and somewhere he could hear angry, indistinct voices. Not fully awake and not knowing where he was, Wolf weakly struggled against an unfamiliar weight that somehow held him fast, fearful that he had either passed out or fallen asleep, locked in some kind of dust-choking, never-ending bad dream. Vaguely he could remember grasping hands pulling him from cold, black waters, half drowned and chilled to the bone.

After crawling from the hole beneath the Leavenworth stockade, Wolf had made his way down to the nearby Missouri River, away from the docks, hoping his trail would be lost in the stinking, high-water bogs that in places formed its muddy banks. But the dogs were not long in catching his scent, and the closer they got, the more relentless their baying pursuit had become, until it seemed they would be tearing at his clothes before he could struggle another step farther. Only his determination to return to the war and the army of the Confederacy had kept him going— that and his determination never again to be locked up in a Yankee prison.

With the baying dogs sounding almost at his heels, he had lunged on into the night, finally plunging headlong into a shallow, stagnant bayou that eventually drained into the large river. The mud had sucked at him, refusing his efforts at further escape, threatening to pull him under as the sulphurous-smelling ooze sluiced around his body, filling his mouth with the fetid taste of the filthy, algae-covered water.

Confused and exhausted he had collapsed in the watery slough, struggling to catch his breath and recover his sense of direction. But feeling disquieting disturbances in the water's coarse surface as unseen things slithered around him in the dark, Wolf had fought to regain his footing and struggled on into the darkness, every part of his being refusing whatever obstacle might deny him his freedom.

The dogs and the men seemed never to give up, racing back and forth through the thick, swampy undergrowth, hour after hour, disturbing nesting birds and sleeping animals lying hid. Finally, after what seemed unending hours of struggle, the clean cold current of the mighty Missouri had caught him, sweeping his half-conscious body out into the river where, at long last, disembodied hands had reached out of the dark and wrestled him from the black, swirling water. They had wrapped him in dusty burlap for warmth and hidden him between coarse, bulging sacks of grain, where he had passed out from exhaustion as they piled more of the heavy bags around and over him. Now, those who had saved him could be heard arguing loudly as angry men stomped aboard the flatboat.

Suddenly Wolf was fully awake, and dark memories of his imprisonment and the struggle to escape through the night flooded his mind. Yankees were boarding the flatboat where he lay hidden, and he was helpless—helpless to defend himself or defend those who had emerged from the darkness to pluck him out of a wet grave. Could there be anything worse than the feeling of helplessness in the presence of one's enemies? Would he never again be able to stand up and confront them alone, meeting force with force, defeating their tyrannical abuses with his own hands?

He did not know the man responsible for saving him, but he could hear his angry recriminations. "You got no call boardin' this here vessel. I got nothin' more'n this here pile of grain I'm takin' down river t' sell at Saint Louie. It's all I got, and nothin's gonna happen to it."

"Saint Louis, my foot. You and these darkies are nothing but southern sympathizers, contraband themselves, more than likely. And my guess is you're delivering this grain to some Confederate port somewhere down river. Somewhere on the Mississippi, maybe. Some Confederate landing someplace south of Memphis is more like it, or even farther south—Vicksburg, maybe. They're going to need it down there. Vicksburg—now that's more like the truth, isn't it?"

"Saint Louie is where we're headin', an' you got no right to stop us. And what's more, these here Negroes are all free men, and don't you be tryin' t' lay a hand on 'em, neither."

With almost every word, the voices grew more bitter and unrelenting. With the sound of men heaving heavy bags aside, Wolf could hear their scuffling, grunting efforts not far from where he lay hidden, and getting closer. With all of the confusion, the sacks seemed to have grown more crushing and the air thicker with dust, making the necessity of lying still almost impossible.

The urge to cough grew as the thick dust filled his nose and throat and the air grew even more mercilessly oppressive. One way or the other, Wolf was convinced he was not going to survive long enough to ever see the light of day again, let alone get back into the war. It was as if all Creation had begun turning against him—again.

"We've got every right. There's a war on, if you haven't heard, and we're looking for an escaped Rebel prisoner. Now, we're going to search this boat if we have to toss every bag of this contraband into the river, and you with it."

"It ain't contraband, I told yuh, and you ain't gonna throw it nowheres. Moses, Hiram, get up on that pile with yer pitchforks. If this here lieutenant wants war, well I guess he's sure enough gonna get it. He's jest declared it on us, from the sounds of it."

For a long moment silence settled across the flatboat, then the Union officer said, "If that's how it's got to be, so be it. Sergeant!" Feet shuffled and weapons were cocked.

The tension on the boat suddenly intensified to the point Wolf knew he had to do something, and he began pushing against the bags that held him fast. He needed air, needed to put an end to this, but he was held so tightly that any movement was impossible. He was about to cry out from anger and frustration when something bumped against the boat, and another voice stopped him.

"Lieutenant Pierce! Hold on there."

"Major, I think there's cause to believe—"

"Just let me have a look-see, Lieutenant," the officer said, boarding the flatboat. Then to the owner of the boat, "Do you mind, Captain?"

"Yuh can look all yer of a mind to, but not a bag of my grain is goin' overboard, and there's nowheres t' restack all them heavy sacks."

"Mmm . . . so I see. Sergeant, put a bayonet on that weapon and hand it to me."

At the sound of the word *bayonet* Wolf sucked in his breath, wishing he could somehow shrink in size. Not a moment later, he heard the blade as it sliced between the sacks somewhere near his feet—repeated thrusts, one after the other, downward, then sideways, each thrust of the blade coming closer, each easy, but with a force calculated to do real harm.

Expecting the worst, Wolf tried to make him self as small as possible. The bayonet slid past his stomach puncturing the sack next to him, its contents spilling around him like dry sand. If that evil blade punctured a bag near his face he would be helplessly suffocated by its contents. The next thrust jabbed along his back, thudding harmlessly into the deck. The next nicked his ear; another half inch and it would have scalped him. The cold edge knifed next to his head again, penetrating the deck on which he lay. With a grunt it was withdrawn.

With each stroke of the bayonet, with each word from the arrogant Union officers, Wolf's determination to survive, to get to where he could wreak havoc on Union arrogance and bullying, grew, and he could feel himself drawing down inside himself, deep down, away from his humanity. The beast was beginning to stir, the old Wolf he thought he had conquered was threatening to again break loose from reason.

Finally, the relentless Union inquisition ended, and Wolf lay with nothing but a bloody ear as evidence of what he had endured. But the damage went far deeper and had for a time threatened his entire being—his soul. It was a line from Shakespeare that for some inexplicable reason broke into the growing darkness of his mind, bringing him up out of that grim place light cannot reach, where no man should go.

Once again, he had escaped the knell that would summon him to heaven or hell. How was it so, and why? Would it have been heaven, or would it have been hell? Actually, he had no idea, but he did have his suspicions, and the thought made him shudder.

Later, when he had an opportunity to reflect upon the incident, Wolf would have cause to wonder about his almost unaccountable deliverance from the persistent Union bayonet—and from himself. One man can have only so many brushes with Shakespeare's fell sergeant without coming at some point to his account. But inside, Wolf knew all too well the real accounting would come later, with a judgment that would be both just and final. How long could his luck, if that is what it was, last?

"Well, I'm satisfied. Here, Sergeant, take this," the Union officer said, handing the rifle back to the soldier. To his subordinate officer, he continued, "I'd have hit something if the prisoner had been under there." And with dripping sarcasm he added, "Oh . . . and I don't think I ripped any of your precious bags, Captain."

"Major, I really think—"

"You're wasting time here, Lieutenant. Now get on with it. I want that man found. Let there be no misunderstanding about that, Lieutenant. I want him found." Whatever else was said was lost amid the confusion of the Yankee soldiers clamoring off the flatboat.

By the time the last Union trooper was over the side, the sky was beginning to lighten with the coming dawn, and the captain turned to one of his two crewmen, the man named Moses, and signaled him to guide their overladen vessel out into the main current. "Time we put some distance betwixt them Yankees and us, Moses."

"Yahsuh, it sho' is. Them Yankees ain't nothin' t' fuss wit'. Not if a body can he'p it, Cap'n."

"Jest you get us as far out in midstream as you can, Moses."

"Yahsuh, I do m' best, suh."

"Hiram, let's you an' me get that poor fella outta there and see if that Yankee Major stuck 'im with that big bayonet of his'n."

With most of the heavy sacks of grain moved aside, the black man unceremoniously dragged a struggling Wolf Striker from beneath the few that remained. "You jest hang on, Mistah," he grunted, ignoring Wolf's struggles. "You's gettin' outta there now."

"You okay?" the Captain asked, as Hiram attempted to brush a thick coating of grain dust from what remained of Wolf's mud-encrusted clothing. "I take it them rags used to be a Confederate uniform."

"He got some blood here, cap'n. Best you have a look-see."

Pushing the black man's inquiring hand away, Wolf hacked, attempting to clear his throat of the dust and dirt he had inhaled while buried beneath the heavy pile of bagged grain and spat over the side. "They're what's left of a Confederate uniform, alright," he wheezed.

Taking a moment to quickly evaluate his benefactors and assess his surroundings, Wolf took a deep breath of fresh, clean air, and in a clearer voice, said, "You'll have to pardon my lack of manners, Captain, but I'll tell you the truth: much longer under those bags and I swear I'd have smothered."

All three men were a good deal older than he would have guessed, and each looked well worn and perpetually worried, but not yet defeated. Extending his hand, he said, "I'm Major Wolf Striker, and I'm afraid you took a real chance on hiding me. If those Yankees had found me, they'd probably have shot all three of you—right after they shot me. As I'm sure you've already guessed, I escaped from Leavenworth—last night, I think," Wolf said, rubbing his temples. "Things are kind of fuzzy. It might even have been in another lifetime"

"Yeah . . . we expected as much, didn't we, Hiram?"

"We sho' did," Hiram said, with his last swipe at the obstinate dust clinging to Wolf's tattered uniform. "Yessuh, we sho did."

"Well . . . Hiram, go open that trunk back there, an' let's see if there's some clothes that might fit our major friend, here. I'll take a look at his ear while he tells us what he's about."

"My ear's fine, Captain," Wolf said, waving the man's hand away and sitting down on a dusty bag. "I'm just a little tired, is all. But to put it as simply as I can, what I'm about, as you put it, is getting back into the war. I'm headed for Vicksburg, and it's my intention to get there just as fast as I can."

"Vicksburg, huh?" the man said, taking an armful of doubtful-looking clothing from Hiram and critically sorting through each piece. "How come Vicksburg?"

"Two reasons, Captain. One, I've got family there—a wife I haven't seen in years, if she's still there, and if she's still alive and unmarried. And two, if there isn't any fighting there now, there soon will be, and it's going to get nasty."

"Well,. I guess so," the boatman said, holding up a pair of bib overalls. "Ain't much, but . . . look here . . . try these. Might not fit, and if they do, probably won't help yuh all that much."

As Wolf accepted the clothing, the captain continued, "There's fightin' all right. Anywhere up and down the Mississippi, the Yankees pretty much control the river, top t' bottom. You jest got a taste of their high an' mighty ways. Anyway, best you get outta them Confederate rags. If we run into more of 'em, maybe we can convince 'em yer one of my men."

"It's that bad, huh?" Wolf said, struggling with the well-worn pair of heavy denim bib overalls that were at least four sizes too big. Between the wounds he had received as the Glorieta battle collapsed around him, and all of the Yankee comforts afforded him in the Leavenworth stockade, he had lost a good deal of weight.

"How long you been locked up, Major?" The captain chuckled, watching Wolf's almost comical efforts. "Folks around here've put up with them peevish Yankees for months now. How come—"

"I was out in the western territories until I got captured," Wolf said, struggling with the heavy garment. "We've had our own Yankee difficulties out there." Pulling the straps over his shoulders and watching the coveralls drop to half mast, he stammered, "What the . . . will you just look? I've lived in tents with less room than this."

"Ain't too stylish, all right," the boatman chuckled, with a quick, appraising examination, "but if yuh pull them straps up through them cinches, they oughtta do jest fine. Truth is, the worse yuh look, the better. Yessir, they'll do jes' fine."

Looking around, Wolf heaved a sigh. "I'll tell you what the truth is, Captain. I will not be caught again, and I don't want you and your men in any danger because of me. It might be best if I got off your boat right here."

"And, what chance would yuh have around here, you a Confederate soldier an' all? You heard that blue belly major, all full of hisself. He wants your hide real bad. You heard 'im. He said as much right out. My guess is there'll be patrols looking for you twenty miles here about," the man said, with a wave of his hand.

"On both sides of the river, more'n likely. Nope. Safest place is right here on this boat, where they already searched—in them overalls."

"Mmm," Wolf hummed, considering the wisdom of the man's advice. "I guess you're right, but what if they board us again?"

"Might, alright. Jest might. They're all over the place. Thicker than gnats on the river at sundown. Yuh see 'em in one kind of gunboat or other almost around every turn, but we'll get as far as we can, least ways off the Big Muddy, here, and down the Mississippi some, too," he said, taking the tiller from Moses.

"Moses, you go forward, there, and help Hiram watch for snags in the river."

"Yasuh, I sho will."

"Though, I gotta tell yuh, it ain't at all that likely we'll be goin' anywheres near to Vicksburg, but you're welcome to stay with us down to Memphis, if'n we can even get that far—Yankees is crawlin' all over Memphis. Most likely we ain't gonna get much farther than Cairo. Cairo's crawlin' with Yankees, too. One way or t'other, though, at some point, I'll have t' stop and sell all this here grain, or take the chance of losin' it, and I sure can't afford to do that."

"It's that bad out here?" Wolf said, trying not to sound too ignorant to this wise old boatman, but wanting to get as much information out of him as possible.

"Worse," the boatman said, spitting over the side, as if aiming at some detested enemy. "Like I say, damn Yankees control most of these waters. Fact is, the Mississippi's theirs from New Orleans all the way up here. Got control of the river at Memphis, last June, I think it was. Vicksburg is all that's left.

"But that ain't the worst of it. Feller name of Grant got control of the Tennessee and the Cumberland late last winter. Took control of a couple of forts, one on each river. Take a boat like this'n up either one of them two rivers now, and yer gonna lose it to them Yankees sure as sunrise. Used t' sell a good deal of stuff up there, too."

"You're turning into an outright river gambler," Wolf observed, beginning to understand the difficulties the man faced. "But I guess you can't just gather up your chips and walk away from this table, can you?"

"A man does what's gotta be done t' keep body and soul together, I guess. I used to be a tinker, too, along with everything else. We did all right, didn't we, Hiram?"

"We was real welcome," Hiram said, his squawky voice a parody of sadness. "We was hardly ever hungry back in them days, huh, Cap'n? Ain't like that no mo', though."

"That's a actual fact." Moses chimed in. "'Ain't it, Cap'n?'"

"Hiram's right. Yessir, folks looked forward to seein' us come up their river, and that's the truth. Them rivers go a long ways back t' the east an' south—even almost into the Alleghenies."

For a long moment, the old river man stopped talking, the weight of his worries more than obvious on his craggy face. Then, almost as if trying to wipe away his worries, he rubbed his face with a darkly tanned and calloused hand, heaved a sigh, and continued. "But, they're gone now. Yessir, they're gone now. Too bad, too. Lots of folks back in there what needs a tinker now and again, not to mention other goods they can't get no other way. Now them Yankees are thick as chiggers—all around. Mississippi? Tennessee? Shoot, the road's as good as open for 'em clear to Vicksburg. You sure that's where yuh want t' go, Major?"

"Sounds as if that's where I *need* to go," Wolf said, at last satisfied with what few adjustments he could make on his tent-like overalls.

"Uh-huh. Somethin's surely needed, and that's a fact."

"But we control Vicksburg. General Pemberton is still occupying the town, last I heard. But where's Beauregard? Where's Bragg?"

"Oh they're out there. Gettin' shoved from one place t' the other, I expect. Get off this boat, and I expect you'll run onto 'em. But more'n likely, you'll run smack into some Yankees first. There's been a passel of fightin' all around Corinth, back and forth over Iuka. Shoot, Shiloh to Memphis, them Yankees is thick as flees on a hound dog's belly. Seems there's one behind every bush anywhere you go."

"But, Vicksburg . . ." Wolf said, almost to himself, the very word tasting like honey on his tongue, his mind drifting back to nearly forgotten days. Vicksburg, a time all but snuffed out as his life had cruelly spiraled out of his grasp and down into a dark, despairing oblivion. A place where all hope had been abandoned—*Abandon hope, all ye who enter here.* And he had.

Yet Vicksburg had somehow remained—a tiny, flickering light in an otherwise stricken life. And now, just the sound of the word brought to his fatigued mind long-lost images of a heaven on earth. Those had been golden days, perfect days: days when the future seemed so bright; days filled with happiness and nights filled with love—a perfect life lost. "I must, you see," he said. "I was raised there. And she may still be there."

"She?"

For a western rancher, a man born to the open places, to the saddle and gun, rail travel under the best of circumstances was a totally undesirable mode of transportation. As far as Clay Ashworth was concerned, nothing could beat the back of a good horse and the squeak of expensive saddle leather, no matter what the distance—certainly not a rattling, aging rail coach.

With each curve of the track, the iron wheels of the slow-moving train emitted an almost unearthly screech, and the wheels on this particular car felt as if each was worn flat, each in a different place.

To top it off, the windows had to be at least partly open or the air in the nearly empty passenger carriage quickly became stifling. As a result, the smoke and cinders from the engine blew with evil determination directly into the car, first on one side, then on the other, changing with every curve in the track.

The big Utahan had moved twice in a futile effort to avoid the smoke and cinders, but to no avail. And rising once more, his patience at an end, he was determined that this move would be the last. Smoke or no, where he landed this time, he would stay put.

"Terrible, isn't it?"

Only his peevish and determined attempts to escape the ambient horrors of the coach could explain how he had failed to realize that there was a woman occupying the space nearest the window, and he had nearly landed in her lap. His impatient behavior became even more embarrassing as he realized that she was obviously what one would describe as a southern belle. And judging by her looks, she was everything such women were said to be.

Even with her face and dress lightly powdered with soot, her beauty remained totally appealing. But it was her large green eyes that immediately caught his attention. Aside from their unusual color, there was a kind of sadness about them that somehow seemed unfair, out of place. "I'm truly sorry, ma'am, and I do apologize. I hope I haven't crowded you," Clay stammered, attempting to rise. "You see, the smoke has gotten so bad on that side of the car, I just had to move. I'm afraid I wasn't looking where I was landing. And you are absolutely correct, it is terrible."

"Please, don't move on my account," she said, her gloved hand lightly touching his coat sleeve. "I do understand—perfectly. The condition of this horrible, decrepit old coach," she complained, as Clay settled next to her. "The smoke, the noise—I mean, really. I do realize there's a war on, but this is almost too much for a civilized person to endure." Her southern accent was as captivating as her beauty, a dangerous combination for a lonely man traveling incognito in hostile country.

It had taken Clay Ashworth nearly a week to make his way from Washington, D.C., to Lynchburg, Virginia—a town roughly a hundred miles west of Richmond and half that again from Washington—where he was at last able to board a train that might possibly get him on his way toward Vicksburg.

Under the best of times, such a trip would have required at least four train changes due to differing rail gauges and a variety of corporate ownership. It was not unusual for track gauges to range from six feet in width down to as little as four feet, ten inches. Add to that uncoordinated and uncertain schedules, and travel was almost guaranteed to be an annoying hassle, even during the best of times.

Thanks to the war raging throughout the South, however, these were not the best of times. Travel for any would-be pilgrim was a precarious venture. And for Clay Ashworth, determined to carry out Mister Lincoln's requests to the letter, the impossibility of his situation was almost overwhelming.

Rail travel south from Alexandria, Virginia, just across the Potomac from Washington was available but would have been far too dangerous, if at all possible. Clay would have had to pass through three Virginia towns that were undoubtedly crawling with rebel soldiers. Even so, he had lost count of the number of mounted Confederate patrols he had encountered before finally reaching the Lynchburg station. Avoiding them had proved more than a little tricky, and on several occasions he had come uncomfortably close to disaster.

The fear of capture had been constantly with him since assuming his false identity and heading deep into Confederate territory. Now, some thirty or forty miles southwest of Lynchburg, on a train that seemed about to shake apart, the likelihood of facing some skeptical Confederate soldiers and being forced to convince them of his loyalties was almost guaranteed, and failure was sure to get him shot on the spot. However, watching this beautiful, sad-eyed southern woman sitting next to him as she complained about her discomforts, Clay began to recognize his obvious good fortune. Who could doubt his credibility if found traveling with her?

"I'm sorry," Clay said, turning to face her more directly, "discomfort is no excuse for bad manners. I'm Braxton Mallory, from Tuscaloosa, Alabama, ma'am."

"Thank you for being so courteous, Mister Mallory. This is hardly the environment for formal introductions, I must say. But such are the conditions bred by this horrible war, I guess," she said, offering a small, femininely gloved hand. "My name is Missus Ellen Parkhill Striker."

Clay was so obviously startled by the mention of her married name, that Ellen Striker smiled, and said, "Is there something wrong, Mister Mallory?"

"Uh . . . no, ma'am. I'm sorry to appear so ill-mannered, but your name . . . I think I once knew a fellow by the name of Striker. However," he said, catching himself, wondering just how much he dared say, given his circumstances, "to be truthful, I can't remember just where or when, or even his full name."

"It's not likely, Mister Mallory . . . unless you've been to Vicksburg. Have you ever been to Vicksburg, Mister Mallory?"

"I'm sorry to say that I haven't. I must be mistaken."

"Perhaps not. It is quite an unusual name. My husband's people are of German extraction. They settled in South Carolina simply ages ago, somewhere around Charleston, I think. They moved west to Mississippi while he was still a very small boy. But I'm quite sure none of them has ever lived in Alabama." Her voice grew wistful, as she continued, "My husband disappeared during the war with Mexico. I've never heard from him since. In fact, not a word about him from anyone."

Clay watched her closely as she spoke. As unlikely as it seemed, it was true. This beautiful, lonely woman was talking about Wolf Striker—the same Wolf Striker.

Turning toward the window, she fell silent for a moment, and then with a sigh, looked back at Clay and, with resignation returning, said, "He has been assumed dead for a number of years, now, Mister Mallory. It's just that it is so hard to let go. But it does seem like such a long time."

"If you'll pardon my forwardness, ma'am, you're still young. It's a shame you—"

The woman turned away, again toward the window, and Clay knew he had overstepped his bounds.

"I'm sorry. I've embarrassed you. Please forgive me, I had no business—"

"No, there is no need," she said, dabbing at her eyes with a delicately embroidered handkerchief, "It's just that Wolf and I . . . well . . . we had such—"

"Please, I've obviously opened a very painful wound. I am sorry."

It is true, Clay thought, attempting to avoid her eyes, *her husband is Wolf Striker.* The odds against such an encounter were absolutely astounding. Yet there was no doubt in his mind. Still, who would have thought that a man like Wolf Striker ever could have been married to such an obviously aristocratic and beautiful woman.

There couldn't be two Wolf Strikers, Clay mused, glancing sideways at the woman next to him, a part of him refusing to accept what had become obvious. The incongruity of it all was astonishing, to say the least.

Ellen Striker dabbed at a very feminine sniffle, and asked, "Are you married, Mister Mallory? Please forgive me for asking," she sniffed. "Mister Mallory?"

Momentarily lost in thought, nearly dumbfounded by the unlikely coincidence of such an encounter and wondering how to save the situation, Clay at last said, "I'm sorry. I don't mean to be any more discourteous than I have been already. I'm just a little chagrined at how forward I have made myself."

"Oh . . . no . . . don't feel that way, Mister Mallory. My goodness, it is I who has been altogether too forward. But it's this horrible war," she sighed, looking away, toward the grimy, indistinct images sliding past the window. "It has torn so many families and relationships apart, filled so many lives with despair and loneliness. I'm afraid my emotions are never far from the surface.

"I don't mean to embarrass you, Mister Mallory, really. But, it's just that the things one was once able to anchor one's life around—family and community, proper relationships—seem completely shattered now. Gone forever, no doubt."

As she spoke, the words began to spill out, as if some barrier had suddenly opened, relieving pent-up pressures that had been locked inside for too long. "After all, where does one look for stability and continuity? No matter where one turns, there is no longer any sense of permanence. I suppose the most distressing thing about it all is the loneliness and sense of separation people feel, as if there is no one a person can any longer trust or depend upon."

Looking directly at Clay she paused, as if searching his face for some hint of understanding, her eyes swimming, then said, "But you see, the truth is, Mister Mallory, it's not just this war. It has been this way for me since the day I lost my husband."

The woman seemed to blur before him, and his thoughts, for the briefest moment, returned to the tiny grave at *Rancho los Librados* and his wife disappearing into the house, leaving him alone. He could still hear the screened door banging closed behind her. "Believe me, Missus Striker," he said, catching himself, "I know something of how you feel. Nothing can hurt more than having your spouse torn from your side—whatever the reason."

"Mmm," she said, her mind still dealing with her loss, almost as if she had not heard him. "You know, Mister Mallory," she said, turning toward him, "I met my husband when he was a cadet at West Point. My, but he was a fine looking cadet. Dressed in his uniform, he quite took my breath away, and he was every inch a real soldier. He rose to senior cadet ranks before he graduated, you know."

"Your husband attended West Point?" Clay asked.

"Oh, my, yes. The day after his graduation, we were married in the chapel there, and all his friends were outside with their sabers arched. It was a true military wedding. I could not have hoped for more. I declare, it was almost a fairy tale, the kind every young girl dreams of."

Clay watched her sad-eyed reverie for a moment. "You know, Missus Striker, wars have a way of turning things upside down," he observed. Somewhat at a loss for words, he added, "Once that first shot has been fired, nothing ever remains the same."

"How unfortunate that is," she said, studying his face, "and I apologize for my forward behavior. It was an impropriety, allowing my emotions to get the better of me this way. You must think me, a complete stranger, terribly rude."

Clay sat silent for a moment, wanting desperately to give her whatever comfort he could, to let her know that she had a friend, someone willing to listen. Then, reacting to the expectant look on her face, he said, "Believe me, there is no need to apologize, Missus Striker. For reasons that may never be fully appreciated, I think the two of us are more than just a couple of strangers on a train. We might just have more in common than meets the eye. After all," he said, a little too offhandedly, "wars have a way of forging strange alliances, and perhaps even stranger friendships."

Looking into her teary eyes, he lightly patted her hand. "But more importantly, they also have a way of revitalizing the past, of removing bygone uncertainties and restoring loss—somehow working miracles, sometimes."

"Really, Mister Mallory?" Ellen Striker said, uncertainly, her eyes searching his for any hidden meaning.

"Yes, ma'am . . . perhaps more than either of us knows," Clay said, looking away, afraid he had said too much, and uncertain whether he could continue skirting around her anxieties without tipping his hand. Somehow he wanted very much to let her know that Wolf was still alive—alive and dangerous.

As if she could not fathom the meaning of his words and was unwilling to pursue them further, Ellen seemed to relax, and said, "Yes, well, because that is so true, one has to wonder if the old refinements, the old rules of etiquette, any longer have meaning in today's world. I mean who hasn't been affected by this horrible war? In such an awful world as this, what norms should govern human interaction, even on so meaningless a level as ours? Certainly, the petty strictures of the Old South no longer apply. I'm afraid the South, the South you and I once knew, Mister Mallory, is truly gone forever, regardless of how this war ends." She sat silent for a moment, then added, "Perhaps that is for the best—in the end, that is."

The depth of her thinking had taken Clay by surprise. The woman sitting next to him was clearly no empty-headed, emotional flower of the Old South. From just this brief encounter, it was obvious that Ellen Striker was woman of surprising discernment, capable of uncommon introspection.

"Two strangers on a train?" she mused, her eyes searching his face. "How often does one have the opportunity to share one's feelings today, no matter how improper it once may have seemed? Especially those feelings where the pain has taken so long to subside."

Listening to her Clay realized that the very fact that a person of such acumen was, or had been, Wolf Striker's wife, was going to force him to reevaluate the man. It was becoming obvious— there was more to Wolf Striker than Clay had been used to thinking. And the more he thought about it, the fact that Wolf was a West Point graduate somehow came as no surprise. There had always been some quality, some almost indefinable something, about the man that, given the circumstances, just did not fit. The longer this conversation went on, the more things fell into place, where Wolf Striker was concerned.

"And for some reason, Mister Mallory, you just don't seem a stranger to me, somehow. I don't know why, but you are the kind of man with whom my husband would have felt some kinship. I just know it."

Her unexpected observation touched Clay in a way he would not have thought possible, partly because he had always sensed that errant, indefinable quality in Wolf Striker that had been so hard to account for. "I don't know what to say, ma'am. Except I take that as a wonderful compliment. I'm sure he's—he was—a fine man."

"Yes. In every sense of the word. And I'm not just talking out of grief. That is long past. It's just that such a man cannot easily be forgotten."

"Oh, yes," Clay said, trying to hide a chuckle. "I think that's very true."

Her unexpected and almost uncanny association of him with her husband, along with her vulnerability and refinement, made Clay want to say more than he should in an effort to give her hope, any degree of respite from her sense of loss, from the obvious grief she denied she still felt.

The fact is, only a few months ago, her husband had not been dead, nor was he missing. Far from it. The man had been very much alive and a threat to all around him. Furthermore, when Clay last saw him, he had been wearing the uniform of a Confederate major. What a study in contrast this man, Wolf Striker, was becoming.

What must Striker have been like when this obviously desirable and aristocratic woman had fallen in love with him—and obviously loved him still? Women, even rich women, women born to high station, have been known to fall for rogues. Such scandals have never been rare, but somehow this woman seemed far too levelheaded, and too refined, to have been swept away by the man

Clay Ashworth knew as Wolf Striker. Why? What could have happened?

Port Rockwell hated Striker's guts and had been determined to see him dance at the end of a rope. Yet even Port, on more than one occasion, had said that there was more to Wolf Striker than any of us knew. And Brigham Young certainly thought so as well.

From all Clay had heard, the man had been known to speak with an educated tongue, knew military strategy and tactics, knew politics and history, and could discuss literature with anyone. Obviously highly educated and gifted, what could have happened to such a man?

And now this. . . .

When last seen, Striker had been fighting for the Confederacy, and if Porter Rockwell's judgment was to be trusted—and it always was—the man seemed somehow to have recovered himself.

The man Clay saw at the battle of Glorieta Pass had fought like a true soldier, not some sort of ravenous, depraved killer. True, someone had shot him, but somehow Clay knew, as only another soldier could know, that Wolf Striker was not dead as he lay there in that burned-out Confederate encampment at Johnson's Ranch. And if that were so, Striker would be back in the war at the first opportunity; and if that were so, Clay was determined to know the man better, come what may.

But even more troubling, why had Striker not contacted his wife? How could he have abandoned such a women as Ellen Striker, a woman so completely in love with him, and left her thinking he was dead? What had happened at Chapultepec that had so changed their lives? Whatever the reasons, Clay Ashworth was determined to find the man and ask him. For now, however, the question troubling Clay Ashworth was, how could he give the woman next to him some hope, however tenuous?

"I asked you a question earlier, Mister Mallory, and you seem to have avoided it. I know it's none of my business, but since we are no longer truly strangers, I must ask again. Are you married, Mister Mallory?"

"I guess it's the war, Missus Striker," Clay said, heaving a sigh, one born almost of despair, "but speaking of one's former life almost makes it seem as if it had never happened. But, yes, I am married. Very much so."

"I thought as much," Ellen Striker said, watching Clay closely. "Is she in Alabama, then?"

Where is she, indeed? Clay thought, the pain again rising. In the past weeks, Connie had never been far from his thoughts, but at least the ache had been partially buried beneath the mountain of dangerous responsibility heaped upon him by the president.

"Oh, my. Has she hurt you, Mister Mallory?"

Clay smiled in an attempt to cover the feelings he had never been able to hide completely. "Not intentionally, ma'am. As you said, it's the war. War does terrible things to all of us. In fact, life does."

"Perhaps when it's over—"

"Will it ever be over?"

The train suddenly jolted and began slowing down, its brakes squealing with the effort demanded of them. Within moments it shuddered to a smoky, hissing stop. Looking out through the grimy window and trying not to appear too concerned, Clay said, "You're not all that determined to get to Vicksburg, are you, Missus Striker?"

"Why . . . yes. Yes, I am."

"I'm afraid there's a good deal of fighting between here and there," Clay said, straining to catch a glimpse of the activity on the tracks that had brought the train to its unscheduled stop. "It could prove to be very dangerous. Even for a woman of your obvious refinement. Perhaps, especially so."

"Nonetheless, I must return home, Mister Mallory. My family is there—at least what's left of them—and I do need to be there with them. And who knows? If what you have said is true—"

"I understand, but—"

The door to the coach suddenly slammed open, and four Confederate soldiers entered the car. Scanning the passengers as he slowly made his way down the aisle, the biggest, a burly sergeant, said, "Truly sorry for the delay, folks, but my men need to see y'all's identification papers b'fore this here train enters the station yard." With his eyes coming to rest on Clay, he continued, "We got reports of a Yankee spy sneakin' into this area, an' we are gonna catch that fella an' hang 'im. Hang 'im real high."

CHAPTER 7

★ ★ ★

For Connie and Emily, the first few days after their arrival at the Salinas ranch had been an emotional time for all concerned—but happy only in part.

For Emily, it had been a rebirth. Until that startling moment when she first glimpsed the Salinas *casa,* and then her brother, Lazaro, Emily's mind had been devoid of any memory prior to the time Clay Ashworth had found her wandering in the desert of the New Mexico Territory years earlier. But the moment she saw the ranch house and Lazaro had ridden up to the coach, it had all come back in full—a flood of emotionally overwhelming memories, vivid recollections of the evil done to her and her family that horrible day the *Comancheros* murdered her husband and sons and left her to die in the desert. And with that flood of memory also came the recognition of Consuelo as a cherished niece. In one moment, one brilliant flash of time, Emily's life had come full circle and was once again whole.

For Connie, the return to her former home had been bitter-sweet at best. Not until she had turned her back on *Rancho los Librados* had she come to realize how desperately she loved her husband. But with the death of their baby, she had been so lost and distraught that no one, not even Clay, had been able to reach her.

Only the thought of her home in Mexico had penetrated that horrible fog of pain, depression, and outright despair. Her father's ranch had always been her place of ultimate safety, the only home she had ever known, the one place on earth where no torment could reach her, a place of culture, joy, and healing. Wounded so deeply, her only thought had been of returning to what she had once known.

Yet each day, as the miles had multiplied between herself and *Rancho los Librados,* recognition of the impossibility of her situation had grown, until she was finally left with the shocking realization of the enormity of her mistake. In a pitiful effort to return to her past, she had left the only man she could ever love sitting alone by the side of that small grave, equally crushed by the death of their tiny, newborn daughter.

The mere thought of her desertion, at the very moment her husband had needed her most, brought tears of shame and pain that would not be held back. Finally, having arrived at her former home, Connie knew where she truly belonged, where she would always belong—with Clay, no matter where.

In the weeks since her return to Mexico, Connie's only respite was to be found in the single, unsigned note she had received from Clay not long after her arrival. It contained only one sentence and bore no signature, but it was in his handwriting, and each time she read those few simple words, her heart would nearly burst with all of the love she had ever felt for him.

I love you, Maria Emilea Consuelo Salinas Ashworth, and I always will.

She had read the short note over and over, until the paper had become so worn his words were nearly gone, but it represented her future, of that she was certain. Emily's assurances were true: one day he would come for her, and if he didn't, she would return to him, if she had to walk every step of the way back to Utah. She had never known such resolve.

But it was the recent arrival of two additional letters from home, *Rancho los Librados,* that had both taken her breath away and clouded her future. Before opening them, she had been sure they were from Clay, and that they would tell her of his coming arrival, but it was not so. One had been from Robby Robshaw, Clay's foreman, and the other from Chet Langtree, *segundo* and top ranch hand at *Rancho los Librados.* Both had assured her that everything was fine at the ranch, she was missed, and the place would never be the same until she returned.

It was Chet's brief letter that both added to her sense of failure as a wife and a mother, and renewed her determination to return to her proper place in the world. Chet reported that a few days after her departure, Clay and Chet, along with Robby, Doctor Richards, and some of Clay's closest Mormon Battalion friends, had joined in a tightly closed circle around that tiny grave, and Clay had given their beloved tiny daughter a name—Victoria Consuelo Emilea Salinas Ashworth. Then, placing a small granite headstone engraved with her name, they had dedicated that precious little plot of ground as a place of rest and peace until the miracle of that future day promised in the scriptures.

It was a perfect name and, like Clay's note, Connie had read it again and again. Each time her heart almost broke. She could see Clay, just as she remembered him, sitting at the side of that holy place, his shoulders heavy with his burden of grief, and alone. Chet's letter said no more, but Connie knew in her heart how her husband must have suffered. His friends had surrounded him in that small circle of love, but they no more could have taken her place than anyone could now take his.

Until Robby's letter arrived, Connie did not know that Clay had gone east at the request of President Lincoln, where he was supposedly working with Allan Pinkerton directly for the president. Since then, they had received only one brief telegram from Clay, not long after his arrival in Washington, D.C., telling them not to worry and not to try to contact him. There had been no further word. However, a recent message sent to the ranch from Salt Lake City indicated that Clay's whereabouts was unknown—he had simply disappeared.

Every evening, just before dinner, Connie would sit in a rocking chair out on the wide, covered veranda of the Salinas *casa,* carefully take Clay's note from its protective envelope, and read the faded words over and over. Then, returning it to the envelope and breathing deeply of the night, she would slowly rock back and forth in the comfortable chair and hold the small letter close to her breast, as if its nearness somehow would bring Clay closer.

Memories of the nights the two of them had spent together enjoying one another in this very place were not long in coming. Just the nearness of his words at this magic hour of the evening gave her a sense of continuity and intimacy that helped her endure the distressing distances that separated them.

The screened door slammed, causing Connie to jump, and Emily, with her hands on her hips, huffed, "Here you are. How come I know right here's where? Night after night, here you are, out here moping, *tú sabes?*"

"Aunt Emily, please don't scold," Connie said, her voice

weighted with emotion. "Something about nights like this makes me feel better, somehow. If it weren't for these wonderful evenings, I don't think I could stand the days."

Each day the two women had grown closer, each understanding the other on a level that in some circumstances didn't even require utterance. Throughout each day they had become so accustomed to speaking English, that only when they were with Lazaro did either of them revert to Spanish, neither of them thinking anything of it.

Being fluent in English, Lazaro soon discovered their ruse, and he quietly informed them that speaking in Spanish around him was unnecessary. In fact, he looked for any opportunity to sharpen his linguistic skills. From that moment on, English became Connie's preferred and soon accustomed tongue.

Sitting down beside her, Emily took her niece's hands in hers and said, "I know you feeling bad, *querida*; but you got to do better. If you no stop bein' like this all the time, you going to get sick, that's what. And that don't do no good for anybody."

Connie sighed, a deep breath of resignation, and looked at her aunt. Then, looking more closely at the woman before her, as if some completely distant thought had suddenly entered her mind, she said, "Aunt Emily, do you believe in God? I mean, *really* believe?"

"Why you ask me such a question like that, huh?" Emily responded, quickly crossing herself. Obviously taken by surprise, she thought a moment and said, "*Sí*, I do . . . I guess."

"I mean, stop and think, Aunt Emily. How Clay found you wandering around in the desert and saved you, keeping you with him almost as if you were being saved, so that when I came to him, you'd be there, and I . . . Oh, I don't know," Connie said, her hand waving slowly in the air, as if she were trying to stir the confusion in her mind into something that would make sense. "I mean . . . I don't know how to describe what has happened, really. Even the loss of our baby somehow made it possible for you to follow me back to Mexico. And then, the moment you see Uncle Lazaro, back comes your memory, and suddenly you are well again. So there was some kind of purpose to it all, wasn't there? There had to be, or it wouldn't make sense, would it?"

Emily sat somewhat dumbfounded, watching her niece, trying to make sense out of Connie's flood of words. "Consuelo, I think I never—"

"I mean, we were all Catholics . . . more or less. Mother and Father and me, and you and Uncle Lazaro—we were all Catholics. Sometimes my family would discuss religious issues, even with dinner guests, but not like this. Not even with our priest or the bishop.

"Father was more of a liberal than a conservative where the Church and Mexico are concerned, and I think that truly affected his thinking. He didn't believe the Church should be so involved in how Mexico was governed, so we really never saw the Church as being particularly central to our lives. Do you know what I'm saying?"

It was Emily's turn to heave an enormous sigh, as if the whole thing was a burden far too heavy for her to bear. "Your Uncle Lazaro is waiting for us, *querida*," she said at last.

Connie ignored the reminder and went on. "It's just that . . . well, it's just that the time I spent in Utah with Clay and his friends. . . ." Connie sighed, her voice trailing off into her own thoughts. Then, glancing down at the two letters resting in her lap, she picked up Chet's, and, as if sensing its true meaning for the first time, tears spilling from her eyes, she continued, "And now, this: how they named and blessed my little girl, our little girl—Clay's and my little girl. Well . . . it's just that I've never thought of things this way before. How beautiful and consoling it must have been for him. And somehow, it is for me, too—just to know it."

"Life got twists and turns, *hijita*, and you and me . . . well, we sure got twisted up in 'em, I think."

"Yes. But look at the miracle for you and for Uncle Lazaro," Connie said, as the two women arose and turned toward the door.

"And for you, too, *querida*. It's going be a miracle for you, too. Just you wait and see."

The two women embraced and, wiping her eyes, Connie said, "It already has been. I don't know how I ever got along without you in my life, Aunt Emily. Right now, things would be unbearable without you. Do you know that? Do you know how precious you are to me right now?"

Kissing her distraught niece on the cheek, Emily said, "Uh-huh, course I know. You no never need to say, *hijita*. Now dinner's on the table, and your Uncle Lazaro is waiting for us."

Every day, her surroundings had taken on a different perspective. Connie knew she had been foolish to have expected things in Mexico to have remained the same, and suddenly it had just become even clearer. With her parents dead, the anchor her father had provided—not just for the ranch, but for the entire region— was gone. Her Uncle Lazaro was doing his best, but unlike her father, he was not the governor. And once again, evil times were breaking forth upon the people of Mexico.

Yet for some reason as yet unclear, she had been meant to return. And in part, she could see the good that had come from it, but whether there was yet more good to come from her return to Mexico, she could not tell. Whatever the benefits to her, she had hurt the man she loved, terribly. One thing she did know, her future lay not in Mexico, but in the Territory of Utah—with her husband, Clay Ashworth.

★   ★   ★

As Connie and Emily entered the house, each with an arm around the other, Lazaro sat watching them from the head of the finely set table, waiting for them as he did at nearly every meal. Having two women sharing his table, let alone his home, was not an entirely comfortable thing, even if they were his closest living relatives. For a bachelor, with two women around the house, things were just not the same. For one thing, they moved too slowly. He always seemed to be waiting, and his burdens were already too many.

Unlike his older brother, the deceased governor of Sonora, Lazaro Salinas had never married. Marriage was not something he had purposely avoided. It was just that he had never stumbled across a woman who struck him as being worthy of pursuit, and as far as he was aware, none had ever felt any differently about him. As the years passed, he had begun traveling, visiting Europe, frequently entering into various lucrative business arrangements, and moving in those circles where politics was of preeminent interest.

Throughout his adult life, Lazaro Salinas's paramount concern had always been for his beloved Mexico, and as his prestige had grown, both at home and abroad, he had been careful to use his influence in furthering the cause of a free and democratic Mexico, wherever and whenever the opportunity had arisen, always exercising the utmost prudence.

As a consequence, over the years, Lazaro Salinas had become a man of considerable stature, one whose opinions were frequently sought by both the powerful and the not-so-powerful. How inconsistent it seemed, then, that daily he should be kept waiting by two women, his sister and his niece.

The world, however, was daily becoming more dangerous, and that was doubly true of Mexico. Early in 1862, sometime after the death of his brother, the three most rapacious of all the European powers—England, France, and Spain—had sent an expeditionary force that landed in Veracruz. Ostensibly, it was a move intended to force Mexico to pay its foreign debts, which Benito Juarez had suspended months earlier. But no one who had the least understanding of world events had been fooled, certainly not Lazaro Salinas.

As with most meals, this one had proceeded quietly, each of the three lost in his or her own thoughts. So when Consuelo looked up from her plate and said, "Uncle Lazaro, Aunt Emily and I have been discussing God," Lazaro was suddenly uncomfortable.

"*God?*" he said, crossing himself, a deep frown darkening his face. "*Madre de Dios,* is that a proper subject for dinner conversation?"

His response, almost a rebuke, caught both women by surprise.

"Is something wrong?" Consuelo asked, dabbing her pretty mouth with her napkin. "Shouldn't He be a fit topic for discussion at the dinner table?"

For a moment, Lazaro did not answer. Studying the two women seated before him, he marveled at the workings of the female mind. Who could explain it? Of far greater importance to him was finding a solution to the very real dangers that were about to envelop them all. Frankly, whether a supreme being existed or not was an extraneous issue.

Lazaro Salinas had never been one to wait for divine

intervention. In fact, where Mexico was concerned, he had seen little evidence of such in the past, and he frankly felt such speculations were a waste of time, a subject best left to the priests and Church fathers. Besides, what did women know of theology? Finally, he said, "*Wrong?* Yes, my dear, much is wrong."

The bluntness of his response took the two women by surprise. Lazaro Salinas was a gentleman, a man of great circumspection, and such sharpness had been unexpected. "It is a dangerous situation we face here in Mexico. I love you both, and your presence here has been good for us all, but I do wish the two of you were back in the Utah Territory, where you would be safe."

"*Safe?*" the two women responded, almost as one.

Replacing her wine glass, Consuelo asked, "Why are we not safe here with you, Uncle Lazaro?"

Lazaro was not accustomed to discussing politics with women, and his response reflected his impatience. "How can you ask such a question, Consuelo? You, an educated woman of uncommon astuteness." But the look of astonishment on her face, that he should address her in that tone of voice, caused him to say less harshly, "Forgive me, Consuelo. But surely you know that the French have invaded our country and are even now marching on Mexico City. When the Juarez government falls, as it surely will, the French will establish a monarchy to which we will all become subject. We are facing a war, my child."

"But . . . here . . . in the north . . . on this ranch? We have always been so far removed that—"

"No more, my darling ladies. This time the war will come to our very gates. The political atmosphere throughout our beloved country grows more dangerous every day. I fear for our future as never before."

"But . . . how?"

"As I am sure you know, it started last year when Juarez suspended payments on Mexico's foreign debt. That was all the French needed. They signed a tripartite agreement with England and Spain a short time later, the intent of which was to compel repayment of the debt."

"But Juarez has already done something about the debt."

"Yes, that is so, Consuelo, and as a result, England and Spain have withdrawn. But the debt was never what concerned the French. All along, certain powerful Frenchmen have wanted nothing less than the complete subjugation of Mexico; and now the French army, having suffered only a few setbacks, is advancing across Mexico."

"But what is being done?"

"General Ignacio Zaragoza routed the French at Puebla last May, but the writing is on the wall, so to speak. There will be no rest until Austrian Archduke Maximilian von Hapsburg assumes what will undoubtedly be the throne of the Second Mexican Empire. In Europe, it is widely known that it has long been his dream to be the first descendent of Ferdinand and Isabella to assume monarchial power on the very continent that has become of such importance for the fortunes of those to whom he is most loyal. He will not rest until that dream is fulfilled."

"Huh," Connie scoffed. "The fortunes of Mexicans are certainly of no concern to him."

"Precisely. You must forgive my bluntness, Consuelo. But just where is this god about whom you and the priests have so much to say? With all of the Church's influence in the past, Mexico is about to suffer under the boot of the French invader. I mean, think of our past humiliations—Spain, the United States, the French. How long does it go on? When will this god of the priests, the god of whom you speak, be on our side?"

Consuelo sat back in her chair pensively watching the worried man at the other end of the table as he confronted the doubts and misgivings her simple question had brought to the surface, a man whom she dearly loved, and for whom she had the utmost respect.

"Well?" Lazaro said, watching his niece closely.

"Lazaro, please," Emily said, her voice softly solicitous. "Don't you see she's—"

"No," he interrupted, raising his hand. "I am interested in Consuelo's answer. After all," he said, his tone half mocking, "it is a theological question of some importance today. If ever Mexico needed divine intervention, it is now. Don't you agree, Consuelo?"

Connie had never seen her uncle so disturbed and unsure of the future. He, like her father, had always seemed so in control, a man whose solidity and constancy had always given those around him a sense of safety and permanence. "I'm sorry, Uncle Lazaro, it is of small matter."

"Is such an issue as this ever *of small matter,* especially in today's world?"

"Mmm. . . . But you see, Uncle Lazaro, I'm not at all sure I'm talking about the god of the priests and Mexican history—at least as we know it, anyway."

"What!?"

"Yes. You see, I recall hearing Brigham Young telling Clay— it was almost in passing, and I never thought about it until now— that Jesus Christ had in fact come here once."

"*Here?*" Lazaro echoed incredulously, unsure of what he had heard. "Come *here?* You mean, *here*—to *Méjico?*"

"*Sí.* Here," Consuelo said, lightly taping the table with a delicate finger. "In *Méjico,* or somewhere close, anyway."

Lazaro stared at his niece. "In all my years, I have never heard of such a thing."

"Mmm . . . nor had I in all of mine."

"Emily?"

"*Sí*. I have it heard, too. Maybe *Méjico*, or someplace to the south—somewhere, anyway."

"Be that as it may," he said, with a wave of his hand, "for now it is not He who is coming, but the French who are coming, and I think there will be no hope of support from any quarter, let alone heaven."

Sensing the futility of any further discussion on the matter, Consuelo nevertheless asked, "But what about Spain or England? Their demands have been met. Won't they do something?"

"Only as it suits their purposes," Lazaro said, returning to his dinner. "For Spain, it will mean revenge. For France, it will be an opportunity to return to North America and to take advantage of the civil war raging in your United States."

Connie thought for a moment. *Your* United States. How good that phrase sounded to her. *Your* United States.

"Consuelo?"

"I'm sorry, Uncle. I was just thinking how good those words sounded to me. They are not yet *my* United States, but Clay is positive that one day, the Utah Territory will become one of the United States and not just a territory. That is what Clay is fighting for at this very moment. And being married to an American will ease any difficulty I might have in becoming an American citizen—especially since my husband is Clay Ashworth."

"Yes. I suppose. Nonetheless, as wonderful as it has been having the two of you here, you should have stayed in Utah. Only harm can come to you by remaining here, especially you, Consuelo."

Both women looked questioningly at Lazaro, not knowing how to interpret his blunt statement.

"What harm can come to me from the French? I have never done them any wrong."

"It is not the French of whom I speak, my dear niece," Lazaro said, pushing his plate away and setting his napkin aside. "Word came only today that Jose Rodriguez Zamora was released from prison some weeks ago. It was thought by some fools in Mexico City that if the French found their loyal henchman behind Mexican bars, they might take some unnecessary revenge when it suited them."

"Zamora. . . ." Connie said, the color draining from her face.

"Yes, the filthy *asesino*. And I'm sure he'll be seeking his revenge here."

"*A qué viene eso?*" Consuelo said, reverting momentarily to Spanish. "What is the point? He has already murdered my parents, *a sangre fría*. What more is there for him here?"

"You, my precious, that's what," Emily said, looking up, unable to hide the fear in her voice. Patting her niece's arm, she continued, "He will be coming for you."

★   ★   ★

"*A toda costa!*" Zamora shouted, startling the other three men at the table. "Do you hear me? I will have her at any cost!"

The four had been eating a late lunch in the dimly lit *cantina,* planning for the arrival of the French troops sometime in the near future. It was a pleasant, quiet place, known for its good food and excellent spirits, especially a robust native wine.

With Zamora's angry outburst, the room had fallen quiet. With the French not yet in Mexico City, the need for circumspection was necessary, and Zamora was too widely known as a European operative of some sort.

Looking around, Zamora became aware that he had drawn unnecessary attention to their table. In a somewhat quieter voice he said, "You must forgive me, but I will have that woman at any cost, and I will have her before the Juarez government falls."

"But why?" one of the men asked, incredulously. "The woman is married and living in *Norteamérica.*"

"*Si.* With a *gringo,* Clay Ashworth," the third man offered.

"No. For some reason she has returned to her home in Sonora. I'm not sure what that means, but it does simplify things."

Two men looked at one another, their glance troubled, and the third said, "Yes, I see."

"When I think of the times I could have killed that Ashworth fellow, I become ill," Zamora said, his voice filled with venom. "It makes my skin crawl. But I will have my *venganza,* and I will have it with her. *A todo costa,*" he emphasized, his voice low, a slender, knifelike finger tapping the table. "At any cost."

"But stop and think. Why—"

"Yes, stop and think," Zamora snapped. "Her name, the family's alliances, their position in the northern part of our country."

"Yes, I see," the older man said, pausing to sip from his glass. "But how?"

"Leave that to me. I have alliances as well. I will take her and burn the Salinas *hacienda* to the ground. When it is rebuilt, it will be my *hacienda* and my seat of government—under Maximilian."

"Yes, these alliances," one of his companions said, his voice subdued. "Might we enquire who—"

"The entire region is torn. Even the wild native tribes are at odds. Believe me when I say, I have a way."

CHAPTER 8

★ ★ ★

WITH NIGHT COMING ON, an exhausted Wolf Striker, cold, hungry, and sick, lay in some sparse grass looking down into a hollow, onto a small, lonely fire struggling for existence beneath the smothering bulge of an enormous black pot. The fire had been built next to a large, garishly painted medicine wagon that barely fit into the shallow, brush-choked gully a few yards below him. Its location was an obvious attempt on the part of someone to prevent being easily seen.

Somewhere off in the distance Wolf could hear the deep, persistent rumbling of what sounded like thunder. Yet the evening sky arching above the dense grove of trees that concealed his hiding place remained cloudless, the air muggy, close, and portentously oppressive. The coming night promised to be uncomfortably humid, chilly, and altogether miserable, making the small, unattended fire at the side of the big wagon more and more appealing.

The rumbling off to the south, however, was not thunder. It was cannon fire several miles distant, but close enough that frequent flashes of light lit up the horizon through the trees. It was Yankee artillery, and there was a lot of it.

Between the struggling fire, its oppressive pot, and the gaudy, oversized wagon, little room seemed left for anything else in the dry, brushy creek bed. The wagon was one of those frequently seen before the war when a circus or carnival passed through town, its tall, wooden sides painted with bright, though somewhat faded colors. Uneven wooden filigreed frills and flourishes ran down all four of its corners and extended the length of the protruding eves and along the center of the slightly peaked roof.

Though the evening was growing late, ample light remained for any observer to make out the messages flamboyantly painted on the wagon's side, and little was left to the imagination. Arched across the top of each side, the wagon boasted its owner's name: **PROFESSOR BRUTUS T. HUSSLEBUSTER and Company**, and beneath that were decoratively listed the many marvels the great man had to offer: **Wonders for the Body and the Mind. Ointments, Unguents, Panaceas, Cure-alls, and Various Medicinal Elixirs.** Farther down, in smaller lettering and less glaring colors, various services were listed. *Upon Appointment, Inquiries into: The State of One's Body; The State of One's Mind; Personal Historical Analysis; and Further Inquiries into the Future.* Then, at the bottom, almost as an afterthought: *Plus, the Charming Miss Adela Goodenuff, Offering Songs of the Heart, a Delight One and All, Also Elocutionary Readings and Wondrous Terpsichorean Presentations.*

For further stimulation, a voluptuous, artfully clad young woman was painted in a reclining pose along the entire length of the base of the wagon, front to rear; and as if that were not enough, signs from the zodiac: stars, moons, and an assortment of mythical animals filled in whatever the remaining space allowed.

Lying there in the weeds, almost too tired and ill to care, Wolf could not help but feel some admiration for the artistic skill exhibited before him. And though he was no proper critic, on the whole, he felt the wagon was, in its own way, a work of art—one that anyone within whose bosom beat the heart of a con man had to admire.

He had been observing the camp for the better part of an hour, and there had been little activity around the wagon. The only exception was a young woman who had come out of the door on the end of the wagon to stir the mysterious black pot, her features hidden by a shawl draped over her head against the damp chill of the coming night. She had been accompanied by a huge black man who disappeared around the far side of the wagon, returning a moment later with an armful of wood, which he carefully placed on the fire so as not to disturb the pot.

The pot in itself was a bit worrisome. It was far too large for cooking soup or a stew, and whenever an occasional ambient breeze wafted across the camp toward Wolf it brought with it a distinctly unappetizing, though possibly medicinal, smell. *Stench* was also a word that came to mind.

His body cramping from the wet ground and feeling the cold more acutely with each passing minute, Wolf was about to rise from his place of concealment when three Confederate foot soldiers pushed through the dense underbrush opposite him and slid down the bank to the bottom of the dry streambed. Stopping to brush themselves off and quickly survey the camp, two stepped to the fire seeking its warmth, while the biggest, a sergeant, climbed the five steps to the wagon's door and softly tapped what to Wolf sounded suspiciously like a recognition code.

From inside the wagon a muffled reply came, and though Wolf could not hear the sergeant's answer, the door opened and the three Rebel soldiers, responding to the sergeant's rude gesture, quickly entered. For the briefest moment a pretty face appeared in the open doorway and glanced about, then the door quietly closed.

Must be the Charming Miss Adela Goodenuff, Wolf mused. *Good enough for what, I wonder?*

Quietly making his way to the big wagon, Wolf crawled beneath it. The floor above him creaked as those inside moved about, their voices muffled to the point that he could only make out an occasional word. Though the space underneath the wagon was cramped, there was room enough for him to shuffle about as he tried to decipher whatever he could.

"Mister, you come out from under there, and be real careful how yuh do it, too." The voice was high-pitched and had a nervous uncertainty to it.

There was nothing Wolf Striker hated more than being caught unaware, but between his head being full of congestion and aching miserably and his trying to concentrate on whatever was going on above him, he had failed to hear the approach of another soldier. "I'm coming, real easy. Just like you said." The Rebel soldier stepped back as Wolf crawled from under the tall wagon and slowly got to his feet. "Where the devil did you come from?" he asked.

"Jest never you mind, and get them hands up in the air." The soldier had a battered musket aimed at Wolf's chest.

"Look, son," Wolf said, taking a step toward the young soldier, "I'm Major Wolf Striker. I'm a Confederate soldier, just like you. So don't go shooting a friend. There aren't enough of us as it is."

Wolf's edgy captor was little more than a boy. He stood a good six or eight inches shorter than Wolf and was obviously an inexperienced, backwoods militiaman or volunteer. A filthy tunic hung from his scrawny shoulders, and no rank showed on what was left of its ragged sleeves.

"Mister, you jest stand yer distance," he stammered nervously, the barrel of his musket waving ominously in Wolf's direction, "'til we get this here settled." Turning, he hollered, "Sergeant! Yuh better come out here—real fast-like!"

It was all Wolf needed. Grabbing the boy's weapon by its barrel and giving it a vicious twist, Wolf slipped his foot behind the startled boy's leg and shoved him backward to the ground, pulling the antiquated gun from his grasp. As the boy's hand jerked free, the musket erupted over Wolf's shoulder like the blast from a cannon, a cloud of black powder liberally bursting across one corner of the wagon, leaving an ugly stain.

With the discharge from the old firearm echoing along the gully, the door to the wagon flew open, and the big sergeant jumped to the ground. Stepping back, his ears ringing from the blast, Wolf dropped the musket across the boy's chest, and raised his hands in the air. "Sorry about this, Sergeant," he said, with a nod toward the stunned young Rebel at his feet, "but I have difficulty standing still when some inexperienced kid is waving a gun in my face."

"Mister, jest don't you move a muscle," the big sergeant snapped, his large navy Colt pointed at Wolf's belly, "and that *kid*, as you put it, better not be hurt."

As the sergeant spoke, his two companions jumped to the ground behind him, followed by a man Wolf assumed was the proprietor of the medicine show, who negotiated the wagon's few steps as quickly as his age and bulk would allow. A moment later Miss Adela Goodenuff appeared at the wagon door. Unsure of her audience, given the circumstance below, she posed in its frame for the briefest moment, then gracefully flowed down the steps in a manner befitting any star of the stage, her unexpected presence completely charming the sergeant's two companions and distracting both Wolf and the sergeant as well.

It was the professor who broke the spell. "Now . . . eh . . . gentlemen, let's . . . eh . . . that is to say, let us not do anything hasty here. I'm sure this gentleman," he said, nodding toward Wolf, "has his story, just as do we all.

"Adela, my dear, would you and your . . . eh . . . two admirers, there, help our unfortunate young friend, here," the professor said, pointing to the prostrate young soldier, "to his feet and into the wagon, where we can look to his needs? I mean, he seems to have experienced quite a shock, I'm sure. Wouldn't you say, Sergeant?"

"Lemme he'p 'im," the black giant said, stepping around a startled Wolf. Where the huge man had suddenly appeared from was anyone's guess. He had materialized like a ghost.

"Leave him be, and y'all just stay put," the sergeant ordered, attempting to retain some control of the situation. "I ain't so sure I'm not gonna shoot this fella right here on the spot, and put 'im out of his misery."

"Well . . . now . . . Sergeant," the professor said, "what would be the point of such impetuosity? Eh . . . would we not thereby deny ourselves the opportunity of inquiring into the meaning of this gentleman's unanticipated presence? Surely there is something to that."

As the professor spoke, two things became obvious to Wolf.

First of all, there was more to this old eccentric than met the eye. Somehow, his exaggerated pomposity was at odds with the intelligent sparkle in his eye.

Secondly, whatever else Professor Brutus T. Husslebuster might be, Wolf sensed that he was likely a man to be reckoned with—the old thespian might make an excellent ally, or a very dangerous enemy. One way or the other, it was altogether likely he was not what he appeared to be.

That being the case, other questions immediately came to mind: what was the good professor doing running around with a circus wagon and a beautiful young girl in the middle of a war, endangering both himself and her? Entertaining the boys? If so, what kind of entertainment? Was he bilking them with whatever he and the girl were offering? Or was there something more nefarious underlying his presence? Or perhaps all three? And what of that big, black, ghost-like character? That he could break a man into bits and pieces was more than obvious.

And what was Husslebuster's relationship with these three Confederate soldiers? Were they here to be *entertained?* If so, why the apparent secrecy?

"As you can imagine, Professor," Wolf said, trying to maintain some degree of equanimity and look as innocent as the circumstances would permit. "I'm in complete agreement with you, sir. I think there is much we should speak of."

"Eh . . . yes. Just so, young man, just so."

"All right, mister, just what *is* your story?"

"Look, Sergeant," Wolf said, turning to face the man as a numbing weakness permeated his body, "I'm on your side, a major in the Confederate army. My name is Wolf Striker, and I escaped from Leavenworth weeks ago. I've been making my way south in an effort to get to Vicksburg. I don't—"

"Vicksburg? Why Vicksburg, and what for? There's plenty of fightin' goin' on all around here," the man said, his hand sweeping a wide arc in the air.

"Sergeant, Grant's pushing for Vicksburg," Wolf said, wiping feverish perspiration from his brow and trying to keep his voice even. "That's where the real fight's going to be, and I need to get there before—"

"If you're who yuh say you are, why ain't you in uniform?"

Wolf's suddenly began to feel as if his head were going to split. He was tired and hungry and sick, and the man's attitude was beginning to grate—and deep inside him, the old monster rolled over and began to stir. That old feeling was always alarming, frightening in fact. *Sing, o Goddess, the anger of Achilles . . . that brought countless ills—*

"Mister?" the sergeant said, leaning toward Wolf. "Are you okay?"

Wolf's hand went to his forehead. *Where did that come from? Anger and its consequences? Putting an end to these fools would. . . .*

His mind raced. Giving in to the old Wolf, the monster he had struggled to bury, would only shatter the dreams he once thought forever lost and were only now appearing possible—if only he could get to Vicksburg—and perhaps Ellen. Just perhaps. Keeping the lid on tight and convincing these Rebels he was one of them was his only real option.

"I'm sorry," he said, leaning against the wagon. "If I could just sit here on this step for a moment, I'll be fine. I haven't eaten or slept in quite some time."

"Here," the sergeant said, reaching in his pocket with an impatient grunt, handing Wolf a lump of hardtack. "I ain't gonna ask yuh many more times, mister. Where's yer uniform, and where'd yuh come from?"

"It's a long story, Sergeant," Wolf sighed, the weeks of deprivation and running, the swamps, the thickets, the muck, all beginning to overwhelm him, "but to make it short, the southern bargeman who pulled me half drowned out of the Missouri several weeks ago gave me these clothes. I had to get rid of what was left of my uniform—it was in tatters, anyway. We were stopped by Union patrols a half dozen times, and these rags helped convince them that I was one of the man's workers."

"Okay, then," the sergeant said, less tension showing in his face but still wary, "what unit were yuh with, and how'd yuh wind up clear up north at Leavenworth?"

"I've been unattached, but when I was captured I had been fighting with a Texas force out in New Mexico. We were trying to move on Fort Union when I was wounded and captured during a fight at Glorieta Pass—out on the Santa Fe Trail. After the battle, the Yankees took those of us who could travel to Fort Leavenworth for incarceration."

"Yuh mean you Confederates lost the fight?" the sergeant said incredulously, mistrust again returning. "And from way out there, you wind up clear to Leavenworth?"

Wolf leaned forward, his elbows on his knees, his pounding head drooping is if it would roll off of his aching shoulders. "I'm afraid so," he mumbled, feeling himself sinking into a dark place. "Most of our men made it back into Texas, I think, but. . . ."

As Wolf slumped to the ground, the professor reached to ease his fall, and without a stammer or hint of befuddlement, while motioning to the big black man, said, "Here now, Big Bill, help me get him into the wagon. I think there is more to this poor fellow than meets the eye. If he is one of us, we need to help him. If he's not, well. . . ."

Wolf's chest felt compressed, as if someone or something

heavy was sitting on him. As he was thrown like a rag doll over Big Bill's shoulder, breathing suddenly became alarmingly difficult, and Wolf could feel himself sinking, into a dark but not unfamiliar place, the voices around him fading with the light.

By some means beyond his ability to comprehend he was slowly floating, no longer touching the earth. There were annoying, indefinable disturbances around him, yet somehow, the darkness was warm and pleasantly familiar, the disagreeable physical sensations slowly seeming to dwindle, and he began to feel a welcome, soothing sense of relief.

But the freedom could not last, and as the dark mist cleared, Wolf slowly realized he was looking up into a pair of bright blue eyes.

"'Bout time you came back t' see us," the girl said, smiling and leaning back.

Rolling onto his side, Wolf struggled to sit up, but the effort was too much. As he fell back on the bed, he felt as if his entire body was filling with pain, as if something thick and hot was being poured into him. His mouth felt sticky and tasted foul, and the ringing in his ears made it hard to hear anything that was being said. Following a cough that racked his body, he croaked, "Where am I?"

Watching him closely, the girl—young woman, really—said, "Right where you been for most of three days, mister. You're real sick, and you need to stay down."

"Three days?"

"Uh-huh. You been mostly sleepin' for three days, kinda outta your head, too. The time or two you did come to, you made no sense at all."

Wolf rubbed his thick head in an effort to clear his thoughts and rid himself of some of the pain. "I take it you're the Charming Miss Adela Goodenuff?"

"Jest like on the wagon," she giggled, "but you ain't gonna see nothin' too fancy. Not yet, anyway. Not in your condition."

"Really?" he said, trying to will his aching body to relax. "That is disappointing. Perhaps when I'm a little stronger."

Reaching behind her, she produced a large cup of steaming liquid. "Oh, sure . . . but that's likely t' take some doin'. Here, drink some of this."

Getting a whiff of the dark liquid, Wolf winced, and leaning on one elbow, asked, "What is it?"

"It's one of the professor's elixirs. That's what he calls 'em, *elixirs*," she said, blowing into the cup. "This'n 'll do yuh wonders, too, if you get enough into yuh."

"Smells like it'll either cure me or kill me," he said taking a cautious sip. Whatever it was, the steaming liquid obviously had a high alcohol content and burned all the way down, quickly producing a sense of warmth and well-being. "Say, maybe I better have a little more of that stuff."

"Um-hmm," she mused, studying his face. "You got a nice face, mister. But you do need a shave." Pushing a lock of hair out of his eyes, she sighed, "A bath wouldn't hurt yuh none, neither."

"Speaking of the good professor, where is he?"

"Oh . . . well, yes . . . not to worry, young man, I'm . . . eh, right here," the professor said, stepping from behind Adela, a worried look on his face. "You have given us quite a fright, I must say. Now, drink up. We must be moving on soon. I mean . . . eh, there have been some disquieting developments while you've been . . . eh . . . shall we say, incognizant of your surroundings."

"Move? Why?"

"Uh-huh. *Move*," Adela said, taking Wolf's empty cup and

refilling it. "Yankees are all around us an' thick as fleas on a hound dog's belly. Them Rebs we was trailin' after have fallen back t' somewhere down the other side of the Tallahatchie, and then the Yankees occupied Oxford, but now looks like maybe they're moving back up t' Holly Springs."

"Yes, I'm afraid what she says is true, and that necessitates our . . . eh . . . shall we say, becoming less conspicuous to any newcomers of the . . . eh . . . wrong sort, shall we say."

The professor's warming concoction had somehow loosened the tightness in his body, and Wolf struggled to sit up. The wagon floor was cold and felt good under his feet, and he began to feel as if he might be able to stand. "You know, I'm beginning to feel like—"

"Ugh-ugh," Adela said, pushing him back down. "You been far too sick, big fella."

"But . . . I'm getting . . . I've been too much of a bother. Oh, . . . why's the room moving?"

"Now, see what you've went and done," Adela scolded, hovering over him like a moth over a flame, attempting to tuck the blanket around him. "A big fella like you needs to rest. Rest, that's what you need, and lots of good food, too. That, and some tender lovin' care," she giggled.

"Eh . . . yes. You see, young man, we need you to get back on your feet. Your falling, eh, into our hands . . . or, eh . . . bed, as it were, was most fortuitous. We . . . eh, that is to say, I need your help."

"My help?" Wolf asked.

"Yes, you see, we . . . eh, that is to say, Adela, had some difficulty with my former assistant, and that necessitated my . . . eh, that is to say, necessitated Big Bill sending him on his way—with some difficulty, I might add. As things now stand, we are overburdened, shall we say, with our efforts to entertain and minister to those who need us most."

"You mean, you want me to—"

"What the professor means is, you're kind of a fast talkin' fella, or you couldn't of got this far after breakin' outta that Yankee prison an' all. What with you bein' a wounded Confederate soldier, too."

"Well, now, Adela—"

"Hold on, now," Wolf said, sitting up. "You mean you follow the fighting and provide some pleasant diversions for the soldiers, now and then relieving them of their money or other valuables in the process. Am I right? And you need me for . . ."

"Well, now, I wouldn't—"

"That's what he means, all right," Adela said, gently wiping the perspiration from Wolf's brow. "How 'bout it?"

"Can you . . . eh . . . deal faro, young man?"

"And where are we headed now?" Wolf asked, unable to prevent a smile from creasing his face.

"Well," Adela said, heaving a sigh, "sounds like Forrest and Van Dorn have been givin' them Yankees fits up north. So, we're gonna move down south. That looks t' be where we're gonna be needed b'fore too long, really."

"What she says is true, Major. The fighting has gone back and forth in this area, from Decatur to Memphis, and things change almost daily, but . . . eh, as you, yourself, pointed out, it's Vicksburg the Yankees are pressing for. Perhaps by staying with us, you . . . eh . . . can eventually get there yourself, and with less difficulty than if you were attempting it on your own."

Wolf's smile broadened into a grin. "Why don't you call me Wolf?" he said, extending his hand to the professor. "And I can deal faro. Nothing like bucking the tiger to get a soldier's mind off of his troubles."

As Wolf spoke, the wagon creaked on its undercarriage, and the door flew open. A large man was silhouetted in the doorway, his features black against the midday light behind him. "Strange place for a circus wagon," he growled. "Just what goes on here?"

It was a Union officer, and voices could be heard behind him. But it was the large army Colt in his hand that left no room for argument.

"Oh . . . eh . . . well, now, General—"

"Captain will do. Just who are you people? And what are you doing here?"

"As you can see . . . eh, Captain . . . we are a small troop of entertainers who also practice the healing arts. It is our hope to . . . eh . . . to provide some relief for you fighting men from your many arduous duties . . . eh . . . now and then."

"Uh-huh. And who's that big fella?" the officer said, pointing suspiciously at Wolf.

Giving Wolf a stern look and shoving him back down onto the bed, Adela stepped in front of the officer, and with a defiant look, said, "This here's my husband, Wilbur, an' he's sick hurt. He ain't quite right in the head, neither. Ain't been for some time now."

CHAPTER 9

★ ★ ★

Amorose and grumpy Orrin Porter Rockwell sat hunched over a pad of paper absently tapping his pencil on the desk, lost in concentration. He had spent the entire morning composing what he thought of as a bill of particulars on the one man who had caused him more misery than any other, Wolfgang Striker. But the more he wrote, the more troubled he became, any kind of resolution always retreating, staying just out of reach.

It had been that way for months. Since returning from Santa Fe, he had thought of little else. The constant worry over Striker was driving him nuts, interfering with his duties, and even keeping him awake nights. Not in the last fifteen years, not since the Saints had fled their enemies in the East and settled in the Salt Lake Valley, had anything troubled him like this Wolf Striker business.

Truth be known, nothing had ever bothered Orrin Porter Rockwell. He had always been a man of action, a man who faced problems squarely and solved them in as abrupt a manner as possible. That's what made this so maddening. When faced with any kind of difficulty, he had just always acted, and for good or ill the problem either died or went away.

But not this. Not Wolf Striker.

On the pad before him, Rockwell had drawn a line down the center of the page. In the left-hand column, he had listed all of the reasons he could think of that Wolf Striker should have been hanged, and why it was unnecessary for him to be feeling any remorse for having shot the man.

Striker was a scoundrel; he had led the murderous raid on Platte River Station; he had killed the Cartwright brothers in cold blood as they attempted to do their duty; the entire town had been destroyed because of his actions; dozens of people had died or been maimed, and all had lost their homes and businesses. And the list continued on. Altogether, it was only right that the man should have been brought to justice as quickly and finally as possible.

Yet the memory of that day at Johnson's Ranch continued to nag at him, almost constantly. He still could see Striker in the sights of his rifle; he still could hear the rifle's blast ringing in his ears; he still could see Striker slump from the horse to the ground like a collapsing bundle of bloody rags. He still could see all of that, but what somehow made it worse was the persistent, gnawing impression that his shot had not killed Striker, that somewhere out there the man was still living and breathing.

On the other side of the line, Rockwell had been careful to list all of the reasons he could think of that Striker should not have been shot or hanged—why the man should have been captured and not killed. And what was really troubling, and of no help in soothing his feelings of guilt or remorse or whatever it was that was troubling him, was the fact that the list for keeping Striker alive just kept getting longer—a good deal longer—than the list in favor of his execution.

But perhaps most troubling was Rockwell's realization that he had come to like the man, a fact that topped his list. As much as he hated to admit it, the two of them were, in many respects, much alike. On top of that, every time Brigham Young spoke of Striker, his words were always tempered with caution, as if he sensed in the man something worth saving. *And if Brigham Young thinks there is something in the man that makes him worth saving, then there must be—simple as that.*

Squeezing his strained eyes shut, Rockwell rubbed his forehead, hoping to ease the nagging ache that had been annoying him with increasing intensity throughout the morning, and his thoughts turned to his wife, Mary Ann. She entered his mind like a cool mountain breeze, offering him welcome relief. *If only she would walk in right now, her lovely, soothing fingers would soon chase the pain away.*

Sometimes, when the hurtin' got bad enough, if he squeezed his eyes shut, he could see stars flying around in his head. But Mary Ann, the one woman in all the world he somehow never would feel worthy of, always knew just what he needed, and just her touch did far more to ease his pains and his worries than any medicine forced down him by some pushy sawbones. She was the one person in all the world who made his life worth living.

Leaning back, his chair complaining loudly, Rockwell tossed his pencil stub on the desk and stretched his aching shoulders and arms in an effort to loosen the ropes of tension that had tightened his entire body. Nothing could tire a man like thinking. In fact, at times it came close to being downright painful. *Far better to be out on a horse, grappling with the kinds of problems a man can get his hands on.*

"You look to me like you're in pain, my bushy-faced friend."

"Wha . . . how long you been sittin' there, Kimball?" Rockwell stammered, blinking to clear his vision.

"Long enough to wonder what had you so absorbed," Ben Kimball said, enjoying Rockwell's discomfort. "I don't think I've ever seen you concentrate so hard you didn't know what was going on around you."

"*Absorbed?*" Rockwell grumped, his fingers finding an itch beneath his beard. "Well, I was just sittin' here makin' a list."

"Mmm . . . so what list could be that important?"

"You ever wonder about that Wolf Striker fella?"

"Can't say as I do."

"Well, I surely wish I could say the same."

"What about him? You shot 'im, didn't you? That usually spells the end for anybody unfortunate enough to get caught in your sights."

"Oh, that's mostly talk," Rockwell said, waving a hand in the air, as if to brush the comment away. "You know that."

"To tell the truth, Port, I don't think I've heard his name mentioned. Not since you got back, anyway. But as I recall, you sort of left President Young and me with the idea the man might not have died at the Glorieta fight. Like maybe your aim hadn't been all that good."

Rockwell leaned back in his chair. "Well, now see, that's just the point."

"What is?"

"Yuh see, I had 'im in my sights, sure enough. And I pulled that trigger all right—"

"Well, that spelled his end right then and there, didn't it?"

Rockwell fell silent, his bushy eyebrows lowering over his pale blue eyes in a troubled frown, his hand absently playing with the pencil on his desk.

"Well, didn't it?"

"Ugh-ugh," Rockwell said, slowly shaking his head. "Leastwise, I ain't so sure. And to tell you the absolute truth, Ben, it's drivin' me up the wall."

Pushing his chair back, Rockwell rose and walked to the window, and for a brief moment wished his life could be as simple and straightforward as the lives of those folks passing back and forth outside his office. Turning, he continued, "I've gone over those few minutes time an' again, and there's just somethin' there . . . somethin' that keeps tellin' me it ain't over."

Ben Kimball watched his bushy-bearded old friend slump back down at his desk. It was disquieting to see this big, tough lawman, a man who rose to any occasion and mastered any problem, so torn by his uncertainties. In fact, it was just plain painful to watch. With a deep breath born of shared frustration, he said, "Port, you got to do something, old hoss. You can't go on like this. You've got to find Striker and put this thing to an end, one way or the other. Either that, or let it go."

Rockwell leaned back and with one finger absently stroked the thick whiskers beneath his nose, as if lost in thought, as if he hadn't heard a word Ben Kimball had said. Finally, looking up, he said, "Mississippi."

"What?"

"Ben, I got a feeling Striker's in Mississippi, and that's where I gotta go, because that's where I'm gonna find 'im."

"Now, where'd you get that idea?"

Rockwell pushed his chair back and began pacing back and forth across the cramped office. "When I first caught up with

Striker, out in that miserable camp in the New Mexico mountains last winter, and wasted my time nursing him back to health, almost every time he passed out or fell to sleep, he kept mumbling something about a woman and Vicksburg. It was always the same thing, over and over. I can't remember her name . . . Ellen, I think it was.

"Vicksburg's in Mississippi, ain't it?" he asked, turning to Kimball.

"Yeah, Vicksburg's in Mississippi, all right," Kimball chuckled. "And from all I hear, so's the Civil War."

Returning to his chair, Rockwell thought for a moment. "Long ways away, ain't it?"

"At least as far as Nauvoo. Maybe farther, and right smack in the middle of a real shootin' war to boot. You stopped to think about that?"

Leaning back, the tension draining from his body, Rockwell said, "I don't imagine Brother Brigham'd appreciate my just up and leavin' like that."

"Not likely," Ben said, with some relief. "It would take you weeks, if not months, to get there, and then it's not likely you'd find 'im, not in the middle of that bloody fracas. Besides, stop and think, Clay's back there somewhere. Nobody knows just where, but he's back there."

"Yeah, that's right, he is," Rockwell said, a sense of relief beginning to ease the pain in his head.

"Who knows? Clay might just stumble across Wolf. He'd not likely shoot the man, but if he could, he'd bring him back here— one way or the other."

"I guess I could settle the whole thing then, if that happens," Rockwell said, with a growing sense of resignation. "Though it ain't all that likely."

Ben Kimball rose from his chair and walked to the door. "Anyway, you know what they say, Port."

"What's that?"

"Ain't no rest for the wicked, an' the righteous don't need it."

"Mmm . . . I fit in there somewheres, I guess," Rockwell said, heaving a sigh. "No matter. Won't be no rest for me 'til I face Wolf Striker one more time and, one way or the other, that'll be the last time. I just hope Clay brings him back—somehow."

The air in the tiny railroad station at Bristol, Virginia, was uncomfortably warm. Given the time of year, the heat was made even worse by the number of passengers crowded into the dingy waiting room. Many waited hoping for space on the next train for Knoxville, some wanting to continue on through Cleveland, Tennessee, to Chattanooga, and still others on to Atlanta.

The wait was ostensibly necessitated by the need to switch trains from the Virginia and Tennessee line to the East Tennessee and Virginia rail line. But no connecting ET&V train had as yet appeared, and there seemed to be no one around who could answer the growing number of questions, the station master having disappeared not long after the arrival of Clay and Ellen's train.

It was over two hundred miserable miles to Chattanooga, requiring at least one more train change, and even then, there were no guarantees that anyone would make it more than a few miles. The entire area to the south was torn by contesting armies. Every mile traveled could be rightfully considered a major accomplishment, and the farther south or west anyone went, the more impossible it was likely to become.

A Confederate officer, his uniform badly stained and worn,

stepped from the cluttered loading dock and crossed the crowded room to where Clay and Ellen Striker sat waiting. "Mister Mallory, if you and Missus Striker would be so kind as to follow me, please."

"Well, Major," Ellen said, irritably, "I'm certainly glad someone finally came. We've been sitting here for simply hours and hours."

With a slight bow toward Ellen, the major said, "I'm most apologetic, ma'am. Things here are somewhat confused, as you might surmise. And, lest I forget, may I introduce myself? I am Major Thomas Farnsworth, at your service."

"What's the big delay, Major Farnsworth?" Clay asked, as he and Ellen rose and followed the Confederate officer through a door at the back of the station. "We've been here for several hours now."

"Union cavalry, Mister Mallory. They've been making too many forays between here and Knoxville over the past few days, blowing up bridges, tearing up track, destroying rolling stock, burning supplies, and generally making nuisances of themselves. They have kept us quite busy, I'm afraid. So much so, it's a wonder any trains are moving at all."

The major led the two weary pilgrims down the street to a clapboard hotel, not far from the train station. The building had obviously seen better times and was badly in need of repair—and a lot of paint. The fancy shingled covering over the front boardwalk sagged on one end, the ornately carved hardwood column beneath it splintered and separated, as if it had been hit by artillery or something equally serious.

But that was not the end of it. The entire roof of the hotel looked to have been badly damaged. In several places large holes had been covered, rather hastily it appeared, by canvas tarps that seemed in constant motion, bulging and fluttering with the slightest breeze.

Carefully observing everything around him, Clay was struck by the amount of damage that could be seen. There was not a building in sight that was not in need of repair. Not only that, the people who passed them on the street looked equally war-torn and haggard. It was obviously a town that had been cruelly victimized by the war.

"It would appear, Major, that the war has found your town."

"Only recently, suh. Since the Yankees overran most of West Virginia, they have been launching forays all throughout southwestern Virginia and eastern Tennessee."

Stepping aside to allow Ellen and Clay to enter the hotel ahead of him, the major said, with a sweep of his hand, "This is merely our temporary headquarters. I apologize for the shabbiness of it all, but it's not permanent by any means." Leading them across the small lobby to a door at the side of the once-elegant registration desk, he said, "If you'll step in here, please."

An older Confederate officer in the uniform of a full colonel rose from behind a desk, the top of which was devoid of any content, not a map, not a paper—nothing. In no way did this appear to be the office of a busy field commander faced with all kinds of logistical problems. The colonel looked to be a man in his sixties and, in contrast to the major, his uniform, though worn, was fairly neat and clean. His graying beard was immaculately trimmed, and as he rose, he somehow exhibited an annoyingly aristocratic demeanor that was completely inconsistent with his surroundings, an exaggerated remnant of the dying southern aristocracy.

Stepping from behind his desk, the colonel swept past Clay and taking Ellen Striker's gloved hand, pressed it to his lips with a courtly bow. Looking up into Ellen's clear, green eyes, he said,

"A true Southern flower in such a bed of thorns as this is a most surprising but welcome sight, dear lady."

"Why, thank you so much, Colonel," Ellen cooed, with a slight curtsy.

"Here, my dear, let me escort you to a chair."

"Why, how very chivalrous of you, sir," Ellen said, leaving Clay's side to settle demurely onto the offered overstuffed chair. "One struggles not to appear shocked when such gallantry arises amid the ruins of war."

"My pleasure, my dear lady, my pleasure," the colonel said, perching on the edge of his desk. "Far too seldom do we have such a privilege as this. You are most welcome, ah assure you."

As the colonel glanced in Clay's direction, the major, attempting to hide his discomfort, said, "Colonel, sir, this is Mister Braxton Mallory, the gentleman Sergeant Harper and his men took into custody."

Before Clay could respond, the colonel's attention quickly returned to Ellen Striker. "Surely, my dear lady," he said, his voice effusive with alarm, "a delicate Southern flower such as yourself was not in any way imposed upon? Not by our southern soldiers, surely?"

"Oh, not at all, Colonel . . . uh?"

"Oh, how rude of me, madam. Ah am Colonel Archibald Spendlove, of the Georgia 10th Fusiliers. Ah am—"

"My, my. Georgia? You are such a long way from home, Colonel Spendlove," Ellen said, her eyelashes fluttering—a little too obviously, Clay thought. "I once had an aunt, Miss Myra Pettigrew, who lived in Atlanta, on Peach Tree Street, near the First Baptist Church, where she attended faithfully all her life. She never married, you know. But then, I don't imagine you could have known her, Colonel Spendlove." With a barely discernible sniffle, she continued, "She died from consumption some years ago. We were very close, and I don't think I'm truly over it, even yet."

"Oh, how awful for you, my dear," the colonel said, fairly overflowing with solicitous concern.

Clay watched this old anachronism, and Ellen's overly theatrical responses to him, almost in disbelief. The drama unfolding before him might have been embarrassing were it not so funny. In fact, it was all he could do to keep from laughing out loud. Having been born in the South, he was not unfamiliar with southern mannerisms, but under the circumstances, this was almost too much. A quick glance in Major Farnsworth's direction revealed his discomfort, as well.

"Yes," she again sniffled. "It was quite sad."

Taking a dainty lace hanky from her purse, and dabbing daintily at the corner of one eye, Ellen turned her head away from the two Confederate officers, and winked at Clay.

Clay had not been able take his eyes away from her. He had never seen anything like it. In a few minutes she had completely captivated the old stuffed shirt. He was putty in her hands. With her thoroughly disarming femininity, she had responded to Spendlove's every word, encouraging him with a demure flutter of her eyelashes, a gloved hand brought delicately to her breast, a weary smile, or some other subtle but highly effective feminine gesture.

The man fairly floated with the music of her beautifully accented southern voice, and Clay would have said she was playing him like a base fiddle at an Atlanta cotillion. Seduced by her every word, her every movement, the old gentleman was hopelessly charmed—hers to do with precisely as she pleased.

Clay had remained quiet, not wanting to break the spell, as

Ellen worked her magic. Even under these circumstance, he had never seen better theater. In his eyes, she could do no wrong. Ellen Parkhill Striker, under the most trying of circumstances, had proved herself to be a woman possessed of enormous talent, charm, and depth—not to mention a low cunning only a female could employ so shrewdly.

At some point, Clay knew the colonel would get around to him, but he was more than happy to wait. It was, however, not long in coming.

"Uh . . . Colonel? Colonel, suh?"

For a moment Spendlove did not respond to Major Farnsworth's unwelcome intrusion. Then, turning as if trying to find the source of some irritating noise, he frowned at Farnsworth, and said, "Major, even you can see I am otherwise happily engaged at the moment."

He's engaged, all right, Clay chuckled to himself. *Roped, tied, and branded is more like it.*

"Oh, Colonel Spendlove," Ellen cooed, one hand reaching out to lightly touch the man's knee, the other delicately fanning herself, "it is frightfully warm in here, and I do believe we have intruded into your terribly precious time far too much."

"Why, not at all, dear lady, let me hasten to assure you. Why I—"

"But, dear Colonel Spendlove, I believe your major, there, would like to point out that unfortunately we do have some rather unpleasant misunderstandings to clear up. And Mister Mallory and I really must be on the next train to Chattanooga."

Nice touch, Clay thought, nearly awe-struck by the woman's calculating political and social acumen. It was his presence that the fuss was all about, not hers. *But why is this extraordinarily beguiling woman so determined to protect me?* he wondered. *What could I have said or done in so short a time to elicit such apparent loyalty? She has no more idea of who I am than they do.*

In a way, the more he thought about it, the more the whole thing became kind of worrisome. Ellen Striker had been an unexpected blessing, from the very moment that Confederate sergeant confronted them until now. But why? Still, given the circumstance, it took little reflection for Clay to realize that it had been nothing less than an act of providence when he accidentally sat down next to her on that train.

"And I really must protest," she continued, a light frown clouding her beautiful features. "You see, the truth is, Colonel Spendlove, Mister Mallory and I were traveling together. I really can't see how that sergeant of yours could have had the temerity to accuse him of being a Yankee spy; not when he was obviously traveling with me—especially in front of everyone in that coach," she sniffed, the flutter of her fan even more pronounced. "It truly was most awfully embarrassing, I must say."

With her unanticipated, though mild, rebuke, the colonel's face grew ashen. "I am so terribly sorry if we have caused you any undue embarrassment, my dear. But we really must establish Mister Mallory's *bona fides,* as it were."

"Yes, well let me assure both of you, especially you, Colonel Spendlove, as a southern gentleman, Mister Mallory's—whatever you called them—can in no way be construed as being contrary to our noble southern cause. That much I can certainly promise you, sir."

"You see, ma'am," Major Farnsworth interjected, sensing the reason for wanting to interrogate Mallory was about to disappear into the fog created by the colonel's increasingly chimerical and self-indulgent confabulation with this beautiful, bewitching woman, "this is a particularly sensitive region of the Confederacy."

"Oh, my," Ellen gasped, a hand to her mouth. "Why, I had no idea. How can that be, Major?"

"Uh . . . well, ma'am, I'm not sure we should—"

"Oh, for heaven's sake, Farnsworth, speak up, man," the colonel huffed. "What possible harm can come from it?"

The look on Farnsworth's face was enough for Clay. Obviously, the man felt it might be possible for a good deal of harm to come from saying too much. That being the case, whatever he did not want discussed was precisely the kind of information that Clay was only too anxious to hear.

"As you wish, Colonel," Farnsworth said, his irritation with the situation more than obvious. "You see, ma'am, there are certain precious minerals in this area we would prefer the Yankees not know about. We, therefore, can trust no one about whom there might be the slightest suspicion. I'm afraid that—"

"You see, my dear," the colonel broke in, "not far from here there are a number of lead mines from which our southern musket balls and bullets are manufactured. Why, it's not widely known, but the Wythe County mines supply our armies with simply thousands of pounds of precious lead."

"Not only that, Colonel," Clay interjected, thinking that the more these men thought he already knew, the less valid their suspicions might seem. Glancing at Ellen, and wanting to move things along, he continued, "The rail line from Richmond through Bristol, here, to Chattanooga, is really our only east-west line through the Confederacy. From Chattanooga, men and materials can be distributed almost anywhere, from the Mississippi to Richmond and anywhere in between. Isn't that so, Colonel?"

"Well, suh," the colonel stammered, "you find me somewhat astonished, suh, I must say. Where did—"

"Colonel, sir," Farnsworth broke in, "I think under the circumstances—"

"Oh, yes. Very well, Major," Spendlove huffed, irritably sensing he had been caught unawares. Returning to his chair, he frowned at the major and nodded toward Clay. "Yes, perhaps we should continue, though I hardly think there's anything to concern us here. Still, perhaps you should ask Mister Mallory a few pertinent questions—very few."

Before Farnsworth could speak, and fanning herself even more briskly, Ellen said, "Oh, dear, Colonel Spendlove. Is that a train whistle I just heard? Could it be true that our conveyance to Chattanooga has at long last arrived? I do hope we—"

"Now look here, Missus Striker," Farnsworth interrupted, the look on his face leaving little doubt he had had enough. "I intend—"

A sudden blast from the street blew the window behind Spendlove's desk, frame and all, across the room, knocking the colonel unconscious to the floor and shattering against the far wall in an explosion of flying glass and splinters.

The concussion from the exploding artillery shot knocked Clay violently to the floor, stunning and disorienting him, but otherwise leaving him unhurt. As his head slowly began to clear, his first coherent thought was of Ellen. Looking wildly about as he struggled to his feet, he spotted her next to the door, a crumpled heap of tattered petticoats, under-linen, and faded velvet over-gown, beneath which one pale ankle was visible.

Farnsworth lay next to her, a pool of blood spreading beneath his head.

CHAPTER 10

★ ★ ★

Aᴄꜰᴛᴇʀ ʜᴀᴠɪɴɢ ʙᴇᴇɴ ꜱᴛᴏᴘᴘᴇᴅ in a driving rainstorm by pickets every few minutes, for over an hour, before reaching the Union headquarters, the frustrated, ungainly rider finally slid from his horse. As an orderly stepped out of the darkness to take his reins, the rider muttered to himself, "A lot of unnecessary bother." He was not all that tall and somewhat large around the girth, soaked to the skin, and completely exhausted from the long, cold ride.

Tripping on a wet tangle of weeds and grass, he stumbled toward the inviting pool of dim light cast from a battered lantern hanging beneath the sagging awning that sheltered the command tent's front flaps.

Two guards stepped in front of him as he ducked beneath the dripping canvas that was beginning to bulge and sag from the accumulating rain water. "Wait here, Professor," the tallest of the two said, stepping into the tent. As the tent flap fell back into place, the other guard moved in front of him, the smile on his face not entirely friendly, his rifle at port arms.

Due to the late hour and the increasing rain, rapidly becoming a torrential downpour, there were few soldiers to be seen around the camp, though the professor knew they were there in very large numbers, which were increasing every day.

Grant's preparations for a three-pronged push south to take Vicksburg, the Queen City of the Bluff, had been scrapped under orders from Grant's superior, General Henry Halleck, and what promised to be a bloody push from the river to take the city was in its beginning stages. A major battle was about to get underway and before that city was taken, if it ever could be, it was going to get costly—for both sides.

Poking a stubby finger at the sagging canvas just above their heads, the sodden visitor said, "One of you boys ought to lift that up so the water can drain off. Looks about to rip. Then where will you be?"

Before the unfriendly soldier could answer, the flap flew back, and the tall guard emerged from a thick cloud of tobacco smoke. "The general'll see yuh now, Professor. Take your hat off, please. And don't take no more time than yuh need to."

In the dim light provided by two lanterns, Ulysses S. Grant sat slumped behind a table covered with maps and numberless papers, all in disarray, a smoldering cigar clamped between his teeth. His elbow propped on the arm of his chair, his chin resting on his hand, and a dense halo of purple smoke enveloping his head, he was flanked by several senior staff officers standing behind him. "Come in, Brutus. You're not an altogether unwelcome sight— even at this late hour."

Ulysses Simpson Grant, known to his friends as "Sam," was a West Point graduate who had marched on Mexico City with

Winfield Scott's army, as had Wolf Striker. Now, after what seemed half a lifetime later, he was rapidly becoming known for his willingness to fight and his downright audacious manner as a field commander.

He was, in fact, rapidly becoming a favorite of Mister Lincoln's, though it was the president's suggestion that had caused Halleck to interfere with Grant's well-thought-out push south to Vicksburg. However, following the bloodbath at Shiloh, amid calls for Grant's removal despite the Union victory, Lincoln had been quick to defend his newfound warrior, arguing, "I can't spare this man. He fights." After months of dealing with McClellan's timid approach to war, Grant seemed like a breath of clear, refreshing air to the beleaguered president.

And there were those on the other side as well who felt much the same. General Ewell, who had known Grant as a cadet at West Point and later in Mexico, thought him the most fearsome of all the Union's officers. He hoped the "Northern people" would never find out about Sam Grant.

Leaning forward, a smile on his handsome, bearded face, Grant said, a puff of cigar smoke punctuating each word, "What've you got for me, Brutus?"

In a few short months, Brutus T. Husslebuster had become the Union's most effective spy in the western theater of the war. No one knew his true identity or where he had come from, but by entertaining Confederate soldiers as they trudged from one battlefield to another, he had been able to glean information that had proved invaluable to the Union as the war progressed.

He especially had become a favorite of many of the smaller cavalry units fighting under Forrest and Van Dorn as they continually raced back and forth across parts of Tennessee, Alabama, and

Mississippi, tearing up track, burning bridges, and attacking overextended Union supply lines.

At the point of exhaustion, small numbers of these mounted knights of the old south would spill into the professor's modest camp for a few minutes of diversion and rest. These were the boys who always seemed to know where the action was, and more importantly, where it was going to be.

Somehow, Husslebuster's big painted wagon of pleasure was never far from the action. Without fail, the adorable Miss Adela Goodenuff would be there to regale tired soldiers with songs, fancy dancing, and other equally appreciated amusements. Wolf Striker, masquerading as Adela's not-right-in-the-head husband, was also there to provide a little friendly gambling at a worn and faded faro table, never allowing any soldier to lose more than a dollar or two at a time.

It was, however, the good professor himself who sent them away with a happy sense of renewal and regeneration. A few swigs from a bottle of the professor's medicinal wonders were guaranteed to ease a multitude of physical pains and sooth a wounded, homesick soul—and loosen a good many trusting tongues, as well.

His was a sympathetic, almost ministerial, ear when a weary, frightened soldier or self-doubting officer needed a supportive word, an insightful interpretation of an otherwise incomprehensible world. And he was always there to provide a reasonable line of questioning, if needed, to help a confused, bewildered soldier find his own true identity in the midst of bloody chaos. But in the end, it was his compassionate, fatherly, and befuddled manner that endeared him to even the most skeptical supplicant—and made him such an effective spy.

The professor pulled a soiled handkerchief from his pocket

and patted his face dry. "At this point, I probably know little more than you, General. I—"

"Sit down, my friend, and let's keep such assumptions at a minimum," Grant said, motioning to an orderly at the back of the tent who immediately pushed another camp chair forward. "You look exhausted." As Husslebuster collapsed onto the chair, the general pushed a mug full of steaming coffee across the desk, and picking up a hipflask and swirling it above the mug, said, "A little added strength, Professor?"

Nodding his appreciation, the professor wiped the remaining moisture from his brow, and said, "As you probably know, General, Porter's push up the Yazoo River was met with heavy small-arms fire from the riverbanks, and his boats finally ran head-long into artillery fire from the Confederate's heavy batteries at Haynes's Bluff. Last word I got was that Lieutenant Commander Gwin, Captain of the *Benton,* was mortally wounded."

"Damn, anyway," Grant grumped, glancing around at his subordinate officers. "Yes, well, we'd heard as much, Brutus, but I appreciate this confirmation."

"But that's not all, General. Very likely as a result of Porter's move, Pemberton has sent two additional brigades to reinforce Martin Luther Smith in Vicksburg. And by now he most assuredly knows of Sherman's Mississippi expedition. There are at least 12,000 men in and around Vicksburg now."

Grant leaned back in his chair, took a long pull on his cigar, as if its glowing end would somehow shed further light on what was beginning to look like a rapidly deteriorating situation. "If Halleck hadn't interfered," he grunted to one of his subordinates, "we'd have done things differently. With a three-pronged approach, we . . . oh, well, spilt milk, I guess."

"But that's not the end of it, General Grant," Husslebuster

said, returning his empty mug to the desk. "Pemberton has withdrawn behind the Yalobusha River to Grenada, and he's been reinforced with another division—10,000 men from Bragg's command. There are now Confederate reinforcements up and down the Mississippi Central right-of-way.

"No matter how you approach Vicksburg, by river or right-of-way, it's going to be a nightmare, General. The city is a fortress, sitting like it does up there on the Chickasaw Bluffs."

"Those cussed bluffs," Grant mumbled, as if to himself, nervously tapping a pencil on his desk.

"Yes, sir. As you know, those two rivers flow parallel to one another almost from Memphis to Vicksburg. And just east of the Yazoo runs that parallel escarpment of clay bluffs—clear down to Port Hudson in Louisiana. Between the Mississippi and those bluffs—they range anywhere from one hundred to two hundred feet high—is the worst terrain imaginable. It's practically all jungle, General. You could lose an entire army in those swamps and bayous."

"Look here, General Grant," an officer said, as he spread a map across the already cluttered table. "Here's what he's talking about."

"And you've also got swamps between the Mississippi and the Yazoo," the professor continued.

"I know," Grant said, cutting Husslebuster off with a dismissive wave of his hand. "I'm familiar with the country down there, Professor. There's no question, it's a nightmare, but we've got to take Vicksburg. Once that's done, we've effectively split the Confederacy, and the rebellion cannot be sustained for any length of time after that.

"The question right now is, where's Sherman? Has he disembarked somewhere north of Vicksburg? Up the Yazoo?

Where? Half the time I don't know what's going on almost until it's over."

Husslebuster cleared his throat and said, "General, I've had Rebel cavalry in and out of my camp for the past week, and the move is to the south. Why, it's as if they're reading your mind, sir. I'm told they're certain of Halleck's strategy, and they're planning on stopping you at the Chickasaw Bluffs, north of the city."

Grant leaned back in his chair, scratching his chin, studying the professor's face. Then, leaning forward, he tapped the table and said, "I'm confident Sherman will take those bluffs, Professor. He's far and away the smartest man I know."

"Perhaps, sir, perhaps," Husslebuster said, carefully watching the weary general's reactions, feeling the need to make his point more forcefully. "But at what cost, sir?

"Two things more, and then I'll take my leave. First of all," Husslebuster said, raising a stubby finger for emphasis, "in order to reach the Chickasaw Bluffs, General Sherman's troops must disembark seven or eight miles up the Yazoo and make their way through that swampy jungle floodplain crisscrossed by a maze of stagnant bayous between the river and the bluffs. Some of those bayous, General Grant, are a hundred feet wide and fifteen feet deep. And the Yazoo itself winds around like a huge snake, just ready to swallow up an invading army.

"Second, sir," the professor said, a second stubby finger joining the first, "the Rebels have occupied a forward line at the foot of the bluffs, where the ground is more open—and that line is four miles long. On the right it's anchored by the Chickasaw Bayou. And believe me, General, that bayou is wide there—impassable, I feel confident to say. On the left, their line is anchored on the very bank of the Mississippi.

"Sir, the Confederates have placed two brigades in front, and one in reserve—ten thousand men in all, General Grant, and more than thirty heavy guns."

Grant leaned back and blew a cloud of smoke up into the darkness at the top of the tent, lost in thought. His original plan for a three-pronged attack would have worked. At least it had a better chance than the way things seemed to be going now. Vicksburg was very nearly impregnable from the north and the west. On the west was the river directly below the cliffs of the so-called "Queen City of the Bluff," and on the north, east, and south were the bluffs—the high ground.

"No matter how you cut it," he said, at last, "there's just no easy way." Pulling a map across the table, his officers closing around, he continued. "But of all the bad choices left to us, the most feasible is beginning to look like an attack from the east."

"But how, General?" one of the officers said. "Trying to go down the Mississippi Central Rail right-of-way is really no longer a sound option, and if we got back to Memphis it would look too much like a retreat. And the river's protected by the Confederate's heavy batteries at Vicksburg."

"Yes," Grant said, his finger absently tapping the map, "but if some of Porter's gunboats could blast us past Vicksburg, perhaps we could secure a landing on some high ground south of the city, then sweep around and advance against the city from the east."

Leaning over the map, Husslebuster could not help but notice General Grant's finger slowly tapping out some message known only to himself. *How ironic,* the tired professor thought. A smile slowly creased his face, as he watched Grant's mesmerizing finger tap on a place called *Hard Times.*

★ ★ ★

The storm had lasted for the better part of a week—wind, then heavy rain turning to a sodden snow that melted as it touched the already nearly impassible, mud-filled wagon roads. It had been a terrible winter for rainfall and high water in the Mississippi Valley, and the further south the Husslebuster troupe of determined entertainers had attempted to move, the worse conditions had become.

Anywhere within the Mississippi River's vast floodplain the weary soldier or pilgrim was faced with cypress swamps, impassible, jungle-like thickets, forests of cottonwood, sweet gum, magnolia, sycamore, and tulip, beneath which the ground was thickly covered with impenetrable masses of creeping vines. To make things worse, the entire area was intersected by a maze of stagnant bayous.

For any hope of success, it had been necessary for the Husslebuster troupe to stay east of the Chickasaw Bluffs, that continuous escarpment that runs parallel to the torn nation's mighty river from Memphis all the way down to Port Holland, Louisiana. Finally, as the drenching day had begun to darken into an even more inclement evening, just at the top of a broad, low hill, the exhausted troubadours had pulled off the road and into a dense grove of trees. The low hill, like an island in a sea of mud, offered them some concealment and an excellent view of the countryside.

Though heavy fighting could be heard several miles to the south, accompanied by a steady drumbeat of cannon fire, Wolf unhooked the big horses and began looking to their needs. As soon as the animals were out of the way, Adela and Big Bill busied themselves assembling the stage, securing it tightly to the front of the wagon. With that done, the two stretched a heavy canvas tarp from the roof of the wagon out to three sturdy poles set at the front of the platform, the longer middle pole establishing a peak to the tarp for drainage. They then strung several lanterns along a rope that hung loosely from one side to the other. When all was complete and the lanterns lit, the small outdoor theater took on a welcome cheeriness that somehow made the war seem less threatening.

Though the fighting was farther away than it sounded, the nearness of the war was unmistakable, and in a perverse sort of way, all that noise meant potential business. Small units of Van Dorn's cavalry were active throughout the area, as well, and with horse soldiers near by, the Husslebuster camp was sure to become busy as the night wore on.

With the horses fed, rubbed down, and tethered farther back in the trees, Wolf returned to the wagon and for a moment watched Adela and her big guardian as they went busily about their tasks. He did not know that much about the girl. In many ways she was a puzzling contradiction, portraying herself in public as a kind of dance-hall girl or worse, but when not performing, she acted as demure and shy as the most well-bred southern belle, though she was becoming more and more forward with Wolf.

From the moment Adela had declared Wolf to be her "ain't-right-in-the-head husband," she had hovered around him like a honeybee around clover blossoms, seeing to whatever she supposed his needs to be. When not performing, she served him his meals, saw to it he never lacked for any comfort, and made certain that his clothes were washed and kept clean.

Annoying as her constant wifely kinds of attentions had become, the beautiful, talented young woman had made Wolf's cover almost absolute, and on more than one occasion she had saved him from situations that would undoubtedly have led to his capture.

For Wolf, the long and the short of it was, the Charming Miss Adela Goodenuff had become a necessity, and there was simply no way around it, a fact made all the more difficult by her increasingly frequent hints that their arrangement ought to be made permanent. Needless to say, it was at those times that Wolf's self-concocted disorientation would appear to become worse.

Because of her, the soldiers—Confederate or Union, depending on where the Husslebuster troupe was at the time—who visited their camp, some frequently, no longer questioned his presence, their glances no longer suspicious. And so far, despite his alleged mental deficiencies, no one had questioned the inconsistency of his paradoxical skill at the faro table.

It was Adela's presence that held the whole charade together—not only for Wolf, but for the professor as well.

Recognizing that fact, Wolf had not asked too many questions about her past, not wanting to raise suspicions about his own. But with her hovering around him almost constantly, making his life far more tolerable than it had been for years, Adela was beginning to get under his skin—in a pleasant, sisterly sort of way. That she was not what she appeared to be was increasingly obvious; that she needed protection and not exploitation was equally apparent.

It was still early in the evening—too early for their nightly business to start—when Wolf set up his faro table under a tarp he had stretched out from the side of the big wagon. He was just lighting the last of three lamps he had hung above the worn, green felt table when Husslebuster rode into camp.

Both Wolf and Adela had begun to worry about their erstwhile leader. He had disappeared three days earlier, with no word of where he was going or when he would return, only the general location where he would meet them. Such disappearances were not that uncommon, but they seldom lasted more than a few hours, and he never had been gone more than a day and seldom overnight.

With a curious sense of relief, Wolf watched the professor as he tied his horse to the back of the wagon, stripped the saddle and tack, and hung a feed bag from the tired animal's head. In the weeks he had been with Husslebuster and Adela, Wolf had developed a certain fondness for the older man, though he could not say why, having never really come to know him.

Husslebuster was one of those men who, for some reason, one could never get close to, despite his befuddled, grandfatherly manner. There was an almost constant furtiveness to the way he went about his business, mixing his elixirs and potions, bottling his ointments, and doing it with the secretive manner of an alchemist out of the dark ages.

Watching the man gently rub the wet animal down, Wolf got the uncomfortable feeling that what was true of Adela was doubly true of Professor Husslebuster, or whatever his name was. The old alchemist or thespian or whatever most assuredly was not what he appeared to be. On top of everything else, there were times when the man's movements, despite his girth, were not those of an overweight, tired, old, itinerant flimflam man—and tonight was one of those times.

Nor were Adela or Wolf allowed into the wagon when the great healer was with one of his needy soldier-patients. Yet, amid all the noise of the camp, as Wolf worked his sometimes boisterous game of faro at the side of the wagon, he could now and then overhear bits and pieces of a hushed exchange between Husslebuster and some soldier, but never enough to understand what was being said.

Adding to Wolf's suspicions was the fact that the professor's private sessions invariably took place while Adela was onstage regaling an appreciative crowd of lonely soldiers with her feminine allure. And during each performance, whether Adela was dancing or singing, Big Bill sat near the wagon door at the back of the stage, accompanying her on his squeeze box or banjo and, Wolf suspected, guarding the door.

The professor's visitors or patients or whatever they might be were allowed in or out of the wagon only between breaks in Adela's performances, and then only one at a time.

As the professor disappeared through a trapdoor set in the floor at the rear of the wagon, the irony of the situation struck Wolf for the first time. *Perhaps that's why I fit in so well,* he snickered to himself, as he watched the trapdoor close behind Husslebuster. *Not one of us is what we appear to be. If it wasn't so worrisome, it'd be downright funny.* In fact, Husslebuster's whole operation just added up to something other than what it appeared to be—something dangerous.

With the coming of darkness, the rain had begun to fall with even greater intensity, and small numbers of weary Rebel soldiers soon began drifting into the camp, finding their way to the gaily lit stage. It had not taken long for the word to spread that there were entertainers in the area, and many of the men were familiar with what the Husslebuster troupe had to offer, having seen them before.

Adela was just preparing to go on when a Rebel cavalry troop of a dozen men rode into camp and dismounted. Among their number were several officers, one of which, a major, handed his reins to a subordinate and, followed by a captain, mounted the steps at the side of the stage. Shoving past Big Bill, the major tapped on the door, and the two entered.

Leaving their horses with a disappointed handler, the other

horse soldiers made their way to the stage, mingling with what was now becoming an eager and impatient audience.

The welcome sounds of Big Bill's banjo brought a wave of applause from the crowd, followed by cheers and shouts of approval as Adela danced and twirled her way to the middle of the stage. As her routine became more and more energetic, men began falling over themselves trying to secure a coveted place at the foot of the stage. Whatever the conditions, her routines of song and dance, not to mention her appealing beauty, could keep any war-weary soldier mesmerized.

Though the ground beneath the tarp protecting Wolf's faro set-up was fairly dry, the tarp itself was beginning to sag from the heavy downpour. Yet despite the rain, none of the men had found his way to Wolf's table. To a man, the wet, tired soldiers were more intent on watching Adela than in parting with what little money they might have. Whatever else could be said about Adela, she was tough competition.

"Step right up, gen'lemens, an' try your hand at buckin' the tiger," Wolf hollered, getting into his role, his speech slightly slurred. Fumbling with a worn deck of cards, he placed the stack face up on the green felt of the faro board, near his right hand.

Three drenched young men—boys, really—glanced at Wolf's faro table, the shelter provided by the tarp tempting them away from Adela's enticing performance. Only the bad weather could account for their obviously reluctant retreat, of that Wolf was certain.

The beautiful young woman was in the middle of one of her more exotic dances, her feet rhythmically tapping and stomping in time with Big Bill's lively tune, the men clapping with the compelling beat of the music. Those who were lucky enough to have found a place at the crowded foot of the stage were intent on getting a peek beneath her whirling skirts and petticoats, hoping to catch a momentary glimpse of a shapely ankle as she danced and spun before them.

As delightful as the men found her performance, the downpour had finally dampened the ardor of an increasing number. "This here game's faro," Wolf said, as several men stepped toward the tempting table and its shelter from the rain, "and there ain't a man amongst yuh who ain't won buckin' the tiger, neither's my guess. Not at this here table, anyways."

Several mumbled their agreement as they fumbled for the few coins they could dig from their pockets, each laying a coin on the game board card he intended to play. It always struck Wolf as sad that so many of these boys had no idea how to lessen the odds of their losing. When honest, faro was a game of pure chance, and though the odds favored the dealer somewhat, the chances for a player to win were not that bad. Still, for Wolf, taking money from these boys was too much like plucking a dead goose.

"On top's the *soda*, gents," he said, sliding the card from the stack to establish a discard pile at his right. "And right there on top's the loser." As he spoke, Wolf slid the eight of diamonds off the top and laid it on the discard pile. "Too bad, fellas," he groaned sympathetically, as he scraped some coins into a barely visible slot cut into the back of the table, where they silently dropped into a padded and safely locked drawer.

Cussing beyond his years, one young Rebel said, "Well . . . that does it fer me, mister. I ain't got nothin' left."

Ignoring the boy's complaint, Wolf declared, "No winners, gents. Leave 'em lay, or play a new one. Eight of diamond's the soda. Time ain't on none of our sides, huh? So lay 'em down, boys, lay 'em down."

"No it ain't," a big sergeant said, as he pushed a smaller man away from the table and laid a coin between the ten and the jack. "An' truth is, I don't think this game's honest."

"Ain't no need fer such talk, Sergeant," Wolf cautioned, bending over the table, studying the man from beneath his eyebrows. "More'n one can play this here *honest* game," he chided, his words slurred. "Y'all step right back over. Here, young fella. House'll float yuh a loan. More of yuhs is gonna make the game more lively, now, ain't it?"

With his continued encouragement, several additional coins were laid on selected cards.

"Them what's stayin' is stayin'," he said, his speech increasingly slurred, as he slid the next card from the top of the deck, revealing the jack of diamonds. "Looks like the sergeant here's a big winner."

As the sergeant snatched his winnings from the table, a cheer went up from Adela's dedicated admirers. Whatever their ultimate motives, between the two of them, Adela and Big Bill always put on a good show. The two never left the stage without wild cries for more coming from the audience.

With the end of the first show, Big Bill began lining the edge of the stage with bottles and jars of the professor's magic concoctions, and the crowd began to split up, some of the men drifting toward the faro table, while others remained by the stage, reading the small cards Big Bill was setting up in front of the goods each described. Still others began leaving the hill to return to their various encampments and the next day's fight.

"We got us some sojur winners over here," Wolf shouted. "Let's have us a little game, boys, 'til that pretty girl comes back t' give us another show. Come on over and buck the tiger, boys."

Inside the wagon, the major slammed a bottle of elixir on the table and said, "Something about this whole set-up I don't like,

Professor. This stuff's nothing but alcohol, that's all. Who the devil are y'all, anyway? And who's that jasper out there doing all the hollerin'?"

As the Confederate officer spoke, his companion moved to block the door, quietly drawing his big Colt navy revolver as he did so, letting it hang unobtrusively at his side.

"Well . . . now, Major," Husslebuster huffed, "I can assure you gentlemen I . . . eh . . . that is to say, we, are here to provide our . . . eh . . . fellow combatants some aide and comfort as we . . . eh . . . pursue our noble Confederate cause."

"That's hogwash. And nobody's leaving here until I know the truth. The Yankees've been out-guessing us too much, and I've got a hunch you 'fellow combatants' just might be the reason. Now I want the truth, and I want it now!"

"Why . . . suh, of what are you accusin' us?" the professor huffed. "Why I . . . I . . . eh . . . why, I'm aghast at the temerity of your accusations and . . . eh . . . implications, suh."

Drawing his pistol, the major said, "Sergeant, get out there and shut this show down. Post pickets and send all the rest of them boys back to their units. Then herd the rest of the professor's so-called Confederate entertainers in here. We're gonna get to the bottom of things, and we're gonna do it now!"

CHAPTER 11

★ ★ ★

P ART OF THE WALL BEHIND Colonel Spendlove's desk had violently burst apart from the blast of the exploding shell out in the street, blowing the window frame across the room where it shattered against the far wall, killing Major Farnsworth and knocking Ellen Striker to the floor unconscious. As more of the splintered outside wall began to disintegrate, the ceiling slumped, threatening to collapse on those trapped beneath it and filling the air with thick dust.

As more shells exploded nearby, Clay crawled from beneath the debris and struggled to his feet. Momentarily stunned and disoriented from the violent blast, but otherwise unhurt, he could see Spendlove behind his desk, partially buried beneath the rubble. But it was the sight of Ellen Striker lying in a tattered heap near the door that brought Clay to his senses. The man next to her was obviously dead, an ugly dark stain spreading beneath his head.

Staggering to Ellen's side, Clay pulled her rumpled clothes away from her face and pressed his fingers into the side of her throat where he felt a faint but steady pulse. Gathering her into his arms, Clay frantically kicked at the jammed door. Then, gathering his strength, he lunged at it with the back of his shoulder. As the obstinate door suddenly gave way, the two tumbled unceremoniously into the empty hotel lobby with the unconscious woman landing on top of him.

Working to regain his feet, Clay lifted Ellen Striker and carried her limp form to the nearest couch. But before he could get her properly situated, a horse unexpectedly clattered through the hotel entryway behind him and into the lobby. Turning, Clay found himself looking into the barrel of a .44 Colt army revolver, and it was in the steady hand of a very determined-looking Union officer. From the looks of him, he was around Clay's age and an experienced soldier—not a man to be taken lightly.

"One move, friend, and I'll blow your head off."

"You've got my complete attention, Captain," Clay said, raising his hands into the air. Then nodding toward Ellen, he continued, "But this woman needs medical attention as quickly as possible."

Not taking his eyes from Clay, the Union captain urged his horse about and, dismounting, motioned Clay away from the couch. "How's she hurt?"

"We were in there," Clay said, nodding over his shoulder, "the Confederate commander's office, when one of your cannonballs exploded out in the street. I'm hoping she's just been knocked unconscious."

Leaning over Ellen, the captain said, "Have you looked her over closely?"

"How closely?"

The officer turned back toward Clay, the look on his face showing a distinct lack of humor. "No time for jokes, mister."

"Well, I was just. . . . Yes, a poor choice of words, under the circumstances."

"Have you determined whether she's bleeding anywhere?" the Union captain said, his growing lack of patience more than obvious. "Broken bones . . . whatever?"

"No, not really. I just got her out here when you made your grand entrance." With a disapproving look from the officer, Clay caught himself, and quickly added, "Sorry, no disrespect intended, Captain. But, by any chance, do you happen to have a physician with you?" he asked, glancing past the man and his horse toward the street.

From where he stood, Clay could see mounted Union troops galloping past the hotel's ruined entryway, and shots could be heard coming from somewhere around the railroad station. From the sounds of things, a heated firefight was taking place.

Taking his horse's reins and starting toward the entryway, the Union officer said, "You stay right here. I see you anywhere else, and I'll shoot you on sight. Understand? I'll find our surgeon and be right back."

As the officer left the building, Ellen cautiously opened one eye. Then, when certain it was safe, heaved a sigh and, struggling with her clothing, sat up and rearranged herself. "My, but you are a brave one, Mister Mallory," she said, her voice steady, betraying no hint of weakness.

Turning at the sound of her voice, Clay said, "Ellen? How long have you—"

"Wasn't that a Yankee soldier, Mister Mallory? Why," she cooed, primly smoothing her dress, "I'm purely amazed that nasty Yankee didn't shoot us both—you, at least."

Searching Ellen's face in an effort to determine what she was up to, Clay sat down next her. "Well, I'm relieved that shell burst didn't rob you of your entertaining powers of observation, Missus Striker, not to mention your puckish southern wit."

"Why, thank you, Mister Mallory. How solicitous of you to be so concerned—and so complimentary."

Not trusting her mood, and very much in doubt as to her present motives, Clay studied her lovely face. In truth, this woman was proving a total mystery to him. *How can she do it,* he thought, watching her watching him. *She's an absolute marvel. And that stupid Wolf Striker? How could he just up and abandon such a woman? What she could add to a man's life if . . .*

Such thoughts were dangerous, and Clay knew it. Ellen Striker was proving to be the most mercurial human being he had ever met, and for that reason alone, she was not to be trusted. And yet her ability to keep a man guessing was just one of the woman's many qualities that made her so totally charming—and potentially dangerous. *I wonder how much she knows? Could she have guessed?*

Finally, looking into her eyes for some clue, Clay patted her shoulder lightly, and said, "Now, Missus Striker, you really should lie back down. You've probably received a nasty concussion, and it's gotten you somewhat confused."

"Mister Mallory, I'm not the least bit confused, though I am beginning to wonder about you. And if you don't mind," she sniffed, waving his hand away, her mood again changing, "I do prefer to sit up. My head is simply splitting, and lying down can only make it worse."

"Yes. That Yankee captain has gone to find a surgeon to look you over."

Turning to Clay, an almost comical look of alarm on her face, she cried, "Whatever do you mean, 'look me over,' Mister Mallory? No Yankee is going to lay a hand on me, much less, 'look me over.'"

"Missus Striker—Ellen—I only meant—"

"Look me over, *indeed*. Why, I declare, I'd rather die first," she huffed.

"But, you've just received a—"

"Oh, dear, my head," she moaned, lifting her hand to her temple. "I mean, really, Mister Mallory. Please don't be argumentative."

"Look, Ellen. . . . May I call you Ellen?"

"After what we've been through together, it's silly for you not to," she sighed, rubbing her forehead. "I truly don't feel myself as yet . . . uh, Braxton, is it?"

"Why don't you call me Brax for short? What few friends I can still claim do."

"Thank you, Mister Mallory, but I really do prefer Braxton."

"I should have guessed."

"It's just that, well, *Brax* somehow seems so—oh, I don't know—inelegant, I think. Even under these deplorable circumstances."

"Oh, well, yes," Clay said, his hand sweeping the ruined room, "We mustn't be inelegant. Not under these circumstances, certainly."

Giving Clay her most disapproving look, Ellen sighed, "You're being rude again, Mister Mallory. Please don't be rude. My head is absolutely splitting."

"I'm sorry," Clay said, immediately regretting his ill-timed attempt at humor. "You're the last person I would ever want to offend. For some reason, circumstances such as these tend to bring out the worst in me."

"Mmm. They do, don't they?"

"Look, Missus Striker, if you and I are going to get to Vicksburg, or somewhere near there, we've got to cooperate with these Yankees. So, please, just let their surgeon determine the extent of your injuries, whatever they might be. He'll at least give you a bromide for your aching head."

"A *bromide?* A *Yankee* bromide?"

"Yes, *a Yankee bromide,*" Clay said, irritation creeping into his voice. "I doubt it will have any political predilections. My guess is they're just like Confederate bromides, so—"

"Please, Mister Mallory, you're becoming boorish again."

"Yes, I'm sorry. But will you please just take what he gives you, and I promise I'll find a way to get us out—"

Accompanied by a medical officer in a blood-stained white coat, the Union captain hurried into the lobby, a sergeant following close behind the two. "Right over there on the couch, Doctor," the captain said, pointing in Ellen's direction. "See what, if anything, is wrong with her. I need to have a word or two with her gentleman friend here."

"Well . . . really, Captain whoever-you-are," Ellen said, attempting to rise, "I'm—"

"Ellen?" Clay warned.

Collapsing back on the couch, she groaned, "Oh, very well—if you must."

Rising, Clay said, "Be careful, Doctor. She'll prove to be a rather uncooperative patient, I'm afraid."

"Now, you step over here with me, mister," the captain said, with a nod away from Ellen and her would-be physician, "and let's hear your story."

Closely followed by the sergeant, the two walked across the room to the once ornate but now totally dilapidated bar. Glancing back at Ellen, who was becoming preoccupied with keeping her Yankee doctor at bay, Clay said, "Captain, my name is Colonel Clay Ashworth, and I'm passing through on my way to Vicksburg on a special assignment from President Lincoln."

"Well, now, that is an unexpected story, *Colonel*," the Union officer said suspiciously. "However, since you're out of uniform and in the company of a southern woman—an all too obviously southern woman, I might add—not to mention being discovered in the headquarters of the Confederate commander here in Bristol, I'm sure you can understand my skepticism. I suppose you've got some proof of what you're telling me."

Glancing in Ellen's direction, Clay experienced a feeling of panic. Given all that had happened, he hoped for just a moment that he remembered correctly which boot contained his Union credentials. Pulling out the wrong set would undoubtedly get him shot on the spot. Taking a deep breath, Clay paused, then reached down into his right boot and withdrew two envelopes. "Here's my commission, Captain. And I'm going to need your help getting the two of us on the next train headed toward Vicksburg. And . . . uh . . . Captain, she—that is to say, Missus Striker—knows nothing of my true identity, nor can she."

Clay watched his captor's face as the Union officer studied the documents.

"Um-hmm," the captain hummed, noncommittally, as he read Clay's commission. Then, after reading the document a second time, said, "Well, Colonel, it looks authentic enough, but let's you and I go have a talk with my commanding officer. He's setting up a command post at the railway station."

Turning, Clay watched Ellen for a briefest moment, unsure of his feelings. He was only now beginning to realize just how protective of her he had become, and the longer he knew her, the

more determined he was to see her reunited with her husband—
assuming Striker was still alive. However, Clay knew if she ever
were to discover what he was up to, everything would be in
jeopardy.

Turning back to the Union officer, he whispered, "Draw your
weapon, Captain."

"Colonel?" the captain said, not sure he understood, and
anxious to be moving.

"Draw your weapon, as if you are taking me prisoner."

Drawing his big Colt, the Union officer stepped back and
loudly demanded, "You're coming with me, mister."

"Yes, but what about her?" Clay said, in an attempt to be
heard across the room.

"Yeah, that's what I'd like to know," the captain growled,
glancing at the obstreperous woman and her increasingly frustrated physician. "She'll be safe enough here, whatever game the
two of you are playing. But for now, you're coming with me."

As they moved toward the entryway, Clay waved across the
room, a gesture intended to let Ellen know he would be back.
Then turning away from her, he confided, "Look, Captain, it's a
complicated story. Missus Striker has no idea who I am, nor does
she know my real name. And the truth is, I need her. She provides
excellent cover. I'll explain all the details when we find your
commander."

Stopping at the hotel's entrance, the two momentarily
watched the confusion at the couch, and the captain said, "Look,
Colonel, since we may be on the same side, my name is Carter—
Captain James Carter." Then over his shoulder, he hollered,
"Sergeant, stay with that woman until I get back or you are
relieved. Without my permission, she's not to leave this room—
not under any circumstance. Understand?"

Clay could not help but smile as the sergeant's face drooped. This was obviously not the kind of duty he was going to enjoy.

"Yessir."

Stepping from the hotel, Clay was shocked at the destruction along the street. The shelling had done considerably more damage than he had anticipated, and Union troops could be seen searching every building in view, rounding up the few remaining Confederate solders who had been garrisoned within the town and any other persons of suspicion. From the looks of things, Bristol had been taken completely by surprise, and the Union force was now in total control—for the time being, at least.

As they approached the railroad station, Clay caught a glimpse of the switching yard, where a wood-burning locomotive and its tender, just coupled to a boxcar, hissed loudly and, with a huge burst of black smoke billowing from its bulbous stack, began backing toward a passenger car already attached to a caboose. It appeared that the train would soon be heading back down track toward Knoxville and possibly Chattanooga.

Perfect, Clay thought. *If I can just convince them to let us be on it.*

Further across the yard, Union troops were busily engaged in tearing up rails and burning ties. And on a side track further down the line, several boxcars could be seen fully enveloped in flames.

"Well, I'll be," the Union commander said, rising from his makeshift field desk, as Clay and his captor entered the building. "Could it really be Clay Ashworth, the pride of West Point?"

"Jake? Is that you, Jake Woods?" Clay exclaimed, reaching for the Union officer's offered hand, the relief in his voice unmistakable.

"Where'd you find this old reprobate, Captain?" Woods asked, his delight at seeing an old friend unmistakable.

"This is hard to believe," Clay declared, with an almost overwhelming sense of reprieve. "This is too good to be true. Why, man, you're the last person I expected to see under these circumstances, Jake."

"That so?" Woods chuckled. "Well, that's war for you."

"Old Lost-in-the-Woods, himself, and a lieutenant colonel, to boot."

"*Old Lost-in-the-Woods?*" Captain Carter echoed, a hesitant grin crossing his face.

Ignoring the captain's obvious delight, Clay declared with relief, "Jake, you'll never know how glad I am to see you right now."

"Old Lost-in-the-Woods?" the captain repeated. "What is this I'm hearing?"

"What you're hearing is the opportunity to spend the rest of this war as a private, if you ever repeat what you just heard in my presence, or mention it to anyone else," Woods chuckled. From the tone of Woods's voice, there was no mistaking his meaning.

"Are you investing this town?" Clay asked, unable to mask the excitement in his voice.

"For the time being, anyway. We need to get control of the rail line between here and Chattanooga. It's the major east-west supply route between the Mississippi River and the eastern Confederacy—Memphis in the west, Richmond in the northeast, and Atlanta and Charleston to the south—and we're either going to get control of it or tear up track for as many miles as possible."

"You're aware of the lead mines, then?"

"Lead mines?"

"Oh, yeah," Clay said, unable to hide his enthusiasm. "And let me tell you, you're going to need more men than I've seen so far, Colonel. The mines near here produce most of the lead for the

Confederacy's ammunition. And you can bet they're not going to lose control of this area. Not without a major fight, anyway."

"For crying out loud, man, where are these lead mines?"

"Get out your maps, Jake. You and your men have stumbled onto something really important, at least as important as this rail line, if not more so. As soon as I could, I was going to get word back to Washington, but with you here, that's obviously no longer necessary. Lincoln is personally interested in this information."

"Mister Lincoln?"

"It's that important. But I'm telling you, Jake, you'd better send for reinforcements fast, unless there are more men already on the way."

"What do you mean?" an alarmed Jake Woods said, studying Clay's face. "I've got a full cavalry squadron here, two hundred and fifty-six men at last count. And that includes two twelve-pounders and two three-inch ordnance rifles."

"Ordnance rifles?"

"You bet," Woods said, his enthusiasm obvious. "Sweetest little weapons you've ever laid eyes on. They only have a three-inch diameter barrel, but with a one-pound charge of black powder, one of those little babies can fire an eight- or nine-pound projectile over two thousand yards. And they are accurate."

"Oh?" Clay said, pretending to stifle a yawn in an effort to irritate his old friend and hide his ignorance of what sounded to be a pretty impressive weapon. Clearing his throat, he continued, "Well, unless I miss my guess, my friend, you're going to need all that and more." Thumping the desk in an effort to add some authority to his words, he added, "And soon."

Watching Clay mix what appeared to be fact with his own brand of fiction, something for which Clay was once not unknown in certain West Point circles, the Union colonel finally said, "Look, Clay, we took this town with hardly any effort at all. I just don't—"

"Jake, there's got to be a large Confederate force garrisoned around here somewhere. The Confederacy could never afford to lose what appears to be their major source of lead."

Grabbing a pencil and a scrap of paper, Woods scribbled a short note and hollered to a subordinate across the room, "Lieutenant, get this off immediately, and make sure they know it's priority—absolutely urgent."

★   ★   ★

A stunned Colonel Archibald Spendlove slowly rolled over and attempted to sit up, wincing at the intense pain in his left arm and shoulder. His arm was obviously broken, and he was covered with what felt like a ton of debris, undoubtedly the reason he had not been found. Outside he could hear Yankee soldiers swarming around the building, and it sounded as if there were hundreds of them.

Cradling his injured arm, the Confederate commander managed to pull himself from under the rubble and struggle to his feet. He could see Farnsworth lying near the open door, dead from the looks of things, and he could hear the Striker woman arguing with someone out in the lobby, a Yankee doctor most likely.

Spendlove's head ached viciously, his arm was completely useless, and with the shock wearing off, the pain was becoming acute. Obviously, medical help was to be found just outside the door, but so was life in a Yankee prison camp for the duration of the war; and no matter what the pain, that was not an option. Turning to the door at the right of his desk, the colonel carefully twisted the knob and pulled it ajar.

The sagging door opened onto a boardwalk, hidden from the street by several overgrown lilac bushes. In one direction, obscured by the bushes, it led to the street; in the other, to outside stairs leading to the second floor of the hotel, where a military telegraph station had been established, bypassing the telegrapher's office at the train station. Aside from convenience for the commandant, the small office was intended to guarantee a greater degree of security for essential military communications. Inexplicably, there was no access to the small room—closet, really—from inside the building.

Having heard no sound from the stairs or the room above, Spendlove stepped out onto the boardwalk and carefully made his halting way to the rickety structure and climbed to the top, agonizingly aware he was in full view from the busy street below. Praying the room had not been discovered, he quickly pushed the door open and stepped inside. Except for the young telegrapher, huddled behind the desk, the room was empty.

"Get up, young man," the colonel commanded. "Is your key alive?"

"Yessir," the young soldier stammered, saluting Spendlove as he got clumsily to his feet, overwhelmed at the presence of his commanding officer. "But the Yankees—"

"Never you mind the Yankees. If we act with dispatch, perhaps you and I can yet save this day for the Confederacy." Scribbling on a small notepad, his hand unsteady, he declared, "Here. Send this message."

★　★　★

In the hotel lobby below, Ellen and her Yankee captor sat waiting, each resentful of the other, the doctor having long given up and gone back to his duties elsewhere. She was the first to break the silence. "Really, Sergeant, one would think you would have more pressing duties, when it comes to attacking an otherwise peaceful southern village, than just sitting here watching me."

"Yes, ma'am."

"Surely there are more brave, outnumbered southern gentlemen to shoot and defenseless homes and buildings to destroy."

"Yes, ma'am.

"Not to mention more innocent women and children to assault and imprison, wouldn't you think, Sergeant?"

"Yes, ma'am."

With each of the Yankee sergeant's stunted responses, Ellen's peevishness grew. Was the man trying to provoke her, or was he just ignorant and rude—like most Yankees? "Who'd have thought it," Ellen snapped. "A Yankee at a loss for words."

"Yes, ma'am."

"Aren't you northern persons, you *Yankees,*" she chided, attempting to force the detestable word out through her nose, "known for your twangy, clipped way of talking through your noses, and for doing so much of it?" Her hopelessly inadequate parody ended in an embarrassing sneeze, irritating her even more.

"Yes, ma'am."

"I mean, really, Sergeant, you—"

Jumping to his feet, the Yankee sergeant waved her silent and asked, "Can you hear that?"

"Can I hear what, Sergeant? And don't wave at me that way— I mean, really."

"That tapping sound," he said, stepping to the office door and pausing to listen, then moving back along the wall toward the couch. "There . . . can you hear it? Why, it's a telegraph! That sounds like a telegraph, and it's coming from somewhere in this building."

For a moment Ellen thought her heart would leap out of her chest. If it were a telegraph, and if this Yankee dullard of a sergeant knew nothing of it, then maybe some brave Confederate soldier was sending a message summoning help. "Well I don't think I hear—"

Grabbing Ellen by the wrist, he pulled her from the couch and headed for the street. "Come on, lady. You're coming with me."

★　★　★

Lieutenant Colonel Woods listened to Clay's story with some amusement, interrupting only occasionally. "And so this woman you're with, she knows nothing of this?"

"No, Jake, she doesn't, and it would be a disaster if she were to find out. The farther I get into Rebel territory, the more I'm going to need her. I'm telling you, Jake, on more than one occasion she's proved to be an answer to prayer. All Ellen Striker has to do is open her mouth and no one questions her southern loyalties—or mine."

"Yeah, well, if you're serious about getting to Vicksburg from here, or anywhere west of here, you're going to need all the help you can get."

"What do you mean? This is a major rail line, isn't it?"

"When the track isn't torn up or the bridges burned," Woods said, rummaging among the papers on his desk. "This purports to be the schedule of the East Tennessee and Virginia Line," he said, uncovering a small booklet, "though such schedules have become a joke."

"But, what about that—"

"That train out there arrived only an hour ago with a few Rebel troops and supplies, but we surprised them. Now, according to this so-called schedule, there won't be another one coming from Knoxville, because this one was supposed to connect with another one coming down the Virginia and Tennessee line from Lynchburg, but that one's not scheduled to arrive until late this evening—if ever."

"If you say so," Clay responded, unable to hide his admiration for Wood's labored syntax.

"I was going to send that ET&V locomotive back to Knoxville and destroy all the cars but one freight and one passenger car. And that's what we'll do—send that one back down the line with you and your traveling companion aboard. That might get you as far as Knoxville. But, I'm telling you, Clay, this whole area, everything from here to the Mississippi is in a constant state of flux. Even if you get as far as Knoxville, you'll have to change trains there—if there's another one to change to."

"Well, are we going right into the hands of the Rebels, or are our people in control?"

"You'll be in our prayers," Woods said, a wry grin on his face. "It's just that kind of thing that makes war so much fun. Between the two of you, one or the other of you should be able to confuse whoever's in control of Knoxville or the surrounding countryside, if anyone is."

"Sir," Carter said, alarm in his voice. "Here comes Sergeant Thatcher, and he's got that woman with him. I told him to stay put, but something must have spooked him."

"Look, Clay, here's what we'll do. I'll place you and your lady friend *traveling companion*," Woods snickered, "under arrest, then have the two of you locked in the passenger car under the pretense of sending you to our headquarters in Knoxville, where you're to be interned."

"We have a headquarters there?"

"One way or the other, she won't know."

"Yeah," Clay agreed, hesitantly. "I hope she'll fall for it."

"Well, if you can come up with something better, Mister Mallory, you'd better do it fast, because here they come."

"No," said Clay, attempting to look defeated, "I'll make it work—somehow."

"Well, how smart can she be?" Jake hissed, at the last moment. "I mean, she's one of those southern belles, isn't she?"

"Let me go, you Yankee brute!" Ellen said, angrily yanking her arm from the sergeant's grip, as the two stumbled into the building.

His chest heaving, Thatcher dragged the unwilling woman up to the desk and, stopping only long enough to catch his breath, said, "Colonel, sir, we got problems."

Getting into his role, Clay spun around and took a wild swing at the sergeant. "Take your dirty hands off of her," he demanded, as the captain grabbed him from behind. Almost twisting free, Clay snarled at Jake Woods, "What kind of an army are y'all running here, Colonel? Assaulting southern women now, are you? Tell that Yankee cretin to let her go."

Waving Clay silent, Woods said, "What are you talking about, Thatcher?"

"Sir, somewhere in that hotel building there's a telegraph. I heard it, sir, and so did she," Thatcher said, giving Ellen a yank.

"Really, Mister Mallory," she said, with a sniff. "I can't imagine what this big Yankee ox is referring to. I heard nothing of the kind, I assure you."

"Leave her alone, you big ape," Clay snarled.

"Telegraph?" Woods snapped. "Captain Carter, you said nothing about a telegraph."

Leaning around a defiant Clay Ashworth, Carter said, "Sir, I had that whole building searched, and nothing was found, much less a telegraph."

"Well, get a squad back over there and take that building apart—board by board if necessary. Find that telegraph and destroy it, and bring whoever's using it back here—and you'd better do it fast, Captain."

As a big sergeant roughly took control of Clay, Captain Carter turned on his heel, and hollering at a lieutenant to gather his squad, ran from the building.

"You Yankees are in big trouble, now Mister Colonel, sir," a defiant Ellen Striker hissed. "Our southern boys won't be long in pickin' your cotton. No, indeed, not now. Isn't that right, Mister Mallory?"

"She's right, Colonel," said Clay, glancing in Ellen's direction, a look of admiration on his face. "Our men are going to be all over this place before you can sing "Yankee Doodle Dandy," mister. "

"Well said, Mister Mallory," Ellen laughed.

"Put these two in irons, Sergeant, and lock them in that second rail car," Woods said, his voice calm, "until I can send 'em on down to Knoxville or Chattanooga—anywhere but here."

"*Chattanooga?*" Ellen replied, unable to hide her enthusiasm.

"Oh, never you mind, miss," Woods snapped. "Your precious Chattanooga will soon be in Union hands. After all, dear lady, nearly everything else is. Your precious Confederacy is coming apart at the seams."

PART THREE

★ ★ ★

CHAPTER 12

★ ★ ★

As Ben Kimball leaned back from the immaculately laid table, an impeccably dressed black waiter removed the dishes from before him. Pulling the delicate porcelain dessert plate toward him, careful not to allow the syrupy golden sauce covering the large piece of apple pie to spill onto the spotless white tablecloth, Ben wished he could loosen his tie. Somehow, his collar seemed to have grown tighter with the last few mouthfuls of his sumptuous dinner. He could not remember when he had last eaten so well—not in the last two months, anyway—and there was just no way this tempting dessert was going to be wasted.

"Coffee, suh?"

"No, thank you," said Ben, smiling up at the waiter. The man had been attentive to a fault, not just in serving him, but in attending to others at surrounding tables as well. He seemed to anticipate their every need, helping women with their chairs, filling coffee cups and water glasses before they were even close to empty. His actions revealed him to be a man of some refinement and as much a gentleman in his manner and the graceful performance of his duties as any of those whom he served.

Ben could not help but wonder as he watched this tall, elegant waiter if the man was an emancipated black, freed by the war, or if he had been born free. Either way, his role in life seemed limited to that of a menial servant. Was this all his future held? Could he ever hope for more? Would the politics of his skin always shackle him? Would this costly war in some way enhance the quality of his life? One could only hope so.

On the other hand, perhaps where he now found himself was so far removed from the terrible life he might once have known as a slave—or could yet know—that he would never think to hope for more. Could it be possible that he didn't look upon his present service as menial? Or was it possible that he saw what he was now doing as an opportunity afforded to few of his race?

With a sigh born of both exhaustion and frustration, Ben rubbed his forehead and reached for his glass of water. He had been away from home too long, and such impossible questions could eat at a man's innards. The true horrors of being enslaved to another human being—of one's body being owned by someone else—were difficult, if not impossible, for any white man to imagine. Stories of families being separated—husbands from wives, children from their parents—of beatings, even of socially sanctioned and unchallenged killings, were revolting to contemplate.

Even so, as a Mormon, Ben Kimball was not unfamiliar with man's inhumanity to man, with what evil blind bigotry could do. In a way most white folks would never understand, he shared a sense of solidarity with the black man who was, once again, refilling his water glass.

Members of his own family had suffered at the hands of vicious intolerance on more than one occasion. It was hard to imagine, but it hadn't been twenty years since the horrors of Ohio, Missouri, and Illinois had led to the torture of Winter Quarters. Then came the unbelievably difficult trek west and the challenge of surviving those first winters on the high desert of the Great Basin, not to mention the scores of faithful who died pulling handcarts across the Great Plains, struggling to reach their long-dreamed-of Zion. How could such suffering ever be forgotten?

Where this destructive warfare between the states was concerned, there were many justifications for the suffering it was exacting, just as there were many forms of slavery. The really interesting thought was that in the heat of the conflict, perhaps even for years afterward, few would ever be in a position to fully appreciate what the war was truly all about—its root provocations.

There were the obvious issues, of course: state's rights or perpetual union; economic inequity or parity between the North and the South; slavery for some or freedom for all—the list was a long one. Yet, the true meaning of the war would never be known or widely appreciated—only to a comparative few. But when, in the entire history of the world, was that not the case?

Ben dabbed at his mouth with a spotless white napkin and pushed the dessert plate away. The dinner had been delicious and the portions generous, despite the war that raged not far to the south—another anomaly. Too much thinking about such issues could ruin one's digestion.

Despite the luxury of his immediate surroundings, there was no escaping the fact that this part of the earth was in upheaval. The reality of it was more than apparent from the numerous large steam-powered riverboats that could be seen from his table near the wide dining room window, each teeming with Union soldiers preparing to be moved downriver. Stern-wheelers, side-wheelers, and flatboats of all sizes were moored alongside the wharfs that cluttered the busy riverfront.

Judging from all that could be seen from where he sat, Grant's assault on Vicksburg was apparently well underway. Though Confederate forces were known to be swarming the countryside between Memphis and Vicksburg, the Union now controlled nearly the entire length of the Mississippi River, from Cairo to New Orleans, denying the Confederacy the men and resources of those rebellious states west of the river: Arkansas, Louisiana, and Texas.

Here in the western theater, Vicksburg remained the only stumbling block, and from the looks of things, it would not remain so for long. On top of that, the very heart of the Confederacy had been made vulnerable through the Union defeats of forts Donelson and Henry, thrusts that opened the Tennessee and Cumberland rivers to the east.

Even to a novice from the western territories, it was more than obvious that the bloody southern rebellion was doomed. It was only a matter of time.

Taking a final glance around the busy dining room, Ben was again struck by the incongruity of his surroundings. Even in the midst of war, the sumptuous Gayoso House Hotel remained an island of comfort and culture, seemingly untouched by the surrounding chaos. With its own waterworks, gasworks, bakeries, wine cellar, and sewer system, the hotel was a marvel of elegant living. The place even boasted indoor plumbing, including marble tubs, silver faucets, and, of all things, flush toilets.

Imagine, flush toilets—a thing almost unheard of. After experiencing such splendor, how could one ever again make the dreaded morning trek to a cold, malodorous outhouse? Ben could hardly wait to get back home to regale his friends with such stories. The exigencies of the human condition paled next to the glory of a flush toilet.

Leaving a silver dollar next to his plate, Ben made his way between the crowded tables and entered the Gayoso House's expansive lobby. For the better part of a week, he had enjoyed these elegant surroundings as he waited for his contact from the nation's capital, but, truth be told, he was anxious to leave the terrible tumults presently racking civilization and return to the comparative safety of the mountains, out in his beloved Utah Territory.

Across the lobby, a Union officer rose from an overstuffed chair and quickly walked toward him. "Are you, by any chance, Mister Kimball?"

"I'm Ben Kimball," Ben responded, accepting the young man's extended hand.

"Yes," the young major said, warmly shaking Ben's hand, "I thought it was you. I'm Jonathan Duncan. Is there some place we can talk where we won't be overheard?"

"Well, Major," Ben said, taking the soldier's elbow and turning him toward the hotel's grand entry, "I'm kind of full after eating too much of this wonderful hotel's excellent food. Why don't you and I take a walk along the riverfront. That way we can see who's paying us too much attention, and I can work off some of my dinner."

The riverfront was teeming with humanity, but a relatively uncrowded path extended along the top of a dike farther back from the river and afforded an excellent view in every direction. Whether they were observed or not, no one could get within hearing distance and not be seen.

Looking around, Duncan took two yellow envelopes from the

inside pocket of his tunic and handed one to Ben. "This contains a message for Brigham Young from the president. As you can see, it's sealed. In fact, both are. I have, however, been made privy to their contents."

"That being?"

"The president received Brigham Young's message some weeks ago. He feels that given the deteriorating conditions in Mexico and the possible impact of European involvement on the American Southwest, and given the fact that Colonel Ashworth in all likelihood will have completed his present mission when he arrives here, there are sufficient reasons for acquiescing to Mister Young's request.

"Upon receipt of these orders," said Duncan, handing the second envelope to Ben, "Colonel Ashworth has been reassigned. He has not been relieved of his rank," the young major cautioned, "nor has he been relieved of his military obligation to this country. Rather, he has been reassigned to duties of his own determination, as related to developments in Mexico and conditions along the existing territorial borders of the United States."

Stopping, the two looked around, and Ben said, "Good. I'm anxious to get it back to Salt Lake City. I'll leave before first light tomorrow."

"I'm afraid that won't be possible, Mister Kimball. The president has asked that you remain here with me, and that you personally hand this message to Colonel Ashworth when he arrives."

"And when will that likely be?" asked Ben.

"There's no way of knowing," said Duncan, lowering his voice. "He is traveling here from Washington by way of Knoxville and Chattanooga. I had hoped he would be here when I arrived. But his assignment from Mister Lincoln was a difficult one."

"And what was that, if I may ask?"

"You may. He was to collect as much field intelligence along that important Confederate supply and communication route as possible and to deliver that information to myself and Union commanders here in Memphis. Of necessity, he's traveling incommunicado, disguised as a Southerner by the name of Braxton Mallory."

"Well . . . what are the chances—?"

"That he won't arrive here at all?"

"Exactly. I mean if he's caught, they'll shoot him on the spot as a spy, won't they?"

"Quite likely. But you know Colonel Ashworth far better than I, Mister Kimball. What do you think his chances are?"

Ben turned and looked out across the busy waterfront and the crowded docks below them. The huge, placid river, nearly a mile wide where they now stood, looked as if no amount of human conflict could disturb its unconcerned passage. "Beautiful, isn't it?" Ben mused, thinking of his friend, and the dangers Clay was undoubtedly facing.

For a brief moment, each was lost to his own reflections, then breathing deeply of the cold air, Ben said, "Clay Ashworth is one of the brightest and most resourceful men I know, a real soldier. I'll wait. He'll be here. One way or the other, Clay Ashworth will show up."

It was well past midnight by the time the sergeant and his small detail had cleared the Husslebuster camp of the remaining Confederate soldiers. All had left to join their units, cold and soaked to the skin from the constant, heavy downpour; not a few went away happily rejuvenated by the musical antics of the

Charming Miss Adela Goodenuff; and a good number stumbled away from Wolf's faro table, broke, grumbling, and threatening to come back and tear the place apart. And to remind them of better times and to ease their fears of the future, those few who could afford such a luxury, departed with a bottle or two of Professor Husslebuster's magically healing elixirs merrily clinking in their pockets.

With the camp empty and the fires nearly out from the rain and lack of attention, the sergeant posted two of his men as guards, sent the rest back to their unit headquarters, and herded Wolf, Adela, and Big Bill into the wagon for what promised to be an uncomfortable interrogation by the major.

The belligerent Confederate officer seemed convinced that the befuddled Professor Husslebuster was a Union spy. One way or the other, he was going to exact a confession, if not from the professor, then from one or all of the others, each of whom he suspected was a spy, as well.

Entering ahead of the other two, Wolf shuffled to the back of the wagon and settled in the darkness next to a small dressing table. Quietly pulling a drawer out from beneath the table, he removed a large revolver and carefully laid it on the floor within easy reach. Then, with Adela protectively hovering at his side, he slouched down and began playing his game of dim-witted lethargy—the innocent fool.

"Now, Professor, we're gonna to get down to brass tacks here, if it takes us all night." Drawing his weapon, a look of pure meanness distorting his face, he snarled, "Whatever it takes, Husslebuster—if that's your real name."

"But, Major, I . . . eh . . . assure you there's—"

"Sergeant, go back there and drag that dancin' slut up here. She'll do the talking, or—No, hold on.

"You back there, the idiot faro dealer," the major, bellowed, squinting in Wolf's direction, any hope for rationality beginning to leave him, "stand up where I can see yuh. What's the matter with you, anyway?"

"You leave him be," Adela hissed, stepping in front of Wolf, poised to strike at anything that threatened her supposed husband. "He's my man, and he ain't right in the head, so you jest leave him be."

"No, now . . . eh . . . see here . . . eh . . . Major. There's no need for such—"

"I'll say what's needful and what ain't," the Confederate officer snarled, turning on the professor, the barest hint of hysteria creeping into his voice. "Drag her up here. We'll soon see what that big fool's made of, when his little wife starts squealin'."

With his arm hanging unobtrusively at his side, Wolf's hand closed around the grip of the heavy pistol. This whole charade was getting tiresome in the extreme—constantly having to play the idiot and putting up with Adela's unwanted, but advantageous, advances. On top of that, he was not so sure himself that the good professor wasn't a Union spy. But now things were beginning to get out of hand and just plain dangerous. It was time to put an end to it—all of it.

Yet, three things were eating at Wolf Striker, keeping him from blowing this infuriating fool's head off before he opened his big mouth one more time. First of all, shabby and unstable or not, the man was a fellow soldier, an officer in the Confederacy.

Secondly, Wolf had to get to Vicksburg and not get shot up in the process. That meant he could not reveal himself as a Confederate officer. If he did, he would undoubtedly get stuck in some nearby brigade or regiment about to go into action. Things from Cairo to New Orleans were rapidly coming apart for the

Confederacy, and Vicksburg was where the last critical fight was about to happen, if it wasn't already underway. No Rebel soldier was going to just walk around in this mess unchallenged.

He had to find a way into the city and not get his head blown off in the process, if ever there was to be any hope of finding Ellen. If his wife was still in Vicksburg—and she was still his wife—she would be in mortal danger. Still, his wife or not, he was determined to find her, and if she'd just let him, he'd get her—get them both—to safety and a new life.

Finally, he could feel the old Wolf—his oldest and most persistent enemy—starting to stir deep down inside—that feral brute that prophets and wise men have warned of throughout the ages. If he ever again allowed the beast to control him, to ever again rise up on all fours, he would forfeit any right to the new life he so desperately desired, a life with Ellen. He would never be free of his past.

The Bard was right, Wolf thought, heaving a sigh. *To willful men, The injuries that they themselves procure Must be their schoolmasters.*

All of that aside, if he gave in to the monster now, no one was likely to leave this wagon alive.

"You keep your dirty mouth shut, you cheap little tart, or you'll soon be—"

"Please, Major, is that . . . eh . . . any way to—"

"You shut up!" the major hollered, turning on the professor, "and get that man up here where I can look at him. Somthin' tells me he ain't the fool he pretends to be. From what I saw tonight, he just deals faro too good."

"He's a dirty cheat," the sergeant sniveled. "Ain't nothin' wrong with his head."

"Don't butt in when I'm talkin', Sergeant. I wanna know what kind of act this fella's puttin' on. In fact, I'm gonna find out what all of yuh are up to."

Lifting the big horse pistol, Wolf started to rise from his chair. It was time to get the party started. One shot from the heavy revolver would quickly put an end to all the noise coming from the front of the wagon. And in the confusion that was sure to follow, he would just slip out through the trapdoor and disappear.

Wolf cocked the big colt and froze. A horse had stomped and blown just outside the wagon, and he could hear others as well.

"You in the wagon!" someone hollered, "Come out here with your hands over your heads, and come out slowly."

"What the—? Didn't you post no guards, Sergeant?"

"Yessir," the sergeant stammered. "One at each side of the camp. They should of—"

"If I don't see some faces out here in the next thirty seconds, I'll order that wagon shot so full of holes there'll be little left of it—or you. Now, start coming out of there, and be just plain careful how you do it!"

"Are yuh Union or Confederate?" the Confederate major hollered.

Hunching down, Wolf waited. If they were Confederate soldiers, the jig was up. There would be no way he could avoid revealing his identity, and that would mean being pressed into service on the spot. On the other hand, if they were Union, well. . . .

A bullet tore through the side of the wagon near the roof, the blast sounding as if a cannon had gone off just outside. "You Rebs get out here! Now!"

That tears it, Wolf thought. *I'm out of here.*

With the major and the others reacting in confusion to the

demands coming from those outside, Wolf crept farther back in the wagon, behind the table, and slowly lifted the trapdoor.

Using the proverb frequently in their mouths, Wolf thought, slipping through the trapdoor to the ground beneath, *who enter upon dangerous and bold attempts, The die is cast, he took the river.*

Why was it, every time he found himself in a tight spot, some line of obscure poetry or classical literature would pop into his head? *I could become a real bore,* Wolf thought, slipping quietly through the trapdoor to the ground beneath. *Those nuns must have done a real job on me.* Actually, there was nothing annoying about it. In fact, given the terrors of the moment, it was kind of a pleasant thing. It was just that he had never thought about it until now, and now was really no time to be thinking about it. *Plutarch,* he thought. *Time for me to light a shuck out of here and, as the poet says, take the river—or something.*

Crouching in the darkness underneath the wagon, all he could see was horses' legs, seemingly numberless horses' legs.

"Come out from under there, Mister," a deep voice ordered, "and lay that nice big hog leg right here on the ground. You even blink wrong, and you're dead."

Chucking the big weapon out ahead of him, Wolf crawled out from under the wagon and quickly found himself surrounded by what looked to be a large detachment of Union cavalry, maybe thirty or forty men, a culled-down company, anyway, and every one of them was pointing a gun at him.

In a matter of minutes the others were out of the wagon and lined up against its colorful side.

"Anyone else left in there, Professor?"

"No, Captain Allen, we are all at your command. I was, however, beginning to think you'd never get here. In fact, this Rebel major here," Husslebuster said, giving the Confederate officer an accusing look, "was starting to get unnecessarily nasty, I must say. He was, in fact, threatening great harm against Miss Goodenuff, and that had me quite worried. She is, after all, a delicate young thing, you know."

"Major, my foot," the Union captain spat. "He's no regular, just one of those deranged, Rebel bushwhackers from across the river. He and that vermin with him ought be shot on the spot."

"Indeed, Captain," Husslebuster huffed in agreement. "You got here just in the nick of time, I can tell you."

Watching the exchange between the Union officer and Husslebuster, Wolf knew his worst suspicions were now confirmed. Professor Brutus T. Husslebuster, now showing none of his usual befuddlement, was indeed a Union spy—and a very effective one, at that.

As for the tearful and Charming Miss Adela Goodenuff, blubbering beneath her name on the side of the wagon and throwing wide-eyed glances at her captives, Wolf wondered just how far her show went. Was she in on it, too? Judging from the looks some of the Union soldiers were casting her way, Wolf felt fairly certain she would bawl and blubber her way out of this predicament. She clearly had taken some of them captive already, and she didn't even have a gun.

"Well, we couldn't do anything until your camp had cleared out and all the Rebs were far enough away that we wouldn't be heard. Seems your show is quite popular among all these Johnny Rebs."

"Yes, well. That, after all, has been the true measure of its value. Isn't that so, Captain?"

In the midst of all the confusion, several soldiers had dismantled the stage and put it away beneath the wagon, while a couple of others had retrieved Husslebuster's two big draft horses and were harnessing them to the wagon. Someone even checked to make sure the faro table was properly stored, something Wolf found surprisingly annoying, under the circumstances. That these Yankees knew what they were doing was more than obvious.

Turning to a subordinate officer, the captain said, "Lieutenant, get these men shackled, and let's move out of here before it starts getting light."

As the Confederate captives were being shackled together, Husslebuster turned toward Wolf. "Oh, by the way, Captain Allen, there's someone here I think you'll want to meet, and he should not be chained to the others." Pointing to Wolf, his pudgy finger a nasty little weapon and his tone accusatory, he continued, "He's not like these others. I want you to meet Major Wolf Striker, a genuine Confederate officer, not mere trash from across the river, Captain. Treat him gently, however. He's a man of some quality."

"*Et tu, Brute?*" Wolf queried, nodding at Husslebuster. Oddly, he should have wanted to kill the chubby little imposter, but somehow he felt no animosity, just disappointment. The world had just ended—Wolf Striker's world—and somehow recriminations, however well-deserved, seemed woefully out of place.

CHAPTER 13

★ ★ ★

N O SOONER HAD CLAY and Ellen stumbled out onto the loading platform, rudely prodded by one of their captors, than the doors of Hades seemed to violently burst open and let slip the dogs of war. Shells began exploding along the outer perimeter of the switching yard, each shattering impact closer to the train station than the last. Nearby a large storage shed blew apart with such force that not a piece was left to flutter back to the powder-blackened earth, and windows were blown out along one side of the train station. And as if the shelling were not enough to send the town's Yankee occupiers into a mass of frenzied confusion, the shrill, distant Rebel cry of rage added an unnerving element to the chaos.

"Oh, damnation," the man behind Clay said, giving him a shove, "here they come. Get moving, you two."

Looking over his shoulder, Clay snarled, "Once more like that, soldier, and you won't have to wait for those Rebs."

"Jest you keep moving down these here tracks," the soldier hollered over the noise and confusion, pushing Clay once more, "and get yourselves into that parlor car over yonder."

The soldier's rude shove, along with the jarring concussion from another nearby exploding shell, caused Clay to stumble into Ellen, knocking the nearly exhausted woman off balance, and with the weight of all her petticoats, her legs failed her. "Oh, Braxton—" she cried, as she lost balance and tumbled across the tracks, "I can't—" Clay reacted too slowly to prevent her fall, and she sprawled headfirst into the oily grime of the rail bed, striking her head on a rail. Struggling to push herself up, she groaned softly and slumped back into the filth, her strength gone, apparently unconscious.

With Ellen lying motionless on the filthy ties, her face and hands scraped, her clothes stained with oil, Clay turned on the Union soldier and shoved him away. "One step nearer, mister," he said, his voice calm, but his tone leaving no doubt as to the reality of the threat, "and I'll kill you with my bare hands, Union soldier or not."

Struggling to gather the dazed woman in his arms, Clay glanced up at the rattled soldier. "Get up there and open that car door," he ordered, "then get back down here and give me a hand."

"But . . . I was—"

"Do what I tell you, soldier!" Clay barked. "That's an order! And help me get her up into that car and settled."

With the sound of small-arms fire coming from somewhere near the center of the town and shells still exploding around the train station, the two struggled to get the unconscious woman up the iron steps and into the parlor car. Gently laying Ellen on one of the heavily cushioned double seats of the once comfortable rail coach, and carefully arranging her soiled clothes, Clay turned to his now cooperative guard, and demanded, "Where's the engineer? Is the steam up on this thing? Your Colonel Woods talked as if this train were ready to pull out."

"Mister, I—"

"*Colonel* to you, solder," Clay countered, pushing past the bewildered young soldier. "Now, let's you and I go see if we can get this train moving, and do it before that fight out there puts a stop to what needs to be done here."

Leaving the car, the two hurried along the side of the train. When they reached the engine, Clay climbed into the empty cab, and while wildly looking at all of the gauges, valves, and levers, hollered back down to the soldier, "The steam seems to be up, all right. You know how to run one of these things?"

"No, sir, I surely don't. I'm guessin'—"

"Hey, you two down there! Whadda yuh think your doin'?"

"Where'd that come from?" Clay asked, looking around.

"Must be the engineer," the soldier guessed. "Wait a second, Colonel, there's somebody up there on that water tower. Why, man, he's gonna be lucky if he don't get hisself killed up there, what with all the fightin' goin' on, an' all."

"Just don't you touch nothin' down there, young fella," the man warned from his perch above the tender. "You hear what I'm tellin' yuh? I'm comin' down there right now—soon as I tie this thing off. Just don't you touch nothin'."

The engineer appeared to be a man in his fifties, and from the looks of him, it was obvious he was in no mood to brook any nonsense where his engine was concerned. "You trying t' get us all killed, foolin' around with something as powerful as this here engine?" he demanded, as he carefully descended from the water tower and onto the engine's tender. "A steam engine is somethin' you don't fool with, young fella. Not unless you got the knowhow, and it don't look to me like as if you do. Neither of yuh, for that matter. Now, whadda yuh want?"

"I'm sorry, but you've got to get myself and another passenger to Knoxville as quickly as possible."

"Oh, I do, do I? And just who the devil are you?"

Clay watched the engineer for a moment, wondering just how to pacify the man and not further offend his obviously proprietary feelings where this belching iron beast was concerned. "Sorry, I didn't mean any harm. Just one look, and it obviously takes someone with a lot more technical knowledge than I have to operate a machine as complicated as this."

Keeping a wary eye on Clay, the engineer climbed down into the cab. "Well, young fella, at least yuh understand that much."

"I do, indeed, and I apologize. Let me explain. I'm a Union officer. Colonel Clay Ashworth's the name," Clay said, extending his hand, "and I'm on a highly confidential mission for the president, and—"

The engineer hesitantly accepted Clay's hand and, with a perfunctory squeeze let it go. "What president, young fella?" he asked, obviously unmoved by Clay's attempt to impress him.

"Mister Lincoln."

The man's tone immediately changed. "Oh, well, yuh shoulda said so t' start with."

"Yes, well, as I was saying, it's absolutely imperative that I get to Vicksburg as quickly as possible."

"Vicksburg?" the engineer snorted. "Ain't likely, son. For a colonel, what kind of greenhorn are yuh, anyway? That place is right in the middle of the dang-blastedist shootin' war you'll likely ever see."

"But I've got to—"

"Don't matter what you *got* t' do, young fella. Closest you're likely to get to Vicksburg is Memphis, and it ain't at all likely you can get even that far."

"Well, one way or the other, I can't get to either place without going through Knoxville, so I'd surely appreciate it if we could get this thing rolling. If you haven't noticed, we're in the middle of a small *shootin' war,* as you put it, right here. And if we don't soon get out of here, we never will."

The man studied Clay's face for a long moment, then said, "Okay, young fella. You gonna ride up here with me? If, so," he said, twisting a worrisome-looking handle, then pulling one lever, his other hand grasping another, "we'll get goin' right now."

"I've got a passenger with me, and I don't want any harm coming to her. I'll be back in the parlor car, where I can look out for her. But I need you to keep this train rolling, and don't stop for anything unless you absolutely have no other choice."

"That's generally how I do things, young fella, 'less there's reason t' do otherwise."

As Clay swung down from the cab, white jets of steam shot out from beneath the engine and with black clouds of smoke ferociously blasting from its stack, the huge iron beast awakened from its slumber. The engine's four big drive wheels fought for traction on the worn rails, and with metal loudly slipping on metal, the big drivers suddenly gained the purchase needed. The engine jerked forward and with its trailing cars and their fistlike couplings banging and clanking in complaint, the train lurched into reluctant movement. By the time Clay reached the parlor car, the train was pulling ahead slowly, and he scrambled up onto the rear platform.

Entering the car, Clay was surprised to see Ellen sitting up, gazing out through the window.

Settling next to her, he asked, "You all right, Missus Striker?"

For a moment Ellen seemed to remain focused on something outside of the car as the scenery began moving past her window, slowly at first, then at an increasing rate of speed. "Ellen?"

As Ellen finally turned toward him, neither the oil and dirt smeared across her face and clotted in her hair, nor the evening dusk, could hide the nasty abrasion and the large bruise on her forehead. Even worse, no amount of rail-bed grime could hide the resentment that darkened her lovely features as she scrutinized his face, her eyes at last locking on his, as if she were looking for something she hoped might still be found there.

"Are you feeling alright, Ellen?" Clay said, sensing the jig was up.

Her mood had changed—abruptly so. Gone was the congenial attitude, the comradery and sense of shared adventure that had brought them increasingly together over the past several days. Most of all, the amusement that had constantly lurked behind her large, green eyes, even in the most trying circumstances, was gone.

It was over, and he knew it. Either she had overheard what went on between him and the Union guard as they struggled to get her and all her petticoats into the coach, or she had seen or heard some of the goings-on at the front of the train. "You took a nasty spill, Ellen, hitting your head on the track the way you did," Clay said, hoping to soften her mood. "You've had me worried."

"Mister Mallory," she at last said, taking a deep breath, "somehow I was under the impression that we—the both of us, that is—were prisoners. Could I have been wrong all this time? Or am I the only prisoner on this train?"

The exhaustion he had fought for so long suddenly flooded his body, and without any energy left, Clay turned away. Sliding deeper down into the seat, his elbow on the armrest and his chin in the palm of his hand, he searched for some plausible explanation, some way to help her understand. How could he justify his having deceived her? More importantly, how could he make her understand what she had come to mean to him over the past few days and just how vital her help had been to his mission and to both of their futures?

"Ellen, I—"

"I suspected as much," she said, her voice flat, her tone dismissive. "I have had my doubts about you, Mister Mallory. Too many things have looked just too coincidental. But today, the way you seem to have commandeered this train, even your attitude toward those Yankee soldiers back at the station. Well, sir, for this poor southern girl, just too many things have failed to add up."

Turning to her, Clay said, "How long have you been awake?"

"Long enough."

"Ellen, I—"

"Please, don't say anything, Mister Mallory," she said, turning toward the window, attempting to hide the tears that were beginning to spill onto her cheeks. "That is your name, isn't it, Mister Mallory? I really don't know what you could possibly say that would make any difference. Not now."

Clay didn't know either, but he knew it was essential to find some way to mollify her, to keep her from betraying him the first chance she got. Yet it was more than that. Her support went far beyond merely insuring his safety. Having her with him, having her support, her goodwill, had become important to him. And when all was said and done, which of them was the guilty party where *betrayal* was concerned?

Ellen Striker was a woman for whom it was easy to develop a true affection. She was nothing like Consuelo, not in looks or personality, and no one could ever take Connie's place, not in this life or the next. Nevertheless, Ellen Striker had grown on him, and the more he had watched her and thought about her over the past few days, the more determined he had become to protect her and, if possible, somehow see her reunited with her husband, Wolf Striker.

The woman had been of enormous help in his making it this far across hostile Confederate territory, saving his hide on more than one occasion, even if she wasn't aware of it. But beyond that, her presence had given his mission new life. The truth is she had given his *existence* added meaning, a kind of renewal that went beyond the raging battle they were rushing toward, even beyond the exigencies of the war itself.

His orders were important, and he would do his duty, come what may; but Ellen Striker, with all her southern charm and wit, had awakened in him a renewed sense of what was most important in life.

The more she had shared with him, the more he had come to know her, the more he had come to see in her a reflection of himself: the loneliness of abandonment, of having had taken from you that which was most precious—the emptiness of love lost. He and Ellen just had too much in common to allow things to come apart at this juncture.

If Wolf Striker was still alive—and he had been very much alive just a few short months past—he and Ellen had to be reunited. Striker had to be brought face to face with his wife, and near as Clay could determine, neither Wolf nor Ellen could have any peace until that happened.

Ellen deserved that much, whether Wolf did or not. She deserved the right to confront the rascal and hold him to account. And the longer Clay had been with her, the more determined he had become to do whatever was necessary to bring that about. That meant doing whatever was necessary to keep her with him, and to get them both somewhere near Vicksburg. Like the man said, Vicksburg is the key—to more things than just the Union cause. There was a kind of personal Confederate cause here, as well.

Noise filled the dark car as the train suddenly jolted, jerking Clay back to the present. How long he had been lost in his thoughts, he was unsure. Exhausted as he was, he may have even dozed. Looking past Ellen's dark form, he could see nothing outside the car. Night had fallen, and the swaying of the coach had probably put her to sleep as well.

The train rattled through the darkness for some time before Clay felt Ellen turn toward him. "Really, Mister Mallory," she said at last, "you are a most persuasive liar." Her tone was not scolding or even critical. In fact, she sounded much like her old self. "Mister Mallory?"

Not knowing what to say, not trusting her mood, and unable to see her features clearly, Clay sat silent, feeling like a kid caught telling stories out of school.

"Mister Mallory?"

"You know, I thought we'd never get out of there," he at last observed, not knowing what else to say. "Those Yankees are an obstinate bunch."

"Oh, stop it, Mister Mallory," she chuckled. "You are such a rogue. You remind me so much of my late husband, it's absolutely painful."

Turning toward Ellen in an effort to see her expression, Clay took a deep breath and plunged into it. "I think you just paid me a compliment, Missus Striker. But you see, I know your husband and, believe it or not, I'm not really sure how I should take it."

Ellen's hand flew to her mouth. "Really, Mister Mallory," she exclaimed, "don't you think that's going a bit too far? Along with all of your other lies and misdeeds, I mean. If that was meant to be funny," she huffed, "I'm not the least bit amused."

"No, ma'am. I'm not trying to be funny. The truth is, I do know Wolf, and as of March last year, he was very much alive."

"Wolf?" Ellen whispered. "You mean, my Wolf? Wolf Striker is alive?"

"When last I saw him."

"Well, that's just impossible." It was the old Ellen, positive and self-assured.

"Oh, no, Missus Striker. Believe me, I know whereof I speak."

"How on earth could you have known my husband?" she demanded, anger beginning to tint her words. "And if what you say is true, why haven't you told me this earlier?"

"Just last year, your husband and I were shooting at each other. Wolf Striker was—*is*, I should say—a Confederate major. We were both locked in a nasty battle out in the New Mexico Territory. The last I saw of him was at the battle of Glorieta Pass."

"You're really serious, aren't you?" Ellen said, her voice again filling with emotion, tears beginning to brim in her eyes. "You mean, he's actually alive?"

"Yes, ma'am."

"But, why—"

"Why haven't I told you before?"

"It would have been the decent thing to do," she declared.

"I guess the time wasn't right and, frankly, I wasn't sure it was my place to—"

"Your place?" Ellen cried, cutting him short. "Well, you should have, you know. But in all of these years," she sniffled, "all of these wasted years, why hasn't he—"

"I couldn't say, ma'am. You see, I never really spoke with him. I just . . . shot at him, actually."

"*Shot at him,*" Ellen gasped. "You mean you actually *shot* at my husband? You didn't kill him, did you?"

"No, ma'am, but a very determined Utah marshal put some lead into him, out there at Johnson's Ranch. I saw it happen, but I'm fairly certain he wasn't killed."

"Johnson's Ranch? I thought you said—"

"I did. You see, Johnson's Ranch was the Confederate supply station and staging area. It was located at the west end of the canyon, and Wolf was in the process of trying to organize some sort of defense when we overwhelmed the place."

"But you're confident he's not dead?"

"It's hard to say for certain, Ellen. He was hurt; that much was obvious. But I'd stake my life on the fact that he wasn't killed."

"Well, you may have just done that, Mister Mallory, or whatever your name is."

"Done what, ma'am?"

"Staked your life on what you've just told me. I had become very determined to point an accusing finger at you when we next encountered some Confederate soldiers."

"I sensed that, Missus Striker. I truly did."

"Very well then," Ellen said, determination adding starch to her words. "If you expect me to lie for you and to further debase myself by helping you—a cussed Yankee—to do who knows what, you must swear to help me find my husband. Is that perfectly understood, Mister Mallory?"

"Perfectly," Clay said, struggling to hide a grin he knew would only serve to irritate her.

"Oh, if I ever get my hands on that man, I swear, I'll kill him myself."

"If you stick with me, Missus Mallory, and help me get to Vicksburg, I'll do everything in my power to help you find him—

at whatever cost. But knowing him as I do, I don't think he'll be that easy to kill. At least, he hasn't been in the past."

"Mmm," she hummed, still absorbing all she had just heard. "Well, if what you say is true, Mister Mallory, when I get through with him, he may very well wish he had been killed back at . . . oh, you know . . . at that place."

"Johnson's Ranch."

"Yes—or wherever."

"Why don't you call me Braxton?"

It was the unearthly squeal of iron wheels assaulting their ears, sounding at first as if the train were just rounding a sharp curve in the track, that began to awaken them. But it was the cars banging together as the train noisily jolted to a stop that brought both Clay and Ellen fully awake.

The train had come to a stop in what appeared to be a large pasture. Leaning across Ellen to peer out through the coach window, Clay could make out several cows grazing close to the tracks, but little else. The early morning sunlight slanting across the grimy glass obscured nearly everything.

As the train noisily shuddered to a stop, voices could be heard over the sound of escaping steam somewhere outside their coach. Before either Clay or Ellen could react, the door burst open as several Confederate soldiers pushed into the car, led by a colonel sporting a large red feather that fluttered from the band of his cavalry slouch hat. It was only then that Clay heard horses stomping and blowing outside in the early morning cold.

The officer looked haggard and tired, his uniform worn and dirty, and as he made his way down the aisle, he brought with him the smell of cavalry, of hard-ridden horses and jaded, war-weary men, odors with which Clay was not unfamiliar. And from the looks of things, the Confederate officer was in no mood for anything he would consider foolish.

"My apologies for interrupting your travels, but—Why, as I live and breathe, it's Ellen Striker. Why Ellen, darlin', you are positively the last person I expected to see when we stopped this train."

"Oh, my gracious," Ellen gasped, her hand flying to her mouth in genuine surprise and delight. "James Earl? Is it really you? Why, I declare," she said, sitting forward in her seat, her southern accent becoming more pronounced with each word, "James Earl Parkhill, you are the handsomest thing in that uniform I believe I have ever seen, and the last man on earth I would have ever expected to see walk through that door."

It was the old Ellen, yet Clay felt little comfort in what he was hearing, knowing the big test was suddenly upon them. There had been no time to prepare, to get their stories straight, and he was certain Ellen was completely taken back by the appearance of an apparently close relative, one to whom she would have to lie if she were to keep her word and maintain their bond.

If Ellen was really determined to find her husband, the effort had just become far more complicated. Lying to strangers was one thing, but to look into the face of someone she knew, maybe even someone close, was something else altogether.

One way or the other, Clay knew his life was now entirely in Ellen Parkhill Striker's hands. As if that were not enough, judging from the man's name and behavior, the two were not only related, they apparently shared a good deal of familial affection. One word from her, and Clay knew his bacon would be cooked. He would be taken out and summarily shot as a Union spy.

Turning his attention to Clay, Parkhill said, "And who is this gentleman, might I inquire?"

Extending his hand, Clay attempted to rise, but the cavalry officer stood too close to their bench and did not offer to move. Settling back, Clay said, "My apologies, Colonel. My name is Braxton Mallory, and I'm most pleased to make your acquaintance, sir."

"Indeed?" Parkhill responded, his manner affable but unyielding. "And what exactly is your business here, Mister Mallory? And sitting next to this lovely woman, as well?"

"Oh, James Earl," Ellen said, catching herself, "it is I who should apologize. I have been so delighted at seeing you that I have simply forgotten my manners. Why my dear mother must be turning over in her grave at this very moment.

"Mister Mallory here is from Alabama—Huntsville, I believe. And being the gentleman I have found him to be, he has been kind enough to escort me to Vicksburg, or as close to home as possible, inasmuch as he is attempting to get there himself. Isn't that right, Mister Mallory?"

"How very interesting," Parkhill said, his eyes locked on Clay's, his tone noncommittal. "And how is it, suh, that you are in a position to make so noble a gesture in the middle of so nasty a war?"

Clay could feel Ellen's eyes boring into the side of his head. From their brief acquaintance, she did not seem to be an altogether forgiving woman, as Wolf might just discover at some point in the future. From everything she had said since their first meeting, Ellen Striker had shown herself to be a loyal southerner. And now, with the arrival of these Confederate fellow travelers, she was once again fairly overflowing with feminine pulchritude. How she was going to react when push came to shove was anybody's guess, and Clay knew his next few words would undoubtedly determine whether he lived or died. Ellen's veracity as a southern sympathizer was on the line. One way or the other, it was going to get very difficult for her.

If the situation was difficult for Ellen, it was even more so for him. Never before had Clay Ashworth allowed himself to be so helplessly caught in such a dangerous a situation. Living a lifestyle as close to self-sufficient as possible, independent in all his actions, how and when he died had previously always been his choice. But now, with his life in the balance, he was totally dependent on the woman seated next to him—a dangerously *Southern* woman, a woman who's feelings seemed always to run close to the surface. Unarmed and surrounded, one wrong move on his part, or one wrong word on hers, would cost him his life.

"Suh?"

"Ah . . . could you and I step outside, Colonel?"

"I think not. We're all loyal southerners here," he said, glancing at Ellen. "Are we not, Mister Mallory?"

"Well, you see, the truth is, Colonel, I'm afraid I have been taking unfair advantage of Missus Striker."

"Braxton?" Ellen gasped, grasping Clay's arm, unsure of what he was saying.

"Really, suh? How very interesting."

"You see, Colonel, I'm on an undercover mission for the president—traveling incognito, as it were, to Vicksburg."

Parkhill stiffened. "What president, suh?"

"Why, President Jefferson Davis, sir. Of course."

Clay felt Ellen stiffen and turn toward the window.

"Somethin' wrong, Ellen darlin'?" Parkhill said, watching his cousin closely.

"Not really, James Earl. I've just been taken quite by surprise, is all. I had no idea—"

"I'm genuinely sorry, Ellen," Clay said softly, turning toward her, his words filled with double meaning.

"Oh," she sniffled, turning and smiling up at Parkhill as she dabbed at her eyes, a moist delicately embroidered hankie in her hand, "it's just this truly dreadful war. In the end, it makes liars of us all."

Parkhill watched her for a moment. "It does indeed, dear cousin. We have to be very cautious about such as that. These are hard times, and they frequently require hard men to make hard decisions."

Scratching his chin, Parkhill turned to Clay. "Isn't that so, Mister Mallory?"

A clean-shaven man, Parkhill's chin always itched when he allowed several days to go by without shaving. But that itch was also a nervous reaction when he became bothered and ill at ease in a situation he felt was just beyond his understanding or control.

"It's an unfortunate fact, Colonel," Clay said, assuming an attitude of mild moral indignity, "that reaches out and touches us all at one time or another. In fact, there are few evils which war does not allow, even encourage."

"Indeed," Parkhill said, his hand returning to the stubble on his chin. "Now, if the two of you will just step out of the car, we'll continue our conversation while my men make ready for us to move on."

"Leave the train?"

"Indeed, Mister Mallory. You must allow us to escort you. You see, there's a bridge out just around the next bend. In fact, several have been burned recently. If you're goin' to get to Memphis—"

"Memphis?" Clay repeated, trying to hide the alarm in his

voice as they followed the colonel from the car. "But the Yankees—"

"Indeed, Memphis. And, yes, the Yankees are in control of much of that area."

"But we must get to Vicksburg."

"I'm afraid, suh, that will soon prove to be impossible. It appears the Yankees are about to lay siege to Vicksburg. In fact, they all but control the entire Mississippi River valley, swarming around Vicksburg like ants on a carcass, I'm sorry to say."

"But how far can you—"

"I think I can guarantee your safety until we get to the other side of Knoxville. It's only a short distance, really. Then perhaps you can secure a train as far as Chattanooga. From there on, you'll just have to make your way as carefully as possible."

"But between Chattanooga and Memphis?"

"It's anyone's guess, Mister Mallory. The question, therefore, arises as to why you need to undertake such profound risks, Missus Striker's presence aside?"

Sitting on the iron steps of the passenger car, Clay tugged off his left boot and reaching inside, withdrew an envelope. Opening the envelope, he handed two pieces of paper to Parkhill. "Here are my orders, Colonel."

Parkhill studied the document and its accompanying map for a moment, then returning them to Clay said, "Yes, I see, Colonel. Well, we shall do all we can to escort you as near to Memphis as possible."

"I'll be most grateful, Colonel," Clay said, folding the papers and returning them to their hiding place.

"There are a number of cavalry troops operating between here and Memphis—Bedford Forrest, Van Dorn, and Morgan. We'll see that you get as close as possible."

"And what about me, James Earl?" Ellen said, her nose in the air. "I am just as determined as Mister Mallory to reach Memphis, since Vicksburg is no longer a possibility."

"Cousin Ellen, what possible—"

"James Earl, it's very personal, and very important, and you are not in a position to stop me."

"This is war, my dear. I am in a position to do many unpleasant things, under the circumstances."

"Nonetheless, James Earl, as a southern gentleman, and an officer of the Confederacy, you'll—"

"Yes, yes. If you're not to be dissuaded, and since Mister Mallory has taken it upon himself to watch over you, perhaps the other side of Chattanooga or Stevenson, Alabama, the M&C line will still be running. That will expedite your mission considerably. Perhaps you both can travel with less hardship and danger— especially for my bullheaded, but delightful, cousin."

CHAPTER 14

★ ★ ★

Clay came suddenly awake. He had heard something, or at least he thought he had. The fires had long since burned low, leaving the camp dark and cold. Carefully sitting up, trying to avoid any kind of sudden movement or sound that would warn some intruder of his awareness, Clay scanned his surroundings. Nothing moved, but he was certain something had awakened him. It may have been the horses, disturbed by a marauding animal nearby or some small creature scurrying around their hooves. But those were precisely the kinds of noises that seldom disturbed his sleep, sounds common to the night in a wild, unsettled place.

For the first week, he and Ellen had stayed with Colonel Parkhill's Confederate cavalry, a culled-down company of some thirty or so men, all seasoned soldiers. They had circled around Knoxville, wide to the north, then cut southwest, careful to avoid any towns or settlements where they might have attracted attention or run into any Yankee cavalry patrols.

Somewhere in the hill country north of Chattanooga, they had rendezvoused with a much smaller Rebel cavalry patrol of a dozen men, and Parkhill had turned Clay and Ellen over to their care. Led by a mean-looking ruffian whose name Clay never learned (the man simply went by the title of *Captain*) and despite Parkhill's assurances to the contrary, he had neither the appearance nor the manner of a Confederate officer.

They had stayed with the captain's patrol for more than a week, taking advantage of the terrain, traveling mostly at night, and hiding out by day. It had been a miserable time, with frequent rain squalls driven by a cold, almost constant, wind out of the northwest.

Making every effort to avoid any contact with Union forces, they frequently had camped with no fire, eating cold food and sleeping under damp blankets. Even so, despite the conditions, they had made good time and were now camped just west of Stevenson, Alabama, not far from the Memphis and Charleston Railroad right of way, the major supply route connecting Chattanooga and Memphis.

At the start, twelve men were riding with the captain, and it was more than obvious that they rode in fear of him. He ruled the gang with a meanness that at times to Clay seemed to border on the irrational. If a man so much as questioned an order by word or glance, the captain's reaction was often swift and vicious.

As the days passed, Clay watched the captain and his men carefully, his hand never far from his gun. Though Ellen had never said anything, sensing her fear, Clay had always kept her close to him, and because of the constant tension, neither of them slept well.

Night after night, the bunch had crawled under their blankets drunk, never loud or boisterous, just sullen. Only the captain remained sober, seemingly oblivious to the hostile moods of his men, his eyes always following Ellen.

Late one night things finally came to a head. Over Clay's objections, the captain had been determined to raid a small, isolated farm for fresh horses, supplies, and whatever else their murderous ways might net them. Bored with their lack of action, the men were nearly delirious with the prospects, and the captain had argued that an army in the field had to forage for its own supplies.

To put a stop to their plans, Clay had pulled both his rank and his gun on the captain. The argument was both brief and violent. When it ended, two of the thugs lay dead on the ground, and the captain found himself looking into eternity, straight down the barrel of Clay's Colt .44, the hammer cocked, and the look on Clay's face leaving no room for further argument.

For the captain, Clay's .44-caliber logic had been flawless. Not wanting to gamble on his fate, the man had backed down, agreeing to see them to a place a few miles farther on, where come morning they could stop a train headed for Memphis.

The captain's disagreeable attitude aside, from Clay's point of view, it was a reasonable solution. With him and Ellen gone, the gang would be free to wreak whatever havoc they wanted, no longer jeopardizing Clay's important mission, nor a southern lady's safety and honor. The captain saw the reason behind Clay's proposal.

Twenty miles or so to the west of their tiny camp lay Decatur, beyond that Corinth, Mississippi, and then Grand Junction, a major rail interchange and Yankee hotbed. Farther to the west, beyond Grand Junction, lay the major river port of Memphis and the Mississippi River.

Now in the dark, the ground beneath Clay's blanket was hard and cold, and something had moved not far from Ellen's bed. He had not slept well—too many nights of not allowing himself to relax, let alone sleep. His senses alert, Clay quietly slipped his big horse pistol from the saddle holster near his head, his eyes searching the darkness for Ellen.

There was nothing to see, only the vague outline of Ellen's blanket. The night before, he had given her his extra blanket, hoping the added warmth would enable her to sleep more comfortably. Thankfully, no movement was apparent. If she remained still, she would be fairly safe if and when the shooting started.

In the darkness near her feet he saw it again, and the black outline of a man blotted out the few stars that shone dimly through broken clouds and the trees. It was the captain.

"Make one move to touch her, and I'll kill you."

"Jest checkin' is all. She's a handsome woman. What's she t' you, anyway?"

"A friend. Now back away, or you and I'll part company right here and now."

"Oh, that's how it is, huh?"

"She's married."

"Married?"

"To a friend of mine, and you don't want to make any more mistakes like that one. You ever heard of Wolf Striker?"

Even in the predawn blackness, the man's reaction was almost palpable. "You mean, *Wolfgang Striker?*"

"Yeah, that's right. Couldn't be more than one like him, huh?"

"That's how come y'all are goin' t' Vicksburg? She's his woman?"

"She's his *wife.* Try to keep that distinction straight in your mind. It'll prove more healthy for you that way."

"Yeah, well, he ain't there. Fact is, he ain't been seen in a long time, not in these parts anyway. Rumor is he's dead."

"Uh-huh. Well, like most rumors, your rumor is wrong. In fact, we're on our way to meet him."

As the captain began to back away, receding into the predawn blackness, Clay demanded, "Stay put. Right where you are."

"I ain't goin' nowheres, Colonel."

"Ellen?"

"I'm awake, Braxton."

"Pull your boots on, Missus Striker. We need to get moving. It's time we parted company with this outfit."

By the time they reached the rail line shortly after sunup, nerves were stretched to the breaking point. In a sense, it had been a bit comical. Clay and Ellen had ridden behind the gang, where Clay, his big horse pistol drawn and his rifle lying across his pommel, could watch the entire bunch. And for most of the way, the captain and his thugs had ridden half twisted in the saddle, not trusting this strange Confederate colonel and watching him closely. There had already been one fallout with him. The big man was just plain dangerous and not to be trusted.

Urging her horse to the edge of the rail bed, Ellen stood in her stirrups and listened for a moment. "Braxton, I think I hear the train. Wasn't that the whistle?"

"Yes," Clay said, motioning for her to move away from the track. "It'll be around that bend at the bottom of the grade any minute now."

"By the time he gets up here," the captain offered, watching the woman as she reined her horse around next to Clay, "he'll be goin' pretty slow. We can stop 'im easy, if he's not of a mind t' cooperate."

"I don't want any shooting, whether that engineer stops the train or not."

"That'll be up t' him, won't it?"

"No," Clay snapped, his manner abrupt. "The train will be going slow enough that one of your men can easily board the engine and bring it to a stop. I don't want anyone hurt. Understand?"

As the engine, its four cars in tow, rounded the bend and began its laborious climb up the steep grade, huge clouds of black smoke and embers belching from its large, bulbous stack, several members of the gang rode up onto the rail bed and dismounted, waving their arms in the air.

With steam hissing and metal grinding and clanking against metal, the huge iron beast lumbered slowly to the top of the hill and shuddered to a noisy stop. Reaching for her horse's reins, unnoticed in the confusion of the train's clamorous arrival, Clay reined about and led Ellen a few yards back from the track and into the cover of a small copse of trees.

For a moment nothing happened. Then suddenly, three shrill blasts of the whistle filled the air as jets of scalding steam shot from beneath the engine, spooking the horses, those nearest the engine bolting in fear and throwing their startled, cursing riders. In the general pandemonium that quickly followed, those few men who managed to stay in the saddle were forced to struggle with bringing their own mounts under control, while attempting to keep the riderless horses from running off.

In the middle of all this turmoil, the double doors in the side of the boxcar just behind the engine's tender were rolled back, and in turn, what looked like a full platoon of mounted Union cavalry jumped from the car to the roadbed. Their shouts and pistol shots adding to the bedlam, they quickly encircled the startled and disorganized Rebel cavalry. Before the dust had begun to settle, the captain and his men were on their knees in the dirt, their hands behind their heads.

Ben Kimball rode forward and dismounted. Walking to the kneeling captain, he demanded, "What have you done with Colonel Ashworth?"

"Who?" the startled Rebel leader said, the look of total ignorance on his face completely convincing, as he gaped at his captors.

"Don't play dumb with us, mister," Major Duncan snapped, dismounting and pulling his revolver from its holster. "You're too near getting shot, as it is, Captain. Oh, yeah, we know who you are, and shooting you here and now would save us the bother of hanging you later. So, I'll ask you just one more time, where is Colonel Clay Ashworth?"

Clay could not keep from laughing, as he again took a bewildered Ellen Striker's reins, and the two rode up to the Union circle. "He's right here, gentlemen."

At the sound of Clay's voice, Ben Kimball turned, the grin on his face betraying his sense of relief. "I'd know that voice anywhere, Colonel."

As Clay and Ellen rode up, the tight circle of Union Cavalry parted, and Clay said, "And to tell you the truth, my friend, I was as shocked as these Rebel raiders to see you fellows pouring out of that boxcar. Though, I must confess, I suspected something might be afoot.

"Oh, and I am sorry," Clay said, with a chuckle of anticipation, "I didn't mean to be rude. Ben Kimball, Major Jonathan Duncan, and Yankee gentlemen, please meet Missus Wolfgang Striker, a genuine southern lady, and one for whose company I have been overwhelmingly grateful for many days now. Were it not for her cooperation, I could not have completed my mission, and in all likelihood I would not be here."

The look on Ben Kimball's face was hard to read as he

climbed back into his saddle. Reining about and leaning forward, as if he were trying to get a closer look at the beautiful woman mounted next to Clay, he cleared his throat, and said, "*Striker?* Clay, you don't mean—"

"Oh, I do, indeed, my friend," Clay laughed. "*The* Wolfgang Striker. The very one you and I have come to know so well and admire so much. And I have all but guaranteed her that you will help her find her husband—as a reward for helping me."

"Me?" Kimball exclaimed.

"Well . . . the two of us, actually," Clay grinned. "I wouldn't shoulder you with such an onerous responsibility, not without wanting to be of some help, at least."

Not fully understanding the levity these two were enjoying, apparently at her expense, Ellen huffed, "Well, I don't wish to be a burden to you two Yankees."

"See," Clay said. "Can you see a resemblance? The way she holds her head, the abrupt manner? Don't you wonder where she might have gotten it?"

"Well," Ellen declared, her color rising, "I should have—"

"Ma'am," Ben said, removing his hat, "I'm Ben Kimball, and I do apologize for myself—and our friend here. None of this is about you, ma'am. It's about us and your husband. The three of us have had a rather strained relationship, as you can imagine. But please rest assured that everything possible will be done to reunite you with your husband."

With all of the horses secured in a cattle car, the captain and his men carefully bound and under heavy guard in the boxcar, Clay and Ellen, along with Ben Kimball and their Union hosts boarded the large passenger car at the rear of the train.

By nightfall they had arrived in Memphis, having experienced no further delays. Upon arrival, the captain and his thugs were quickly and unceremoniously herded down to the river and locked up on the already crowded prison barge. And Clay and Ellen, in a more leisurely manner, were led to their respective rooms in the imposing Gayoso House Hotel, where each enjoyed a hot bath and clean clothes in anticipation of a sumptuous dinner in the hotel's elegant dining room.

All of this was to be at the expense of the United States government, an arrangement that left Ellen Striker far from comfortable. Regardless of her affection for Braxton, Yankees were, after all, Yankees; and in her heart, she remained a decidedly determined Confederate lady.

Ellen Striker could hardly remember when she last had enjoyed a leisurely soak in a steaming tub. The water was hot—almost too hot—the soap plentiful, and after washing her hair, she had nearly fallen asleep right there in the elegant, enameled tub.

After drying herself off and slipping into the robe that she found hanging on the back of the bathroom door, Ellen walked to the large window overlooking the Mississippi River and its teeming shoreline. The riverfront just below the hotel was lined with docks jammed almost side by side, many of them obviously temporary, and each with a steamboat of one kind or another moored to it. Those that did not have a steamboat, had barges tied to them, most being loaded with large, ominous-looking crates. Several barges had been loaded with large artillery pieces, each cannon with its caisson tucked backward beneath its barrel and tightly secured.

A much bigger barge had been tied farther up the shoreline than any of the others, drawn well up on the river's muddy bank and tied off on several large trees. It was nothing more than an oversized flatboat, but it appeared to be some kind of make-shift stockade. Around the edge of its sizable flat deck, a substantial-looking fence had been erected, and the boat was crammed with men.

Because Memphis was a Union stronghold and because a handful of Yankee soldiers appeared to be standing guard around the barge, the prisoners crammed on the flatboat were obviously Confederate soldiers, a fact that made Ellen Striker extremely uncomfortable.

It was just a guess, but Ellen presumed that was where the captain and his men had been taken, though she could not make them out from her vantage point. By the time she and Braxton—Colonel Clay Ashworth, rather—had left the train, the boxcar holding the Rebel raiders was empty, and no explanation had been offered as to their whereabouts—not that it mattered. From the moment the train stopped, the Yankees had been in control of everything, including her. It was just one more indication, but from all she had heard and seen, the southern cause was all but lost.

As depressing as the sight was, Ellen could not take her eyes from the prison barge, despite the fact she was late for her dinner appointment with Clay Ashworth—or whatever his name was—and his two Yankee cronies. Finally, heaving a sigh, and not wanting to become more depressed than she already was, Ellen started to turn away when something, or someone, on that crowded barge caught her eye.

Though the barge was too far away to clearly make out any of the men's features, one of the prisoners somehow seemed to stand out. He was at the rear of the boat, back where it stuck out into the river. The crowd was less pressing there, and the man kept pacing back and forth, like a big bear in a circus wagon. He even looked like a big bear. That's why the man had caught her eye; her husband also resembled a big bear. In fact, at certain intimate moments, Ellen had always called him her honey-bear.

Ellen's breath caught in her chest. From this distance, not only did that man down there look like a big bear, despite the fact she could not discern his facial features, he looked just like Wolf Striker, her honey-bear. There was something: the way he held himself, the way he walked as he paced back and forth, some combination of mannerisms—something.

She hadn't seen the big lummox in nearly twenty years, but Wolf Striker was the kind of man one did not easily forget—especially if you were his wife. Especially since she had waited all these years to get her hands on him.

Fuming anew over his never having attempted to contact her and not really caring how she looked, Ellen combed out her hair and hurriedly dressed, her mind a storm of vengeance. She could almost feel her claws growing. Yes, if that was Wolf down there, she would claw his eyes out. No, not good enough. Where could she get a gun? Maybe Clay Ashworth, or whatever his name is, would let her use his.

But wait, what was the best way to do this? Just walk up and shoot him? Wait until he walked off the boat and claw his eyes out? Use a sharp knife? A butter knife? A spoon? How? One way or the other, if that really was her honey-bear, he was going to pay his dues, and she would see that it was deliciously painful.

Closing the door to her room and sliding the key into the pocket of her dress, Ellen hurried toward the staircase, her agitated mind refusing to let go of all that had happened.

She knew there had been a court-martial held against Wolf, though for what she had never been told. But that was all. As far as she knew, he had not been imprisoned or shot. He had simply disappeared, and try as she might, neither the Army, nor anyone else, could tell her—or *would* tell her—where he was.

But at no time since his disappearance had she thought, even for one moment, that Wolf had been killed in Mexico. How she had known he was still alive she could not have said, but through the years she had remained adamant. It was one of the reasons she had never remarried, though she had had plenty of opportunities. And now, something deep down inside told her in no uncertain terms that big oaf down on that prison barge was her husband.

Well, he was back, and now it was her turn.

Reaching the fence at one side of the filthy barge, Wolf turned and started back to the other side, shoving two men out of his way. The prison barge was crowded to the point that a man hardly had room to move, and he was in no mood for niceties. The place smelled of unwashed bodies, open sewage, and many other delights that war imposed on otherwise civilized men. There was only one way to survive such circumstances and that was to give no man the edge. It was bully or be bullied, and fighting those old inner urges, Wolf had continually paced back and forth along the barge's fenced perimeter until his feet ached, feeling his situation fairly impossible.

Stopping, Wolf ran his hand along the rough-cut pine enclosure, estimating its height to be ten or twelve feet. It wasn't the first time he had studied the fence, but he couldn't help himself. The separate planks were not joined, some having gaps between them as wide as six or eight inches. Though substantial, the enclosure was so poorly thrown together that it was hard to fight the temptation to try to escape. In fact, it almost looked as if that's what his Yankee captors were inviting him to do.

Wolf grunted, searching for options. *Cussed slots are too narrow for a man to push through,* he thought, *and the fence is too high to climb.*

But that wasn't the worst part. There were guards everywhere. Even if a man managed to break some of the planks and force himself through or climb over the top, he would undoubtedly be shot before he hit the water. But there had to be a way. He had gotten out of worse places than this, and his time would come.

Turning, Wolf looked up toward the gigantic hotel that dominated the riverfront. There were people strolling along a walkway that apparently stretched the length of the dike between the hotel and the river. He watched as a few stopped to peer down into the open barge, gawking at him and the other prisoners, as if they were wild animals caged in a filthy pen.

He could even see a woman looking out of a window up on what looked to be the third floor of the hotel. At this distance he could not make out her features. Maybe it was his imagination, but the woman almost appeared to have singled him out, standing up there taking some kind of perverse pleasure in observing his misery. The fact that she just stood there watching irritated him, made him itch, in fact. If he, somehow, could ever get his hands on her, he might just forget the progress he had made in learning to control his temper.

Turning, Wolf again started to pace, but stopped, his eyes drawn back to that window. She was gone, and it was probably a good thing. The urge to make a hateful gesture in her direction had nearly overcome him. Still, her having been there was not an altogether unpleasant thing.

Damnation, he thought, his mood for some reason suddenly

moderating. *I wish she were still up there. She kind of looked . . . oh . . . I don't know, kind of pretty, her obvious rudeness aside.* For some reason, the woman's image would not leave his troubled mind, and Wolf's face softened. *She kind of reminded me of—*

The noise from a sudden commotion at the other end of the boat broke into Wolf's thoughts. Three Yankee guards had entered the enclosure, and one had climbed up onto the guard's platform at the front of the barge. "Is there a Wolf Striker among you southern gentlemen?" the man hollered, his tone sarcastic. "Wolf Striker! Come forward, and do it now!"

Sullenly, Wolf made his way to the front of the crowded barge, shoving men out of his way. Whatever this was about, maybe it would be the opportunity he was waiting for—a chance to escape.

The guard looked down from his perch, as Wolf approached the platform. "You Wolf Striker?" the man demanded.

"I am. *Major* Wolf Striker to you."

"You're comin' with us, *Major Wolf Striker*," the man said, his attitude mocking.

As Wolf struggled to stifle a suitable reply, one that only would have served to get him into even more trouble, one of the guards took him by the arm and shoved him toward the gate.

"The Commandant wants to see you, Reb. You can count yourself lucky, though."

"Really. And how's that?"

"You'll need t' get deloused and cleaned up before you can enter his office."

"Lucky me. What's this about, anyway?"

"How'm I supposed t' know?" the man said, giving Wolf a rude push down the gangplank to the muddy riverbank, where two more guards surrounded him. "Jest keep movin', Major Johnny Reb, or you'll be in no shape to see the big man or nobody else. Besides, chances are you're gonna hang—or maybe somethin' even worse."

★   ★   ★

Clay watched Ellen Striker glide down the hotel's sweeping staircase, a picture of Old South, antebellum elegance. She was truly a compelling woman, brimming with aristocratic beauty and grace. And on more than one occasion since meeting her, he had thought that, were the two of them not married, she would be a hard woman to ignore. But he was very much married, and that was another story, a problem that yet remained to be resolved, as one day it would be.

"Ellen, you are a vision," Clay said, his admiration genuine and more than apparent. "As tired as you must be, there isn't a woman in this hotel who could stand next to you without wanting to run and hide, and you'll have the eye of any man lucky enough to be near you."

"More Yankee lies, Colonel Ashworth?" she cooed, her deep southern accent growing more syrupy with each word. "That is your name this evenin', isn't it, Braxton, honey?"

"Now, Missus Striker, please, it's—"

"I know, I know," she said, taking his arm. "You needn't say it, Colonel. It's the war. Oh, my, the sins we do cover with that awful phrase."

As Clay and Ellen approached their table, both Ben Kimball and Major Jonathan Duncan rose, each bumping into the other hurrying to hold her chair.

"Gentlemen, please," she cooed demurely. "You both are most gallant, but a little decorum would be nice, too—under the circumstances, that is. After all, I am your prisoner, am I not?"

Young Major Jonathan Duncan was truly smitten. "No, ma'am," he gushed, "you're surely not. But I almost wish you were."

"Why, Major," she purred. "Oh, I am truly sorry, do tell me your name again, Major."

"Jonathan, ma'am. Jonathan Duncan, ma'am—at your service."

"My, such gallant words, young Major Jonathan Duncan."

With growing amusement, Clay watched the exchange between the mature southern beauty and the young, almost breathless Union officer. He shook his head. It was absolutely amazing how Ellen could so quickly dominate a situation, especially among men. Not only was Duncan smitten, she also had the undivided attention of Ben Kimball, though his reactions were somewhat more subdued.

Things quieted as the first course of their meal was served. Ellen, though elegant in her habits, was obviously starved, as were the men, and the food was delicious.

As the second course was being served, Ellen turned to Clay and, daintily dabbing her mouth with a large white linen napkin, said, "I must confess some sense of guilt eating all of this delicious food, and in such surroundings."

Unfortunately, Clay took the bait. "And why's that?"

"Well, after all, Colonel . . . it is Colonel, isn't it?"

Setting his fork aside, Clay watched her more closely. Knowing Ellen Striker as he did, things seemed to be taking a turn that called for caution. "Yes, ma'am, it is. And my real name is Clayborne Raynor Ashworth, Clay for short, as you very well know, Missus Striker."

"Oh, do let's forgo the formalities, Colonel," she said, absently buttering a roll. "You must continue calling me Ellen. It's just that, well, nowadays, it being wartime and all, things do have a nasty way of changing, almost without warning. Isn't that so, Colonel Clayborne Raynor Ashworth, Clay for short?"

"I'm sure you're about to make a point here?"

"Well . . . in such uncertain times, it's just that a lady must try to understand her surroundings and her circumstances as best she can. Don't y'all agree?"

"Well, Missus Striker, Ellen, let me hasten to assure you, you most certainly are not our prisoner. Quite the opposite, in fact."

"Really?" she cooed. "How nice."

"Indeed. In fact, you are free to go where and when you like. However this is a war zone, our present surroundings aside."

"Mmm," she hummed, taking a dainty sip of water. "Well, then, speaking of circumstances—who is a prisoner of whom, an' all—tell me all about that big ol' barge down below us on the riverbank, the one crammed full of Confederate gentlemen."

"Ma'am," Duncan broke in, "we were going to wait until after dinner to talk about that, ma'am."

"How thoughtful, but do let's talk about it now."

Clay took a drink of water and cleared his throat. "Wolf is on that prison barge, Ellen."

CHAPTER 15

★ ★ ★

I T HAD TAKEN THE BETTER part of an hour, but a freshly scrubbed Wolf Striker now sat in the empty waiting room of the Memphis Commandant's office wondering what to expect next. To add to his discomfort, since his arrival two very unfriendly armed guards had never taken their eyes from him.

This whole thing made no sense. Surely, if they were going to hang him, they'd have done it by now. The drop to the end of a taut rope is just as deadly for a dirty man as it is for one freshly bathed and shaved.

After being taken from the barge, he had been briskly escorted to a large, empty shower room where a Yankee supply sergeant had provided him with soap, a razor, and a cracked mirror. Upon emerging from the shower, and feeling like a new man, Wolf was handed a stack of clean clothing by the same sergeant, including new underwear, a clean shirt, and a pair of coarse, freshly laundered pants, the kind worn by civilian jailbirds.

Words could never describe how good a change of clean clothes can feel, though it angered him that he could not face whatever was about to befall him in uniform. By the time he was dressed, Wolf had begun to wonder if he was about to meet Lincoln himself.

He had not had a change of underclothes since he was taken captive at that traitorous Professor Husslebuster's camp. Even worse, he had not worn a clean uniform since the battle of Glorieta Pass, and he had worn it to rags. The clothes Husslebuster had provided him had all but fallen apart as he literally pealed them off in the shower room. Though given a fresh pair of socks, he was still wearing the same badly worn boots, the leather stiff and cracked, each sporting a hole in its sole. Yankee or Confederate, shoes or boots were at a premium. In this war, a man was lucky not to be running around barefoot, and many were doing just that.

Given the lateness of the hour, the otherwise busy waiting room was empty, but Wolf could hear voices through the door to the commander's office. It was clear that an argument had been going on, though in the last few minutes things seemed to have settled down. Twice he had asked his guards what it was all about, but each time he had received only hostile grunts.

Without warning the door to the post commander's office swung open, and a master sergeant he had not seen before motioned to him. "Step this way, Major Striker."

Wolf was not prepared for what he saw as he stepped into the inner office. Standing behind the commander's empty desk was Clay Ashworth, in the uniform of a Union full colonel. Ben Kimball sat next to the desk, and both men were grinning like Cheshire cats.

Hardly skipping a beat, Wolf said, "Where's Rockwell and his

265

rope? Your bushy-faced marshal friend would make this reunion almost complete."

Both men chuckled, and Clay declared, flatly, "Oh, knowing Porter Rockwell, he'll get his chance. But not quite yet."

Pushing a chair toward Wolf, Ben said, "Have a seat, Major. We've got some earnest haggling to do before this night is over."

"Haggling?" Wolf said, the shock of unexpectedly seeing two of his former antagonists slowly wearing off.

"That's right," Clay said, leaving the desk and sliding a chair around, where he would be face-to-face with Wolf, "and I don't think you'll find it altogether unpleasant."

"Not if you're of a mind to cooperate in your own best interests, that is," Ben asserted, the frown on his face threatening to break into a grin. Ben Kimball was not known for keeping a secret, not for any length of time, at least.

"Well, not so fast, Ben. Remember, we've had to deal before with this . . . this . . . let's see, what was it she called him?"

Ben scratched his chin. "Uh, lummox, Clay. I think the word was *lummox*."

"Lummox," Wolf repeated, half aloud, not quite sure he understood. Only one person on earth had ever dared call him that, and there was a time—a wonderful time—when she did it quite often.

"My word, Clay," Ben chided, "look at the man's face."

"Wolf, do you need a whiff of smelling salts or something stronger?"

"I think he's going to pass out, Clay," Ben chuckled.

"Lummox," Wolf whispered, more to himself than to his two would-be tormentors, a grin slowly spreading across his ruddy, freshly shaved face. Looking up, he stammered, "Lummox, you say? Someone called me a lummox?"

"Not just someone, Wolf. Ellen is here—here in the hotel. Your wife is waiting to see you, Wolf."

"Not *see* him, Clay," Ben said, fighting to hold a straight face, "*kill* him. I think she said she was going to kill him. Remember? When we left her, she was still mulling over just how to do it. Remember?"

"I believe you're right, Ben. The instant she saw him, I think she said. One way or the other, he's a dead man, I think she said."

"*Here? Ellen's here?*" Wolf stammered, emotions threatening to overwhelm the big man, emotions he had not felt in what seemed a lifetime. "In this hotel? She's going to kill me right here? After all these years, she still wants to kill me? Here in this hotel?"

Ben could not help but laugh out loud. "Try to get a grip, man."

Clay held up his hand, bringing Ben's merriment slowly to an end. "Yes, she is, Wolf. Ellen's here in this hotel. But before you see her, we need to talk."

"I knew it was she," Wolf declared, to the surprise of the other two. "I saw her, you know. I saw her up in that third-floor window, from down on the barge. She was just staring down at me. I just knew it was Ellen."

"How?" Ben chuckled, struck by the novelty of what he was hearing. "You were down on the river, down on that crowded barge. Must have been over a hundred yards or more. And how many other prisoners were crammed in there with you?"

"Oh, you don't know Ellen. No one else could be that judgmental—even from that distance," Wolf asserted. "I just knew it was Ellen. Even after she disappeared from that window. Don't misunderstand me, gentlemen. After all these years, after all that has happened, there could never be another woman in my life. I love my wife more than words can say, but she could be very difficult."

"Yes. I know your wife," Clay chuckled.

"You know her? You know Ellen?"

"Besides, I'm a married man, so I know just what you mean," he added, his mood suddenly sinking, as visions of the precious few months he had spent with Connie streamed through his mind. "Yeah, I'm a married man myself."

Pausing for a moment to rub his eyes, forcing his thoughts of Connie to the back of his mind, Clay looked up and studied Wolf's troubled face, wondering how to proceed. He *did* know how the man felt, and for that reason, at this moment, his own emotions were not far from the surface.

The man before him was a portrait of bewilderment, clearly having been taken by surprise. "Well, you've got a lot to account for, Major Striker, especially where she's concerned. Still," Clay chuckled, his spirits lifting, "your multitude of sins, crimes, marital shortcomings, and general ill behavior aside, we think your ornery hide is still worth saving."

"Saving? Me?"

"Oh, yes, and *save* is the appropriate word, all right," Clay declared. "You, sir, are on your way to some godforsaken military prison, whether you know it or not. Without our help, you're going to spend what's left of this war rotting away in some hellhole, with little or no hope for survival."

Wolf studied his hands, not wanting to look at either Ben or Clay, not until he could get his emotions under control and his thoughts together. "Oh, I'd find a way," he said at last, looking up. "Up to this point, I always have. I escaped from Leavenworth, as I'm sure you already know."

"Yes, we know," Clay said, all traces of humor gone from his voice. "They caught the guard that helped you, by the way. Right now, he's enjoying that same Leavenworth hospitality, but from a different perspective. And as a matter of fact, the Leavenworth commanders know you're here. But I think, inasmuch as you've already escaped their care and keeping, there is another prison somewhere out on the East Coast that they have in mind for you. And from what I hear, it will make Leavenworth look like a picnic in the park."

With a deep breath, Wolf leaned back in his chair, watching Clay and Ben closely. "All right, what are my options?"

"At this point, precious few," Clay declared. "We want to take you back to the Utah Territory, where you'll be tried for the atrocities committed at Platte River Station."

Wolf looked away, his mind returning to the flames and agony that had been Platte River Station. Shaking his head slowly in denial, Wolf flatly asserted, "I wasn't the one who caused that town to burn, and if I'd had a chance, I would have stopped it from happening. The whole thing went up in flames the second or third night we were there, as I recall. There was no way of stopping it. It was over almost as quickly as it began."

"We know all of that, Wolf. We know it was Jubal Hathaway who was responsible for how things went down—the murder of the Cartwright brothers, the destruction of the town, and the deaths of so many. But you also need to understand that for us, the Cartwright brothers were special. You could have been a little less vicious in the way you disposed of their bodies."

"Yes, I'm not proud of that," Wolf sighed, his hand going to his forehead, as if he were trying to rub away some deep pain. "The more I've thought about those days, the more the deaths of those two men have eaten at me. They were real soldiers, if you know what I mean. I recognized that right at the start. They were good lawmen, just doing their duty, and they deserved better. But then, so did nearly everyone else I encountered back then."

"Mmm," Clay hummed, half aloud. Studying Wolf's troubled features, trying in some way to measure the man's sincerity, he at last said, "Jubal Hathaway shot himself, by the way. I doubt you knew that. He tried to ambush our column in the foothills west of Platte River Station, on our way back to Utah. Didn't work, though," Clay concluded with a deep breath. "Your friend, Porter Rockwell, showed up and saw to Hathaway's peculiar needs."

"Well," Wolf said, almost dismissively, "I certainly can't say I'm sorry to hear of the little monster's passing. I tried to watch out for him, keep him under control, but he was beyond help; and in his twisted little mind, he hated you Mormons beyond all rationality. The truth is, Jubal Hathaway deserved what he got, however he got it.

"But you must understand, Colonel Ashworth, from my point of view, I was acting under the legitimate orders of the Confederacy. Captain Beauregard Mayfield—a West Point graduate, I might add—was in command of the entire expedition, though I'm afraid I did little to ease the man's burdens. The point being, we constituted an invading army in a time of war, under the orders of a lawful government that was—and is—fighting for its legitimate independence."

"We know that, too, Major, the legitimacy of the southern rebellion aside. In fact, we're pretty sure we know your entire story, clear back to Mexico. That's why we're willing to see you get a fair trial and, hopefully, acquittal."

"*Acquittal?*"

"Look, Wolf," Clay said, shifting forward in his chair, "we hold no grudges. In fact, we want to see you exonerated. To that end, Brigham Young has gotten the permission of President

Lincoln to extradite you back to Utah, and General Grant has agreed. I have the papers right here with me," he said, patting the breast pocket of his tunic. "But it can happen only under certain circumstances."

"And those are?"

"You must give me your parole—your absolute promise as a Confederate officer and gentleman—that you will not try to escape, but that you will accompany us to Salt Lake City, where you will stand trial.

"If you agree, for your trip west, I have a new uniform here for you, including a new pair of boots. You will travel with Ben and myself—and your wife, if you can fix that problem—unshackled and under minimal guard. At all times you will be shown the respect due an actively serving field-grade officer."

"So, I'm a prisoner of war, then?"

Clay took a deep breath and thought for a moment. "No, not really." With a chuckle, he concluded, "Actually, you've been captured by the Mormons, Wolf. We're willing to let it go at that—if you are."

"A uniform, you say?"

Reaching for a box that had been placed out of sight on a table behind the desk, Ben laid it in front of Wolf, and said, "The uniform of a Confederate major, fresh from a Confederate supply depot that recently fell into Union hands."

"Mmm," Wolf sighed. "I'm afraid there's a lot of that going on."

"Spoils of war," Clay declared. "But there remains an even weightier matter for you to consider, Major Striker."

"Yes," Wolf said, a slight smile on his lips. "When do I get the pleasure of facing my wife and her feminine retribution."

271

"You agree to our terms, then, Major Striker?" Clay demanded.

"You have my word," Wolf said, extending his hand. "Not just as an officer of the Confederacy, but as a grateful friend."

"Done!" Clay declared, shaking Wolf's hand, as Ben Kimball stepped up to participate in the honors.

"I can hardly wait," Wolf exclaimed, as Clay and Ben left the room.

Breaking the string around the box containing his new uniform, Wolf ripped away the heavy brown wrapping paper. Ever the poet, his heart full, he could not hold back: "'A woman move'd is like a fountain troubled,'" he crowed aloud to himself, "'Muddy, ill-seeming, thick, bereft of beauty, And while it is so, none so dry or thirsty Will deign to sip, or touch one drop of it.'"

"Did you hear that, Clay?" Ben snorted, closing the door.

"Yeah," Clay chuckled. "Sounds like Shakespeare. The man's a marvel. Definitely worth saving."

"Maybe so," Ben concluded, "but I don't think I'd want to be in his shoes right now."

"Not if he's dumb enough to 'deign to sip, or touch one drop of it,'" Clay laughed.

"Oh, yeah, she's a 'fountain troubled,' alright," Ben concluded, no longer able to contain himself.

★　★　★

Three newly joined allies stood outside Ellen Striker's door on the third floor of the elegant Gayoso House hotel, their mood solemn, as if one of their number were about to go to his execution. They had stood there for what to each seemed an eternity.

"You sure either of you won't come in with me?" Wolf whispered.

"Not a chance, soldier," Ben declared.

"We're friends, but friendship can go only so far," Clay solemnly declared.

"Yeah. You're lucky we came this far," Ben asserted.

"That's the truth," Clay agreed. "From here on, you're on your own, Major. Come to think of it, you don't even have your saber for protection."

"Let's get out of here, Clay," Ben snickered.

Abandoned in the dimly lit hallway outside his wife's room, watching his so-called friends retreating back toward the stairwell, a nervous Wolf Striker found himself vacillating somewhere between fight and flight. At this moment, for an experienced soldier, flight seemed the more prudent option—just a hasty, cowardly retreat.

It had been so long. And for her, it had been so unfair. Why she hadn't divorced him and remarried was more than he could fathom. After all these years, he could be nothing more than a stranger to her; and at this moment, he felt small, small enough to just slither under the door. How was he to explain himself? What could he possibly say? Did the words even exist that could adequately express the shame and remorse he felt? The horror of Mexico; the years of running; his life as a mercenary; none could have included her. He had been a fugitive, a fugitive from the law, from his own conscience, and from God. What on earth could he say to her? Would she even allow him to say anything? How much he missed her? How much he loved her? Anything?

Standing there alone, his heart in his throat, the only answer to the questions flooding his mind was his undying love for the woman on the other side of that very solid-looking door. There was nothing else, no other reason, no other excuse—only his love. And suddenly, at this moment, she was more important to him than life itself. But then, she always had been. That was the shame of it all. She would always be the center of his universe.

If he lost her now . . .

"Well," he mumbled half aloud, as he raised his hand toward the door, "standing here only makes it hurt worse—like waiting to go into battle."

For a man his size, the knock seemed tremulous and uncertain. It was almost embarrassing.

"Come in." The voice seemed far away, hardly audible, almost as if he were hearing it out of the past, across all those lost years.

Taking a deep breath, Wolf opened the door and stepped into the room. It was dark, with only a small lamp dimly burning on a table near the large window. And yet there was a fulness in the air, a feeling of expectancy, a sense of her nearness, her fragrance, her aura, her presence, everything she ever brought into a room, everything she had ever brought into his life.

And then she was there, hardly an arm's reach in front of him, appearing out of the shadows like a small beautiful apparition, the most perfect being he had ever seen. "Wolf? Is it really you?" Her voice somehow seemed tiny, and feminine, almost as if she were afraid to breathe, but it was her, his wife, his Ellen.

"Yes, darlin'," he stammered, tears suddenly burning his eyes. "It's me. I've come home."

How long they stood motionless there in the darkness, neither could have said, for neither of them was aware of the moment they silently came together. It just happened, something so natural no thought was necessary, his big arms enfolding her as she disappeared within the embrace each had spent what seemed an eternity longing for.

In the sweet totality of that embrace, words lost all meaning and became unimportant, the years of anger and loneliness melting into the night. They just stood there, holding each other with an intimacy, a oneness, that denied any past separation and healed all feelings. They were at last together, as each knew they must always be.

At some point in the soft sweep of the night, Wolf had gathered Ellen in his arms and carried her to the room's one big, overstuffed chair. There snuggled under a large, soft quilt, Ellen curled against her husband's chest, the two emotionally exhausted lovers had fallen asleep.

With the early light of morning came a new awareness, a new urgency, and Wolf brushed a curl of hair from his sleeping wife's forehead and kissed her tenderly on each eyelid. She was the most perfect thing he had ever seen or touched, and he mourned the years he had denied himself being with her.

Her complete, loving acceptance of him back into her life and the sweet perfection of the night somehow made it necessary that he explain himself, fully and openly, nothing held back. If he didn't, there would always remain the need to make things right, to account for his absence, to explain why he had done what he had done—or failed to do.

She had to know, to understand, that what he had done—his failure to return from Mexico, his life of self-denial, all those years of skirting the edges of the law—was because of his love for her. She had to know that it was because he would have done anything to keep his shame and embarrassment from staining her that he had disappeared and that it was out of bitterness he had turned to a life of violence and degradation.

Stirring, with a soft, southern, and completely feminine sigh, Ellen murmured, "Wolf, honey?"

"Yes, darlin'."

"I've missed you so, honey-bear."

At the thought of the pain he had caused her, the big man heaved a great sigh, almost a sob. Attempting to stifle his emotions, he whispered, "We need to talk, sweetheart."

"Yes, you do."

"We need to talk about all those years."

"Yes, you should."

"I have to explain."

"Yes, you must."

"I love you, Ellen."

★   ★   ★

A sumptuous Sunday brunch had been laid out in the hotel's elegant dining room, where Clay and Ben—both having made a second shameless trip to the heavy-laden serving table—were seated, indulging in scrambled eggs, biscuits and gravy, and a generous helping of sausage and bacon, their plates filled to capacity. Before them on the table were bowls of fresh fruit, a crock of butter, jars full of jams and honeycomb, and a large plate of hot toast.

Their formally clad waiter had just poured them each a glass of cold, fresh milk when Wolf and Ellen entered the crowded dining room and approached their table.

As the handsome southern couple walked across the carpeted floor, heads turned and the room fell silent. Given the current hostilities and the number of blue-clad Union officers in the room, the arrival of a smartly uniformed Confederate major with a beautiful woman on his arm was totally unexpected. Whether from astonishment or good manners, no one had risen to object, and as Wolf and Ellen arrived at Clay's table, the tension in the room began to ease.

"In the midst of war and misery, the table of a king," Wolf grumped, his disapproval more than obvious.

"No guilt here, Major Striker," Clay flatly declared, as he and Ben rose to greet their guests, "if that's what you're trying to imply. I've known famine, and I've known plenty. War quickly teaches you to accept the plenty when it's offered—and do it with gratitude."

"It does look rather vulgar," Ellen opined, looking around, "when you think of where I found Wolf, only yesterday."

"Won't you please join us?" Ben said, gesturing to the other seats.

Clay added, "Yes, please do. The real crime would lie not in thinking of where Wolf was only yesterday, but in letting all of this delicious food go to waste."

Turning toward the buffet and giving Wolf's sleeve a tug, Ellen said, "He's right, sugar. Come on. It looks wonderful."

Wolf stood watching his wife's too hasty retreat from virtue, clearly torn. "Oh, well," he said, turning to join her, "'Let the world slip, we shall ne'er be younger.'"

"Whatever," Ben said, as he buttered a piece of toast and reached for a crock filled with peach jam.

"Mmm," Clay said, his mouth full of sausage and gravy, "Shakespeare —again," he mumbled, reaching for his napkin.

Ben looked up, watching Wolf and Ellen as they helped themselves to the buffet. "I guess so," he said, taking bite of bacon. "Isn't there anything that old Englishman didn't write about?"

The breakfast was delicious, and talk came easily. By the time they had finished eating, the four were as comfortable with one another as if they had known each other all of their lives.

As they were pushing back from the table, a corporal entered the room and quickly approached Clay. "Colonel?"

"Yes," Clay said, turning toward the young soldier. "What is it?"

"A telegram, sir." he said, handing Clay a yellow envelope. "I'm to wait for a reply, sir."

Tearing open the envelope, Clay quickly read the short message, his face growing pale.

"What is it, Clay?" Ben Kimball asked, with growing concern. "Bad news?"

Clay slumped back down in his chair, staring across the top of the telegram, his face ashen. "It's from President Young. Connie has disappeared. The Salinas ranch has been burned, her uncle severely wounded or killed, and Connie and Emily taken captive—they think by Jose Rodriguez Zamora."

PART FOUR

★ ★ ★

CHAPTER 16

★ ★ ★

NEARLY TWO MONTHS AFTER receiving that devastating telegram in Memphis, Clay Ashworth sat at the edge of the majestic Mogollon Rim. Behind him lay miles of densely timbered land, running nearly to the edge of the south rim of the Grand Canyon of the Colorado River.

Miles below him, shimmering in the heat of late summer, spread the vast Sonoran Desert of the Arizona Territory. From where he sat, nothing could be seen in the brightness of midday but a vast, seemingly barren wilderness. It was a dangerous place in a dangerous time.

But Clay was a true westerner, a man intimately familiar with the deserts and mountains of the American West. One of a very few to have explored the wild, broken country south of his ranch in the valley of Utah Lake, Clay was at home in the wilderness that now surrounded him. He had been in the saddle for days, pushing himself, two horses, and a pack mule hard to cover as much territory in a long day as possible. But it was wild, demanding country, broken by deep gorges and raging, unnavigable rivers.

No more than a handful of mountain men and explorers had seen those precipitous canyons, let alone attempted to explore them. Of those who had, not a few died in the attempt. If the unforgiving terrain had not killed them, the Indians had.

There were few established trails, and those were known only to the Ute, the Navajo, the Paiute, or those whom they chose to help. Clay Ashworth was such a one, widely known among the hostile tribes as a friend to the Indian. For years, the cattle on his ranch had fed those of any tribe who were hungry, free for the taking. There was timber to warm their lodges, and water was plentiful, available for their families and livestock. None was turned away.

In return, his home was known as a sanctuary of Indian culture, filled with Navajo weavings and silver work, and the pottery and basketry of numerous tribes, all brought to him over the years by those whom he had befriended. When others sought to rid the land of the Indian, Clay Ashworth had offered them help, sat in council with them on matters affecting the land and the game to be found there, and intervened where possible when they were unjustly threatened.

Two days of hard riding found Clay far out into the wilds of the Arizona desert, a dangerous place of contrasts regardless of the time of year. During the day, the sun blazed down out of a cloudless sky with a ferocity that would almost bake a man's brains right inside his skull. The nights, however, often turned bitter cold under a velvet black sky alive with sparkling, diamond-like stars. And night or day, the air was so clear, a man could almost see forever.

For the uninitiated and the experienced alike, the desert

provided a kind of beauty that had to be experienced with great caution, for in all its forms, it was potentially deadly. Beyond the heat of the day and the cold of the night, nearly everything that lived and thrived in the desert was a potential threat and could kill a man.

Hardly a form of vegetation could be found that did not have thorns, thorns that almost sought an opportunity to stick, sting, or cut anyone or anything that ventured too close. The danger of a nasty puncture wound was very real.

By contrast, however, the desert was capable of sustaining human life in unexpected ways. The prickly pear cactus could be used for food in desperate times, as could the saguaro. And water—the single most precious resource known in the desert—could be wrung from the meat of the barrel cactus.

Reptiles and serpents of almost infinite variety were found in large numbers, both venomous and benign—the rattlesnake, in several hostile and equally deadly varieties, and the deadly coral snake being among the more feared. In addition, there was the Gila monster, looking like a plump, benign, beautifully beaded bag, its powerful jaws deadly. The list could go on and on. Wise was the pilgrim who knew the desert and its many moods. For those unwise in its ways, the desert was a very dangerous place.

But by far, the greatest threat to any white man venturing into that world of infinite dangers was the Apaches, always on the move, and always alert to any opportunity. The name *Apache* applied to a number of different tribes and bands throughout the Southwest, but regardless of which, the mere mention of the word was enough to strike terror into the heart of any pilgrim even remotely familiar with Apache ways.

The unforgiving desert aside, Apache hatred for the white man had become a truly dangerous threat, and not without justification. Only their loathing of Mexicans exceeded their hatred of the white-eyes. Mexicans had been the enemy of the Apache for many generations, raiding their camps for women and children to be sold into slavery, killing the men, torching their wickiups and camps, running off their horses and livestock, and causing as much human misery as possible. A man could get rich selling Apache scalps almost anywhere in Mexico.

It was into this cauldron of hatred and heat that Clay Ashworth rode. But his was a resolve that could not be denied, not by the dangers of the desert and not by the dreaded Apache. Consuelo, his Connie, had disappeared, and without her, his life could hold little meaning. Alone, he had buried their precious newborn daughter, and he was determined to find his wife, reclaim her love, and build their lives anew back in Utah, back at *Rancho los Librados.*

That was not all, however. Along with Consuelo, Emily— Clay's long-time housekeeper, friend, confidant, and Consuelo's newly discovered aunt—had disappeared as well. Nor had Lazaro Salinas, Connie's beloved uncle and overseer of all the Salinas holdings, been seen since being wounded in the attack and fire that destroyed the family hacienda.

From what little Clay had been able to discover, the assault on the Salinas ranch had been sudden and vicious, carried out in the middle of the night, and with absolutely no warning. The reasons for the attack and the identity of the attackers had not been determined, though a band of Apaches was rumored to have been involved. It amounted to little more than rumor, but apparently a small group of Mexicans had led the attack.

If true, that left unanswered and perplexing the question of why such an assault had taken place. The loyalty of the Salinas family always had been to the people of Mexico, not to the French nor any of their European allies. And from what little Clay had been able to surmise, it was unlikely that there had been any French involvement. Consuelo's father, the late *gobernador* of the northernmost state of Mexico, was not, however, a man free of controversy. He had been known to favor an alliance with, perhaps his state even becoming a part of, a new California, a position that was in itself not without its detractors. That issue, however, had been laid to rest with his death and the subsequent arrest of his murderer, Jose Rodriguez Zamora.

None of this was of any help where Clay was concerned. The whereabouts of the family, if they were still alive, seemed to be a mystery. It simply appeared as if they had been caught up in the political unrest sweeping the country and had disappeared. But Clay Ashworth knew there was more to it than that. What had happened was not about French imperialism, nor California politics.

Jose Rodriguez Zamora was at the bottom Connie's disappearance and that of her family. The whole thing had his unsavory smell about it. From the very beginning, Zamora had been determined to have Consuelo and the Salinas holdings, thus assuring for himself a position of power in northern Mexico when the French finally took control. But that was not going to happen. One way or another, Clay Ashworth was determined to find his loved ones and put an end to Zamora's ambitions—once and for all.

It was late in the day when a trail-weary Clay Ashworth rode into Apache Wells, a small, lawless border town resembling nothing more than a pile of bleached bones drying in the middle of the Apache-infested desert, an obstruction in the trail where none could pass unseen.

He had been here before, and nothing had changed. The place

consisted of little more than a ramshackle feed store and stable, both located directly across a narrow, dusty trail from a false-fronted, two-story, clapboard building boasting a sign above its sagging covered boardwalk that read: *H-O-T-E-L.*

Maria's Cantina, the only public eating place to be found anywhere south of Tucson, was an afterthought attached to the north wall of the hotel. It consisted of worn plank flooring supporting a rough frame of warped two-by-fours and covered with a sun-rotted canvas tarp. The ramshackle cafe boasted a squatty wood-burning cook stove at the rear and three dilapidated trestle tables, each of which could accommodate four or six customers, if they were on friendly terms.

What little there was of Apache Wells was presided over by Maria, of *Maria's Cantina,* a large, buxom woman who stood well over six feet tall and outweighed Clay by at least fifty pounds. That Maria knew her way around and would brook no nonsense from man or beast was more than obvious and attested to by the fact that she survived where few could. As far as Clay could tell, she was the town's only citizen.

"Say, I remember you," the big woman said, swatting a fly on the counter, as Clay walked into the tiny hotel lobby. "Must be more'n a year now since you walked through them doors."

"That's about right," Clay responded, dropping his saddlebags on the floor next to the front desk. "And just like the last time, I need a room, a bath, and a meal."

"Well, the rooms are still upstairs, right where they was the last time you was here, and the bath you still gotta find for yerself. You remember the routine?"

"Yeah," Clay chuckled, "I remember."

"Take any room yuh want. As yuh can see," she said, her fat hand sweeping the empty room, "the crowds have thinned out some. You go on about yer business, and I'll take care of your horses and gear, they're safe enough with me. I'll have some steak and beans ready for yuh in the cantina—when you've had yer bath, that is. Then we need t' talk some."

An hour later, a freshly bathed and shaved Clay Ashworth sat mopping up his second helping of Maria's thick, brown sugar, pepper-laced baked beans, when the big woman sat down across the table from him. "You know the Salinas ranch ain't there no more, don't yuh? The hacienda, least ways. Burnt t' the ground weeks ago. Walls might still be standin', though."

"I've heard," Clay said, wrapping a thick slice of juicy beef and a generous scoop of salsa in a large flour tortilla. "How much do you know about what's happened down there, Maria?"

"Well, sir, it'd be easy to dismiss it all as just more Mexican misery. Seems like Mexico'll never know anything but pain and misery, I guess."

"The French?"

"Oh, them French are there, all right. A Catholic *padre* came through here on a donkey a day or two ago," Maria said, pouring herself a large cup of tarlike coffee, and refilling Clay's. "Said he was fleein' Mexico." The big woman huffed at the thought. "Fleein' Mexico on a donkey," she snorted, spilling some of her drink. "Can you imagine? Anyway, this here *padre* said everything was in, uh . . . *chaos,* was what he called it. Yeah, *chaos,* and he was headed for one of the missions over in the New Mexico Territory—if the Apaches don't get him first. The silly old fool.

"Anyway, he said that Juarez and his cronies are gone. Tucked their tails and ran, I guess. Seems his army got whipped down around Puebla somewheres, and the French army's headed for Mexico City, if it ain't there already. They was probably smart t' get out while the gettin' was good."

"Mmm," Clay said, studying Maria's wide, life-worn face. "Maria, have you ever heard of a man by the name of Jose Rodriguez Zamora?"

Maria sat frozen for a moment, staring at Clay over the cup she held to lips. "Why do you want to know about Zamora? That's one mean *hombre*—pure poison, and then some. I heard his political cronies got 'im outta prison some months back, around the time them French landed."

"Is he in with the French?"

"Last I heard he was—has been from the start, hear tell. Wants Sonora all to hisself. Wants t' be governor, from what I hear, when the French take over. But what's worse, he's teamed up with a band of renegade Apaches."

"Apaches? You mean Cochise has—"

"Never said nothin' about Cochise, now did I? Nah," she said, waving her hand for emphasis, "Zamora's been runnin' with Chuh—and a meaner little savage never lived, if I do say so myself, and I'm one-quarter Apache." Stopping to refill her cup and vigorously scratch under one arm, she grumbled. "Cochise? He won't have nothin' to do with Chuh, and he knows Zamora was one of them what was workin' Apache slaves in the mines south of here."

Clay looked up, his face darkening with anger. "But those mines are closed, aren't they? Is Zamora back down there again, trying to work any of them with Apache slaves?"

"Could be, but it gets worse. Seems there's more money in an Apache's scalp down south of the border than in workin' him to death in some mine. And that evil little Chuh is helpin' him. If Cochise ever got his hands on that bunch, he'd skin 'em all, and hang what's left of 'em on a mesquite bush."

"Where's Cochise now, Maria?"

The big woman watched Clay for a moment, then snickered, "Cochise? Shoot, Cochise is the wind. He's nowhere and he's everywhere, and he'll be right in yer face when yuh least expect it."

"Do you think I could find him?"

Maria almost laughed out loud. "Pilgrim, more'n likely, between here and where you're headed, he's gonna find you, and I gotta tell yuh, he ain't in no mood t' talk to no white man."

"Yeah," Clay said. "I've seen plenty of Apache sign between here and way north of Tucson, but I've managed to avoid any contact with them. Came close a time or two, but if they saw me, I was lucky."

"If you saw them, it ain't likely they didn't see you, pilgrim."

"There was a cavalry patrol headed the same direction. I camped close a couple of nights in a row. That's probably the reason."

"Look, I keep callin' you a pilgrim, but I know that ain't so. You got lots of savvy. Still, you need to understand, these are bad times down here. Cochise is at war with all whites, not t' mention Mexicans. Since them bluecoats murdered Mangas Coloradas and his son, and wounded his wife, the Bedonkohes band has joined up with Cochise and the Chokonens, and the whole bunch of 'em are on the warpath. Oh, there's been talk of an armistice, but there's been too much killin'. Cochise ain't of a mind t' stop. Not now."

Taking one last bite of Maria's delicious beans and washing it down with the last of his coffee, Clay pushed back from the table. "Well, Maria, thanks for everything. I know what you're saying is true, but I've got no choice. I'll be out of here before daybreak. If Cochise hasn't caught up with Zamora, I'm going to. If Consuelo is alive and unhurt, whether Zamora lives or dies will be entirely up to him, but one way or the other, his days on the loose are numbered. And if he has harmed my wife or those with her, there is no force on earth that can save him. Cochise isn't the only one on the warpath."

"*Forbear to judge,* Clay Ashworth, *for we are sinners all.*"

Standing in the cantina's open flap, silhouetted by the setting sun behind him, the speaker's features were hard to make out. But the big, square shape and the voice were unmistakable.

"Wolf Striker?" Clay said, slowly coming to his feet. "What the devil—"

"More talk of war, Clay?" The big man said, making his way to Clay's table, where he sat down next to Maria. "It's a good thing I showed up, then. That's my specialty, as well you know." Giving her a wink, Wolf reached for a cup and poured himself some coffee. "Relax, man," he said, a huge grin splitting his face. "Believe it or not, I'm here by way of assignment."

"You're what?" Clay said, sitting back down at the table.

"It's a long story, my friend. You sure you want to hear it?"

"Well, the night's young, and you're the last person on earth I expected to see walk in here. Let's hear it, Wolf."

"Uh-huh . . . I'd kind of like to hear it, myself," Maria said, going to the stove, stoking the fire, and refilling the coffee pot. "This place is startin' to get downright crowded."

"Well, okay," Wolf chuckled, "not being one to just barge in unexpected like this, I suppose you both deserve an explanation. You had no way of knowing, Clay, but I was acquitted by that military court out at Camp Floyd, and your testimony was a big help, as were all of the others who came to my defense. Believe it or not, I've never known what it's like to have such friends.

"But I guess the point is you had been gone only a few days when the acquittal was handed down. Frankly, it did come as a bit of a surprise, though along with all of that supportive testimony, it helped that most of the officers on that court-martial board had been comrades in arms at one time or another.

"In the end," Wolf said, watching Maria return with a pot full of hot coffee, "the military, us bluecoats, as you put it," he grinned, giving Maria another wink, "are a brotherhood of sorts, Civil War or no. Especially if you have West Point in your background, as Clay here well knows. Two of those guys were even ushers when Ellen and I got married."

"Why doesn't that surprise me?" Clay asked. "But in the past couple of years, frankly, nothing has really surprised me about you."

"Oh, then, here's another bit of news. There's a whole troop of U. S. Cavalry just making camp a half mile or so back up the trail," he said, jerking his thumb over his shoulder. "I hooked up with them several days ago. Good thing, too. I don't know this country hardly at all. It's been years."

"But, why? How?"

"Your great friend, Brigham Young, asked me to follow you down here and help you get things straightened out—sort of as my penance, was the way he put it. But when he and Ben Kimball told me the whole story, well, after what you did for Ellen and me, there was no way I'd let you come down here and get yourself killed all by yourself."

"Why, man, I thought I'd made good time. How in the world did you—

"Your President Young, an amazing fellow, saw to it that I got hooked up with another amazing fellow, a man by the name of Hamblin. Jacob Hamblin's his name. Either of you ever heard of him?" Wolf asked, looking from Clay to Maria.

"Yes, I know him. He's a good friend," Clay affirmed.

"Heard of him? Why, I surely have heard of him," Maria

declared. "He's big medicine amongst most of the southwestern tribes. Why, he—"

"Well," Wolf said, laying a calming hand on the big woman's fleshy arm, "it was he that got me down through all of that Navajo and Hopi country.

"And you're right as rain, Maria. That man is a regular Indian himself. It's not hard to see why anyone would think he's big medicine. He knows the country like the back of his hand, and he seems to speak all of their languages, Paiute, Navajo, Hopi. I don't think I've ever heard the likes.

"Anyway, because of him we made better time than I would have ever thought possible. Then I got hooked up with that cavalry patrol out there, near one of the Mormon settlements, up on the Salt River, and . . . well . . . here I am: dirty and tired, but willing." Looking at Maria, he declared, "And I could sure use something to eat."

"Well, make yourself comfortable, stranger," the big woman said, returning a wink and making her way back to the stove. "You've come to the right place. It's all warmin' on the stove."

"Wolf," Clay said, scratching his chin, "I can't say I'm not glad to see you, but I couldn't have been more surprised if Abe Lincoln himself had just walked through that tent flap."

The Apache camp, a *gotah* of nine wickiups and a sweat lodge, lay hidden in a narrow box canyon high up in the Sierra Madre Mountains of northern Mexico, a dozen miles from where the Salinas hacienda had once stood. It was the camp of the renegade Apache, Chuh, and his small band of Chokonen Apaches. It also served as the current hideout of Jose Rodriguez Zamora.

The camp was protected on two sides by steep canyon walls densely timbered with pinion and juniper, manzanita, and prickly pear. At the rear of the camp a sheer cliff of unbroken granite soared above a pool of clear, cold water, constantly replenished by a generous seep at the base of the massive formation.

Near the mouth of the box canyon, where the mountain slopes were steepest and formed a natural choke point, a three-sided pole corral had been erected. Only four horses remained in the corral, nibbling at what little was left of the sparse grass at the base of the nearly vertical slope. High above the camp, hidden under an ancient juniper tree that hung precipitously out over a rock ledge, a solitary Apache lay watching the camp. One of Cochise's trusted scouts, he had lain there, motionless and invisible, blending completely with his surroundings, since before sunrise the day before. Waiting and watching as Chuh and his braves had ridden out.

For an Apache, patience is inborn and silence is among the highest of virtues. He had been sent to find Chuh's camp and ascertain its strength, and he would not leave until he could provide his leader with whatever information the great chief desired. If necessary, he could remain hidden and unmoving for days, without food and needing very little water.

Several days earlier, while searching for Chuh's camp, the scout had stumbled across some of the renegade Apache leader's murderous handiwork. Chuh and his band had struck several outlying ranches, leaving them in flames and killing and scattering whatever livestock they could find. But that was not all. The scout had found Chuh's murderous ways indiscriminate. Before they were through, the renegade Apaches had raided a few Indian camps for scalps, as well, leaving only death, heartbreak, and ruin in their wake.

The scout had followed their bloody sign until he located Chuh's hidden canyon: something only another Apache could have done without fear of discovery. Quickly finding the best place for observation, the trusted scout had stoically settled down to fulfill his leader's wishes. Late on his first day above the camp, the scout unexpectedly had discovered that there were Mexicans somewhere in Chuh's camp. Though he had seen only one—a lean, mean-looking man with a narrow, sharp face that resembled an ax—he knew there were more. He had heard them, and he would not leave until he knew how many and who they were.

It was late on the second day when his questions finally were answered. Except for a few women who were busy tending cooking fires in anticipation of the return of their men, the camp was empty. Some were flipping corn tortillas and laying them to cook on hot rocks nestled in the glowing coals of their fire pits. Bowls of food were also nestled among the hot coals of each fire. It was a deceptively peaceful scene, where all appeared in harmony with nature.

The unmistakable sound of a vicious slap, followed by a woman's scream, came from one of the wickiups on the far side of the camp, and angry voices could be heard. Though the words being spoken were in Spanish, they could not be understood for the distance. There was little doubt, however, in the Apache scout's mind as to their meaning.

Then, without warning, the heavy deerskin flap that covered the entrance to the wickiup was thrown back, and the sharp-faced Mexican stepped out. His voice was loud and threatening, and many of the women in the camp scurried in fright to the far side of their fires and watched with caution.

Turning and leaning back into the wickiup, he snarled, "I will be back in a few days, and you will do as I say. I'm tired of your impertinence, Consuelo. You will soon learn your proper place and how to speak to your husband, and it is I who will teach you."

"No, Jose!" the woman screamed from inside. "Never! I will die first!"

Straightening, and letting the flap fall back across the wickiup's opening, the man turned to walk away, spitting back over his shoulder, "I am losing patience with you, Consuelo. But you will not be the one to die." Stopping for a moment, he spun about and, stepping back to the wickiup, lifted the hide covering. "No, little one," he cooed, "it will not be you who will die. You will watch Lazaro die slowly, as he should have died months ago, and then it will be the old hag's turn. Your aunt, no? And in the end, you will do as I say. Think on it, little one. It will not be a pretty sight."

"You murderer! You *asesino, bárbaro!*" Consuelo screamed. "Kill us now because I will never submit to your filthy touch—no matter what you do, or how you do it!"

Dropping the hide covering in place, Zamora turned and walked away, the sound of Consuelo's sobs almost like music in his ears. "Oh, little one, I think you will," he exclaimed, his voice almost melodic. "Their screams will soften your heart, if not your head. You will see."

"Without me, you pig—you *cerdo*—you will have nothing!"

For a moment, Zamora stiffened, stopping in his tracks. He knew she was right, but now was not the time. When he returned, there would be time enough to deal with her. She had no idea what harsh lessons awaited her. "A few days only, little one," he sang.

CHAPTER 17

★　★　★

It was a little after noon when Clay and Wolf rode up to the edge of the deep, wide arroyo where the coaches and wagons of the Salinas party had been attacked by Apaches as they were returning to Mexico from California. Here it was, nearly a year and a half before, that several had made a last-ditch stand, holding off the Apaches until the others could get away. Those that remained had been slaughtered.[6]

Among them had been young Toby Bennington, ostensibly Senator Gwin's administrative assistant—how he had hated being referred to as the senator's *aide*. While serving on the senator's staff, Bennington had been recruited by the Pinkerton agency to act as an undercover agent on behalf of the Lincoln administration in an attempt to determine the extent of the senator's involvement in the California separatist movement.

Bennington's secret work had probably cost him his life. He was traveling with the Salinas party as the senator's representative in his effort to cement an alliance between California and the Mexican state of Sonora. Bennington had gone, however, with the intent of derailing any such alliance. However, not long after crossing the border into Mexico, the Salinas party had been attacked by Apaches, and Toby was among those left behind and killed.

Whether the senator had ever suspected Toby's infatuation with Gwin's wife, Mary, was unlikely. It had amounted to nothing more than a young man's romantic fantasies about a beautiful, intelligent, and inaccessible older woman. It may also have been a way for Toby to strike back at his boss, a man he considered to be a condescending, egotistical, self-possessed traitor to his country.

Toby's attentions toward Mary Gwin had not been altogether unreciprocated. Approaching middle age, she had found his flirtations an amusing boost to her ego. However, in the end, what with Toby being sent to Mexico and the needs of California being of paramount importance, Mary had put an end to their somewhat lopsided affair.

"Will you look at that," Wolf said, removing his hat and wiping the perspiration from his forehead and hatband. "It looks as if a wagon train has been attacked down there sometime past."

Spurring his horse down into the deep gully, Clay affirmed the obvious. "Yeah, it happened more than a year ago. Let's get out of this heat, and I'll tell you the whole story. We can make better time after the sun sets and the heat is not so oppressive. We need to give these horses a rest."

Reining up next to what was left of a coach that had been turned on its side, the two riders dismounted and tied their mounts to a wheel.

As the two loosened their saddle cinches and climbed into

what little shade the ruined coach could provide, Wolf said, "Apaches?"

"Right. Cochise and his tribe, a Chiricahua band no doubt. They've been running wild in this part of the country for a long time now. I'll tell you one thing, you don't ever want to tangle with them. It may not look like it, but most of these folks got away," Clay said, his hand sweeping what was left of the Salinas wagons. "Those who didn't, I buried over there against that bank, under those rocks."

Wolf took a long pull on his canteen, wiped his mouth, and said, "Well, I'm waiting to hear the whole story. From the looks of things, it ought to be a good one."

It was early evening when Clay concluded. "So, now you know. That's how I met Consuelo and wound up at Glorieta. It's also how I met Cochise."

Wolf looked around uncomfortably. "You think you can still rely on this Cochise fella's gratitude?"

"We shouldn't count on it, judging from what Maria said."

"Yeah, I'd say so. Well, anyway, that was some story, Clay," Wolf observed. "It just proves an old Striker theorem."

"Don't tell me, a *Striker theorem?* What's that?"

"Yeah, a theorem. You know, a proposition that is not self-evident, but can be proved from accepted premises, and is—"

"Oh, stop it," Clay chuckled. "So, what is this theorem of yours?"

"There's no such thing as coincidence, my friend. Things don't just happen. There's a reason for everything under the sun, and something good comes from even the worst of circumstances."

"A philosopher," Clay said, shaking his head. He would never admit it to Wolf, but the more the man was around, the more Clay liked him. "You're a man of hidden depths, Wolf Striker."

Wolf laughed and said, "You know, Porter Rockwell once said the same thing to me—and then he tried to hang me."

Throughout the hot afternoon, the two men had moved with the ruined coach's shadow, seeking relief from the heat, until their backs were to the gully's western edge. And as the sun began to slip behind the hills to the west, a cooling breeze sprang up, catching the sand and scuttling it across the floor of the arroyo.

After the intense heat of the day, the light breeze and the whisper of the moving sand had a soothing effect on the two men, lulling them into a sense of contentment.

Behind them, a small avalanche of gravel and sand spilled down the steep sides of the deep, rocky arroyo, and a horse blew.

Glancing over his shoulder, Clay breathed, "Don't look now, but we've got company—the worst possible kind."

"I see them. They're turning away."

"Yeah. To find a way down here from that side," Clay said, getting to his feet. "Lucky for us, the bank is too high and steep. They've got to go upstream about a half mile to either cross over or get down here to the bottom. Let's not wait for them, *amigo.*"

"I hear you."

Cinching up their saddles and swinging aboard, the two gave spur to their mounts, and Clay hollered, "Anything good going to come from this, philosopher?"

"Remains to be seen."

"Some theorem."

Urging their horses to a full gallop, the two riders rode headlong down the deep arroyo, the clatter of their horse's hoofs echoing off its narrowing rocky banks. The horses ran with surprising ease, and the cool air whipping the two men's sweaty faces gave an unwarranted sense of well-being and enjoyment. But it was not to last.

"Follow me," Clay hollered. "There's a way up out of this dry wash just around the next bend."

"What then?"

"We head for the hills—real pronto-like."

"One good thing has come from this already."

"What's that?"

"At least those Indians back there are going the opposite direction."

"They're not just Indians—they're Apaches. And if they catch us, they're going to make anything you've ever heard about other tribes pale by comparison."

Just where the deep wash made a sharp bend to the west and deepened, a narrow game or cattle trail had been worn into the rocky, precipitous cutbank, leading up and out. Narrow and unstable, the trail made for a brief but dangerous climb and forced a rider to slow almost to a walk.

Reining in, both riders eased their mounts up the treacherous trail and over the top, where a large band of mounted Apaches sat in a semicircle waiting for them. There was nowhere to go.

For a few brief moments, no one moved, only the two horses pranced nervously in place.

"Are we dead?" Wolf whispered, his body tense, his mind searching for some way out.

"No. And that's a problem. It probably won't be long before we'll be wishing we were."

"Let's rush them," Wolf offered, unable to rein in his deviant sense of humor. "Wait until they find out how much trouble they're in."

"I guess we ought to do something to get the party started," Clay agreed. "On my word, we charge them."

"On your word? Why on your word?"

"Because, I'm—"

As the two nervous white men spoke, the semicircle of Indians directly in front of them parted, and a tall Apache mounted on a magnificent mottled gray horse rode through the opening. It was Cochise.

"Is that him?"

"That's him."

The scene was almost surreal. With the appearance of the great Apache leader, the sense of confrontation that had charged the air immediately diminished. Though no word was spoken, lances were lowered, and the horses ceased their nervous prancing, dropping their heads to nibble at the sparse grass at their feet.

With a barely perceptible gesture, Cochise reined his horse about and the Apache band crowded tightly around the two white men, leaving them no opportunity for escape. Neither could do anything but move with the small band of Chiricahua Apaches; there were no options.

It was late when they rode into Cochise's *rancheria.* As Clay and Wolf dismounted, their horses were taken from them, and the two white men were led to a small wickiup where, with no more than a couple of gestures, they were told to stay put. The message was unmistakable.

Wolf sank cross-legged to the hard-packed dirt floor. "What now?"

"I don't know," Clay said, shaking his head and dropping next to Wolf. "But at least we're not dead—or worse."

"*Or worse?*"

"Oh, yeah. You know the stories. Apaches can take a long time making you wish you were dead."

With a groan born of bone-tired weariness, Wolf leaned back

on his elbows. "Yes, I know. And right now I'm truly regretting all those years I could have spent with Ellen."

"Mmm," Clay said, regarding his friend through the dimness inside the smoky hut, his mind reviewing all that had happened. "Believe me, friend, I know how you feel. But somehow I think we might just get out of this."

"You do?" Wolf said, sitting up, his spirits lifting. "What makes you think that?"

"Your theorem, remember? If they were going to kill us, they'd have started the party back—"

Before Clay could finish his thought, the hide drape that served as a covering for the wickiup's entrance was thrown back, and a squaw shuffled in with two steaming bowls of food. She set them on the dirt floor, across the fire from Clay and Wolf. Turning back toward the entry flap, her disdain for the two white men more than apparent, she grunted perfunctorily. "You eat now. No time later. Cochise, he come soon."

"You think they're fattening us up?" Wolf said, peering into his bowl. "What do you think this smelly stuff is?"

"I don't know," Clay said, dipping a couple of fingers into the steaming concoction, "but it's got to be better than starving, and right now I'm starving. Ouch! It's hot, whatever it is."

"Lamb. Lamb stew is what it is," a man said, entering the wickiup. "And the hungrier yuh are, the better it'll taste. At least that's been my experience."

Clay began to rise, and the man put a hand on his shoulder, easing him back to the ground. "Eat up, Clay Ashworth. You're gonna need all the strength you can get, you and your friend."

"Now, that doesn't sound good," Wolf said, sampling some of the greasy stew.

"Name's Tom Jeffords, and it ain't gonna be all that bad." The man was tall and spare with reddish hair, and he sported a beard of considerable length for a man his age. In the smoky gloom of the wickiup, Clay guessed him to be somewhere in his early thirties.

"I'm sorry, but you took us by surprise. Another live white man is the last thing I expected to see," Clay said, taking a careful mouthful of the hot stew.

"I ain't *another white man,*" Jeffords chuckled, his manner open and friendly. "I'm about Cochise's *only* white friend, at least the only one left alive, as you put it. And, like you two, I'll last only as long as he trusts me. That's a fact you might want to keep in mind."

"What on earth are you doing here?" Clay asked, cautious in how he said things. Jeffords was obviously a man to climb the mountain with. And there was no question he and Wolf were in need of someone who knew his way around. "We're grateful for just the sight of you."

"That's the truth," Wolf agreed. "For the first time," he continued, glancing at Clay, "I'm beginning to feel like we just might get out of this alive."

"Remains to be seen," Jeffords said, a grin creasing his rugged features. "There's a lot of water t' go under that bridge—before the end is known, that is."

Before either Clay or Wolf could respond, the flap flew back again, and Cochise entered. He nodded and sat cross-legged between the fire and the door, his dark eyes assessing Clay and Wolf. Without blinking, the Apache chief began speaking.

Jeffords cleared his throat and translated. "Cochise says because of what you did for his people, he will help you one last time."

"*One last time?*" Wolf said, his eyes going from Cochise to Jeffords.

"How?" Clay asked, watching the Apache leader closely.

Cochise looked up at Jeffords and spoke briefly in Spanish, his speech and manner brisk.

"Says he knows where your woman is."

Clay started to rise when Jeffords stopped him. "Never get up before the chief does. Ain't mannerly, and we don't want to upset Cochise, now do we." It wasn't a question.

Settling back to the ground, Clay smiled at the Apache leader and said, "No, sir. We surely don't. Do we, Wolf?"

"Not I," Wolf said, wanting to say more, but knowing when to keep quiet.

Rising, Cochise turned to leave. He stopped near the doorway and spoke briefly in Apache to Jeffords. Glancing back at Clay, he lifted the flap and stepped out of the wickiup.

"We'll be leavin' before sun-up," Jeffords said, turning to follow Cochise. He paused and looked back and said, "Yuh should have yer wife back by noon tomorrow and be on your way back t' the Utah Territory."

Though Wolf had seemed to sleep, it was the longest night of Clay's life. The thought of at last finding Consuelo, not to mention Emily and Lazaro, never left his restless mind. He'd never felt more helpless, not knowing where she was or how to go about finding her, or even if she were still alive. It was not in his makeup to just sit and wait on others. For him, patience had been a skill hard-learned but never really mastered.

When the flap was at last thrown back and Jeffords stepped into the wickiup, it was still dark outside. "Squaw's bringin' some food. Eat it, and then we can go."

"Eat?" Clay exclaimed. "Why, man, I have no appetite. Let's get going."

As an Apache woman entered and set two bowls on the ground, Jeffords said, "It's gonna be a long day, and who knows when you'll see food again—if ever. Come on now, eat up. Yer wastin' time."

"He's got me convinced," Wolf said, gulping down a mouthful of whatever it was in his bowl. "Dying is one thing, Clay, but dying hungry is something altogether different. Napoleon was right, an army travels on its stomach."

Faced with the futility of his position, Clay reached for his bowl and managed to get down several mouthsful. It was greasy and had some corn in it, along with some stringy meat. "There, that's all the room I've got, Napoleon or not," he said, wiping his mouth on his sleeve. "I have no idea what it was, but you tell that poor woman it was truly wonderful."

The sun was nearing mid-sky when Cochise held up his hand, bringing the small band of warriors to a halt. Turning to Jeffords, he spoke briefly in Spanish.

"Cochise says Chuh's camp is near. Up through that draw. Ain't no other way in nor out; it's a proper box canyon. The scout says your woman was there early yesterday. So was the Mexican *bandito* that's holding her and her family."

"Well, what are we waiting for?"

"Now, hold on, Clay," Wolf said, resting a hand on his friend's arm. "You go charging in there, and you're likely to get Consuelo and the others killed." Turning to Cochise and Jeffords, Wolf smiled half apologetically. "Clay's just anxious to get his wife out of there, that's all. What's the plan?"

Taking a deep breath, Clay turned to Jeffords, and asked, "How do we know they're even in there?"

Cochise smiled, and pointed to the ground. "Old tracks," he said, for the first time addressing Clay in English. "Nobody come out. Maybe one day."

Clay got off his horse and studied the ground, fighting a sense of self-disgust. He was in too big a hurry, and he knew it. He could read sign as well as the next man—if the next man wasn't an Apache. "I should have taken the time to look myself," he said, glancing in Wolf's direction as he remounted.

"Gents, what's gonna happen is likely t' get kind of bloody," Jeffords said, a look of concern on his bearded face. "These here Chiricahua want Chuh's hide t' hang out on a Mesquite bush for all to see and feed what's left of 'im to the buzzards. So, best we let Cochise do the thinkin'. That'll save you from gettin' yourself and your friend, here, killed *and* increase the likelihood of your savin' yer woman and her family."

"You know as well as I do, Clay," Wolf mused, "victory is purchased by blood—usually lots of it. And it looks like Cochise's enemies are facing sure destruction. I don't know about you, but anything less wouldn't be near good enough for me."

"Mmm," Clay sighed, half to himself, "von Clausewitz." Looking at his friend, he said, "Okay, from all I know about Cochise, the man knows what he's doing. What are we going to do? More importantly, when and how are we going to do it?" he asked Jeffords.

With a brevity of words typical of the great Apache leader, Cochise divided his band into three groups. Two were dispatched up the sides of the canyon above the renegade encampment, one group on each side. The third, a smaller group of eight men, remained in the canyon's narrow mouth leading to the encampment. This group would be led by Cochise himself. On a prearranged signal, the attack would begin.

Cochise waited only until he was signaled that his men were in place on each side of the box canyon, above Chuh's camp. Then, with a scream that could cause a white man's skin to crawl right off of his bones, the Apache leader dug his heels into his horse's ribs and charged through the canyon's narrow mouth.

Hearing their leader's piercing scream, the Apaches above the encampment began their war cries, launching a hail of arrows down into the canyon as Cochise and his band thundered into Chuh's camp, with Clay, Wolf, and Jeffords hot on their heals. With the noise and confusion coming from every direction and the deadly flight of arrows raining from the sky, the renegade Apaches were taken completely by surprise, quickly throwing down their weapons.

Storming through the camp, Cochise brought his mount to a sliding stop directly in front of Chuh's wickiup. Dismounting on the run, his large knife held throat high, he hit the ground just as the entry flap was thrown aside and the little renegade ran out. Falling onto his back was the only thing that kept Chuh from impaling himself on Cochise's knife.

Clay, Wolf, and Jeffords also dismounted. Grabbing Clay by the arm, Jeffords said, "This way. She's in that wickiup back there."

They ran forward, but before Clay could reach the wickiup, the flap was thrown aside and Jose Rodriguez Zamora stepped out, holding Consuelo by her hair in front of him, his knife to her throat.

Consuelo saw her husband and cried, "Clay!"

With a vicious yank of Consuelo's hair, Zamora silenced her, and tiny beads of bright, red blood formed on her beautiful neck. "One more step, and I will kill her, *señor* Ashworth. I'm tempted to do it anyway, just to see the look on your *gringo* face."

Clay nearly lost his balance as he skidded to a stop some ten feet from his wife, and a deathly silence settled over the camp.

"Let her go, Zamora," Clay warned, his voice barely above a whisper. "Let's you and me settle it. Right here and now." Moving slowly to his left, he growled, "You know, our old score, when I could have killed you—you the great swordsman—at will. Killed you at your own game. You were no man then, Zamora, and you're no man now, cowering behind a woman's skirts."

"One more step, *gringo,*" Zamora said, giving Consuelo a shove to their left.

"One more step and what?" Clay said, following her captor with his eyes. "You'll kill her? Why don't I think so?" he sneered. "If she dies, Zamora, so do all of your big-man plans for ruling northern Mexico when and if the French take over. Consuelo Salinas is your ticket to the top, and you know it."

"My name is not Consuelo Salinas," Consuelo shouted, attempting to pull free. "It's Connie Ashworth!"

"Shut up, little one," Zamora snarled, jerking her by the hair, "or you die right here."

"Careful, Zamora. Don't damage the goods. You're nothing without her, and you know it. Only she and her family name will smooth the way for you among the people of Sonora, not to mention these Apaches."

As Clay spoke, Zamora prodded Consuelo around Clay toward the canyon entrance. "If my French allies are not already in Mexico City, they soon will be, *gringo.* Then we shall see what it takes to rule northern Mexico—and she's going with me. Unless, of course, you force me to kill her right here in front of you. And don't think, with all of your words, even for a moment, I won't do it."

"If you get out of here alive, Zamora, there is nowhere on

earth you can hide. I'll find you, so help me, and you won't enjoy it when I do."

Cochise stood with his foot on Chuh's neck, holding the little renegade pinned to the ground. At his signal, Cochise's men had moved back. Nothing was to be done that might result in the woman being hurt or killed. Their time would come.

Unobserved, as the confusion of the camp's capture had come down to the hate-filled, explosive confrontation between Clay and Zamora, Wolf had backed into the canyon's narrow defile and melted into the shadow of a deep overhang. There was no way he was going to let his friend get into a knife fight or worse with this self-styled Mexican *abogado del diablo.* If the man got this far, he would get no farther, not with Consuelo, perhaps not even with his life.

Reaching the narrow opening of the canyon, keeping Consuelo between him and Clay, Zamora backed out of sight. Then turning, he pushed the woman ahead of him into the narrow defile, the force of his rude shove causing her to stumble and nearly fall.

"Careful, little one," he said, reaching for her. "We must hurry, and I—"

As Zamora leaned forward, reaching to again grab Consuelo by her hair, a massive fist seemed to burst up almost from the canyon floor, completely filling his vision in the split second before shattering his nose, lifting him from the ground, and launching him back into Clay Ashworth's hard-toed boot.

As Clay's boot slammed into Zamora's back, Zamora suddenly felt as if a kidney had just exploded. For a brief moment the agony was excruciating. Then, mercifully, everything stopped as he fell forward, unconscious, landing face-down in the dirt.

In all of the dust and confusion, panic close to overwhelming her, Consuelo was unsure of exactly what had happened. Zamora had shoved her and was reaching to grab her as she stumbled, even had his fingers in her hair, when without warning, something huge loomed up out of the shadows, and she heard the crack of knuckles on bone, and Zamora was suddenly flying backward, away from her.

Then she saw Clay.

Squealing, tears suddenly springing to her eyes, Consuelo scrambled along the prostrate man's back, her heels digging in for traction, and leapt into her husband's arms.

They clung one to the other with a desperation that each felt to the marrow of their bones. "Never again, my love," Clay whispered. "Never again."

She pushed herself back and looked at her husband's face. "No, never. I love you, Clay Ashworth."

"I hate to barge in on something like this," Wolf said, tapping Clay on the shoulder, "but aren't there others?"

Wiping the tears from her face with her palms, Consuelo turned, pulling Clay by the hand. "Over there. That wickiup back by the cliff."

Before they could reach the squatty thatched hut, the flap was pushed aside, and Cochise stepped out, Emily in his arms and Lazaro limping behind him.

Clay gently took Emily from the Apache's muscular arms. She was weak, and lack of water and food had robbed her of her voice, but her smile seemed to light up the entire camp. "She's going to be fine," Clay asserted, his heart feeling a lightness he had not known in months, "and so is Lazaro." Giving Wolf a nod toward one of the fires, he said, "We need to get some water and food into them. Then it's time to get out of here and start rebuilding."

CHAPTER 18

★ ★ ★

I<small>T WAS AFTER MIDNIGHT</small>, and Clay and Consuelo sat wrapped in a large blanket under the same gnarled old apple tree where she had found him wounded, unconscious, and slumped over his horse's neck so many months before. It had been a long day, one of many, and though both were exhausted and comfortably snuggled together, for both sleep refused to come.

"When can we go home, Clay?" Consuelo asked, pushing away from her husband to better see his face. "I'm anxious to see where our baby is buried. I miss her more every day, and I need to spend some time with her. And, Clay Ashworth, we are both going to settle down and enjoy what is left of our lives—together."

"Mmm," Clay sighed. "We've got a good many years left, if I have anything to say about it—together."

"Uh-huh, but when?" she persisted. "Tomorrow or the next day? Wolf is anxious, too, you know. He told me that for him, it's as if he has a new bride waiting for him."

311

"I know just how he feels," Clay said, pulling her back down to him. "We'll hurry. I'm anxious to get back as well. Within the week or so, for sure."

Not liking Clay's noncommittal attitude, Consuelo looked up. "Why so long, my husband?" she said, warming to the discussion. "There is nothing here for us. Uncle Lazaro has his *vaqueros,* and the work on the house is nearing completion. All of the livestock have been rounded up, and his Andalusian breeding stock is once again safe. The ranch will soon be back in business."

"Yes, I know," Clay said. He paused for a while before saying, "You know, your Uncle Lazaro wants Emily to stay here with him."

Consuelo pushed herself away from him and exclaimed, "Is that what's bothering you? Do you think for one moment she would leave you, Clay Ashworth? She loves you like your own mother. For that matter, she's the nearest thing to a mother either of us has." Leaning back against the tree, she fell quiet for a moment. Then with a dismissive wave of her hand, she quietly declared, "Uncle Lazaro knows it, too. He doesn't really believe she'd stay, not after all these years and not after all that has happened."

Glancing up at her husband, she could see the smile on Clay's face, and she knew she had won. "So, you see, if that's all that's stopping us, we can leave tomorrow."

Up the road, through the ancient orchard, behind the charred brick and stucco walls, the old hacienda was gone. In the past few weeks, under Lazaro's skillful but at times overbearing direction, and with the invaluable help of both Clay and Wolf, a new and even more graceful *hacienda* had risen out of the ashes. The tile roof was on, the outside walls had been stuccoed, the latest in glass windows had arrived and were installed, and he and his *vaqueros* were now in the process of putting the finishing touches to the interior. With Emily and Consuelo's feminine input, the big ranch house was shaping up as a place of Hispanic elegance and comfort.

Gone for Consuelo, however, was any remaining sense of belonging. Her parents were dead; the old home she had loved so dearly was gone; nothing of value was left. Nor would it have mattered if anything had survived. Her life now lay elsewhere, at home with Clay—in Utah.

Drawing his wife back into his arms, Clay said, "Well, then I suppose we ought to get packed and get going. I don't think we'll get any argument from Wolf."

That settled, Consuelo fell silent. When she finally spoke, her voice was choked with emotion. "I received only two letters all the while we were separated."

"*Two letters?*" Clay asked.

"Yes, in all those months, only two letters—one from Chet and one from Robby," she sniffled, dabbing her eyes with the blanket. "When they told me how our baby was buried, what you were faced with, what you did—my heart broke for you, alone by yourself. I should have been standing there with you when she was laid to rest. I don't know how I could have been so selfish, so cruel."

For a moment, Clay did not respond, his own heart suddenly full and unsure whether he could speak at all. "I thought I'd lost you, Consuelo," he said at last. "First our daughter, then you."

Consuelo leaned up, pulling his face down to her. "Not for a moment have I ever stopped loving you, Clay Ashworth," she said, kissing him with all of the feeling she had in her. Then, pushing him away, gripping him by the shoulders, and looking squarely into his eyes, she flatly declared, "And one more thing.

Stop calling me Consuelo. I'm your wife, Connie Ashworth. We are going to be *norteamericanos* together. Both of us."

Clay could not hold back his chuckle and said, "You have no idea how much I love you."

Finally, letting him go and sinking back into his arms, Connie sighed. "Perhaps I do. You're my husband, Clay Ashworth, the father of our child. There could never be another man. Why I did what I did, to this day I can't say. Not even to myself. It's just that everything seemed broken—me, our child, you, everything. It was horrible, and I ran away from it all, when a real woman would have stayed."

"Now," Clay said, kissing her forehead, "I don't want to hear any of that kind of talk. You did what you had to do, and it was probably for the best. Anyway, that's all behind us."

"Can you ever forgive me?"

"Forgive you? There's nothing to forgive.

"Besides, look what's happened as a result. You and Emily found each other, and Emily found her memory and her family. And soon we'll all be on our way back to Utah—this time to stay."

"Yes," Connie said, snuggling closer. "This time to stay."

"On top of that, Cochise by now has settled Zamora's hash. He won't be heard from again."

"I shudder every time I think of that horrible man," Connie said, loving the warmth of the man next to her and the protective feel of his arms around her. "How could I ever have been so wrong about anyone?"

"The man wasn't what he appeared to be, Connie. Lots of folks were taken in by him, not just your parents and you. Zamora was a true villain, in every sense of the word."

"Anyway, it's all over," Connie sighed, "and I could not be happier, my husband."

"Mmm," Clay agreed. "Wolf was right."

"Wolf? Our big Wolf? Right about what?"

"There is no such thing as a coincidence, and even from the worse situations something good will always arise. He called it the *Striker theorem.*"

Connie chuckled. "The Striker theorem, indeed. That idea has been around as long as I can remember. It's as old as the rocks."

"I know," Clay agreed, weariness creeping throughout his exhausted body. "But let's not tell him. The big lummox thinks he thought of it."

"*Lummox?*"

"Yeah, lummox. That's what his wife, Ellen, calls him when she thinks he needs some straightening out."

"*Lummox,*" Connie repeated to herself, as Clay drifted off to sleep. Such a word had its uses.

★ ★ ★

The coach came to a clattering halt, dust swirling high into the air and drifting in through the windows, settling on Connie's and Emily's clothes, as Clay leaned out of the window. It was midday, and they had been on the road for hours. The sun was hot, and he could see nothing.

"*Señor* Ashworth," the driver called, "better for you to come out here—quick!"

"Yeah, and make it fast, soldier," Wolf hollered from his place up next to the driver. "We got us a couple of unexpected guests." Wolf had chosen to ride shotgun next to the driver all morning, shunning the stuffy confinement of the coach.

Irritated at the heat and the delay, Clay threw open the coach door and stepped out, urging the women to remain inside. Wolf had never called him *soldier,* and his tone was a little too worrisome.

Cochise sat astride a beautiful mottled gray stallion in the middle of the rutted road, his right hand held high. On his own horse, Tom Jeffords sat next to him.

As Cochise lowered his hand, mounted Apache warriors suddenly appeared, quickly surrounding the coach, throwing even more dust into the air and further unsettling the coach's nervous team. Clay thought again how uncanny it was the way these warriors could suddenly materialize, almost out of nowhere, swarming around any unsuspecting pilgrim like a band of deadly ghosts.

There had been no war cries, and hardly a sound could be heard as Cochise urged his horse forward, Jeffords reining his mount alongside. Glancing at Cochise, then at the coach's window where Connie's worried face had appeared, Jeffords gestured toward Clay and Wolf, and explained, "Didn't mean t' startle yuh none, ma'am, but the chief here's got some words for these two fellas."

As Cochise began speaking in Apache, the circle parted, and an Apache brave urged his pony up out of a nearby arroyo, two beautiful mottled gray stallions in tow. Both horses were identical to Cochise's mount, and both were outfitted in beautiful, heavily silvered Mexican tack.

Listening to Cochise, Jeffords shifted in his saddle and cleared his throat, obviously not entirely at ease. "Well . . . the chief here says he's grateful for what you two fellas, and the *señora* there," he said, nodding toward Connie, "have done for his people. And he ain't gonna forget it, neither."

As Jeffords spoke, Clay watched Cochise closely. The big Apache appeared reserved and not entirely friendly. And a glance in Wolf's direction told him that his friend was feeling a bit edgy as well.

Clay said, "Tom, you tell—"

"Uh . . . I ain't exactly through, Clay," Jeffords interrupted. "There's more.

"While Cochise is mighty grateful for all you've done, him and his people are still at war with all white-eyes, not to mention Mexicans. Nothin's changed that. Now, these here horses are his gift to you, and they make things square. He knows how much us white-eyes set store by a fine horse, not the same as Apaches. Also, he says you got safe passage through all Apache lands, but it would be best if yuh didn't return. He says—"

"Clay," Connie whispered from the coach window, "what about Uncle Lazaro?"

Cochise frowned at the interruption then spoke abruptly to Jeffords.

"Oh . . . yeah," Jeffords said, leaning to listen closely to Cochise's words. Then, "Cochise says the *señora's* uncle and his ranch'll be safe from Apache raids, so long as him and his *vaqueros* are honest with the Apache. But there ain't no other Mexicans what'll ever be safe. There's just been too much bad blood betwixt 'em."

Almost before Jeffords had stopped speaking, Cochise abruptly turned and rode off, his band of warriors following.

Jeffords held his horse for a moment and said, "You can trust Cochise, *compañero*. His word's solid gold." Then reining his horse about, Jeffords rode off, disappearing in Cochise's dust.

At some point in the confab, the two big grays had been tied to the luggage rack behind the coach, each stomping the earth impatiently.

"Well, my friend, that's something you don't see everyday," Wolf said, climbing down from the coach.

"No, you don't," Clay agreed, watching the dust settle where their Apache benefactors had ridden off into the nearby hills. "Are you thinking what I'm thinking?"

Wolf took a deep breath, and handed the reins of one of the big grays to Clay, while mounting the other. "I'm thinking these are two of the most beautiful horses I've ever seen, and from the way they are outfitted, I'd say they had previous owners."

"Yeah. That's just what I was thinking."

"Uh-huh. Anyway, you can't tell 'em apart. But more importantly, soldier, I'm thinking we ought to get out of here—*pronto*. That big Apache didn't look any too friendly, gift horses or not."

"You're not going to say what I think you're going to say?" Clay said, swinging into the saddle.

"You mean something about looking a gift horse—"

"If you do, I swear I'll shoot you."

"Nope. What I was going to say is that I'm thinking we ought to get out of here—right now, while the getting's good."

"Right now?" Clay said, swinging his beautiful mount around to the side of the coach. "This is no time to look a couple of gift horses in the mouth. Huh, Wolf?"

"Right now," Wolf said, signaling the coach driver. "One more like that, and I'll shoot *you*."

"I don't think my wife would let you get away with anything like that, you old *lobo*," Clay said, winking at Connie, her pretty face framed in the coach's window. "Let's go home."

EPILOGUE

★ ★ ★

"PRESIDENT YOUNG, I HAVE TOLD no one of these things," Wolf said, his hand reaching for Ellen's and receiving the squeeze of support he knew would find there. "Not all of it, anyway—not like this. Not in the last twenty years."

Brigham Young had watched the man closely, sensing that in some horrible way, a terrible wrong had been done him, and whatever its details, that wrong had reached out and very nearly destroyed the lives of countless individuals, certainly those sitting before him. "But, Wolf, at the original court-martial, didn't any of these facts come out?"

"It was the times, President Young. I don't know how else to explain it. Recognition of that fact is probably behind the court's favorable decision a few weeks ago. To some extent, anyway. Several of the men on this last court-martial board were there originally."

As he spoke, Wolf's eyes seemed to focus on something far

away—Mexico, the ugliness he had spent the last decade and a half seeking to escape. The march across Mexico had been a nightmare. The assault on Mexico City, while successful, was unbelievably difficult. What happened at Chapultepec was just part of the same exhausting, thankless torture. That court-martial was, in some way, a part of the resolution of the war, and more for the benefit of the Mexicans than any attempt to really get at the truth or reach a truly just or equitable solution.

Momentarily lost in the nightmare he had lived, Wolf fell silent. It was Ellen's light squeeze that brought him back. "At any rate," he said, straightening in his chair, "in all of the confusion caused by the war—the violence, the politics, the misery—I was an obstacle best brushed aside. I saw that all too clearly, so I guess I just gave up. But I didn't quit. I got out, escaped with nowhere to go, really. All I knew was the army, the military way of life that I loved. I did the only thing I could do. "

"But your fellow officers," Clay said, after feeling a light nudge from Connie. "I don't understand why they couldn't do anything, didn't—"

"No, it was better to just disappear while I had the opportunity. And that's what I did—just disappeared. I couldn't go back to Ellen in disgrace, convicted of such crimes, not and drag her down into my morass. The future I faced was just too uncertain."

"Wolf, darlin'," Ellen whispered, her cheeks damp with tears, "you know I'd have gone into Hades with you and done all I could to help you."

"I knew that then, sweetheart, and I know it now," Wolf said, reaching over to lightly brush her tears away. "That's why I could never allow your life to be ruined—not for my sake. You were still young and could move on."

"*Move on?* Move on, indeed," she huffed. "Move on to where?"

"The best solution for both of us—at the time, anyway—was to find a way to do what I know best, wherever I could sell my peculiar services. So, I became a mercenary and sold my soul to the highest bidder. That was something you could not have been a part of, my love. I did what I thought was best—for both of us."

"Nearly twenty lost years, young man," the Mormon prophet observed, his tone a combination of sympathy and accusation.

"Painfully true," Wolf said, studying the face of the man across the table, "and I am more than aware of that fact. Oddly enough, however, it was our current Civil War that gave me renewed hope and opportunity. War sometimes has a way of doing that."

"The Striker theorem?" Clay said, smiling at his friend, hoping to ease the tension that had developed as Wolf told his story.

"Absolutely," Wolf chuckled. "That's why it's a theorem. Something good will always arise from the worst of circumstances, and there's no such thing as coincidence. All of this bad luck, bad judgment, personal misery, injustice, whatever you want to call it, eventually led me right to those Confederate headquarters at Apache Canyon in New Mexico. Right then and there, the door to both the future and the best of my past opened. I was commissioned a major and given an opportunity for redemption in what I will always consider to be an honorable cause. And just look around to see where that has led."

"I guess war does have its compensations," Clay said.

"War and its compensations, indeed," Connie huffed. "War is a terrible thing, and I will never understand why God allows it to happen. How can a loving God do such a terrible thing?"

321

"Because he loves us, Missus Ashworth," Brigham Young said, his reply perhaps a little too immediate and final.

"*Loves us?*" Connie said, taken back by the Mormon leader's abrupt response.

"Yes. God—our Father in Heaven, if you will—does not cause war. We do that to ourselves, one man to another, one nation to another," Young said, his finger lightly tapping his desk. "The Creator of this world has nothing to do with it, except to give men the commandments they violate all too freely. He allows us to exercise our agency. If mankind kept his laws, lived his gospel, there would be no war—ever."

"I swear, that is the strangest thing I've ever heard," Ellen sighed, wanting to avoid any argument, but feeling the same deep-rooted frustrations Connie was expressing. "I lost my husband to war for the better part of twenty years, because the God of this world loves us?"

"Yes and no, Missus Striker. You lost him largely because of man's refusal to live God's commandments."

The room fell silent for a moment. Then sitting forward in his chair, his voice filling with the enthusiasm that comes with unexpected enlightenment, Wolf said, "Yes. I see what you're saying, President Young. Think of it. It's so painfully simple. All of the problems faced by man on this earth—in any age, in any culture, at any level of society—would disappear if each of us, each individual, merely kept the Ten Commandments. I've never thought of it quite like that before."

Brigham Young's chair squeaked, as he leaned forward. "In the Church, we call it moral agency or free agency. However, the word *free* is somewhat misleading and even inappropriate, its common usage aside. Agency is anything but free. When not properly understood, ignored, or just abandoned, moral agency can be terribly costly, as in the case of war—our present Civil War, or any other."

"No," Wolf asserted, his mounting enthusiasm obvious. "On the contrary, it is *always* costly, President Young, because agency demands discipline. When you think about it, freedom—the right to choose—always demands discipline from those blessed with it. It must be exercised with wisdom and restraint, or it is lost and becomes something condemning."

"You know," Clay said, watching Wolf, then turning to Brigham Young, "if you come to understand that principle in that way, you can almost predict the future—in a general sense, I mean. What a marvelous political concept."

"It is," Wolf said. "It goes way beyond von Clausewitz or Sun-tzu, or any of those you and I have studied, Clay. It's a principle of policy every leader should see as fundamental to excellence in government and certainly in military affairs."

"It goes beyond the political or military aspects of life," Young flatly declared, tapping his desk. "It's theological—pure religion and undefiled, if you will—having the broadest and most basic application in all human affairs.

"Because that is true," the Mormon prophet continued, "our present difficulties were predicted in some detail thirty years ago."

"What?" Clay and Wolf said, almost in unison.

"Look," Young said, turning to lift a book from the table behind his desk, "you four are not members of the Church, so it's not my intention to preach. But from what has been said, please allow me to read this. In fact," he said, opening the book and handing it to Connie, "it might be best if you read it, Missus Ashworth. I think it might help to clarify the problem you expressed earlier. Would you mind reading where I've marked?"

As Connie took the book from the Mormon leader's hand,

their eyes locked, and in that brief moment she sensed a depth of love and concern that surprised her. From the moment she first met him, many months before, Brigham Young was not what she had been led over the years to expect, and with each encounter her respect for the man had increased. In fact, over the past months, she had come to love him as a leader and as a friend, even as a father figure. Doubting his words, for reasons she did not yet understand, made no sense at all.

Taking the book, Connie turned it around in her hands, examining it closely. Then, clearing her throat, she began reading, "*Verily, thus saith the Lord concerning the wars that will shortly come to pass, beginning at the . . .*" Stopping, she looked around at her friends and then at President Young. "I don't believe what I'm see-ing here," she said, pressing the book to her breast. "It's too—"

"Too what, sweetheart?" Clay exclaimed. "Keep reading, for heaven's sake."

"Yes. Don't stop now," Wolf declared. "Keep going."

"*. . . at the rebellion of South Carolina, which will eventually terminate in the death and misery of many souls; and the—*"

"*Rebellion of South Carolina,*" Wolf and Ellen repeated simultaneously, looking into each other's eyes.

"Amazing," Clay said, watching Wolf's reaction. "When was that—"

"Written?" Young said, finishing the question in the minds of each couple. "The Prophet Joseph Smith received that revelation in 1832," Brigham Young quietly declared, "more than thirty years ago now."

"You know, President Young," Wolf said, his voice subdued, yet filled with intellectual excitement and curiosity, "it has been a long time ago, but for a very short time I thought of studying for the Catholic priesthood, and I find this very interesting. I've got to look into this much more deeply."

"Oh, no you don't," Ellen gasped, the look on her pretty face eliciting a chuckle from the others. "I'm not losing you again, not over some idea like that."

"Let him delve as deeply as he likes, Missus Striker," the prophet chuckled, "and you dig into it with him. This doctrine, and many like it, will never require that kind of sacrifice from either of you, not once you've found the truth. Quite the contrary, in fact."

Connie turned the book over in her hands and began leafing through it, stopping now and then to briefly examine a page. "What book is this, anyway?"

"The *Doctrine and Covenants*," Young responded. "It has also been known as the *Book of Commandments*—at an earlier time."

"I must have a copy," Wolf declared. "I've got to get into this."

Reaching behind him, the Mormon leader turned and handed several books to Wolf and to Clay. "Here, for you both, my friends. There are three of them, the revelations of the ages—at least those presently given to us. I'm sure you're all familiar with the one, the Bible; but to understand what we have been talking about, you must study the other two as well. Take them with my blessing. And brethren, study them with your wives."

"Kind of like walking into a brick wall, isn't it?" Ben Kimball said, feeling the need to make his presence known. Entering the room unnoticed in the middle of the discussion, Ben had chosen to remain silent, watching the excitement grow as the conversation had progressed. "When certain truths hit you head-on, it can give you kind of a numbing feeling."

"Is that what that feeling is?" Ellen remarked, looking at the others. "I thought the room was just getting too warm."

"Oh, Ben," Brigham Young said, seeing the young man for the first time. "Have you had any luck in finding Marshal Rockwell?"

"No, sir, and I've looked everywhere. In fact, no one seems to have seen him for several days."

"That's something I've got to set straight, President Young," Wolf said, handing his books to Ellen. With the mention of Rockwell's name, a feeling of unease, almost foreboding, had entered the room for the first time since their meeting with the prophet began. "Believe it or not, I feel a real bond there."

"Yes, I've heard all about him," Ellen sighed, "his determined efforts to hang you and all. I can hardly wait to meet the man. I mean, really, Wolf, honey. How can you possibly—"

"But don't you see, my sweet? It wasn't until I came up against Porter Rockwell and these men," Wolf said, squeezing his wife's hand, nodding at Clay and Ben, "and others like them, that I discovered there were men similar to myself, or at least the kind of man I once wanted to be—solid men with the kind of values I once held dear."

"Well, in Porter Rockwell you ran headlong into the best," Young said, smiling at Clay and Ben.

"But where is Rockwell, President Young? I need to make my peace with him. Somehow, I feel a real kinship with that bearded rascal, and I need to seek his forgiveness for everything I put him through. Believe it or not, I think he has the soul of a true Christian missionary."

"Porter Rockwell?" Clay and Ben chortled, in unison.

"Our Porter Rockwell?" Ben Kimball laughed, elbowing Clay. "The same ornery, irascible Porter Rockwell the rest of us all know and love so much?"

Their reaction brought chuckles from everyone in the room

but Wolf Striker. "Well, I guess you'd just had to have been there, to come to know him the way I came to know him, to understand what I'm talking about. The man could have killed me a dozen times over, but he couldn't bring himself to do it. He could have left me to die in the snow, but he suffered through a horrible New Mexico blizzard and unbelievable cold to save me—for hanging, to be sure. But his heart wasn't in it, I can tell you."

Ben looked at Clay, and snickered, "First chance we get, we need to take another look at Brother Port."

"Yeah," Clay chuckled. "Maybe we just haven't looked closely enough."

"Yeah, but the old coot would need a shave for us to get any kind of look at all."

"Dangerous thoughts, brethren," Brigham Young said with a warning wink. "Despite the fact he has always needed a shave and a haircut, it's not a matter for jesting where he's concerned. If it were possible, the devil himself would die a horrible death trying to give Porter Rockwell a shave and a haircut."

"Oh, it just wouldn't be the same," Ben said, a questionable tone of nostalgia in his voice.

"What wouldn't?" Clay snickered.

"Old Port with a clean face."

"Yeah," Wolf grumped, "too bad he isn't here to defend himself. I've got a hunch he could make life a real misery for anyone that got too familiar, and I speak with some experience."

"You know, of course," Brigham Young said, making an effort to bring the visit back to a more sober spirit, "it was Porter who shot you at Johnson's Ranch."

"I've guessed as much, but knowing him, well, somehow, I don't think he really tried. Otherwise, he'd have left leaving no doubt."

"Mmm," Young hummed thoughtfully. "Well, that is something you'll need to straighten out with him when the time comes. As for me, knowing Port as I do, somehow I'm not so sure. I know our good marshal regretted having shot you, but as to why you were only wounded, I can only guess.

"But, Wolf," President Young hastened to add, "Porter was not sent there to do what he did. I want you to know that. As far as we knew, he was going to bring you back here to Salt Lake City for trial. Only then could an appropriate decision be made as to your future."

"I've never doubted that, President Young," Wolf said, glancing affectionately at Clay and Ben. "Not knowing these men as I do."

"Well," Brigham Young said, rising from his desk. "I've enjoyed this conversation very much, and I'm glad you're all back among us—this time to stay, I hope."

★   ★   ★

The meeting with Brigham Young had been extraordinary, and the two couples stepped down from the porch with a view of the future none of them had ever had before. For each, life was truly just beginning.

"I'll get our carriage," Wolf said, not waiting for an answer. "The three of you wait right here. Ellen and I want to take y'all to dinner."

"Striker!"

At the unexpected sound of Porter Rockwell's strident voice, Wolf spun around, shoving his startled wife back through the compound gate. The .44 Smith and Wesson Russian struck Wolf squarely in the chest and dropped to the ground at his feet.

"Pick it up, Striker," Porter Rockwell said, his voice low, filled with the ugly emotions that had boiled within him over the past months. "It's time for an accounting, Mister Striker."

Wolf glanced down at the gun lying at his feet and then at Porter Rockwell, and something started to stir deep down inside—the old evil wanting its freedom once more. Would he ever be free of it? "Go back and stay where you were, sweetheart," Wolf said, as Ellen attempted to step in front of him. "Back of the wall, sweetheart, please."

"No, Wolf, I—"

"Stay outta the way, ma'am. You can't save him. Not now. It's a sad fact, but your man has committed a crime for which he's gonna have to pay, and it's time to balance the books."

"I've been acquitted, Marshal Rockwell," Wolf said, his voice even and unemotional. "What happened at Platte River Station has been determined to have been an act of war. Bloody, mean, perhaps avoidable, and certainly regrettable, but an act of war, nonetheless."

"Them two boys weren't soldiers, and neither was you."

Wolf stood staring at the bearded man threatening to kill him. All he could see were Rockwell's piercing blue eyes, cold and determined. "True enough," Wolf said at last, his manner easy, almost as if he were in agreement with Rockwell's determination, "but I was acting under the orders of two duly constituted officers of the Confederate States of America, one of whom lost his life there, as well. Have you forgotten? We were carrying out the military policies of a nation at war."

Wolf's words carried force, but somehow lacked conviction, and for the briefest moment his eyes clouded over, as if he had drifted off into another world. Then, "If there were any way to restore those two men to life, to restore that entire town, I would do it—at any cost."

Rockwell's finger tightened on the trigger. "Pick it up. The time for talk has long gone. Now's the time t' meet your maker, Wolf Striker."

Stunned from the suddenness of the unexpected confrontation playing out before them, and urging Connie behind the compound wall, Clay said, "Don't do this, Port. Not now. This isn't right, and you know it."

Reeling from the sudden shock of what was happening, Connie spun about and ran back into the Young compound.

"It's his time, Ashworth. It's his time."

"Thanks, but do stay out of this, Clay," Wolf said, never taking his eyes from Rockwell. "There's been too much killing in my name, and I don't want any more. Too much has happened, and I can't go back. Seems as though any kind of happiness is always just beyond my grasp. So when it comes time for judgment, Marshal, I'm truly tired and more ready than I have been in the last twenty years, I guess."

"Pick it up, Striker."

"Oh, pull the trigger, Rockwell," Wolf said, impatience replacing resignation, "and get it over with, man. How many opportunities to put me away permanently have you had since this all started? Two, three, more? This time, try to do it right.

"I'll tell you the honest truth, Marshal, I'm tired of wondering just what my standing is with the Lord. I've asked too much of Him for too long, and I need to know; I want to know. You, of all people, can understand that, can't you, Rockwell? The nagging doubts regarding one's salvation and the constant worry, especially late at night—they weigh a man down. Isn't that so? You of all people are in a better position to appreciate my feelings than anyone here. So, go ahead, Mister Avenging Angel, and pull the trigger. Grant me the kind of relief only a welcome death can bring."

"Don't you trifle with me, Striker. Ain't no two people less alike than you and me."

"Really," Wolf chuckled. "Too bad there's no time for talk. We—"

"No! No time for talk. Not now. Now, for the last time," Rockwell hissed, "pick that piece up, or so help me, I'll gun you down where you stand."

"No!" Ellen screamed," running to Wolf's side. "You can't do this! The law has freed him, and you're not the final judge, no matter how you've been hurt."

"She's right, Porter," Brigham Young said, stepping through the compound gate, Connie close behind. "Don't do this, old friend." The Mormon leader's voice was uncharacteristically gentle as he spoke, an odd mixture of authority, understanding, and compassion, a quality that somehow seemed for a moment to suspend time. "It would be murder, Orrin—and you know it."

In spite of himself, Rockwell had to look away to see who was talking, but the dusk of the fading day had turned to a moonless night, and only the outline of the man could be seen standing in the gate.

"Think, Orrin," the voice continued, "would you kill a man who's life lies before him—for the first time, really?

"Just stop and look at the beautiful woman standing next to him, the one person in this world who can truly save him. Don't deny her the opportunity, and don't deny him the blessing. Don't interfere with the miracle that has not yet fully run its course."

At the sound of the prophet's voice, the tip of Rockwell's

weapon dipped slightly, and the tension in the air, in some barely perceptible way, seemed to begin dissipating, however slowly.

"Think of Mary Ann, and what she has done for you. What would your life have been without your wife, or hers without you. Stop and think, Porter.

"Destroy their lives, and you will destroy your own soul. You will be the one to answer, Orrin. And what would be the point of that? Certainly not justice, not redemption, not restoration or absolution. Only misery could follow such an act of hateful vengeance.

"Ask yourself, Port, what would the Savior do?"

For what seemed an eternity, no one moved. Finally, Rockwell relaxed, almost seeming to shrink in size. Slowly, holstering his gun, he walked the few short steps to where Wolf Striker stood, stooped down, and picked up the Russian. Rising, he stuffed the heavy weapon behind his belt and stood looking at the man he had pursued for so long, the one man he both hated and admired, their faces only inches apart in the thickening darkness.

No one spoke. No one dared even breathe. Finally, Rockwell, his voice drained of emotion, said, "I should have killed you when I had the chance, out there in the New Mexico mountains, Striker, before I saw you were nearly dead, anyway. I should have shot you right then."

As Rockwell started to turn, Wolf Striker grabbed his bearded antagonist by the shoulders and pulled him into a huge bear hug. Then, releasing his stunned captive and standing back, Wolf said, "You and I are brothers, Orrin Porter Rockwell, two tortured souls struggling to escape a darkness that we both have known too well.

"The truth is, Porter Rockwell, we're kin, and you know it, too. Somewhere down deep, we're brothers of a kind, and neither one of us will ever be rid of the other. I'm willing to live with that, whether you are or not. Fact is, I wouldn't have it any other way."

Clay looked at the two women standing next to him and whispered, "Now, that *is* scary."

WORKS CONSULTED

★ ★ ★

Ballard, Michael B. *Vicksburg.* Chapel Hill, N.C.: The University of North Carolina Press, 2004.

Bokenkotter, Thomas. *A Concise History of the Catholic Church.* Revised Edition. New York: Doubleday, 2004.

Caroli, Betty Boyd. *Inside the White House.* New York: Canopy Books, 1992.

Cartmell, Donald. *Civil War 101.* New York: Gramercy Books, 2001.

Cowley, Robert, ed. *With My Face to the Enemy: Perspectives on the Civil War.* New York: G. P. Putnam's Sons, 2001.

Delaney, John J. *Dictionary of Saints.* 2d ed. New York: Doubleday, 2003.

Editors of Time-Life Books. *Echoes of Glory, Illustrated Atlas of the Civil War.* Alexandria, Va.: Time-Life Books, 1998.

Emery, Michael, and Edwin Emery. *The Press and America: An Interpretive History of the Mass Media.* 7th ed. Englewood Cliffs, N.J.: Prentice Hall, 1992.

Flood, Charles Bracelen. *Grant and Sherman: The Friendship That Won the War.* New York: Farrar, Straus, and Giroux, 2005.

Fuller, John Frederick Charles. *The Decisive Battles of the Western World.* Vol. 3. *From the American Civil War to the End of the Second World War.* London: Eyre and Spottiswoode, 1956.

Furgurson, Ernest B. *Freedom Rising: Washington in the Civil War.* New York: Alfred A. Knopf, 2004

Harsh, Joseph L. *Confederate Tide Rising: Robert E. Lee and the Making of Southern Strategy, 1861–1862.* Kent, Ohio: The Kent State University Press, 1998.

Keegan, John. *Intelligence in War: Knowledge of the Enemy from Napoleon to Al-Qaeda.* New York: Alfred A. Knopf, 2003.

McDonald, Forrest. *States Rights and the Union: Imperium in Imperio, 1716–1876.* Lawrence, Kans.: University Press of Kansas, 2000.

National Geographic Historical Atlas of the United States. Text adapted by Ron Fisher. Washington, D.C.: National Geographic, 2004.

ENDNOTES

★ ★ ★

1. It was Teddy Roosevelt who, at a later time, insisted that the president's home become known and for all purposes be referred to as The White House.
2. For an elaboration of this story, see Hainsworth, Brad E. and Richard Vetterli. *Heroes of Glorieta Pass.* Salt Lake City: Deseret Book, 2005.
3. This previous escape from Leavenworth was detailed in, Hainsworth, Brad E. *End of the Rope.* Springville, Utah: Cedar Fort, Inc., 2000.
4. See *Heroes of Glorieta Pass.*
5. See *The Doctrine & Covenants of The Church of Jesus Christ of Latter-day Saints.* Section 87.
6. See *Heroes of Glorieta Pass.*